SO MUCH FOREVER

JAFE DANBURY

SO MUCH FOREVER

www.JefePress.com
Ordering Information
Quantity sales: Special discounts are available on quantity purchases by corporations, associations, and others. For details, you can contact the publisher and author at:
jefepress@yahoo.com
jafe.danbury@yahoo.com

Orders by U.S. trade bookstores and wholesalers:
Please contact Jefe Press or visit www.JafeDanbury.com

ISBN 978-1-7333440-1-2 (print)
First Printing, August 2024
Printed in the United States of America

Cover concept by Jafe Danbury
Cover design and formatting by Damonza.com

Praise for Works By **JAFE DANBURY:**

*The Other Cheek: Boy Meets Girl. Girl Beats Boy.
Just Your Typical Love Story...*

Leaving Phoenix (Book 1 in The PHOENIX Series)

✗ (Book 2 in The PHOENIX Series)

Praise for JAFE DANBURY'S debut novel
The Other Cheek:

FINALIST, "Best First Novel" category,
2020 Next Generation Indie Book Awards

"This read to me as a desperately written burn book no one was supposed to read, how real and honestly it was written, absolutely sucked me in with the emotional rollercoaster that was this man's life. Such a page-turner with how flawlessly this book flowed. My only wish was that I could read this book over for the first time. You won't be disappointed if you read this book. Bravo!"

~ BECCAH, AMAZON REVIEW

"Jafe Danbury is a superb writer, riveting my soul to every turned page...Oprah Winfrey must interview Jafe on her Super Soul Sunday program. Everyone should read this superbly written story.

~ ELAYNE SILVA-REYNA, AUTHOR OF *WOLF DREAMER OF THE
LONGEST NIGHT MOON*

"Jafe's page-turner is a first-class read I would recommend to everyone fascinated by the extremes of human tolerance and abusive behavior."

~ R. GOODWIN

"An intense, sometimes-brutal novel about acknowledging and escaping an abusive relationship."

~ Kirkus Reviews

"The characters are so well defined. Jafe writes with true feeling for his characters. Although a very entertaining read for anyone, I can also see how this book could serve as a beam of hope and a beginning of healing for anyone found in the same situation."

~ P. Minnich

"Danbury is reaching an audience not often addressed in realistic fiction...I absolutely flew through Danbury's work, absorbing one of Rich's emotions after the other and fearing Tami right alongside him. I recommend this book to anyone who has survived abuse, thinks they may be a victim, or knows and loves someone who is dealing with a controlling significant other. Danbury is making important strides with *The Other Cheek*.

~ Literary Titan

"*The Other Cheek* by Jafe Danbury throws light on the existing but ignored aspect of domestic violence. This book challenges us to see the vice of domestic violence from a broader perspective. I loved how realistic this book turned out to be. Its authenticity comes from the fact that nowhere did I find it going overboard. In fact, the story remained true to its intent and shook me. It also strengthened my faith in the belief that not all that appears is true. There could be something more malicious and horrifying beneath the surface."

~ "Top 10 Fiction Reads of 2020"
~ K. Gautam, Bookish Fame

"Danbury strikes the nail on the head with this one. I would give a copy of this to the guy in your life about to start dating. Maybe to the guy you suspect is in a similar situation. This is for women too. For every woman who has a man she loves in her life. This is Danbury's debut novel, and I dare say we will be reading much more from him in future, at least I hope so!"

~ The Book Dragon

"Wow! *The Other Cheek* is a great book! Spousal abuse is a tough subject, and male spousal abuse practically a hidden subject, but the writing is superb and opens up new understanding and levels of compassion for victims."

~ J. Templeton

"Kept me turning pages...beyond that I also gained a better insight to see how this type of abuse starts, grows, and morphs into something beyond the victim's control. Thank you, Jafe Danbury!"

~ N. Bozzo

"Yes, this is a story of domestic abuse, but there is also a deeper meaning. It is also a story of hope, a story of making it through to the other side, a story of "the other cheek." I stayed up past my bedtime reading this one ...that doesn't happen often. This book definitely comes from the author's heart, and I totally respect him for putting his story 'out there.'"

~ M. Ammons, Goodreads review

Praise for *Leaving Phoenix:*

GOLD, "Mystery/Thriller" 2023 Reader Views Literary Awards

FINALIST, 2022 IAN Book of the Year Awards

GOLD, 2022 Reader Views Award

FINALIST, 2022 Readers' Favorite Book Awards

GOLD, 2021 Literary Titan Book Awards

"This novel is likely to earn strong reviews by word of mouth. Now is precisely the time for this novel. It is intense and often gripping to read, but it is also highly satisfying as you put yourself in the shoes of a young woman who must unravel her past and face a dark truth. Jafe Danbury displays a well-crafted treatment of tone and pacing, as well as a well-fleshed-out protagonist that you will truly care about. Danbury kneads the tension slowly, allowing Phoebe to accumulate resilience and intelligence as she gets closer to the truth. A must-read for any lovers of suspense and mystery, *Leaving Phoenix* is a heart-pounding and profoundly suspenseful novel that reaches an enormously satisfying arc."

~ Readers' Favorite Book Reviews

"Wow! What a phenomenal book! I don't have many 'favorite books,' but this one has been added to my very short list! I had such a hard time putting it down, but I did have to sleep and interact with my family, LOL."

~ Travel Thru Books

"The author is a skillful writer with a sure-footed knack for keeping the narrative moving. A significant element of this is Danbury's decision to delve in detail into the individual backstories of his characters, ranging from Phoebe's grandfather to the Pirate himself. These extended flashback sequences provide a welcome shading to Phoebe's own tale as it progresses, and they further highlight the author's ability to craft moving, believable characters. Liam's story, in particular, the tale of a good man hitting rock bottom and finding his way back to the world, works as an effective narrative counterpoint to the book's main plot threads. A tense and involving tale of a young woman seeking revenge and finding a family."

~ KIRKUS REVIEWS

"Danbury is a master storyteller. Phoenix's life is nothing short of a miracle, and the intricate plot he lays out for his main character traces her life from conception through her fearless resolve to find her mother's killer at any cost. Phoenix is a phenomenal main character and is a picture of strength and determination. The relationship she is able to form with her grandfather after two decades with her adoptive father is touching and quite amazing. In addition, her willingness to relive the past is truly a testament to her incredible strength of character."

~ LITERARY TITAN

"Jafe's writing really knocked me. This book has a very well-constructed story. It captures the readers from the beginning with a storyline that gets better and better as you turn each page! It was interesting and captivating from the start."

~ LAURA, GOODREADS REVIEW

"A well-edited story alive with striking images, sharp dialogue, and the pain and promise of self-discovery. Deep character development and welcome lighthearted moments lead the way in keeping the pages turning. The mystery is believable, and the characters are lovable with well-thought-out character arcs and a relationship to story development. Any mystery fan who loves a mostly fast-paced narrative with a splash of romance will find this is a rewarding addition to to-be-read lists."

～ Book Life Reviews, Publishers Weekly

"Both thrilling and captivating, this story checks all the boxes for an addictive, heart-pumping read. Complete with a soundtrack of classic rock road trip songs, *Leaving Phoenix* provides the reader a glance into the complicated journey of a young woman's attempt to find her identity. All of us have faced similar experiences entering adulthood, and this book perfectly captures the feelings of vulnerability, fear, and excitement that mix together to form a beautiful mess of emotions that guide us each on our journeys. Buckle up for an amazing read that you won't want to put down - and wrap your arms around nostalgia and youthful audacity."

～ B. Boone, Goodreads

"Can't wait for the movie! *Leaving Phoenix* is an excellent read that is suspenseful, happy, sad...hard to put down! Jafe is an excellent writer who makes sure the characters, music, time periods, personal experiences, settings...everything fits together! An amazing read! I also recommend his first book, *The Other Cheek*."

～ Audrey, Amazon review

Praise for **X**:

"Willing to take on some of the seedier sides of life, Jafe takes us inside the criminal minds of people who think nothing of kidnapping other people's children. A parent's (grandparent's) worse nightmare is realized by Phoenix, Curt, and Pop Pop when their angelic Rose is snatched right out from under Phoenix's nose. Just as *Leaving Phoenix* was a page turner, *X* will keep you up at night, flipping pages to discover what happens next. Keep 'em coming, Jafe!"

~ L. CONKLIN

"Jafe Danbury's construct of a potentially horrific story takes the reader through a major roller coaster of fear and trauma that breaks through with a surprising resolution. The plot trajectory was so fascinating that I could barely put down my cigar while reading (my favorite combination of activities). Many thanks to Jafe for such an amazing journey through the *Phoenix* series! I'm very much looking forward to Book 3!"

~ C. TALLEN

"I love the fact that Phoenix's story has continued. While it's a traumatic subject, it was handled gracefully and with heart. The characters are so very well written and they're down to earth and relatable. My favorite part is the music references. Gave me ear worms where some of the songs wouldn't go away. Mr. Danbury has a true gift for writing and I'm excited to hear that there's going to be a third book to this series!"

~ L. A. WILCOX

"Jafe Danbury has such a relaxed and enjoyable style of writing. Despite serious topics, he peppers his story with humor and musical references. As a resident of Arizona, I especially appreciate the many location references, all very familiar to me! I highly recommend this book and look forward to #3 in the series!"

~ SUSAN B.

"Jafe Danbury's thriller, *X*, sinks its claws into you from the beginning and doesn't let go, using multi-perspectivity to keep you in its grip. With surgical precision, this author stitches together a series of heart-pounding events that keep the pages turning feverishly late into the night. You're left breathless as the plot plunges into shadowy danger, ratcheting up the vitalizing suspense with exquisite timing. *X* will leave your pulse racing and your heart aching. You'll find yourself holding your breath as Phoenix and her family confront impossible choices. Phoenix's family has fierce love that burns like a torch, lighting their way through the darkest moments. The bonds between them are unbreakable, even as sinister forces threaten to tear their world apart. Jafe Danbury's ruthless, unputdownable thriller is not easily forgotten."

~ TAMBI SMITH

"A sensitive topic handled very well. As the second in a new series, this one definitely came out swinging and never stopped! Such a sensitive topic but handled with a lot of care and discretion, great foundation and now the series is twisting and turning in a way I can't stop reading. I love the way this author writes. I can envision the people and backdrops in every scene as well as hear the soundtrack he lays. Looking forward to the third installment!!"

~ Colleen Curtis

"It was such a pleasure to follow Phoenix and Curt into their next story...until the moment it became every parent's worst nightmare! Then it was a nail-biting, gripping, totally engrossing ride feeling every moment of fear, determination, and faith along with these characters as they dig deep to take a stand against predators. What can they do, and is there any hope? Read it now to find out. Jafe Danbury draws you into his characters and delivers intense thrillers with heart...and unforgettable moments of humor just when you need it most. Another nail-biting thriller with heart from Danbury!"

~ Natalie Brown

"Never underestimate a mother's wrath…Danbury picks right up where he left off with these characters, guiding us into this latest adventure with a narrative style that is somewhat casual, effectively descriptive without being overly so, and most uniquely his own voice. The characters are as much defined by their banter with one another as through any physical description, save for Phoenix's and Rose's matching locks of fire, and their commitment to finding Rose and seeing her home safely is absolute. The story is fast-paced with plenty of hand-wringing obstacles before reaching a conclusion that will have you on your feet and cheering, all set to the soundtrack of a mix tape with a central theme of vengeance. Danbury is no stranger to handling sensitive topics in his previous books. In *X*, he navigates the perverse world of child abduction and human trafficking with care, mercifully never spelling out that which is most frightening left to our own imaginations. As with any good writer, he improves with each outing. Can't wait to see what he comes up with next! Two thumbs WAY up!"

~ DARIN MILLER, AUTHOR OF
THE DWAYNE MORROW MYSTERIES

"Against all odds, this sequel surpassed all my expectations. In fact, as much as I loved *Leaving Phoenix*, *X* blew it out of the water and that's saying a mouthful because *Leaving Phoenix* rocked my world and had me pondering the fate of its characters long after flipping the last page. This sequel not only delivered but it delivered like a rock star! Jafe's writing skills reached new heights in this one. He fearlessly tackled a sensitive subject, one that I find very hard to think about, let alone read, and knocked me right out of the literary stratosphere. I also want to applaud Jafe's gift for description. Seriously, this guy knows how to paint a vivid picture with words. Every scene, every detail, it all just deepened my adoration for his writing. Bravo and a loud cheer, Jafe, you seriously outdid yourself!"

~ M. OLIVER

An Unforgettable Sequel That Leaves You Breathless! "*X* catapults readers back into the gripping world of Phoenix and Curt with heart-stopping intensity. Jafe Danbury once again proves his skill as a master storyteller, weaving a tale of relentless suspense and gut-wrenching emotion that will leave you on the edge of your seat from start to finish. As Phoenix and Curt find themselves facing every parent's worst nightmare, the stakes are higher than ever, and the tension is evident with each turn of the page. Sharp and gripping as ever, Danbury draws readers into a world where danger lurks around every corner, and nothing is as it seems!"

~ MANDY S.

"A fast-paced page-turner with sequences that are the stuff of great cinema."

~ D. LARRABEE

"Danbury's expertise in crafting a riveting tale shines through, making *X* a book that's difficult to put down. His flair for suspense keeps readers on the edge of their seats, continually urging them to turn the next page. For its engrossing plot, well-rounded characters, and gripping narrative, *X* comes highly recommended as one of the most remarkable reads in recent memory."

~ LITERARY TITAN

This book is dedicated to a very dear soul, Blair Boone.

Arguably one of my biggest fans via my Facebook author page, Blair became an honored friend and, eventually, entrusted some of her own writings with me, seeking my input, which I gladly provided. They were good, showed promise, and I was looking forward to seeing more.

Blair was nothing short of evangelical when it came to her praise and enthusiasm for my work, and truth be told, I never felt worthy of it. But she remained a steadfast supporter, and she shined her light generously and brightly. Her smile was always a mile wide.

In fact, it was Blair who once jokingly said, "You should name your next book starting with a weird letter. That way you can get recommended on those A-Z book lists more often."

The message was replete with the laughing emoji, but you can file this under *Great Minds Think Alike*, because the book I was in the process of writing at the time became what is now Book 2 in *The Phoenix Series*: **X**.

Sadly, Blair is no longer with us, but she left an indelible mark on me and, certainly, many others.

A true phoenix in her own right, I like to think she's soaring now. Flying high, flying free.

Thank you for sharing part of your brief time here with me, Blair.

You've made an impact...so much forever.

"Be kind, for everyone you meet is fighting a
battle you know nothing about."

~ Wendy Mass

SO
MUCH
FOREVER

CHAPTER ONE

DESERT PALM APARTMENTS
SURPRISE, ARIZONA
WEDNESDAY, APRIL 1, 2009

BEADS OF SWEAT had formed on her brow, and the old, threadbare Minnie Mouse tank top felt heavy. A loud and persistent housefly buzzed her moist, unshaven armpit for a third time, tickling her awake.

Tempest Cage shooed the pesky fly away, faceplanted to her other side; the black sleep mask peeling away. She blinked the cobwebs from her eyes. The room was atypically bright, and warm, for what should be her usual, still-dark-at-five-thirty wake-up, and a supernova of sunlight breached the cheap miniblinds. *What the hell?*

Her seventies-era flip clock stared back at her with a straight face, even though it was lying when it declared it was 2:17 AM.

The clock wasn't illuminated, and the flipping number

tiles had parked themselves at the stated time. She reached over and gave the appliance a sharp smack.

Did we have a power outage? She picked up her cheap Timex from the nightstand and got her confirmation: 9:55

What...the...fucking fuck!!

As if it wasn't bad enough living in a town named Surprise, it also happened to be April Fool's Day, and she didn't need the double-whammy today. This had to be some kind of hidden-camera joke, and she wasn't finding any humor in it. At all.

"Abby!! Wake up...we're late for school!!" she called out to the seven-year-old occupying the cheap futon in the apartment's other bedroom. No response. *Shit.* Tempest was sprawled sideways across the queen bed and, being a statu-esque five feet eleven and a half, her legs hung off the mattress at mid-calf. She propped herself up, got to the seated position, and her feet found the flipflops that awaited them.

Flipping and flopping, she hurried down the short hall and peeked her head into the doorway. "Abigail, get up, honey. Mama overslept. Got to get you to school...."

And me to work! Damn it.

She winced as she removed her Minnie tank, noting the spot of blood on its back before tossing it in the laun-dry basket. Standing at the bathroom sink, she did a quick assessment, deciding there wasn't time for a shower this morn-ing—let alone shaving her pits. It wasn't like they'd reached the Rapunzel level, she decided, and the blouse she'd selected from the closet would obscure them well enough until tomor-row. *Jeezus....*

Tempest hastily rolled on some deodorant and slipped the blouse over her head so her daughter wouldn't see the tell-tale belt mark and bruising on her back. She knew full well her daughter had heard the whipping she'd received over the weekend—the walls were thin in this six-hundred square foot hovel—but she still wanted to spare her the visual.

She splashed cold water on her face, jolting herself awake, and quickly patted it dry. Lucky for her, at thirty, she still had a youthful, natural beauty and could crank it up to stunning if she wanted to. She rarely employed much in the way of makeup, and today was no exception.

If she had a dollar for every time she'd been told she could be a runway model, she'd be set for life. The term "glamazon" had been floated by more smooth-talking creeps than she could count and in more bars than she cared to admit. Bullshitters, all. She shuddered at the thought.

Where are all the nice guys?

Yeah, right....

She maneuvered her considerable honey blond mane into a chip clip, letting the remainder cascade down to her well-toned shoulders. *It'll have to do.*

"Abby? You up? Come on, honey...got to move!"

Why didn't anybody call me? Tempest thrust the electric toothbrush into her mouth and ran it around all thirty-two of her perfect teeth as she grabbed her cellphone off the nightstand. The iPhone's display wouldn't even power on. *Dammit.* She replaced the toothbrush back atop its dead charger and rinsed her mouth.

"Mom?" the tiny voice asked from the doorway.

"Yeah, baby, what is it?" Tempest replied as she applied her lone embellishment: strawberry lip gloss.

"Am I going to get in trouble for being late to school again?" Abigail asked. Her blond hair was still in yesterday's ponytail, and she had already dressed herself in a mismatching ensemble. Her mama took three seconds to assess her outfit and decided it would have to be fine. No time to get changed. "No, honey. It's not your fault. The electricity went off while we were asleep. It'll be fine, okay?" she replied as she slipped her toned legs into a pair of Lucky jeans. *Real lucky.*

"Can I have some Froot Loops?"

"Mm...no time for that this morning, sweetie. Quick, brush your teeth."

"I did. But I'm hungry," Abby complained as her mom ushered her to the tiny kitchen.

"Here," her mother countered, grabbing an opened box of strawberry Pop Tarts from the cupboard and handing her one. "We can't toast it because the power's out. Best we can do."

Abigail hesitated before taking it from her. "What about my lunch?"

Tempest exhaled through ballooned cheeks and handed her daughter another one. "Put this one in your backpack, honey. Sorry. We'll do better tomorrow... got to go."

As she scooped her car keys off the counter, she noticed a handwritten note affixed to the fridge door by a Mickey Mouse magnet. The chicken-scratch missive looked like it had been scrawled by a caveperson. In a matter of speaking, it had:

> You coulda at least paid the fuckin electrick bill.
>
> That's the one bill you said you'd take care of and you didn't.
>
> Is it that hard? I work my ass off and wake up to no power!

Good thing my phone alarm went off or I woulda been fuckin late.

Pay the dam power company and get it turned back on TODAY.

D-backs game's on tonight and Tommy's coming over to watch it with me.

Better be fixed when I get home! And pick up some beers. You know witch ones.

Working over in Gillburt at the golf club.

Call me later. Get the power back on!

Tempest shook her head as she crumpled the note from her Neanderthalic partner, Prince Charming—who in reality went by the name of Richard Franco.

Dick!! She tossed it across the kitchen as she ushered her daughter outside, slamming the door behind them.

POP'S AUTOMOTIVE
GILBERT, ARIZONA
WEDNESDAY, NOON

Phoenix Martinsen cradled the office phone's handset under her dimpled chin as she wiped the oil from her tiny hands with a shop towel. She'd just remedied a Land Cruiser's elusive oil leak and was equal parts proud and relieved.

After several rings, she silently willed the person at the other end of the line: *C'mon...pick up.* Like magic, the next ring bore fruit.

"Hey, honey," Curt Martinsen answered. "Everything okay there?"

"Hey, sweetie. Yeah, just wanted to check in. I know you've got to get back in a few. Are the monkeys behaving themselves today?"

"Ha! Well, it's April Fool's Day, and they're having fun with it, as you can probably imagine. Somebody switched the colored tops on all the dry erase markers, and I found a big rubber spider inside my attendance folder. Other than that, we're good."

"Glad to hear it," she said with a chuckle. "Just wanted to remind you of Rose's therapy appointment at 3:45. You still good with taking her over there today? If not, I—"

"Yeah, I'm good. I'll get her there. Got a bunch of papers to grade and I'll be on the computer for a while after dinner though, sorry. Report cards are due, plus parent/teacher conferences. Oy..."

"No worries, I know. Pop Pop already volunteered to pick up a gonzo order from Los Dos Molinos, so that's a plus."

"Sweet. Uh, please remind him: no beans on my super burrito," Curt said with an embarrassed laugh. He'd learned his lesson the hard way that morning in church a while back and would apparently never live it down.

"*No beans for Curt*...check!" she acknowledged, returning a knowing giggle. "Hang in there, honey. Spring Break's just around the corner."

"Roger that!" he said just as the school's bell system began to chime. "Okay, gotta go round up a bunch of second-graders, honey. See you at home with our little angel in tow. Love you!"

"Love you more," she replied with a smile she hoped he could pick up on.

He had and returned one through his voice. "Have a good rest of the day, baby. Mwah."

"Mwah." Phoenix returned the handset to its base. She paused, reaffirming their decision to switch Rose over to the same school where her dad taught. It had turned out to be both practical from a carpool standpoint and therapeutic as a fresh start for their daughter, especially after everything Rose had been through while a first grader at her previous school.

Phoenix made her way around the corner to the shop's sink where she worked up some proper suds on her hands. As she scrubbed, a quick look to the mirror provided a chuckle as she regarded the blob of grease on the end of her button nose. She'd worry about that later. She was starved and had a date with a garden veggie sandwich on Dutch Crunch bread.

DEPARTMENT OF TRANSPORTATION
GLENDALE, ARIZONA
WEDNESDAY, 12:50 PM

The unscheduled trip across town to pay the power bill had taken up the lion's share of Tempest's already-short lunchtime. She had caught a fair amount of grief for being two hours late, and it hadn't been the first time. She sat in her beater 1977 Dodge Tradesman cargo van and nibbled the perimeter edges of her room-temperature strawberry toaster pastry as she ruminated on the need for a change.

Change wasn't anything new to her. God knew she'd experienced more "change" than a vending machine, none of it planned, and seemingly always spontaneous in response to various emergency situations. This would be no different, except it was getting increasingly difficult to transplant herself with a school-aged daughter in tow.

Richard—*Dick*—had all but smacked the living shit out of her again, and the previous bout's bruising had pretty much healed just in time for more. The memories never healed, though. The smackdowns were always for minor violations of his code, and it could be something as simple as not keeping the fridge stocked with his favorite light beer on game night or forgetting to pay the electric bill. She'd reached her wits' end with this arrangement, one that had been casually forged out of convenience after a drunken meet-up at a local saloon in Peoria six months prior. *How hard is it to find one nice guy, for God's sake?*

Tempest grabbed a nearly empty prescription bottle from her purse, shook a couple of aripiprazole into her hand, and swallowed them with a bite of her Pop Tart. She tossed the rest of her wannabe pastry out the window and watched a couple of sparrows spar over it as she manually cranked the window up. She had to get back inside to finish the remaining two and a half hours of her shift in hell. There were vehicle registrations, license renewals, liens, and a myriad of other vehicle-related customer service fires to put out.

It was like the *Star Wars* bar in there sometimes, and she wondered how some of these people ever got the green light to operate a motor vehicle in the first place.

After work, she'd have to have a little *chat* with...Richard.

LA JOYA ELEMENTARY SCHOOL
APACHE JUNCTION, ARIZONA
WEDNESDAY, 2:45 PM

Curt waved to the last of his parent pickups as they exited the long parking lot that ran the length of the campus, in front of the office building's entrance gates. The bus riders had all found their respective numbered chariots, everybody was accounted for and where they were supposed to be, and his day's responsibilities had officially just ended. All but one. He turned to the tiny person holding his left hand.

"You ready, sprout?"

"I'm not a sprout! I'm a little girl!" came the giggle from Rose, as this continued to be her little game—both with her daddy and her beloved grandpa, Pop Pop. Her otherworldly ginger hair had been tied into a glorious ponytail and was adorned with a white ribbon today, and as she beamed her smile to her daddy, it revealed a recently vacated spot where a tooth had been. She looked not unlike a jack o' lantern.

"Oh, you're right! Sorry, pumpkin!"

"Hey!"

"Just kidding. C'mon, honey. We're going to see Miss Julie and then we'll go home and have Mexican food, okay?" He added a huge smile to help sell the excitement of the agenda as they reached his chestnut brown Ford F-150, which had never run better since Phoenix overhauled it. He helped Rose into her booster seat and strapped her in.

"I don't want messagin food tonight, daddy. Can I have a hamburger?"

"A *ham*-burger?" he replied, confirming the belt's final *click*. "A ham-*booger*?!"

"Not a booger, silly! That's gross! Can we go to Wiley's... please?" she asked, employing the impish expression she used to great effect—the one that almost always got her what she wanted from daddy.

"Hmm...Wiley's..." he pondered. A glance to his watch told him they'd probably have time if there wasn't any traffic. It was only a couple of blocks from the therapist's office in Mesa, on South Alma School Road. "Okay...but it'll be our little secret, okay?"

"'Kay!" She bounced up in her safety seat a few times. He might as well have told her they were going to Disneyland.

"Here we go," he said, smiling over at his little angel.

"Here we go," she parroted.

There wasn't a day that went by when he didn't realize just how lucky they were to have her back home safe.

She'd been through a lot.

God knows, they all had.

WILEY'S BURGER
MESA, ARIZONA
WEDNESDAY, 3:35 PM

Traffic through Mesa was a bear today, and Curt had been weighing contingency apologies in the event they had to wave off Rose's favorite burger place and go straight to the therapist's office. But they had just enough time, he figured, and the therapist's preceding appointment almost always ran long anyway, necessitating that they wait for several minutes in the lobby.

He pulled his truck into the drive-thru queue and turned to his tiny co-pilot. "We'll have to be quick, honey. You want your regular Cub Burger?"

"Yes, please," Rose chirped back politely. She had better manners than most children her age, and Phoenix's lessons in common courtesy had been paying off. "Oh, and friends fries too. Please," she added, selling it with a smile.

"And *French* fries...okey-dokie, artichoke."

"I'm not an arti-joke!" she corrected with a giggle.

Friends fries. He smiled to himself. The car ahead of

theirs began to pull forward, closer to the window, and Curt closed the gap. They were third in line. His fingers nervously tapped the steering wheel, as if that would somehow expedite things. A glance to his rearview mirror showed a van pulling in behind them.

"I almost forgot to ask: how was your day, sweetheart? What did you learn? Anything new? Anything fun?"

"It was April Foods Day, and we're learning to tell the time on a clock. We got to read a story...and math was fun," she recalled.

"Yes, April *Fool's* Day," he replied, rather distractedly as he returned his gaze to the rearview. The driver of the van, an otherwise-attractive young woman, appeared rather frenzied and discernably stressed—almost to the point of crying. She was clearly having a bad day. Her young passenger, a girl who looked to be about Rose's age, sat next to her and appeared to be playing with her phone. *How old is she? Seven? And she has a phone?*

The car ahead pulled forward and Curt followed suit, speaking their order into the menu board's microphone. He wasn't having anything; he was saving his appetite for some righteous Mexican fare, so Rose's order should be quick, he decided.

ONE CAR BEHIND...SECONDS LATER

Tempest was counting a wad of one-dollar bills in her lap while simultaneously glancing up to monitor the movement of the truck in front of her. Working at the Department of Transportation, she couldn't help but notice the vehicle's personalized plate. It was automatic for her, plus she had a photographic memory, and they were like little puzzles for her to figure out:

LVG PHX

Leaving Phoenix? A little lame, but cute...leaving Phoenix... don't blame you, dude!

She also noticed the driver glancing at her through his mirror. He looked like a big guy. Cute, even, but it was hard to tell. *Is he checking me out?*

CURT'S TRUCK...SAME TIME

The train of cars crept ahead slowly. Curt's eyes shifted frontward as he watched the driver ahead of him hand his payment to the window attendant who, seconds later, reciprocated with a sizeable bag of food. As that car exited the drive-thru, Curt snuck another glance to the rearview. The woman looked like she was about ready to pull her hair out as she conversed with an unseen order taker via the talking menu board. He shook his head and pulled up, stopping at the pick-up window.

A moment passed before the plexiglass slid open and a fresh-faced young girl of about sixteen smiled and prompted, "That'll be five-twenty-five, sir."

"Sure thing," Curt said, pulling out his wallet. "Oh, one more thing, if you don't mind."

"No problem. What can I get for you?"

"It's not for me, actually. I...I'd like to, uh...I'd like to pay for whatever the woman behind me is ordering as well. It looks like she's having a tough time, and I just wanted to pay it forward, if you know what I mean. May I do that, please?"

"That's very kind of you, sir. Sure, let me add her order to your total and I'll get your receipt...one moment," the girl said. Curt glanced to his watch. They'd be a couple of minutes late, but he wasn't too concerned. "Okay, your total, including the next person's order, comes to twenty-two-seventy."

"Wow...um...okay. No problem," Curt said, digging deeper into his wallet in search of a twenty to augment the fiver sitting on his lap. "Here you go," he said, handing her the money. "Thanks."

"Sure. Your food should be up in a minute or two," she replied, smiling as she closed the window.

Curt let his eyes travel back to the mirror, and it didn't look like the woman's situation had improved much. He was glad he could offer this small, anonymous, random gesture of kindness. Maybe it might help as an attitude adjustment. You never know.

The sound of the window sliding open, and a paper sack being thrust his way, got his attention. "Here you are, sir. And your change...your receipt's in the bag. Thank you for choosing Wiley's!"

The window slammed shut and Curt handed Rose the bag. He rolled up his window and pulled out of the queue. Part of him wished he could see the reaction on the woman's face when she got to the window, but they had three minutes to get to the therapist's office.

Have a nice day, he silently wished her.

CHAPTER TWO

COYOTE GULCH GOLF CLUB
GILBERT, ARIZONA
STILL WEDNESDAY, 4:15 PM

TEMPEST RARELY HAD occasion to come out this way, but this was where the Dick said he was working, and judging from the piles of tree branches and palm fronds piled along the frontage road leading up to the golf course, she knew he couldn't be too hard to find.

The road here had the occasional pothole, so with her free hand she steadied the two large, drive-thru iced coffees that occupied the van's cupholders. Abby had already inhaled her mystery nuggets, large fries, and a milkshake, and Tempest's Big Wiley burger was fighting for space with the large fried zucchini in her stomach. Another bump. "Shit!"

"Mom!" Abby admonished without looking away from her tiny phone's screen. She was tilting it back and forth, obsessed with a basic game called Cube Runner on her iPhone

3G, a Christmas gift Santa had relented to after so much clamoring for one.

"Sorry, honey," Tempest said. She reached down to take a sip of her iced coffee, making damned sure she didn't pick up the wrong one. A moment went by before an excruciatingly loud grinding sound got her attention. It was coming from somewhere off to her left, and she followed the sound. As she pulled to within a hundred yards, she came to a stop and cut the engine. She looked over to Abby. "Let's go say hi," she said, opening the door.

"Do I have to?" Abby protested.

"Just take a minute, c'mon," she replied, closing the door.

"Fine," Abby muttered, rolling her eyes as she stepped out.

The grinding noise got exponentially louder as they approached, Tempest carrying the two iced coffees with her. Abby barely looked up from her screen and only long enough to check her path between tilts of the phone. "Watch where you're walking," her mother advised.

"I am..."

They walked up to the man operating the machine and Tempest put her arm out, signaling Abby to stop. He wore heavy industrial ear protection, gloves, and goggles. With his back to them, he remained unaware of their presence as he fed a sizeable clump of vegetation into the woodchipper. The grinding sound was painfully loud, and the air was thick with particles of pulpy wood and debris. Tempest whistled loudly. No reaction.

As the last of the branch entered the chamber of the shredder it quickly vaporized and the noise dissipated, leaving only the whir of the machine's feed wheels. The man turned around, seemingly startled to see company out here.

At a tick above six-foot-two, Richard Franco was lean but sinewy and didn't have an ounce of body fat. He took a step forward and exuded the danger of a rattlesnake, surely a close cousin.

He removed the muffs from his ears and hung them around the back of his neck, then pulled the goggles away and wiped the sweat from his brow with his flannel shirt. He stuffed his work gloves in his hip pocket. "Well, looky here! To what do I owe the pleasure?" he asked.

"Thought you could use something cool to drink," Tempest replied, holding out the full drink cup, which had two napkins wrapped around it. "Ice is a little melted, but still cold. Here." She approached and handed it to him.

"Very thoughtful of you," Richard the Dick said. "Beer woulda been even more thoughtful, but I'll take what ya got." He hadn't shaven in days and the hair that protruded from beneath his ball cap was greasy and full of wood pulp. He peeled off the napkins and removed the cup's plastic lid, letting the napkins fall to the ground as he tossed back a long gulp of the cool beverage. "Did you get the power back on?"

"Yeah. There's beer in the fridge too."

Richard looked at her as he lowered the cup. "Atta girl. See, that wasn't so hard." He turned his gaze to Abby, who still hadn't looked up from her phone even to acknowledge him. "Abby! Hey...come here, girl. I won't bite. What's so interesting on your phone there?"

"Nothin'...just a game," she replied.

"Just a game. Hmm...can I see?"

"I guess," she said with a shrug as she joined her mother. She handed him the phone.

"You just tilt it? That how the game works?" he asked.

"Yeah."

"I see. What'll they think of next? You know, when I was your age, we didn't have gadgets like this to play with. We played outside, climbed trees, played sports, and whatnot, and when we weren't playin' outside, we were workin' outside. We had chores. Responsibilities..." he said as he attempted to play the lame game. "Ah, sorry...I think I just lost it for ya. I've never been good with this shit."

"Please watch your language around my daughter."

"Oops...forgot...sorry!" he said disingenuously, with a cheesy smile. He looked closer at the device in his hand. "Fancy...must've cost your mama a pretty penny. Apple 3G...."

"Can I have it back?" Abby asked.

"Ooh...now you see, when I was your age, we also had something called *manners*. Not that you'd know anything about those. Maybe your mama hasn't taught you them yet. Sometimes I think she could learn a little respect too." He punctuated the last with a stern look to Tempest.

"Please, just give her back the phone," Tempest interjected. She didn't like where this conversation was going, and one thing she'd learned about living with this asshole was that he was unpredictable as hell and could turn on a dime. She'd thought having Abby with her might make him a little less so, but he quickly demonstrated she'd been wrong.

"Sure," he said, reaching out as if to hand it to Abby. As she reached out to take it, he quickly pivoted and tossed it like he was shooting a three-pointer in basketball. Only there was no hoop, only the chipper, which instantaneously turned it to microparticles of plastic in half a second. "Oops!" he said, turning back toward them with a sheepish grin. "My bad."

"You asshole!" Tempest barked, violating her own rule about language. "What the fu—"

He held up his hand to pause her. It also served as a warning. "Ah-ah...language...."

Tempest knew better than to escalate things further when he was like this, and she put her arm around her daughter, who was now crying. "We'll get you another one, honey. You go back to the van, and I'll be there in a minute, okay?"

Abby was now bawling, her shoulders heaving as she turned and headed back to the vehicle. Tempest watched her until she disappeared behind the tree line where they'd parked. She spun back around.

"Why the hell would you do that to her? She's *seven*...she did nothing to deserve that, you bastard."

Dick tilted his head slightly, which she knew to be a dangerous indicator of what could likely follow. He tossed back the remainder of his tall drink and wiped his mouth with the back of his hand. "I'm sorry...if I didn't know better, I'd say you just called me a bad name...what was it? I think you said... *bastard?* He took a step closer, his menace evident.

Tempest took a slight step back and studied him. She had expected the xylazine tranquilizer in his drink to be faster acting, and as he took another step closer, she noticed a change in his breathing. He paused, attempting to steady himself, and now had an odd expression on his face. It became clear he was losing both control of his own body and the upper hand.

"You okay?" she asked, even though she knew the answer.

"What the hell was—?"

Guess I forgot to tell you that, before we met, I used to assist at a vet clinic.

The drink cup slipped through his fingers and dropped to the ground as he involuntarily took a knee. He looked up at Tempest, who now towered over him. She was backlit by the sun, and he could only make out her silhouette. He felt helpless as he shaded his now-blurry eyes.

"Guess things just didn't work out between us, *Dick*. Too bad, so sad. You just couldn't play nice, could you? That's all I wanted. Just be a *nice* guy...you know? But I guess that's too much to ask, isn't it? You're just another in a long string of disappointments."

"I...baby, I'm—"

"Sorry?" she interrupted. "If you only knew how many times I've heard that. She took a moment to regard the pathetic man now kneeling before her as she noisily slurped the last of her own beverage through the straw. "C'mon, let me help you up."

Abby was all cried out when her mother emerged from the tree line several minutes later and entered the cab of the van. Tempest fired up the ignition and the air-conditioning before turning to her daughter, whose eyes were red-rimmed. "I'm sorry, honey."

"He's so mean!" Abby responded, her hate for him evident. "Why do we have to—?"

"We don't," her mother answered. "Not anymore, okay? We had a little talk, and we don't have to put up with him after today." She cradled Abby's cheek with her palm. "It'll be just you and me now...and your new phone after next payday," she added with a tired smile.

"Promise?"

"Promise." Tempest rolled up her window, which helped lessen the noises coming from the overtaxed woodchipper. She clicked her belt and checked Abby's before slowly pulling back onto the frontage road. As they exited the property she turned to her daughter. "Want to go see a movie?"

"*Monsters vs. Aliens*?" Abby responded hopefully.

"You bet! And you can pick out the candy!" Tempest replied, a long-overdue smile returning to her face.

POP POP'S HOME
GILBERT, ARIZONA
WEDNESDAY, 5:20 PM

The kitchen door opened and David LaFlamme—"Pop Pop" to family—entered the house carrying the repurposed Modelo beer box that contained several takeout orders of food from their favorite Mexican place, Los Dos Molinos—the one on South Alma Road, in Mesa. The screen door gently closed behind him with a click as he placed the box atop the counter.

"Food's here, guys!" he called out, which triggered the stampede of four-legged rescue dogs from down the hall. The family chihuahua, Prick, emerged first, followed by a tiny, wind-sprinting, off-white blur of scruff, Sidney. Galloping in right behind was Luke, their beloved German shepherd who made his entrance with all the grace of a bull in a china shop.

"Whoa! Whoa! Hey! Watch where you're going, Luke!

Geez oh Pete!" Pop Pop admonished, adding a laugh. "This is not for you guys, I promise you that!"

Phoenix came into the kitchen and picked up the tiny terrier, Sidney. "Come here, little thing...one, two...hop!" she said as she carried the rotisserie chicken-sized ball of fluff to her crate in the corner of the room and placed her inside. "Luke...on your place!" she directed firmly, pointing to the large dog bed in the far corner.

He complied with gusto, jumping atop his designated station, completing three spins in the process in hopes of earning a treat. His floppy tongue hung out, creating a smile that was hard to resist on your best day.

"Good boy," Phoenix praised. "And you, you little stinker..." she said, picking up the petite alpha of the pack, Prick, "...on your bed...and you stay there...it's not time for treats yet." She kissed his little head and lowered him to the tiny donut-shaped bed in the remaining corner. The little guy's name was fitting, yet they didn't use it around young Rose. To her, he was known as *Rick*.

"Thank you," Pop Pop sighed.

"Gawd, that smells good," Phoenix said, pulling out the several Styrofoam containers and spreading them out on the counter. "Which one's mine?"

"Should be marked as *PHX*."

"Yep...thanks, Pop Pop!"

"My pleasure, sweetie. Where's Curt?"

"Right here," the lumberjack of a man replied as he entered the house. "Oh, yes," he said, smiling in response to the aroma filling the room. He turned to Pop Pop. "You remembered the no—"

"No onions...no beans...roger that!" Pop Pop replied as he shot a grin at Phoenix.

"How's the grading coming, hon?" Phoenix asked.

"Slow...good, I guess. End-of-second-trimester madness. It's a pressure cooker."

"I'll bet," Pop Pop said. "Got a super carne burrito with your name on it. Literally, your name's on it," he added, handing him the giant, Sharpie-inscribed, foil-wrapped tube of goodness.

"Yes."

Phoenix turned toward the hallway. "Rose, honey. Dinner's ready...come on, baby!"

"Not hungry," came the tiny voice in response.

"What do you mean you're not hungry? Pop Pop brought Mexican food. He got you a cheese enchilada and a taco."

Curt gave Phoenix a sheepish grin. "Um...my fault. Rose really wanted to go to Wiley's after school and my defenses were down. I'll eat her enchilada."

"And I'll eat her taco," Pop Pop said, kindly volunteering his help.

"Oy," Phoenix muttered, a knowing grin forming.

"Come sit at the table with us anyway, sweetheart," Phoenix said, loud enough to be heard by Rose, who was playing with dolls in her grandpa's office/sleepover room.

"'Kay," Rose answered. A moment later, the seven-year-old elf materialized, jumping up first into Pop Pop's arms, then making the rounds delivering elf-like kisses to her mom, then her dad, who had to bend way down to reciprocate her hug.

As Rose took her designated seat at the table, the grown-ups exchanged stealthy glances with one another. It had been not quite fourteen months since...since they'd almost lost her, and they were constantly monitoring her behavior, looking for any subtle signs of post-traumatic stress she might exhibit. Being kidnapped, transported across state lines, witnessing two bloody murders, and escaping a den of pedophiles—all while missing the opportunity to sing in the winter program at school during Christmas week—that was a lot to process for a then six-year-old.

From outward appearances, Rose seemed fine tonight, and they all took their seats as Phoenix distributed their entrees and sides, which now completely covered the dinette table. Phoenix would have questions for Curt later regarding Rose's therapy session today. That could wait until after she'd been tucked into bed, as now was the time to enjoy a nice meal with family.

With great ceremony, Pop Pop slowly opened his own container, the one that had been labeled: *Junior*. His new favorite dish, it was by no means a junior-sized portion; it was dubbed the *Junior's Special* after a former employee there. It was a tweak on Pop Pop's other favorite entrée, the adovada ribs, which were tender pieces of pork served in Los Dos's signature flaming hot red sauce. This time he'd ordered it "junior's way," rolled into flautas, which had him salivating like a rainbird sprinkler.

Curt finished unwrapping his burrito and had it halfway to his mouth when Phoenix gently touched his arm, interrupting his bite.

"Who'd like to say Grace?"

24

KOKO CINEMAS
QUEEN CREEK, ARIZONA
WEDNESDAY, 6:35 PM

Abby's eyes were glued to the screen as she watched the 3D computer-animated monster comedy. She was also glued to the large bucket of faux-buttered popcorn in her lap. She hoisted another greasy fistful to her mouth and crunched it noisily as several kernels missed their mark and fell to the floor.

Tempest stared straight ahead, finding the movie beyond mindless as she absently popped the occasional Milk Dud into her mouth. If there were to be a pop quiz about the movie afterward—and she prayed Abby wouldn't want to discuss it—she would clearly fail as she had completely tuned out as soon as the theater went dark an hour before.

She had shit to figure out, and this was her uninterrupted window of time to do so. She took slight comfort in the knowledge that she had paid the electric bill in cash, and that the bill was in Dick's name, not hers. No utilities were in her name, and the apartment had been his long before she and Abby had even moved in. There wasn't really any beer in the fridge; she'd lied about that. And if Dick's hillbilly friend, Tommy, really did come over to watch the game tonight, he'd find there was nobody home. *Doesn't that loser have a TV of his own?*

It was still Wednesday—April Fool's Day. Seemed fitting with how the day had played out. *Jeezus...Dick had been a fool.*

One thing that was good about her current job, she reminded herself, was that she had weekends off. Till then, she wouldn't have much time to shop their options, but they still had a roof over their heads—for now—and a certain threat had been removed. Still, they'd need new digs, and quick.

Abby laughed loudly, bringing Tempest's attention back to the present moment. She reminded herself to stop by the Circle K store on the way back home and pick up some provisions. At the bare minimum, her baby deserved to be sent to school with a proper lunch, and they sure couldn't live on friggin' Pop Tarts.

POP POP'S HOME
THE COTTAGE
GILBERT, ARIZONA
WEDNESDAY, 9:40 PM

Phoenix had tucked Rose into the single bed in Pop Pop's guest room/office, where her daughter liked to sleep some nights. It was a good arrangement, as she and Curt were still occupying the humble granny unit—a studio—adjacent to the main house. With Rose now a second grader, their tiny abode seemed to get smaller by the day. They hoped to be approved for a bigger apartment soon, as they were starting to bust at the seams.

Curt buttoned up his grade reports, placed them in his backpack, and closed the lid on his school-assigned Dell laptop. His eyes stung from hours of pouring over endless English-language and math assessments, and it was all he could do to brush his teeth after a long day made longer.

"Done, honey?" Phoenix asked softly, half asleep.

"Almost...sorry to disturb you."

"Mm...no problem. I already set the alarm for you, and Rose's lunch is in the fridge."

"Thanks."

"*Jeezus*," Phoenix said, suddenly wide awake.

"What? What's the matter?"

"There's a ginormous friggin' spider on the ceiling!"

"Where?" Curt asked as he turned away from the sink. He looked up. "Wow...that's a big one, all right."

"Can you get it, please? Like right now, before it rappels down and eats me alive?" she asked with a shudder.

"Yeah, let me get the stepstool," Curt said as he retrieved the folding three-step apparatus from the closet. "What can I swat it with?"

"Don't swat it! Catch it. Can you get a jar...or a glass or something, please? Oh, shit...he's moving...he's almost...he's right over the bed! Hurry...crap!"

Curt removed his toothbrush from the glass on the counter and positioned the stepstool near the foot of the bed. He climbed up onto the second step and hovered the glass below the thumbnail-sized arachnid. After counting to three he made his move, thrusting the glass upward against the textured "cottage cheese" ceiling. He had him and, with a little maneuvering, managed to get the critter into the bottom of the upright glass.

"Ewwww! Take it outside and let it go in the bushes, honey! Gawd, it looks like a tarantula," Phoenix declared, pulling up the blanket as if to hide.

Curt smiled as he carried the offending creature to the door and went outside. He was one of those people who had never developed a fear of spiders. A mouse, on the other hand, would probably have him standing atop the table, screaming like a girl, but he'd never tell Phoenix that.

"There you go, little guy," Curt said as he relocated the spider to its new digs. "And don't come back," he added, closing the door behind him, rinsing the glass, and putting it back where it belonged.

"Here I come to save the day!" he sang in his best Mighty Mouse voice.

"My hero," Phoenix said with a smile of relief.

Curt climbed into bed and met her in the middle, pulling up the covers to make sure his lady wouldn't get cold.

"Thank you, honey. What would I ever do without you to protect me?" she said, rewarding him with a kiss.

"It's my job, and we do what we can," he replied with a warm smile, returning the kiss. He rolled onto his back and liberated a sigh he'd been holding in since that morning. It had been a long day, and he was burned toast. "Sorry," he said through a yawn.

"No worries. I know how tired you are."

"Mm...'night, baby," Curt said as he rolled toward the nightstand, his arm outstretched.

"Sorry, hon. Can I just ask you one thing real quick?"

"Sure. Shoot," he said, turning back toward her.

"I meant to ask you earlier: what'd the therapist say after Rose's session today? Anything new we need to know about?" Phoenix asked.

"Not really. She mentioned Rose is still triggered by the color red, having witnessed the big guy in the bear trap, no doubt. Jeez...and in some of her play therapy, she still calls one of the dolls *Willie*."

"Poor baby...yeah, it'll take a while...for all of us...we can't put a time limit on it."

"I know," Curt agreed. "I'll take that drawing you found—the one with what looks like blood in the snow—with me to next week's appointment..." he added, his voice trailing off. It was beyond all their comprehension to understand why these traumatic events had happened to their family.

Phoenix put her arm around Curt and kissed him softly. "We have Easter coming up soon. We'll do something fun, reconnect...it'll be good for us all, don't you think?"

"Absolutely. Plan on it," he managed through a yawn. "Goodnight, sweetheart," he said as he switched off the bedside lamp atop the two-drawer file cabinet that was their nightstand.

"'Night," Phoenix said as she rolled over to her other side. "Love you."

"Love you more."

CHAPTER THREE

COYOTE GULCH GOLF CLUB
GILBERT, ARIZONA
THURSDAY, APRIL 2, 6:22 AM

THEY WHIRRED UP to the second tee, parking their two golf carts just off the path. This foursome was comprised of close friends, all hacks—with the possible exception of Jimmy Huff, who could drive the ball a country mile if he didn't slice the damned thing.

Jimmy and his pals, Gary, Pete, and Jack were all in their late sixties and recent retirees. They tried to get together for a round once a week—usually Thursdays, as they had better luck getting their desired tee time and they could get breakfast in the Clubhouse. To them it was just good to be out enjoying some sunshine, fresh air, and a little birdsong. And it was a good excuse to have a Bloody Mary with their omelets.

Jimmy's cart mate, Gary, studied him as he set his tee and placed his Titleist ball atop it. According to the sign it was 340 yards to the pin, and Jimmy hoped to at least meet it halfway on his drive. He turned his gaze to the fairway, then back to his ball and, after a shake of his hips and a moment's deliberation, he swung his Callaway driver with everything he had in the tank.

The ball exploded off the tee with that sweet *ping* sound you wanted to hear but, instead of heading straight, it immediately went off course, sharply off to the right and into some trees.

"Damn it to hell!" he barked. "Sliced it again! Anybody see where it went?"

"Yeah," Gary said. "Went into the rough by that group of palms," he said, pointing. "Wanna hit another?"

"Nah!" Jimmy replied, shaking his head as he retrieved his tee. "I'll play it where it lies and take the penalty."

"Suit yourself," Gary said as he approached the tee box. "You hit the hell out of it, though; I'll give ya that. I'll be happy if I hit it seventy-five yards with this thing," he added with a grimace directed at his garage sale "1" wood.

With all tee shots now in play, Gary navigated his and Jimmy's cart toward the clump of trees he believed his partner's ball had disappeared into. "Should be right in there, somewhere," he said, offering Jimmy a little encouragement. "Got an extra ball with you in case you don't find it?"

"Yeah," Jimmy said with a groan as he headed into the thicket. There were palm fronds and clumps of vegetation seemingly everywhere. "Where the hell are you?" he muttered as he began his search.

Gary, from the comfort of the cart, lit up a Marlboro Light and turned his attention to the others, who were studying their second shots from mid fairway. He inhaled a deliberately deep drag from his cigarette, savoring it, as he'd just started smoking again after a year's pause. Indulging his habit on the golf course helped him keep this little secret from his wife, who would kill him if she found out—if the cigarettes didn't beat her to it.

A moment later, Gary heard a scream. It was unlike any scream he'd ever heard. It was a man's scream, he was certain of it, but it almost didn't sound human. He climbed out of the cart, throwing his ciggie to the ground as he stared at the treeline where Jimmy had entered, only to see his partner come running out with his eyes wide and a look of abject horror on his face.

IN THE ROUGH SOMEWHERE
BETWEEN THE 2ND AND 3RD TEES
THURSDAY, 8:32 AM

Detectives Jeffrey Ramage and Bethany Moser of the Gilbert Police Department had received the call and, upon arriving at the scene, had each thrown up their breakfasts.

They were joined by Kevin Parks, manager of the golf property; Tim Welch, owner of the tree-trimming service; a police photographer; and two emergency medical technicians who were busy doing their assessment.

Jimmy and Gary sat on the stump of a dead tree, twenty

yards away. There'd be no more golfing today, especially since Parks had closed the entire course two hours before.

Ramage was a husky man. He had one of those Flintstones-like necks that seemed to morph straight from his shoulders. With his crewcut and solid frame, this former varsity wrestler and standout of the Arizona State football team looked like somebody you wouldn't want to mess with.

Not by design, he'd allowed himself to pack on an extra twenty pounds of celebratory weight gain in the past year, having helped crack a high-profile interstate child-trafficking case, and he had plans to learn about the benefits of a salad bar. Now in his early forties, he couldn't remember the last time he'd visited one.

He wiped his mouth with a handkerchief. "And who found...him?"

Parks cleared his throat and pointed over to where Jimmy was sitting. "Mr. Huff, there. He and the rest of his foursome are regulars here. Jimmy's ball apparently went into the rough here and...." He shook his head as his voice trailed off. "It's a hell of a thing."

"Yep, like you said...helluva thing," Ramage replied, looking back over at the equipment and the bloody carnage that was like something out of a horror movie. The brush chipper was a trailer-mounted machine and painted in a faded, school bus yellow. It was far from new, from all appearances, and it had seen a lot of action. It was now covered in blood spatter and looked like Jackson Pollock had been commissioned to repaint it.

Ramage turned to the other man, Mr. Welch. "Can you tell me how long, uh, this employee had been working for your company, sir?"

"Dick—sorry, Richard—Franco has been with me for about six years now. Never any issues or problems, and no accidents. Until...."

"Victim's ID was in the cab of the truck. Checks out: Richard Franco, age thirty-seven, six-foot-two, hundred-eighty pounds. Address in Surprise," Detective Moser interjected as she joined them.

Moser was in her mid-thirties and a single mom of a now six-year-old daughter. As a result, she had taken a special interest in cracking the interstate kidnapping and pedophilia ring with her partner. Together, they made a great team and had earned their promotions.

Ramage nodded to acknowledge her findings and took a step closer to the woodchipper. Protruding from the in-feed chute was what was left of Mr. Franco, and he was nowhere near six-two anymore—not by half.

His legs hung down, as his lower torso rested on the lip of the feed chute, which was elevated two feet from ground level. Blood, minced flesh, and pieces of bone were everywhere—especially at the discharge chute, which fed into a dump truck.

Ramage loosened the too-tight collar of his shirt and fought down another wave of nausea before asking his next question. "So, he was an experienced worker, no safety violations?"

"Very experienced, yes, sir. And no, no safety violations. We usually work in two-man crews, for safety reasons, but the other man had gone home early due to illness."

"We'll want to talk with him later," Ramage replied.

"Sure thing. Hector Rodriguez is the name; I'll get you his contact information."

"Thank you," Ramage said as he scribbled into his

notebook. "How about the machine? Can you explain how it works, briefly?"

"Sure, well, it's a Blizzard Model 12," Welch began. "Real workhorse, with a solid safety record. All our employees go through a vigorous safety program and Franco's worked with this rig for...probably five, six years. Doesn't make any damn sense," Welch said, shaking his head. "Wouldn't wish this on anyone."

"And how does one operate it?" Ramage asked, redirecting him to the question he'd posed.

"Sorry. So, this is the in-feed chute. The operator feeds the branches into it manually and a set of feed wheels grabs the vegetation and feed it into the rotating blades attached to the chipper drum inside."

"What safety equipment do they wear? Goggles?" Ramage asked.

"Goggles, yes...hearing protection...and gloves," Welch replied. "Always."

Ramage furrowed his brow and cocked his head as he pointed to what looked like a deviation in protocol. There, partially obscured by the flannel shirt, were what appeared to be two leather gloves hanging out of Franco's right hip pocket. "I guess not always...."

Welch's jaw slacked as he now saw this anomaly. He shook his head in disbelief, rubbing his face, taking a full minute to collect himself. Ramage and Moser exchanged glances.

"This is unusual then?" Ramage queried.

"Very," Welch replied softly. "He would never operate the machine without gloves on."

Ramage jotted a few notes into his pad and gestured to

the photographer to grab some more shots. "Sorry to have interrupted, sir. You were telling me how the machine works."

This safety violation, on top of everything else, had left Welch white as a sheet. He turned to face Ramage, and his expression broadcast his level of distress. "The chipped wood—er, that's what it's designed for, for wood, obviously—is uh..." Welch paused, shuddering at the thought of what had happened here.

During this, the more senior of the EMTs looked over to Ramage and shook his head as he removed his latex gloves, indicating there was nothing they could do here. Ramage acknowledged this with a nod then put his hand on Welch's shoulder.

"It's okay, sir. Take your time. This is a horrible tragedy and, understandably, very upsetting to lose an associate this way."

"Yes...um...well, the chipped wood is ground up, almost instantaneously, and blown through a discharge chute and into...into the dump truck bed," he managed, pointing to it.

"I see," Ramage said softly. "And the machine wasn't running when the victim was found here this morning?"

"No, sir. The motor would've eventually shut down when...something...large...got stuck in the...chute," Welch said softly. His mind was already envisioning the insurance ramifications.

Ramage closed his notebook, pocketed his handkerchief, and nodded to his partner.

"Thank you, Mr. Welch," Ramage said, handing him his card. "We'll let you know if we have further questions."

"Sure," Welch said as he pocketed the card and initiated a much-dreaded phone call to his insurance guy.

"What now?" Moser asked her partner as they began walking back toward their vehicle. Moser had her almost-shoulder-length blond hair gathered into a perfect ponytail and was glad she'd worn comfortable shoes today, as her typical heels wouldn't have negotiated this terrain very well. She tipped her Ray Bans as she looked at him. "Who gets the pleasure of...you know...?"

"Since the EMTs couldn't extract him here, he'll have to be removed from the chipper at the coroner's office, after the machine's dissembled. Welch will be there for that. He knows the machinery better than anybody. Won't be pretty though, I guarantee you."

"No, I'm sure it won't," Moser said, stopping in her tracks.

"What is it?" Ramage asked.

She bent down to get a closer look at something that caught her eye. "Looks like a drink cup," she said, nudging it with a gloved hand. "Guy liked his iced coffee from Wiley's, I take it."

DEPARTMENT OF TRANSPORTATION
ARIZONA MOTOR VEHICLE DIVISION (AZ MVD)
GLENDALE, ARIZONA
THURSDAY, 8:56 AM

Tempest ejected the Iron Butterfly eight-track tape from the under-dash mounted Muntz stereo and silently cursed the idiot whose car had stalled on the freeway on her way here. She'd dropped Abigail off at school with plenty of time to spare, and here she was, now scrambling to get inside before her shift started.

If there was a plus that came from being stuck in traffic, it was that it had enabled her to hear the entirety of the Butterfly's seventeen-minute-long opus, "In-A-Gadda-Da-Vida" and, more importantly, Ron Bushy's nearly three-minute drum solo. The drums were absolutely tribal, which was perfect for her post-kill mindset this morning.

Still, it was annoying to have the lengthy song fade out in the middle of Track 1, then have to wait several more seconds for the little piece of metallic tape to pass the tape head and click it to the next track...only to have it slowly fade in again and resume the song in Track 2. She had the same complaint with the clueless formatters when it came to breaking up the guitar solo in Lynyrd Skynyrd's epic, "Free Bird." It was the nature of the format, which was lame by design, and at almost the size of a paperback novel, an eight-track tape was decidedly less portable than its competition, the cassette tape.

But there it was. She was old-school that way, plus she still had a gazillion of them thanks to the many mail-order, *13 Tapes for Only One Dollar!* membership offers she'd exploited over the years. Some memberships were in her own name, a couple under her goldfish's—Goldie—and several were under her then-dog's, Rufus. The company never checked, and over a few years' time, she'd amassed a huge collection and managed to outrun the collection agents.

Tempest stuffed the tape into its designated empty slot in the open carrying case. The narrow case had two sides and was designed to hold twenty tapes, with ten on each side in vertical rows. It was one of four identical cases she kept with her in the van, hidden under a quilted blanket, and she'd rotate the tapes as her mood suited her. She still had several full boxes of them in storage.

She set her vintage 1984 Care Bears lunch box on the passenger-side floor of the van and covered it with a light jacket. This wasn't one of those cheap knockoff lunch boxes; this was the real deal, the original Aladdin-brand one, in near-mint condition, and with the "pop-top" thermo bottle. She was taking no chances after her Berenstain Bears one was stolen a few months back.

She retrieved her go-to beverage, a fresh iced coffee, from the cupholder, locked the van's door securely, and ran toward the building.

There were already a dozen people standing outside. *Shit!*

Allison Peck, Tempest's supervisor, couldn't resist giving her a little stink-eye as she let her in through the front door and relocked it. "Glad you could make it," she said under her breath as Tempest breezed by.

"Sorry, traffic," she replied, and it was true this time.

"Yeah, well, Paige called in sick, so it's just you and me this morning."

"Mm...okay," Tempest said, slightly out of breath as she stashed her backpack under her chair at Window 2. "Thanks for turning on the computers. Give me two minutes and I'll be ready," she added as she urgently pecked at the keyboard to log in.

Allison glanced at the clock on the far wall: 9:02. "Okay, make it quick," she said, monitoring the growing crowd outside. One minute later she got the response she wanted to hear:

"'Kay! Let 'em in!" *Shoot me now....*

AZ MVD PARKING LOT
GLENDALE, ARIZONA
THURSDAY, 1:05 PM

Tempest climbed into her van and rolled down both front windows to allow some cross-ventilation while she ate her lunch. There was just a hint of a breeze, and it was only in the low eighties outside. She found that she strongly preferred spring here, especially coming off a brutally hot summer last year in this hellish place.

She had to expedite her exit plan, she decided—especially after yesterday's...hiccup.

The van was where she ate her lunch five days a week. She didn't really have the gift of gab and, even if she did, her coworkers weren't people she'd want to spend any more time with than absolutely necessary. They shared a workplace, but they had their separate windows, thank God, and that was where it ended as far as she was concerned.

Thus, the van was her little sanctuary for thirty minutes, Monday through Friday.

She unfastened the latch on her lunch box and extracted the sandwich she'd made the previous night. Even though she'd felt exhausted when they got back to the apartment—post-shopping run, post-movie, and post-killing—she'd soldiered on, and assembled both her and Abby's lunches for the next morning.

She regarded the singular beauty of the item in her hands as she removed the plastic wrap. It was not only her go-to, work-week sandwich, but it had been a favorite since she was a kid, and she made them exactly like her mother had: apple butter and mashed banana on white bread with the crusts cut off.

Her side dishes rarely varied either: an individual serving of fruit cocktail and a stick of string cheese. The thermo bottle did a decent enough job of keeping her sweet tea cool, thanks to the few ice cubes she'd dropped into it before leaving the apartment.

She glanced at her Timex. *They've definitely found him by now.* She allowed herself a brief replay of yesterday's events and was satisfied there wasn't anything to tie it to her.

A sharp knuckle rap on her rear window jolted her almost into tomorrow and just shy of cardiac arrest. Her head spun toward the sound, and she was only semi-relieved to see that it was her coworker, Paige, standing there with a goofy grin. And not a cop.

"Jeezus, Paige," Tempest barked, her pulse pounding like a jackhammer. "You scared the friggin' crap out of me!"

"Sorry!" Paige replied. She couldn't have been too sorry because the grin remained. Her closely cropped jet-black hair and unfortunate bangs gave her a goth vibe, while a series of ill-advised piercings helped sell it.

"I thought you called in sick."

"I did. But I feel better. Not contagious or anything..." she said, now leaning in the window.

"Good, well..." Tempest said as she returned her attention to her masterpiece.

"Just had a bad case of the runs this morning," she added with a genuine smile now.

Tempest looked down at her sandwich, which had now been irreparably tainted; not only for today, but...forever. "Uh, thanks for sharing...that," she muttered with a frown that couldn't possibly convey her true level of upset. She hastily rewrapped the sandwich and tossed it back in the lunch box, opting for the cheese stick. "Look, I'm on my lunch, Paige...I'll see you in about twenty minutes, okay?"

"Yeah, sure," Paige replied breezily, failing to pick-up on Tempest's annoyance with her. She gleefully spun on her heel and, almost skipping, headed toward the building where her dream job awaited.

Paige was clueless, which was her way, yet Tempest couldn't help but think this pathetic, rail-thin, twenty-something goth creature must've been dropped on her head as a child.

GILBERT POLICE DEPARTMENT
THURSDAY, 1:35 PM

Detective Ramage hung up his office phone and, turning to his partner, shook his head.

"Anything?" Moser asked, pushing aside the pieces of kiwi in her deli fruit salad. She'd eaten everything else in the bowl, but she didn't understand people's attraction to kiwi.

"Coroner had a hell of a time extracting the remains of Mr. Franco. Welch supervised a couple of his equipment guys, and they had to disassemble the chipper—the blades, discharge chute, and the drum, anyway. Took a while, as you can imagine...got what's left of him out of the machine. Still going through the hot mess in the dump truck. God knows, I wouldn't want that damn job," he replied, tossing his untouched chilidog into the trash can.

"Positive ID, though?"

"As well as they could determine. Coroner was able to find a chunk of Franco's jaw. Enough to make a confirmation via dental records, anyway. They're checking into his files now, see if they can find any next of kin."

"Okay. Anything else we should be pursuing?" Moser asked.

"Let's sit tight for the moment and wait till we hear back about any family he may've had," Ramage said, rubbing his face. "Can you imagine? Pretty sure that'll be a closed-casket deal," he added.

"You think?" Moser agreed, pushing away the bowl.

"Other than the wallet you found in his vehicle, not much else to work with. Coroner said there were tiny remnants of electronics—what appeared to be pieces of a couple of cell phones he must've had on him."

"A couple?"

"Different colored plastic housings, he said, but the fragments are quite small. Might not be anything useful, but they're trying to sift 'em out from...you know...from the rest of...the stuff."

"Yessiree...you sure can paint a picture, partner."

"Guilty on that point," he replied, picking up his notebook and tapping it. "Call me wacky, but something tells me Mr. Franco—with his safety record—wasn't one to forget his gloves."

LA JOYA ELEMENTARY
APACHE JUNCTION, ARIZONA
THURSDAY, 1:40 PM

Curt walked back to his classroom, having just supervised the dispersal of the monkeys in his charge. Thank God for "minimum" days. The bus riders were in their assigned coaches and parents had picked up the remainder. He unplugged his laptop computer and stuffed it and its charger into his shoulder bag, along with the folders he'd need.

The days leading up to the end of a trimester were always crazy, and he was looking forward not only to a break, but also celebrating both Easter and his daughter's eighth birthday. He had another minimum day ahead of him, plus a full slate of parent/teacher conferences to get through, then he was home free.

He turned off the lights and locked the door. He didn't have far to go to collect Rose; she was in Miss Kay's class, directly around the corner. She was standing in the open doorway, interacting with a parent who was collecting her son.

"Hi, Mr. Martinsen," she said, greeting him with a warm smile. "I'll bet you're here for your precious Rose!"

"Daddy!" Rose's excited squeal came from inside the classroom as she ran up to him, jumping into his arms.

"Hey there, sugar pie!" he said with a big daddy grin.

"I'm not a pie, silly!" Rose said, correcting him.

"Sorry, honey buns."

"Hey!" she squeaked back with a laugh.

"How was your day, honey?" he asked, holding her at eye level and rubbing noses.

"Good!" she said. "Look what I made!" she added, signaling she wanted to be put down.

"What'd you make, angel?" Curt asked. He watched as she rifled through her backpack, then looked up at her teacher. "How's she doing, Margie?" he asked quietly.

"We had a pretty good day," she replied softly, as to not be heard by Rose. "Other than a few tears after the second recess...."

"Oh? Anything happen?" he asked.

"Here, Daddy! Look!" Rose emerged holding a particularly well-executed drawing of a colorful Easter basket with all the trappings.

Curt turned to his daughter and regarded her masterpiece. "Wow! You did this, Rose?!"

"Uh-huh!" she affirmed with a proud beam.

"Do I get to see?" Phoenix asked excitedly as she walked up. She'd left work early to retrieve Rose, since Curt had to stick around for conferences.

"Hey, honey," Curt said, looking at his watch. "Right on time," he said with a smile.

"Mommy! Mommy!" Rose squealed as she ran into her mother's arms. "Look at my picture!"

"Wow, honey...you are an amazing artist! Did you have a good day?"

"Uh-huh," Rose replied.

"We'll have to put this up on Pop Pop's refrigerator when we get home, okay?"

"Yay!" she replied, carefully replacing the artwork into her pack with her math worksheets.

"Anything I miss?" Phoenix asked.

"I was just telling your husband that there were a few tears today," Miss Kay replied.

Curt gave Phoenix a peck and returned his attention to the unfinished conversation. "Anything we need to know about?" he asked Miss Kay in a concerned whisper.

"No... I think she was having a conversation with her imaginary friend, Willie, again. I overheard her say his name just before she started crying."

"I see...thanks for bringing that to our attention. I'll mention this to her therapist when we see her next week."

Margie responded with a nod, her bright smile returning. Her eyes were always smiling, Curt noted.

"Thank you," he said before turning back to Rose. "Ready, Freddie?"

"Hey!" she answered with a laugh. There was no end to their little game and Curt was glad at least that had survived the ordeal they'd all faced a year ago at Christmas.

She placed her tiny hand in his gigantic one as they walked toward the parking lot. Phoenix took her other hand. "You and daddy like my drawing?" she asked.

"Are you kidding? We love it!" she promised. They

approached Phoenix's Road Runner and stopped at the passenger door.

"I'll give you a call when I'm done with the last conference, honey. Should be home in time for dinner, but...."

"No problem," Phoenix said. "Just leftovers tonight."

"Sounds perfect," Curt replied. He turned to his tiny munchkin and picked her up as Phoenix opened the car door. With a broad smile, he hoisted Rose into her seat and buckled in his precious cargo. "You are amazing, Rose, you know that?"

"I know! You are too, daddy...and you too, mommy, you know that?" she parroted back as he clicked her belt.

"Yes, we do," came the collective parental chorus. And all three of them meant it.

Phoenix gave Curt a quick hug and walked around to her door. "See you at home, sweetie."

"Yep. What's left of me, anyway," Curt said with a tired chuckle.

"See you later, alligator," Rose called out as Phoenix pulled away.

"In a while, crocodile!" her daddy replied, waving until they left the lot. He looked at his watch. First conference was scheduled to be in thirty minutes. *Let's do this.*

CHAPTER FOUR

DEPARTMENT OF TRANSPORTATION
WINDOW 2
GLENDALE, ARIZONA
THURSDAY, 3:35 PM

O N ONE HAND, Tempest was grateful Paige had recovered from her intestinal maladies enough to come into work. Just having her there, though, let alone stationed only a scant few feet away at Window 3, was brutal on any given day. Today's seemingly endless stream of customers, however, had been one for the record books, and much more manageable thanks to goth girl.

Tempest glanced up at the clock. The only remaining customer was now at Window 3, thank God, which gave Tempest a few minutes to decompress from her shift.

Her last customer had just walked away: a prissy, self-important, gum-smacking blond bimbo with a painfully obvious set of store-bought breasts that strained against her Arizona State tank top. She'd impatiently endured the long line, her constant eyerolls telegraphing her discontent, and upon reaching Window 2 to renew her driver's license, she'd been all attitude, which Tempest wasn't having. Not today.

When it had come time to take her picture, Tempest made it a point to snap the worst possible license photo she could, choosing an unflattering moment during the gum chewing, assuring four years of humbling embarrassment and misery upon receipt of the document in the mail. Tempest smiled at the thought of the chick, a few weeks from now, pulling her license from the envelope, her expression one of abject horror and, Tempest hoped, accompanied by tears.

She had another twenty minutes until her shift ended and knew Abby would be in good hands, doing some kind of art activity with the after school program until she got there. Which left her with her thoughts, idle hands, and a keyboard to play with. She was pissed at how things had ended with Dick. He'd made his bed though. *Too bad, so sad....*

Tempest could feel her serotonin levels starting to tweak, and she couldn't risk an emotional flare-up. Not here. She looked around and, seeing nobody was paying attention, fished a couple of pills from her purse and popped them in her mouth. A quick swig of sweet tea helped send them on their way to her bloodstream.

Her thoughts went back to the situation she faced. She and Abby couldn't stay there. Not now. The Dick had forced her hand and now she needed to uproot. Again. Out of necessity, she'd gotten good at it. In recent years, she likened herself to a hermit crab, molting and changing her shell about once a year—sometimes sooner, especially when she left a body in her wake. Her mind went to a verse from her favorite Emitt Rhodes song, as it often did.

Somewhere, someone special just for me....

Her fingers found the keys and began pecking around in the AZ MVD site. She paused when the vehicle license plates search window popped up. *What was that truck's goofy personalized plate yesterday? The cute guy...he'd been checking me out!* She smiled to herself as her photographic memory came up with the desired info within five seconds. Against better judgment, she typed it in:

LVG PHX

A few seconds went by before the information populated her screen, and it was accompanied by an exceedingly good license photo. Those were rare. The guy was several inches taller than her: six-foot-four, it said. *Nice.* An address in Gilbert. *Okay.* And his perfect smile complimented his sparkling eyes. *Those teeth.* It was a nice-looking face. A *kind* face.

Somewhere, someone....

Her lips curled into a smile as she whispered, "Hello, Curtis Martinsen...."

POP POP'S HOME
GILBERT, ARIZONA
THURSDAY, 6:35 PM

So much for a "minimum" day. This, by anyone's measure, had to qualify as a maximum one.

Curt pulled the F-150 into the long driveway, proceeding to his designated spot at the far end and off to the side, nearest the garage. He switched off his headlights and killed the engine and just sat there for the better part of a minute to lick his wounds. Day One of conferences had run long, and he was spent.

Pop Pop's truck wasn't in its spot, and Phoenix's Road Runner was safely tucked in its place of honor in the one-car garage. The last vestiges of a great sunset were fading to gray.

Curt sighed and, with great effort, opened the truck's door, grabbed his computer satchel, and headed into the main house. He hoped there might still be some leftovers saved for him.

From her vantage point across the street, two houses down, Tempest had watched the house—and Curt's arrival—from the comfort of her extra-long, 127-inch-wheelbase Tradesman van. She'd been waiting here for over an hour, but valuable intel had been gathered tonight, confirming the information she'd gleaned from the database. She started the van and pulled away, turning on her headlights only after she'd reached the end of the block.

"Can we get Wiley's now?" her passenger pleaded, pre-occupied with the new iPhone 3G her mama had surprised her with.

"That's what you want, baby?" Tempest replied quietly. She turned to give her daughter a smile, but Abby was glued to her screen and only nodded.

Getting Abby's new device on the way home had been the right call. Now that she didn't owe Dickwad her share of rent money, buying this gadget had been a no-brainer purchase. "Sure, honey."

Phoenix sat at the dining table and watched in amazement as Curt wolfed down a second self-constructed burrito, having incorporated the remains of both the carne asada and chile verde, along with the rice and beans she'd saved for him. He'd sworn off the beans for the longest time, and tonight's indulgence would make for a noisy cottage tonight. Phoenix made a mental note to crack open all the windows.

"Care for a wafer-thin mint?" she joked, replicating the French accent used by the waiter in the infamous Monty Python skit.

Curt's mouth was way too full to attempt a comeback, so he shook his head. She waited several seconds until he'd swallowed and come up for air. He wiped his mouth with a paper towel and chuckled weakly. "I'm good, thanks, babe."

Luke was sitting next to Curt's elbow, working him with his soulful brown eyes. It worked every time, and Curt shared a tiny bite of his carne asada with him. "That's it, buddy."

"How many conferences you got left for tomorrow?"

"Mm...nine, I think. Something like that. Got through

about half of them. One no-show, and a few late shows. Can't wait to be done," he replied, taking a long pull from his Dos Equis lager. "Hoping to be done earlier tomorrow."

"Pop Pop's talking about doing some barbeque, so I hope so," Phoenix said.

"Did I hear somebody mention barbecue?" Pop Pop chimed, letting the screen door close behind him as he set two full paper grocery bags atop the counter. "'Cause I've got the goods!"

"Hey, Pop Pop!" Phoenix acknowledged.

"Hey, guys," Pop Pop replied, setting down his keys.

"Hey...hope you won't be mad, but I finished off the left-overs," Curt said, sounding just short of apologetic.

"No worries, Curtis," Pop Pop replied, chuckling as he got himself a beer from the fridge. He knew Curt hated anyone using his full name almost as much as he himself disliked being called David. "Mind if I join you two?"

"Please do," Phoenix said, clearing away the evidence before returning to her seat, placing the plastic vial of Beano at Curt's station. "I was just about to tell Curt that I picked up these today!" she added, dangling a keyring that held three color-coded keys.

"What? Wait—you got 'em? That's awesome!" Curt replied enthusiastically.

"Yep. Two door keys, one mailbox," she replied eagerly, removing one of the door keys and handing it to him. Put it on your ring before you lose it."

"Roger that," Curt said, grimacing a little as he worked to slide it on to his less than cooperative keyring. "Nice touch with the orange key marker on it," he added.

"Yeah, well...mine's got a green one...don't want you getting too easily confused," she said with a chuckle.

"There," he said, smiling back as he jingled the keys.

"The manager called and said they'd completed the carpet install and the paint. We can move in anytime. Timing's perfect with next week off, and we should be able to get our stuff in there in half a day. Not that much, really."

"Please tell me we got—"

"The one with the doggie door? Yep!" she said. "Luke might find it a little tight because the previous renter got the installation approved for her corgi, but the little guys will definitely like it once they get the hang of it. It's grandfathered into the lease, so...."

"Never underestimate Luke's ability to squeeze through a small place," Curt said, smiling as he gave their shepherd a pat on the head.

"Patio's not huge, but we should be able to fit a decent grill, plus I can have my succulents. It'll be great."

"Perfect," Curt agreed.

"That's amazing, you two. Don't get me wrong; I'll miss having you here in the cottage, but after...what...eight years... you deserve a bigger place. With a bedroom door and a proper kitchen, at least," Pop Pop said, tipping his beer bottle to meet theirs. "Cheers!"

"Cheers!" Phoenix and Curt responded in unison. "And we'll only be fifteen minutes away, so it's not like you'll never see us!" Phoenix added with a reassuring smile.

"Roger that," Pop Pop said. "When you planning to move stuff over?"

"Not before Monday. Right, babe?" Phoenix answered, looking over at Curt.

"Yeah. Monday sounds good. Even Tuesday. I dunno...but

shouldn't be a big deal. I just need to survive this week," he replied as Phoenix's fingers gently combed his forearm hair.

"Let me know how I can help. Two trucks are better than one, right?" Pop Pop offered.

"We'll see. Thanks," Curt said, clinking bottles again. He turned to Phoenix as he changed the subject, lowering his voice. "How did Rose seem tonight?"

"Pretty good. Good appetite, anyway. She had her cheese enchilada, plus half of mine. I think the new apartment will be a good thing for her. For all of us."

"Hope so," Curt said. "I'll go peek in on her and let the other dogs out of purgatory while I'm at it," he added, carrying his empty beer bottle to the counter. On his way to the hallway, he dipped down and kissed Phoenix's forehead. She loved that and her smile confirmed it.

"Be sure to check out the artwork Rose made for you, Pop Pop," Phoenix said, gesturing to the masterpiece affixed to the refrigerator door.

"My goodness, will you look at that," Pop Pop replied, beaming proudly. "My granddaughter is brilliant...like her mother," he added with a smile at Phoenix. He didn't let up, but he was already beginning to process the separation anxiety.

"Where's my bunny girl?" Curt called out from the hallway just before reaching the office/guest bedroom.

"Hey!" came the sing-song-y response. "In here, Daddy!" Rose said, looking up from her art pad with a broad smile as he entered the room. Curt was happy to see that, and as he settled onto the floor next to her, he engaged her in a long hug.

From her seat at the table, Phoenix was listening to the exchange with a smile.

"Love you, Rosebud," Curt said.

"Love you more," Rose chirped.

"Doubt it," he replied. "So, show Daddy what you're working on, sweetie."

"Okay, so this is you...and this is mommy...and this is Pop Pop...and Luke...and Rick...and Sidney... and this...is Willie."

CHAPTER FIVE

DESERT PALM APARTMENTS
SURPRISE, ARIZONA
THURSDAY, 9:05 PM

TEMPEST HAD TUCKED Abby in an hour before and had gotten no complaints about the early bedtime, thanks to the new electronic babysitter, Abby's replacement iPhone 3G.

Best money I ever spent.

This gave Tempest time to quietly pad around the hovel and empty her clothes from the main bedroom's closet and dresser drawers. She did a half-assed job of folding things—apart from two cocktail dresses she kept in their hanging bag—as she hurriedly stuffed the lion's share into the packing boxes she'd kept flattened under the bed. She'd used these same boxes for more moves than she cared to remember, and she couldn't wait until she could be done with them, once and for all, and finally call someplace home...for reals.

Somewhere, someone....

Tempest didn't have much in the way of possessions. It was mainly her two boxes of clothes, plus four pair of shoes, and a half dozen necklaces—each a gift from various former boyfriends. Other than that, she kept her prized possessions: a stuffed bear from her youth, her toiletries, and her Conair professional-grade hair dryer. She'd add that to the box in the morning after she'd used it. Same went for her funky, pre-disco era alarm clock, which she had more confidence in now since she'd paid the electric.

The kitchen would be a one-boxer, as she sure as hell didn't want to take any of Dick's shit. The dishes, pots and pans, the toaster...all his. The knife holder, she'd take. It was something Dick had hated anyway, probably because it was called *The X – Voodoo* model and consisted of a molded, blood-red plastic figure of a human male standing atop a matching round base, with an assortment of five knives protruding from its torso and lower limbs, plus one through the head. It was the only kitchen item she cared about and it was a keeper. She set it into the box.

Tempest tossed two boxes of Pop Tarts in with it, along with the new box of Froot Loops, and some generic honey grahams. Two sets of utensils found their way into the box as well—they weren't savages.

She plucked her Disney magnets from the fridge door—souvenirs from her and Abby's one and only trip there three years before—then scanned the room for any other telltale signs of their existence. She wiped down the fridge handles, countertops, and cabinet doorknobs with an all-purpose spray cleaner she'd gotten at Dollar Tree.

Abby wasn't yet in the loop as to their exodus. But it wasn't her first rodeo, either. Tempest could have her daughter's things boxed in ten minutes and would do so while she was showering in the morning.

A quick look inside the fridge confirmed there was a little milk for the morning, along with some mayo and enough bread for their sandwiches. The jar of apple butter taunted her from its perch in the fridge door. With great ceremony and crushing sadness, Tempest grabbed the apple butter jar and tossed it into the trash. *Damn you, Paige!*

Killing the kitchen light, she padded back to her room, ran the electric toothbrush for several minutes, and set her alarm, along with a backup.

Tempest flopped back on the bed, her head sinking deep into the feather pillow. She extinguished the light and allowed her mind to perform a checklist to make sure she wasn't forgetting anything. Other than making sandwiches in the morning, and taking out the trash, she felt as prepared as she could be. She didn't have the next step planned out— not by a longshot—but she rarely did, and she'd figure it out as she went. That, it seemed, was both her specialty and her lot in life.

Goodnight, Tempest. She rolled onto her stomach and pulled up the covers. She was asleep within seconds. Her subconscious was already at work, doing its thing.

Somewhere, someone....

POP POP'S HOME
THE COTTAGE
THURSDAY, 9:35 PM

Curt was busy flossing his teeth, his thoughts already on the next day's conferences. He was happy to have finally dislodged the particularly pesky morsel of carne asada that had now chosen the bathroom mirror as its landing place.

Phoenix ran the tape gun along the seams of another freshly packed moving box and stacked it against the far wall, along with many others. She brushed the hair out of her eyes and set down the tool. "This is getting real!"

Curt spit the foam into the sink, rinsed, then wiped the schmutz off the mirror. "Sure is, honey. Can you believe it? After all this time?"

"So many memories in this little space. Ours, together, plus my own before I knew you. I'll miss it in a way, but I'm excited to make the move."

"Same here," he replied as he came in for a hug. "A real kitchen will be a huge upgrade, not to mention...a bedroom... with a locking door. Know what I mean?" he asked with a lascivious grin. He kissed Phoenix's neck.

The gesture was probably the closest thing to real intimacy they'd made time for since their spontaneous Valentine's date-night lovemaking session, two months prior, in the backseat of the Road Runner during a drive-in screening of *Paul Blart: Mall Cop*, and that had been helped along by the thermos of Cosmos they'd brought along.

For the past year and some change, all of their attention and efforts had been focused on keeping Rose emotionally healthy after her traumatic ordeal and at the expense of their own needs.

"I do indeed know what you mean," she said, kissing him. "Think you can hold on to that thought for just a few more days?" she asked, gesturing to their sleeping soon-to-be eight-year-old nestled in the middle of their communal double bed.

"Mm...guess we'll have to," Curt replied with a sigh and a tired smile. "Precious angel," he said softly, looking back over at Rose. "Thank God we have our family back together. Nothing's more important than that."

"Nothing." Phoenix nodded in agreement, melting into her gentle giant's massive arms. "I love you so much, forever, Curtis Martinsen."

"S. M. F., back to you, sweetie."

GILBERT POLICE DEPARTMENT
RAMAGE'S OFFICE
FRIDAY, APRIL 3, 9:05 AM

Detectives Moser and Ramage stood at the round table, having completely abandoned the savory croissant breakfast sandwiches she'd brought in. The photos spread across the tabletop had something to do with that, as they had just come from the coroner's forensic exam of the deconstructed woodchipper, the lower torso, and a sizeable bin containing the minced remains of Mr. Franco.

"Good God," Ramage muttered, trying not to spew his coffee all over the color 8x10s.

"Lord, have mercy," Moser said under her breath. Her hand covered her mouth, and she didn't know whether to cry or go blind. These were the worst images either of them had ever experienced in their combined years on the force.

"The jaw piece there," Ramage said, pointing to the close-up photo. "At least they were able to confirm dental from those couple of teeth. Poor bastard...."

Moser had seen enough. She looked up from the photos and turned to her partner. "Anything from the drink cup?"

"Besides Franco's prints, there was only one other—a partial—and it's probably from the gal at the Wiley's drive-thru," Ramage replied, scanning the report. "But..."

"What?"

"...the gloves. I can't get past the fact he wasn't wearing 'em."

"You think it's possible somebody else did this to him?"

"Anything's possible...we both know that after that shit-show in Idaho."

"Want to run by Wiley's?"

"Mm...yeah, but first," he said, consulting the address he'd written on his notepad, "how about we take a little drive out to Surprise?"

LA JOYA ELEMENTARY
APACHE JUNCTION, ARIZONA
FRIDAY, 9:18 AM

Mr. Martinsen was in the middle of his lesson on contractions when the phone rang in Room 8.

"Phone!"

"Phone's ringing!"

"Phone, Mr. Martinsen!" came the chorus of helpful notifications. It was as if they thought their teacher was completely deaf.

"Thank you, everyone!" he replied, holding up his palm as he gestured them into silence. "I want you all to try the next one on your own while I answer the phone. You can do this! Quietly, please. Got it?"

"Got it!" came the choral response.

"Mr. Martinsen," he said as he picked up.

"Mr. Martinsen, sorry to interrupt, it's Kelly in the front office."

"No problem, Mrs. Bozzo. How can I help you?"

"I know it's a bit odd, especially on the day before we go to spring break, but I'm sending someone over to your room. A new student. Brenda will be bringing her—"

A knock on the classroom door seemed to confirm this. "I think she may be here."

"Door, Mr. Martinsen!!" was but one of the helpful alerts coming from the peanut gallery.

He put his hand over the mouthpiece. "Guys...I can hear. Thank you."

"Sorry to add this to your day, and to your roster, but

63

the other second grade classes are maxed out. You okay with this?" she asked.

He could sense her pleading through the receiver, and he would do anything for Kelly. "Sure, why not?" he replied with a smile in his voice. "I'd better get the door. Thanks for the heads-up, Kelly...er, Mrs. Bozzo."

"Great, thanks!"

He placed the handset back in its cradle and walked to the door. He flipped open the locking mechanism and the door swung wide as Kelly's very capable office mate, Brenda, greeted him with a smile. She had a student file in one hand, and her other hand rested on the shoulder of a young girl.

"Mr. Martinsen, I'd like to introduce you to your new student, Abigail. Abigail, this is your new teacher, Mr. Martinsen."

"Hi," she said, looking up at the giant before her. She only mustered a half-smile, as she was every bit as surprised about this development as her teacher was.

"Hello, Abigail. Welcome to Room 8," he said, employing his best *welcome* smile.

"I like to be called Abby."

MEANWHILE...
POP POP'S HOME
FRIDAY, 9:35 AM

Phoenix had taken the day off from her gig at Pop's Automotive. She'd remedied the Land Cruiser's mystery leaks and replaced both the brakes and shocks on the Buick Skylark in her charge, so her boss—her dad and the shop's namesake— had given his blessing.

Today's gig would be dropping a few packed boxes off at the new place, making a run to the Goodwill, a vet visit, and finishing the mountain of laundry. She'd already walked the pack, and they were good and tired. She could hear Luke snoring from his crate in the kitchen.

As Phoenix peeked her head around the corner to watch him, she noticed three of her missing socks in the crate with him. He had a bit of a foot fetish when it came to his mom's socks, and she chalked it up to his abandonment issues. *Good thing you're cute, Luke.*

She smiled as she quietly retrieved the socks, shaking her head as she added them to the laundry pile. She finished separating the whites from the bright colors Rose often wore and checked everyone's pockets, including her own, before placing the items in the washer's tub.

As she got to Curt's favorite shirt, a light blue, short-sleeved button-down, she fished out a piece of paper from the breast pocket. It was a receipt from Wiley's, and she was just about to toss it in the trash when, upon closer inspection, she noticed a few anomalies. Some of the items made sense. Others not so much.

"What were you...feeding an army? Since when do you like zucchini?" she muttered. "And what's with the two large iced coffees?" She shook her head and set the receipt aside as she grappled with the heavy jug of detergent. "Nuggets? Really?" She'd have to ask Curt about it when he got home. She started the washer's cycle and switched off the laundry room light.

As she also had to take Sidney in for her dental appointment, she grabbed her tiny crate as she exited out to the garage.

Phoenix popped open the Road Runner's sizeable trunk. It was mostly filled with already-sealed, medium-sized packing boxes. Adjacent to them sat an almost-full donation box with its top still open, beckoning for something else to be added to it. *Why move to the new apartment with stuff we no longer need?*

As she scanned the garage shelves, her eyes rested on the clear plastic bins of Christmas decorations. Staring her in the face was Rose's snow globe. With all the secret chatter her daughter was still having with the deceased giant who had been one of her kidnappers, Phoenix didn't hesitate to remove the item from its storage bin and place it with the other donatable items.

Phoenix slammed the trunk, then placed Sidney's crate in the rear seat, securely buckling it in. "There you go, pipsqueak."

A series of low growls came from the scruffy rug rat, which puzzled her owner. *Too early for the mailman.* Phoenix shrugged, knowing it didn't take much to set her off. Sidney could hear anything. *A butterfly must have farted in the deepest part of the Amazon rainforest.*

Sidney always enjoyed going for a ride in the car but was now on full alert, barking bloody murder. Being a rescue, Phoenix wasn't entirely sure what her DNA profile was, but her best guess was a terrier/Tasmanian devil mix. She'd ask the vet.

"You hush now. There's nobody here, you little stinker," Phoenix said, closing the car door. Sidney growled in protest; she wasn't convinced.

Phoenix shushed the little girl one last time as she opened the garage door. "See? Now don't you feel silly?"

She stood there for a long moment. With her eyes closed and head tilted skyward, she let the warm morning rays of sun caress her face, her freckles. It was going to be another glorious Arizona day, and it reminded her just how much she enjoyed springtime here. She drank in the sunshine for a full minute, her smile of gratitude impossible to miss.

Even from across the street.

As the Road Runner backed down the drive toward her, Tempest scooched down in her seat as to not be seen. From the van's side mirror, she watched as the tiny redheaded driver pulled away, the throaty orange car disappearing down the street.

Who the fuck *are you?*

Tempest executed a slow, three-point U-turn, falling into place about a hundred yards behind.

Tempest maintained her following distance as the Road Runner zigzagged through light traffic, stopping briefly at the Good Will drop-off container in the parking lot adjacent to the grocery store.

She watched as the tiny driver emerged from the vehicle, retrieved a box from the trunk, and handed it to the young man attendant. He handed her a receipt in return, and she was on her way. The stop took less than a minute, which was good, because Tempest didn't have all day.

Glancing at her watch, Tempest figured she could maintain her tail for another twenty minutes or so, if need be. She had hoped to get to the gym for an overdue workout this morning before work, but something more pressing had come up. She could go after work, maybe. It was called Anytime Fitness, after all.

After nearly losing her in traffic twice, Tempest locked in on the distinctive rear end of the orange muscle car and made a few aggressive maneuvers, as necessary, in order to maintain her surveillance position.

The next stop was at an older, two-story apartment complex about ten minutes from the store. The Road Runner pulled into the covered parking structure and proceeding to the end space by the rear of the building.

Instead of following her into the lot, Tempest pulled the van along the curb and got out. She stealthily followed on foot, taking advantage of a parked minivan for cover, as she watched Phoenix pull the first box from the trunk and round the corner to the rear of the complex.

Tempest walked as briskly and quietly as possible, arriving at the corner of the building and peeking around it just in time to see her tiny target set the box down outside a nearby door and fumble for her keys. She tucked her head back and listened until she heard the door close before poking her head around to get a look at the number on the door: 133. She filed that nugget of intel into her photographic memory bank and hustled back to her van.

Tempest sat curbside with her window down for several minutes, slunk down in her seat and glancing at her watch on occasion. She was running out of time and just about to abandon her mission when the sound of the trunk lid slamming got her attention. A moment later it was followed by the vroom of the muscle car's engine. The Road Runner materialized, exited the lot, and turned back onto the street, at which time the van followed suit.

A scant two miles later, the Road Runner turned into the driveway of an automobile repair shop. Tempest glanced up to the sign: POP'S. Slowing the van, she watched as the driver pulled the orange beast into an end spot near the Dumpster, hopped out, and proceeded inside.

Okay then.

DESERT PALMS APARTMENTS
SURPRISE, ARIZONA
10:05 AM

Mrs. Sawyer, the onsite manager, stood on the landing of the exposed walkway, just outside Richard Franco's apartment. It was the only place she could enjoy her cigarette while the detectives went about their walkthrough, as smoking was expressly prohibited inside the units.

She hadn't had much to tell them about the tenants. The rent was paid on time, and other than a few complaints from the next-door neighbor about TV noise and a couple times about a raised voice, Franco seemed to have been a decent enough tenant. Better than that downstairs asshole—the one with an illegal muffler on his Camaro, anyway.

"Almost done?" she called out to them. She had paperwork to catch up on, plus she was missing her favorite soap on her tiny office TV.

"Just about," Detective Moser answered, loud enough to be heard from the bathroom area adjoining the larger of the two bedrooms.

Detective Ramage walked up to his partner. "Anything?"

"Not much," she said, her gloved finger running along the bathroom counter to the sink area where she noticed a few small brown stains. She studied them for a few moments, noting their characteristics. The droplets were small, and few, and their shape and hue weren't consistent with blood stains, at least visually. She'd seen her share. Still, it might warrant a follow-up investigation with the chemical reagent, *Luminol*, to rule anything out, she noted.

Since she'd also dyed her own hair more times than she cared to admit, a cheap box of hair color seemed a more likely source of the stains. She switched her attention to the bathroom cabinet.

"Old Spice, some Mitchem deodorant, ribbed condoms... guy stuff. You?"

"Nah. Second bedroom's closet's empty. So's the chest of drawers," he muttered, his stomach growling loudly.

"Did you see a file cabinet anywhere, phone records... anything?"

"Not a trace of paper, other than on the roll by the toilet. There was an empty plastic file box in the bedroom closet, but nothing left behind. Seems somebody may've cleared out in a hurry."

"I'll call it in, get the forensics crew to give the place a closer look. Might be some latent prints that don't match his."

"Roger that."

"So...we done?" Moser asked.

"Yeah. Think so."

JUICE BLAST
SURPRISE, ARIZONA
10:35 AM

Detective Moser was pleasantly surprised she hadn't received much pushback on her suggestion. She and her partner stood in line at the recently opened Juice Blast, as it was only a couple of blocks from the Desert Palms complex.

They'd finished talking with Franco's apartment manager and Ramage's blood sugar was starting to tank. As they hadn't been able to enjoy their breakfast sandwiches, no thanks to the coroner's photo dump that morning, this seemed like as good a place as any to recharge their batteries.

"You been here before?" Ramage asked her, his stomach growling.

"Not to this one, but they have a few other locations. So, yeah. Pretty good smoothies."

Ramage perused the menu board and felt like he'd lost a bet. "Is that all they've got? Nothing...solid?"

"It's a juice bar."

"I'm seeing a lot of veggies and stuff I've never even heard of."

"Yeah, well...think of it as a salad in a glass. You can get fruit added to it, so you won't be too traumatized. C'mon, it'll be good for you!" she replied with a smile of encouragement.

"You say so...."

There were a couple of industrial-grade blenders already whirring with nutritious concoctions. As the detectives reached the counter, a new blender was being fired up a few feet away, its blades groaning loudly against the stubborn stalks of kale, celery, and raw beats being fed into them.

"May I help you?" the bubbly juice bar attendant asked, her voice barely discernable above the grinding of root vegetables.

Ramage turned to his partner, and his expression told her he not only knew nothing about juice bars, but that the noises were also bringing back horrific flashes of poor Mr. Franco's demise.

"We'll just take, uh, two number sevens. And add some strawberries to his, please."

"Two number sevens, one with strawberries...got it. That'll be twelve fifty five. Those will be right up," the girl said cheerfully.

Moser turned to Ramage; his expression was ashen. "You okay?"

He nodded as he dug out his wallet and handed her a twenty. "Um, I'm gonna go grab that table by the window."

"'Kay," Moser replied, handing the girl the cash and retrieving the change. She stuffed two singles into the tip jar. As she waited for their order, another blender fired up and she watched as whole carrots, celery, and kale were pushed into the top of the vessel. She too was finding it impossible not to think of what must've transpired at the golf course.

Ramage took another pull from his large, clear plastic drink cup. The beets had trumped all, turning the concoction a blood red. He looked out the window.

"What do you think? Pretty good, right?" Moser asked.

"Meh...strawberries were a good call, but I'd skip on those beets next time," he replied with a grimace. "You don't think they taste like dirt?"

"No! I love me some beets. Always have," she replied. "I'm proud of you for trying something healthy," she added with a smile.

He nodded slightly; he was secretly proud of himself as well. He turned to the window, then back to her as he changed the subject. "So, tell me. What do you make of the apartment manager's statement? What she said about a young woman living there?"

"Seems Franco might've had a girlfriend."

"If so, she wasn't on the lease. No trace of a girlfriend, no personal belongings, from what I could tell. I mean, you're a woman. Anything seem unusual? I miss something?"

"Well, there were only a man's clothes in the closet. Same with the dresser. Kitchen seemed tidier than I would imagine Mr. Franco keeping it, but then I didn't know the man. Might've been a neat freak, who knows? Still, it's hard to say if he'd had a female companion living there recently."

"Okay, what about the kid? The girl? Said she was, like, seven or eight. Both blond. Do you think this was a mother and daughter? She'd seen them a couple of days ago. Did they make a hasty exit? And if so, why?"

"I do find that curious. Mother's tall, she said. Like six feet, athletic build. Kept to herself," Moser said, taking another sip. "Might no longer be a blond, though."

Ramage's brow furrowed. "What makes you say that?"

"Just that it looked like there might've been some traces of brown hair dye in the bathroom sink. We girls notice stuff like that."

"Good eye. Partner. Forensics will—"

"Already on it."

Ramage nodded thoughtfully. "I'm gonna go out on a limb here... I don't figure this Franco guy for having been the vain type. You?"

"You never know, but his driver's license photo made it appear not. Kind of an ill-kept salt-and-pepper rat's nest."

"So, the roomie—the girlfriend—might be a six-foot brunette then..." he muttered, scribbling a note into his pad.

"Possible. Trash cans were emptied, so...we can't be certain of that."

"Yeah," Ramage said, noisily slurping the remains of his smoothie. "We may want to come back another time, later in the day, when we can find some of the neighbors home. They might have something to add."

"Hope so."

"In the meantime, since we're out here anyway, I say we check out the local elementary schools. See if anybody matching the girl's description may've been recently pulled from the roster."

DEPARTMENT OF TRANSPORTATION (AZ MVD)
WINDOW 2
GLENDALE, ARIZONA
FRIDAY, 11:05 AM

Tempest settled into her chair and began inputting a search into the AZ MVD system. There were only a couple of customers now, and they were being assisted by her associates at Windows 1 and 3.

She'd lied to her supervisor about having a doctor's appointment this morning, but it had allowed her to handle a couple of important matters. She took a quick sip of her iced coffee as the screen began to populate with the desired information. Her brow furrowed.

Phoenix. What kind of name is that? Phoenix Martinsen... could be his sister? Whoever you are, your registration's due this month. Tempest looked up from the screen and noticed two new customers had materialized. She'd have to pursue this a bit later. She switched screens and feigned a smile. "May I help you?"

AZ MVD PARKING LOT
12:10 PM

Tempest liberated her sandwich from the lunch box. It was her Plan B—maybe even Plan C—sandwich now that her traditional apple butter concoction had been forever ruined for her. She pulled off the plastic wrap and, like a great white ruining a sea lion's day, sunk her teeth into the crustless tuna on white. She chewed furiously. *Needs pickles.*

She dug the prescription bottle from her purse and tossed back the last two aripiprazole. *Shit...need a refill!* These didn't seem to be helping much more than the bupropion had, but she'd run that course of meds and didn't like what it did to her libido. She'd continue to self-medicate until she found something to take the edge off and made a mental note to call her doctor. If he was even still talking to her after her last visit. She was pretty sure she still had some Valium in her toiletries bag.

Tempest was still fixated on what—more like, *who*—she'd seen at the Martinsen house this morning. The car, she'd discovered, was a 1970 Plymouth Road Runner, and its munchkin driver was listed as being four-foot-eleven. *What the hell?* She was beginning to wonder if this was A-Z or OZ....

Still could be his sister...or he might just have a thing for dwarves. Is the circus in town?

Tempest, sensing something, turned to her left and started at the sight of the smiling goth girl standing a foot away from her van's door. "Jeezus!! Paige!! What the fucking fuck?!"

"Hi! Sorry...didn't mean to scare you!"

"Too late!" Tempest snapped, lowering the window. "What is it, Paige? I'm trying to—"

"I know...I know. Sorry. I just wanted to ask if...um...you wanted to, you know, hang out sometime...?" Her awkward expression only served to confirm Tempest's hypothesis about childhood head trauma. Tempest scrunched her brow. *Is she asking me out now?*

"Uh, can we...this isn't a good time, Paige. Thanks, but, uh, I've got a *lot* going on right now, okay?"

Paige's smile hiccupped for a moment before she recovered. "Oh, totally understand. Maybe some other time, then."

"Maybe..." Tempest lied. She held up her sandwich to remind her coworker this was her lunch break and her sacred private place to enjoy it.

"Okay, then," Paige said breezily, flashing another smile. "Love your hair color by the way!" she added before walking away. Tempest continued to watch her unfortunate coworker as she headed to her equally unfortunate looking Ford Fiesta.

Tempest shook her head as she wolfed down the remainder of the sandwich and grabbed a cheese stick. Her mind returned to current events. It had been a manic morning, would likely be a crazy afternoon, and anything beyond that was still in an insane state of flux.

She looked over her right shoulder and surveyed what was left of her existence: it was all stuffed into a half-dozen pathetic, very used moving boxes and a few plastic bins in the rear cargo area. *Jeezus....*

She powered up the eight-track player and was immediately blasted with what had been her morning selection, "Twisted" by Joni Mitchell. She yanked out the blue tape cartridge and stuffed it into the empty slot in her carrying case.

She had about ten minutes left of her break and needed to clear her head. Her fingers walked down the spines of her collection until they came to the one she wanted—and needed: a self-titled masterpiece of an album by a relatively obscure genius who was widely compared with Paul McCartney: Emitt Rhodes.

She inserted the cartridge into the player, hit the track selection button twice to get back to Track 1, then leaned back into her seat as she waited for the second song to cue up.

It began with a very brief and simple guitar intro, which always brought a smile, before giving way to an infectious

Beatle-esque arrangement of piano, guitar, bass, and drums—
all played by this multi-instrumentalist pop sensation and
recorded in his home studio. The vocals were sweet and the
chorus sublime; one would swear it was Paul singing a hidden
Beatles gem.

It was her soundtrack. Her affirmation. And, out of necessity, it had long ago become her mantra. She closed her eyes
and let the melody wash over her, and the lyrics penetrate her
like a prayer, for what had to be the millionth time.

The lyrics spoke of something she'd never experienced,
not by a longshot, but she held out hope anyway. She clung
to its promise because it might one day germinate into truth.

It had to.

She murmur sung along with the tape, forever faithful—
evangelical, even; its simple message serving to nourish the
seed she'd planted years ago. The gospel according to Emitt.

Somewhere, someone special just for me

Somewhere, someone special must be

Somewhere, someone special just for me (somewhere, someone)

Somewhere, someone special must be

Somebody made for me, somebody made for you

Somebody made for me, somebody made for you

Ask and you'll receive

Dear God in Heaven, won't you help me, please?

Somewhere, someone special just for you (somewhere, someone)

Somewhere, someone special, it's true

Somewhere, someone special just for you (somewhere, someone)

Somewhere, someone special it's true

Somebody made for you, somebody made for me
Somebody made for you, somebody made for me
Ask and you'll receive
Dear God in Heaven, won't you help me, please?

CHAPTER SIX

LA JOYA ELEMENTARY
APACHE JUNCTION
FRIDAY, 1:50 PM

M R. MARTINSEN WAVED back at several of his bus riders as they anxiously awaited their circuitous ride home. The students' Spring Break had officially started fifteen minutes before, and he looked forward to his own starting upon wrapping up the last of his conferences.

He looked down and smiled to the one remaining child awaiting pickup, the new girl, Abby. She wasn't smiling, nor did she seem particularly excited. Curt scanned the parking lot.

"Your mom should be here any minute, Abby," he offered. He was just throwing out a comforting thought, as it wasn't based on any intel he possessed. He hadn't yet met her parents, but he knew Kelly would have made it clear that today was a minimum day due to conferences.

Abby stared straight ahead, her eyes scanning the parking area, the street.

"What kind of car does your mommy drive, honey?"

"Van. Dodge, I think," she replied. She began futzing with her iPhone.

"What color?"

"Kind of white, I guess," she said.

"Okay, I'll keep an eye out with you," he said, glancing at his watch. "If she doesn't come in another ten minutes, we'll go to the office and you can wait for her there, okay?"

"I guess," she replied with a shrug of annoyance. "She's late a lot."

"Mm...so, what does your family have planned during the Spring Break? Anything fun?" he asked, trying to keep things positive.

"Nah, no plans. Nothing fun," Abby replied truthfully. She'd forgotten what fun was.

Just then the kind-of white Dodge van approached the driveway, pausing for a bus exit.

"She's here," Abby said, looking up at him. "Bye!"

"You're sure that's your mom's car?" Curt replied, needing confirmation that it wasn't some random stranger.

"I'm sure...bye!" she affirmed, as she began walking toward the vehicle.

"Abby, wait. Stop, please. I'm coming with you," her teacher replied firmly as he fell into step alongside her.

Abby looked up at him, her expression telegraphing her thought: *whatever.*

With the angle of the sun, it was hard for him to make out the driver. As a teacher—and a parent—he had to be vigilant, especially after nearly losing his own daughter to evildoers.

Shading his eyes as they approached the van, he waved and smiled.

"Hi, I'm Abby's new teacher, Mr. Martinsen. I just wanted to introduce myself," he added, extending his hand to the driver through the window.

"Hi, I'm...Abby's mom. Nice to meet you," Tempest replied, half-smiling back as she returned the handshake, much of her face shielded behind the oversized lenses of her dark, flea-market sunglasses.

She collected her hand from the yummy man's soft-yet-firm grip. *Oh, my gawd.*

Tempest hadn't intended this to be his first impression and she silently cursed herself for her stringy ponytail and ball cap. And she was devoid of her lip gloss. *I must look like shit.*

Abby continued around the front of the vehicle and climbed into the passenger side.

Tempest turned to Abby. "Seatbelt," she said, waiting for the click before turning back.

"Abby had a good first day—well, it was a half day—but I think she'll like our class," Mr. Martinsen said.

"Great."

A slightly awkward moment went by, the gap filled by the unhealthy idling of the van's engine. When it seemed a more elaborate response might not be coming from the parent, he glanced at his watch.

"Well, nice to meet you. I've got to get ready for conferences here in a minute but just wanted to say hi. Abby, we'll see you when you come back after the break, okay?"

"'Kay," Abby grunted, having all but tuned out anything outside her phone's display.

"You folks have a nice Easter," he said, flashing his genuine smile.

"Thank you. You as well," Tempest replied with a half-smile

as she nudged her sunglasses up the bridge of her nose and began to pull away.

Tempest glanced at her mirror and saw Mr. Martinsen waving goodbye. *Wow.*

She turned to her daughter.

"So, it sounds like you had a good day," she said.

"It was okay...he's my new teacher," Abby replied, completely unenthused.

"I know, honey," Tempest said, shaking her head. "*Hello...* Earth to Abby... We just met, silly. Do you like him?"

"Yeah, I guess."

"Good..." Tempest replied softly, a secret smile forming as she gave her Dean Martin eight-track tape a nudge, resuming its play. She hummed along as Dean crooned his 1966 hit, "Somewhere There's a Someone."

Still squinting, Curt finished his wave and let out a sigh as he thought about the busy day that lay ahead. *Four more hours, Mr. Martinsen...four more hours.*

PARADISE FOUND MOBILE ESTATES
SUPERSTITION SPRINGS/EAST MESA, ARIZONA
FRIDAY, 2:45 PM

Abby worked on a large order of nuggets and sipped her chocolate shake as she kept herself entertained with her electronics. Tempest had placated her with a quick visit to Wiley's drive-thru because she knew her daughter wouldn't be any too excited about where they were heading. Nor was she, for that matter.

Tempest took comfort in her Emitt Rhodes eight-track, as she often did, and the album was nearing the end of its third complete cycle. "Ever Find Yourself Running" played softly in the background, and once again, Emitt's lyrics were nailing her mood, his questions pinning her down:

Ever find yourself running, running, running away

Ever find yourself hiding from the things that you feel

Ever hear yourself crying, crying, crying to someone....

"Okay...you win...yes, I do...thanks for asking..." Tempest answered under her breath, reaching down to remove the tape cartridge from the deck. As she pulled it out, a long loop of its magnetic tape cascaded from the opening, extending from the tape's housing like so much extruded pasta, fatally stuck in the player's machinery.

"Dammit!" she blurted, tossing the ruined cartridge onto the dash.

"Mom!" Abby scolded, her face still glued to her phone's screen. She hadn't seemed to mind the endless music loop too much; at least she didn't say anything, but she always called her mom out for swearing.

"Sorry, honey," Tempest replied. It wasn't the end of the world; she had another copy. Tempest took a deep breath and slowly exhaled her sigh as she turned the corner.

Abby finally looked up from her phone, and the sky-high cluster of palm trees told her where they were going. "Mom! No!!"

"Abby...."

"I don't want to go to Grandma's!"

"C'mon, she hasn't seen you in a long time, and besides, there's a swimming pool there!" Tempest said with more excitement than she herself was feeling.

"I don't want to go swimming!" Abby protested.

"It'll be fun, and we can order a pizza later!"

"I just ate! And I didn't even bring a swimsuit!"

"I brought it, honey! It's in the box, with all your things, behind your seat," she said, trying to sell it with a broad smile. "We'll just stay for a little while," she lied.

"All of my things are in that box?" Abby cried out, craning her neck to look at the van's meager cargo. "Are we homeless again?!"

"We're not...*homeless*, honey. We're just...needing to... make another change, okay? It'll be fine, honey, I promise."

"That's what you said last time," Abby said, sinking into her seat as they pulled up to the driveway entrance leading into a several-decades-old mobile home community.

Tempest lowered her window and pulled into the sprawling wannabe oasis that had seen much better days. *Paradise Found? More like God's Waiting Room.* It looked sadder than she remembered. She couldn't recall if it had been two years or three, and she didn't want to be here any more than her daughter did, that was for sure.

The van slowly crept along the circuitous driveway path and Tempest couldn't help thinking that each unit looked sadder than the last. An elderly couple leaned into their walkers as they hobbled along the edge of the pavement. The man was particularly frail and looked to be breathing with assistance from an oxygen line attached to a bottle. These desert tortoises were way overqualified when it came to the homeowner's association stipulation of a fifty-five plus community, and surely there would be another vacancy any day now.

They drove past the meager pool area where three octogenarian women with swim caps were standing waste deep in the water. One was wearing water wings.

"Mom...."

"Here we are, honey," Tempest said, pulling into one of the two guest parking slots nearest the dreary, gray doublewide. The unit's number, 88, was nailed on to the wood trim where it joined the porch, its paint left faded and peeling from the unrelenting Arizona sun and an indifferent owner. A few weathered potted plants fought for survival and were losing the battle. This was it.

Tempest was momentarily startled when she checked in with the mirror on her visor. She'd forgotten she was a brunette today. She applied a coat of her strawberry lip gloss and flipped the visor closed. "C'mon, Abby...let's go say hi."

"Fine-*nuh*," came Abby's snotty, elongated response as she undid her seatbelt and hopped out. Tempest did the same, and as she closed the van's door, the tortoise couple slowly shuffled by, craning their necks suspiciously. *Don't worry...I'm not the coroner.*

Tempest flashed a fake smile at them and knocked on the unit's door. Abby stood behind her. "Please put your phone away, honey." This got an unseen eyeroll as Abby complied.

Tempest hadn't called beforehand, so it remained to be seen how the reception committee would react to this surprise visit. She had a pretty good idea though.

Desperate times call for desperate measures, Tempest. A minute went by with no indication there was anyone home. Tempest turned, put her arm around her daughter, and was just about to step off the porch when she heard the door open behind her.

"Well, well...look what the cat dragged in," came the gravelly voice.

Tempest closed her eyes and silently counted to five before turning toward the source. She manufactured a smile. "Hello, Mother."

The woman staring back at her had visibly aged since Tempest had last seen her. At sixty-six years old, she was considerably younger than most of the demographic here, but forty-plus years of that had been as a very loyal two-pack-a-day Pall Mall Red consumer.

Her skin was leathery and weathered beyond her years, thanks to a combination of sun, tobacco, and her favorite libation, Maker's Mark. Her eyes were alert, scanning Tempest carefully as if assessing a threat. "Almost didn't recognize you. What the hell happened to your hair?"

"Good to see you too, Mother. Just thought I'd change things up a little," Tempest said, ignoring the insult. "You remember Abigail, of course," she added, prompting her daughter to make eye contact with her adoring grandmother. Abby looked up at the enfeebled woman who, at four-foot-seven, wasn't that much taller than she was. "Abby, can you say hello to your Grandma Vicky?"

"Hi," she said meekly.

"Abigail...why, look at how big you are," Vicky replied. "Of course I remember my only granddaughter," she said, looking back up at Tempest long enough to fire a scowl across the bow before returning her gaze to the precious youngster standing before her. "I'm not that old," she muttered. "And you're even more beautiful than I remember," she said, smiling now through discolored teeth that reminded Abby of one of her Crayola crayons, and it wasn't the white one.

"Such a lovely child," the woman said softly. "Your mother used to be too."

Then what happened? Tempest almost said in response to what was clearly meant to be another jab, but she bit her tongue. She'd been on the receiving end of her mother's barbs for most of her adult life, so she knew them when she heard them. *Pick your battles, Tempest.*

"You're probably thirsty," Grandma Vicky said to Abby. "Why don't you come inside, and I'll fetch you some sweet tea. Or some juice. Would you like that?" she asked. Abby looked up at her mother, who gave her a nod. "Okay then," Vicky said, opening the door wider so her granddaughter could enter. Vicky followed her inside and let the screen door slam. "You might as well come in too," she said without looking at Tempest. It wasn't an invite as much as it was an afterthought.

Story of my life.

Unit 88 was a two-bedroom double-wide that appeared to be frozen in time, while struggling to decide which decade it should belong to. The once off-white walls, as well as the drapes, had long ago surrendered to the beige of tobacco stain, and the empty twenty-gallon fish tank's former occupant, a puffer, had succumbed to the secondhand smoke of another puffer. The shag carpet was a bit worn, but appeared clean enough, its brown tones forgiving.

"You can sit there, honey," Grandma Vicky said, pausing to cough as she pointed to the loveseat. "Let me just move this big scrapbook here," she added, grabbing the hefty album and casting Tempest a shifty glance while she was at it. Tempest picked up on it, finding it curious.

"I'll bring you a cool drink. I have apple juice and lemonade," she offered.

"Lemonade, please," Abby said, her dormant manners making a rare appearance.

Tempest was still standing as she had yet to be shown any such hospitality. Her nostrils flared; the place smelled not unlike an old chimney. She watched as Vicky placed the album on the floor near the slider and shuffled into the tiny kitchen.

She pulled a glass pitcher from the brown side-by-side refrigerator and placed it on the yellow ceramic-tiled counter as she retrieved a plastic tumbler from the dish strainer. The drinking glass was fifties era, while the pitcher was straight out of a Kool-Aid advertisement, only minus the smiley face.

"What do you want?" the kitchen troll called out.

"Me? I'm fine, thanks," Tempest replied.

"Suit yourself," Vicky said, pouring lemonade into a second tumbler.

Abby looked up at her mother and Tempest responded with a tight smile as Vicky entered the spartan living room with two glasses. She placed one on a round plastic coaster in front of Abby and carried her own over to the tiny side table, sliding a full ashtray off to the side to make room for it. Across the room, an old TV was playing a soap opera with the sound off.

Vicky plopped down into her well-used, gunmetal gray recliner and looked up at her daughter, who was still standing there awkwardly. "Well, are ya going to sit or just stand there?"

Tempest flashed a hint of a smile as she squeezed onto the loveseat, next to Abby. She placed her hands on her knees and rubbed the moisture from her palms. She was screaming inside. "How have you been, Mother? Sorry to just show up unannounced, but we were in the neighborhood."

"Were you now?" Vicky replied, not quite a scoff. "That's very kind of you to check in on your dear ol' mother," she said, lighting up a Pall Mall with her trusty Zippo. She took a deep drag and exhaled. The room almost immediately filled with smoke.

Abby winced as the cloud came her way. "Would it be okay if I opened the slider?" Tempest asked.

Vicky nodded her approval as Tempest got up, stepping over the stack of books on her way to the patio door. She rolled the glass door across its tracks and returned to her seat. "Thank you," Tempest said.

Vicky turned to her granddaughter. "Tell me, child, what grade are you in now? First? Second?"

"Second."

"Second...well, that's terrific." She took another deep puff and exhaled a cloud as she continued. "I think the last time

I saw you...you were maybe four," she said. Her smile disappeared as she turned a judgmental look toward Tempest. "That's a long time without seeing family."

"It is. I'm sorry," Tempest conceded. "Work's been keeping me busy. And...life too."

"I see," Vicky said, pausing long enough to enjoy three more drags from her grit before continuing. "You still with that fella...what's his name...Andy...in Peoria?"

"You mean Randy. No, that didn't work out. Lost his job, started drinking pretty heavily, and wasn't treating us too well."

"Where are ya now then?" Vicky pressed.

"Now," Tempest began, pausing to suppress an urge to laugh at the absurdity of recent developments. "Well, we've been over there in Surprise since...I dunno...must be last October, I think," she added, wishing for an to end this line of questioning. "Not the best situation, I'm afraid."

"Well, that's too bad," Vicky eventually replied. It sounded neither judgmental nor sympathetic. She could've just as easily responded with, "Huh." A moment went by before she felt compelled to insert her dig: "You've always known how to pick 'em."

I sure picked one hell of a mother! Tempest's fingers clenched around her kneecaps.

"Started Abby in a new school today. Over in Apache Junction," Tempest said instead, attempting to sound positive. "Closer to her grandma," she added, trying to sell it with a smile to them both.

"Well, well," Vicky said, looking to Abby. "Sounds like your ol' grandma might just get to see you more often then," she said. "Maybe you can come over some days after school and go swimming. How would that be?"

Abby's smile was strained, but it was the best she had. "That might be nice," she lied, with a nod.

Vicky was staring harder at Tempest now. Assessing. Judging. Tempest's nervous ticks never went unnoticed by her mother, nor did the rather wild look in her eyes. She'd seen it before. Plenty of times.

"Tell me you're not self-medicating again," Vicky said softly but directly.

Tempest shot a look back at her and shook her head subtly, her mouth a tight line. It was a warning shot: *don't go there*. She opted to change the subject.

"Speaking of the pool, Mother, I think Abby might like to go swimming while we're here, wouldn't you, Abby? That is if it's all right...?"

"If you have a suit with you, I suppose that would be just fine," Vicky replied, directing her attention to Abby. "Or you could use one of mine," she added, her laugh triggering a coughing fit.

"We have hers. Excuse me, I'll just go get it," Tempest said as she stood, exiting through the front door and into some fresh air.

"We have a lifeguard," Vicky said, smiling at Abby. "His name's Larry. I think he's eighty, but an excellent swimmer, I'm told. I think he fancies me."

Abby returned the smile awkwardly, taking a sip from her lemonade.

Tempest rifled through Abby's worldly possessions, which were few. She pulled out last year's pink one-piece swimsuit, hoping it still fit Abby. She was growing like a weed. "Why do you always have to be such a fucking bitch, Vicky?" she muttered through clenched teeth as she exited the van and made her way back to the lion's den.

She let herself in and found her mother in the kitchen, cutting off the crusts from three sandwiches.

"Not for me, thanks," Tempest said.

"It's your favorite, and my neighbor, Sonja, made the apple butter...you're sure?"

"Yes, thank you." She didn't feel like elaborating.

Vicky wrapped the third sandwich in some plastic wrap, placed it in the fridge, and carried the two others on paper plates to the living room. Tempest followed and took her seat next to Abby. She gave her daughter a stealthy reminder nudge.

"Thank you, Grandma," Abby said. She waited several moments before taking a small bite, then nudged her mother back.

"I used to make these for your mother, Abby, when she was your age. She always wanted the crusts removed, and I still make them that way. Not sure why," Vicky said, puzzled to think of it.

Tempest looked around the room while the others ate in silence. She didn't see any photos of herself displayed anywhere, and she was fine with it. There was a five by seven inch framed photo of her beloved childhood pet, Rufus. A sweeter labrador you could never meet, and it had absolutely crushed her when her father had dropped it off at the pound while she was at school one day. *Bastard.*

Her mother's raspy voice brought her back to the present.

"Did your mother ever tell her how she got named Tempest?" Vicky asked, wiping her mouth with a paper towel.

"No," Abby replied, looking at her mother and gauging her expression.

"I don't think I've ever been told that either, Mother," Tempest said incredulously. "Is there some weird, unusual story about my name I don't know about?"

"I wouldn't say weird...it's not weird. It's just interesting. At least I think so," Vicky replied, now turning toward her grand-daughter. "You see, a long time ago, when your grandpa and I were married—I know you didn't know him, but he and I got married and were living in a godforsaken place called Kentucky. Ken-*tuck*-y—pretty far from here, Abby. I can show you on a map later but don't feel like getting up just yet."

"That's okay," Abby answered, her disinterest already rising to the surface.

"Anyways, about the time I was fixin' to have my baby—your mama there," she said with a quick head turn as if clarification was necessary, "we'd been having some awful weather, for about a week. Maybe longer. Probably ten days...I mean, it was nasty. Wind was howling, roof felt like it was going to blow clean off the house. Rained nonstop for days on end..." she added, pausing as she relived the memory. "Road was muddy, washed out...couldn't get to a hospital."

"What'd you do, Grandma?" Abby asked, fully invested now.

"Well, only one thing we could do. Go down into the cellar. Kind of like Dorothy's family in *The Wizard of Oz*. You remember that movie?"

"Yes, Grandma."

"Well, that's what we did. We were down there for two days, in the dark, listening to what sounded like the end of the world out there. She was stubborn, that baby...like she didn't want to come out. Finally, had me a little girl. Your mother there. Your grandpa and I had planned to name her Alice, but with everything goin' on, we went with something that seemed more appropriate: Tempest...means *storm*. A *violent storm*...and that's how your mama got her name," Vicky said, turning toward Tempest. "I'd say the name fits her perfectly."

Tempest looked back into her mother's eyes and searched them. She felt nothing. Certainly nothing remotely close to love. It wasn't hate, either. She'd long ago let go of that poison, at least when it came to her feelings about her mother. No, what she was feeling was more like...pity...mixed with disgust.

The hatred she still had, she reserved that mostly for her father.

"Wow...thanks for telling me about my origins, Mother. I rather like my name. Always have," she said, denying her mother the pleasure of ruining it.

"Yes, well..." Vicky muttered, fumbling for her pack of smokes that had lodged in the edge of the chair's cushion. "How about we get you changed, Abby, and I'll introduce you to Lifeguard Larry."

Grandma Vicky had decided she was overdue for a swim herself and put on her lime green and black one-piece swimsuit. Lifeguard Larry had taken notice last time she'd worn it.

Tempest had passed on the invitation to join them, stating her desire to nap on the couch while they were enjoying themselves.

She wasn't the least bit tired though. And she had things to do.

Now that the coast was clear, Tempest went back out to the van and brought Abby's box of belongings into the house.

She placed it in the corner of the second bedroom, which was primarily a storage place for various things, including the canister vacuum cleaner, a seldom-used exercise bike, and an old broken treadmill, its belt stacked with several boxes.

She recognized a few of the boxes as being her own, having asked to store them "for a week, tops," several years before, during another hasty move. She found the one she was looking for and opened it. Just as she'd left them: the remainder of her treasure trove of eight-track tapes she'd collected during her music club membership years. She was pretty sure she'd only paid the equivalent of a buck, cumulative, for her various memberships, and her frequent moves made it hard for the collection department.

There were over a hundred tape cartridges in the box, and after sorting through them all, she was happy to find that she still had several copies of the self-titled Emitt Rhodes album, which quickly eased the pain of having had one eaten by the deck. She grabbed two of those, along with another Dean Martin one, and some Patsy Cline.

She reclosed the box, placed it neatly atop the stack on the treadmill, and took the tapes out to the van. While there, she grabbed her hanging clothes bag, some fresh underwear—her Victoria's Secret ones—along with her make-up case and Conair hair dryer. She knew where her good shoes were, so she'd get those later.

Not knowing just how long the swim party might last, Tempest kicked things into high gear as she stepped into the tiny bathroom, hanging her clothing bag on the empty robe hook on the back of the door. She shook her head several times, as if it might somehow reboot.

Her prescription meds were running low, and she had

been experimenting with different combinations and doses out of necessity. Her psychiatrist had, years before, told her that her diagnosed borderline personality disorder was something she would be dealing with for the rest of her life, and because of her stubbornness, he considered her his most difficult patient.

Borderline personality disorder? So...not an actual *personality disorder...but* almost... borderline...*as in,* not quite *a disorder.* That had been her argument with him, and her therapy sessions ended shortly thereafter.

That's how she saw it and how she'd long ago framed her reality. She had never accepted the clinical definition because it labeled her as *borderline between neurotic and psychotic: BPD.*
Not me!

Tempest stared at herself for a long minute in the medicine cabinet's mirror and didn't like what she saw. She looked sleep deprived and haggard, and that wouldn't cut it. No, she would have to dial it up a notch or three.

She flipped open the mirrored cabinet door and smiled. There were about a dozen prescription bottles staring back at her. She didn't have time to thoroughly read the labels, but she recognized a couple that were painkillers, another that was clearly Valium, and several others she wasn't familiar with. Not wanting to be obvious, she shook several from each bottle into her hand and placed them the odd collection of meds into a zippered side pouch of her makeup bag.

She replaced the caps on the bottles and returned them to their rightful places, or at least close to where she'd found them, on the two shelves.

A quick peek into the shower revealed there were decent-enough shampoos and conditioners for her purposes, as well as a bodywash. She pulled a fresh towel from the under-sink cabinet and, after letting the shower water reach temperature, brought her disposable razor in with her. She had legs, pits, and a vajayjay to attend to.

And you only get one opportunity to make a good first impression.

Vicky noticed it first. As she and her granddaughter made their way back from the pool, she could see the empty parking spot where the van had been parked. She said nothing as they approached her unit.

"I'll bet you could use something cool to drink," she said, placing her hand on Abby's shoulder. "Would you like that?"

"I guess," Abby replied as they reached the porch. "Hey. Where's my mom's car?"

Grandma Vicky looked over at the empty parking place, pretending to have just noticed. "Not sure, child. Maybe she had to go to the store or something," she said, not believing her own answer. "Come on inside. We'll get changed and you can show me how that fancy new phone works."

"'Kay," Abby said as they walked inside.

Vicky closed the screen and the front door, and all her senses agreed that Tempest hadn't left for a simple grocery run. The rear slider had been closed and relocked. She walked down the short hall to the bathroom, where she found a wet bath towel piled atop the bathroom counter. For someone who had, decades before, become completely comfortable with her own deadly carcinogens, Vicki took offense at the whole double-wide now reeking of a cloud of perfume and hairspray. She opened the small bathroom window and turned on the vent fan.

She scowled as she tossed the used towel in the hamper and set out a fresh one for Abby. "You can get changed in here, honey. Larry keeps the pool chlorine pretty strong, so you might want to take a shower first. There's a towel on the counter here for you," she called out.

"'Kay," Abby replied from the living room. She was distracted by her phone's display, which indicated there weren't any missed calls or messages from her mother.

Don't leave me here!

LA JOYA ELEMENTARY
APACHE JUNCTION
OUTSIDE ROOM 8
FRIDAY, 4:50 PM

The door swung open, and a young Hispanic couple stepped out into the open hallway, followed by Mr. Martinsen. He pushed the door against the wall-mounted latch, left it in the open position, and shook hands with them both.

"Thank you so much for coming, Mr. and Mrs. Reyes. As I said, Katy's a joy to have in our class and I'd like to thank you again for fostering her enjoyment of reading at home. That makes all the difference, and I hope you'll encourage her to find opportunities during the break to do so."

"Thank you, Mr. Martinsen," Mrs. Reyes replied with a warm smile.

"Yes, thank you, sir. Katy loves having you as her teacher," her husband added, shaking his hand vigorously. "We'll definitely have her keep up with her reading log next week."

"Perfect," Curt replied. "I hope you all have a wonderful break and a Happy Easter."

"You as well!" Mrs. Reyes said, waving. Curt returned the wave and smiled as they walked away.

Whew!

Conferences were officially over. And Spring Break—*Easter Break*—had officially begun! He stuffed his laptop and charger into their satchel and zipped it closed. He looked around to make sure he wasn't forgetting anything.

A knock on the door frame got his attention as Margie popped her head in.

"You all done?" she asked.

"I am. Stick a fork in me!" he replied with a tired chuckle. "You heading home?"

"Yeah, but a couple of us are going to have a well-deserved adult beverage first and wanted to ask if you'd like to join us," she replied, selling it with her hard-to-resist grin and an eye twinkle.

Curt looked up at the wall clock. *Not quite five. Dinner's at six thirty.* He cocked his head as he assessed the proposal. "Where you guys going?"

"Just down the hill, to Rocky's. You know it, right? You pass it every day."

"I've never set foot inside, but yeah. I know it. How soon are you leaving?"

"How soon can you be ready?"

"How about right now?" he responded with a grin as he dangled his keyring. "Just got to lock up."

"Yay! See you there!" she chirped. As she turned to walk away, she nearly collided with another woman much taller than she. "I'm sorry, I didn't see you standing there," Margie said.

"My fault," the woman replied quietly, smiling as she watched Margie turn the corner. "No problem at all," she muttered to herself.

Tempest may have been too late for a conference opportunity—and there wasn't much to confer about, really, when your child has only been there for one day—and a minimum one at that. She'd found out everything she needed to, however. And this presented a much better scenario.

She knew exactly where Rocky's was.

It was only a ten-minute drive and Curt calculated he could imbibe in one cocktail with his cohorts and still be home in plenty of time for Pop Pop's legendary grill fest. At the intersection, the light turned red, which presented the opportunity to punch in the number. It picked up on the third ring.

"Hey, honey," Phoenix said, sounding slightly out of breath. "You all done with conferences?"

"Yeah, sweetie. Just finished, leaving school now. You sound winded. Everything okay?"

"Me? Yeah. Just bringing in a few things from the car. New vacuum, on sale. And..."

"And...?"

"I was going to surprise you, but...I got us a toaster oven! Also on sale."

"Sweet. Maybe we can break it in next weekend."

"Let's do that. Oh, and I took some stuff to Goodwill and

while I was out, dropped off a few of our packed boxes over to the new place too. Love the smell of fresh carpet."

"Been so long, I can hardly remember," Curt admitted. "Fresh paint's nice too, I'll bet."

"Definitely. So, what time you going to be home?"

"Well...if it's okay with you, I've been invited to have a quick drink at Rocky's with a few other teachers, then I'll be home. Dinner's still six thirty?"

"Six thirty, yeah. No problem, honey. Just having one, I hope, because I'm *not* coming to the station to bail you out if you get pulled over," she said with a chuckle. Her husband was a large man and not a huge drinker, so her concerns were small. *Still.*

Curt picked up on her chuckle, but he also knew her statement to be true, coming from a non-drinker with zero sympathy for DUIs. "Yeah, baby. Just the one. Promise. Should be home by six fifteen, tops. Need me to pick up anything?"

"No, we're good! See you in a little bit, honey. Love you."

"Love you more," Curt replied as the light turned green. "So much forever," he added as he ended the call and proceeded through the intersection.

Three car lengths behind him, a kind-of-white Dodge van followed suit.

ROCKY'S TAVERN
JUST DOWN THE HILL
5 MINUTES LATER

The parking lot was already mostly full, and it confirmed: *It's five o'clock somewhere!*

Curt pulled his F-150 into an available spot along the south side of the building and stashed his computer case under the passenger seat before hopping out and securely locking the vehicle.

Across the lot, the van backed into its spot, buried amongst the other cars and directly facing the front door to the establishment. Sunset wouldn't be for another hour plus, so Tempest slunk down in her seat as to not be visible. She watched Curt enter, then looked at her Timex. She'd give him a couple minutes.

Margie had scored a highly coveted pub table for four and gestured to the empty chair. "Mr. Martinsen's in the house!" she squealed. She stood and initiated a hug, which Curt returned before turning to greet the two other teachers he knew from school. They were both in the fourth-grade department, so he didn't really hang with them, other than at staff meetings, but they'd always been friendly enough to him.

"Glad you could join us," Tiffany said with a smile. She was already on her second Cosmo. Short and stocky, she was in her mid-forties but looked older. The job was kicking her ass in her twentieth year.

"Thank you," Curt said, returning the pleasantry. He turned as the other teacher stood and initiated a handshake that could crush walnuts. It was Mr. Alonzo, an athletic and reasonably attractive man in his early forties. Not everybody could pull off the look, but his hair had prematurely grayed, and it totally worked for him. Curt was embarrassed to think he didn't even know his first name, but the man saved him from any awkwardness.

"Hey, Curt....Mark Alonzo. Join us! You survived the conferences...well done. Say, what are you having?"

"Wow, uh...thanks, Mark. I'm kind of jonesing for a margarita after the day I've had." He looked around and didn't see any servers. "I'll go grab one at the bar. Be right back... save my seat, please."

"You've got it," Mark said, returning to his.

The place wasn't large—far from it—and as Curt navigated the pub tables on his way to the bar, he was just glad they'd gotten there when they did, especially it being a Friday. The jukebox was blasting, and somebody had surrendered a few quarters to share Molly Hatchet's "Flirtin' with Disaster" with everybody. The song selection generated a grin as he remembered Phoenix's reference to it on the way to their fateful first dinner date to Fandango, several years back, in California.

The barstools were all taken, save one, which provided the only approach to the bartender. The young woman appeared to be in her mid-twenties and her platinum blond hair and deep tan complimented her very tight *Rocky's Tavern* tee. The place was hopping, and as she collected money from a customer and turned to operate the register, Curt got a chuckle out of the slogan on the back of her shirt: *Rocky's. We spill more drinks than others serve!*

104

When she turned back, Curt caught her eye and smiled. "What'll you have, hon?" she asked.

"Could I get a top-shelf margarita, please?" he answered loudly enough to be heard over the blaring music.

"Rocks?"

"Uh, yes. Rocks. Thank you."

"Want a floater of Patron for five bucks more?" she asked, leaning forward enough so that her perfect store-bought breasts kissed the countertop. It almost always helped make the sale.

"Why not!" he answered with a smile. "Still counts as one drink, right?" he chuckled.

"Yes, it does...be right up with that!" the barkeep said with a wink.

Curt let out a sigh. The smile remained on his face, as it felt good to unwind a little.

"Good call with the Patron," an unfamiliar woman's voice said.

Curt turned toward the voice, which had come from one barstool to his right. He wasn't prepared for the source, and the flashing hiccup in his expression gave him away.

This woman was stunning. Even seated, she looked atypically tall. Her hair was almost a mahogany brown and styled in cascading curls that graced her toned shoulders. The sparkly blue cocktail dress was short, had plunge in just the right places, and out of the corner of his eye he could tell it also revealed very toned thighs.

Her makeup was impeccable, but not overly done. This was a natural beauty, and as she spoke again, his eyes gravitated to the source of her sultry voice. A devastating smile revealed perfect, pearly-white teeth framed by glossy strawberry-toned lips. "The Patron. Good call," she repeated, offering up her best smile. The overall effect was intimidating. A thunderstrike.

Curt blinked, a bit hypnotized and didn't know how to respond. He was clearly outmatched here, as was every guy who had tried to make eye contact with her in the last several minutes. "I'm sorry...um, thanks," he managed, feeling like a complete idiot. He wished he'd worn his wedding ring, but he usually didn't wear it to work, as he'd have to take it off every few minutes to put hand sanitizer on his hands.

"I'm Tempest," she said, offering her hand.

"I'm...Curt," he answered, reciprocating her handshake before repeating himself like a dweeb at his first middle school dance. "Curt."

"Mm...nice name. Pleasure to meet you, Curt." Again, with the smile that hit him like the second tranquilizer dart from a blowgun.

"Here you are...one top-shelf margarita with Patron floater," the barkeep said as she placed his drink atop a Rocky's paper coaster. "Did you want to start a tab, or...?"

"Um, I don't think so. Here," he said, fishing out a twenty. "I don't need change," he added as he handed her the cash. Little did he know there wouldn't have been much to return. "Thanks," she replied, flashing a quick smile as she walked down the bar.

"Come here a lot...Curt?"

"Me? No. Not much of a drinker. Never even been in here before," he confessed.

"Me neither," she lied, taking a sip from her diminishing gin and tonic. Curt noticed that her drink was on its last legs. "May I buy you a refill?" he asked, sensing it was the gentlemanly thing to do.

"That would be lovely, Curt," she said, touching his hand lightly as she smiled. "Thank you."

"No problem," he said. He caught the barkeep's eye again, smiled, and pointed to Tempest's glass. A wink and a nod acknowledged his request. He turned back to Tempest. "On its way!" he said too loudly as the Molly Hatchet song ended, providing the room with a few seconds of blissful peace.

"You're sweet," Tempest replied softly, taking advantage of the moment. The jukebox selection segued to Bonnie Raitt's "Something to Talk About." *Perfect.*

Curt turned back around to his tablemates, catching Margie's eye. He held up his index finger as if to say *Be right there!* She gestured back with a *hang loose*, accompanied with a smile. *No worries.* He mouthed back: *Thank you.*

He spun back around just as another gin and tonic arrived and was parked atop a fresh coaster in front of Tempest. "Here we are," the gal said.

"Thank you," Curt said, placing another twenty on the bar.

"Ahh, come to mama." Tempest directed her smile back to Curt before adding, "It's great to meet you...officially... cheers!" She lifted her glass, offering a toast.

"Cheers," Curt said, his mind racing. *Officially?* He clinked her glass and took a sip of the delicious concoction. "Oh, yes...."

"See?"

"You are very wise," he replied. A long moment went by. "I'm sorry, but I think you said, 'great to meet you *officially.*' Have we met?" He cocked his head like a confused puppy.

"My apologies. Yes, we have. Just once though and only for a moment," she teased.

"And that was...?" he asked, taking another sip.

"Earlier today..." she teased.

"Today...."

"A few hours ago, in fact" she said, fluttering her extended lashes as she smiled.

"I'm...pretty sure...I would've remembered...that," Curt said, a bit embarrassed, and feeling a hint of buzz coming on. He'd skipped lunch. "Today. You say we met today...was I there?" he added with a chuckle.

"Yes, though I don't think I properly introduced myself, Mr. Martinsen," she replied, adding a provocative dollop of sexy to the mystery.

"Wait...you just called me by my last name. Almost nobody calls me *Mr.* Martinsen. How do you know that?" he asked, his brow furrowing slightly, his smile intact.

"At school," she replied, laughing between the bite sized morsels of information she was feeding him. "After...."

Curt paused to replay his afterschool parking lot ritual. It took him several seconds.

"Nuh-*uh*...wait. That wasn't you in the street...in the van...picking up...?"

Tempest nodded along in response to each bit of recollection. "My daughter. Yes. Your new student, Abigail."

"Who likes to be called—"

"Abby!" they both said in unison.

"Wow! That was *you*?! I mean...we talked! I...I didn't—"

"Well, I was in a dreadful tee-shirt, and a ball cap. I wasn't wearing this dress, but, yes, that was me, Curt...Curt Martinsen," she said, ratcheting up the seduction a notch. "Small world sometimes."

Somewhere, someone. Curt nervously took another swig

and shook his head. "Amazing," he said softly. His buzz was starting to come on a little stronger and he knew he had to throttle back; he had to get home. "Are you going to be here for a little bit longer?"

"At least long enough to finish my drink, yes," she replied.

"I...uh...I'll be right back, if you'll excuse me," Curt said, standing up. "Save my seat, please."

"Count on it," Tempest said with a smile. "I'm not going anywhere."

Curt smiled, nodded, and headed off to the restroom. As he did, Tempest looked around, then quickly opened her tiny clutch purse, unzipping a compartment in the inner lining, where she fished out a couple of tablets of flunitrazepam. In some circles it was referred to as "roofies," while also being widely known as a "date rape" drug.

Tempest was pretty familiar with the drug, having been involuntarily introduced to it by a Swiss doctor whose bed she'd found herself in one morning; her only recollection being that he'd bought her a drink at the bar the previous night. She'd been alarmed by the drug's potent effects on her and, after kicking his ass, she disappeared from his hotel room with a full bottle of them. *Thank you, Dr. Burckhalter.*

Using great stealth, she passed her palm over Curt's glass and watched as the pills found their way to the bottom. She picked up his glass and pretended to take a sip while actually using her own plastic cocktail straw to agitate the tablets, so they'd more quickly dissolve. He'd be back any minute, she knew, so she replaced his glass atop the coaster.

"Would you like another?" the barkeep asked, materializing out of nowhere. *Jeezus!*

"Um, no...thanks so much. We're good for the moment,"

Tempest said, dismissing her with an ingenuine smile, just as Curt returned.

"Hey there," Tempest said, looking up at him. "Everything okay?"

"Yeah...yeah. Just splashed a little cold water on my face. That must've been some floater of Patron," he replied. "Empty stomach, y'know."

"I do know that," she said, gesturing for him to sit. "How about we at least finish our cocktail. I'd hate for our conversation to end so soon," she added, her fingers brushing his hand again.

Curt looked over to the recently vacated bar table. "Oh, man...my friends left, and I didn't even notice. I didn't say goodbye...I suck." He tossed back a swig of his drink, deeply disappointed in himself.

"You don't suck, Curt Martinsen..." Tempest said, seizing the moment. She leaned in, whispering in his ear, "...but I do." She ran her tongue across her strawberry lip gloss. "I have an idea. How about we free up these two stools so somebody else can have them and we can move over to your friends' table and finish our little drink? How's that sound?"

Curt blinked slowly. He found her eyes and they were absolutely penetrating him, piercing him mercilessly. She smiled again, having saved up her best for this moment. "Come on," she said, grabbing both their drinks and leading him over to the pub table.

Curt was losing perspective, sense of time, and willpower. He nodded his compliance as he followed her to the table. "I've got to...barbecue..." he muttered.

Once they were seated, Tempest began more closely observing Curt's mannerisms. The roofie was taking effect, and soon he'd be putty in her hands. She put her hand on his and began running her finger seductively along the hairs of his giant fingers.

"I need..." he muttered.

She handed him his glass. "Here, hon. You must be dehydrated after your long day," she said, prompting him to take an involuntary sip.

"No...I need..." he mumbled.

"What do you need, Curt?" she asked in a sexy tone, looking around to see if anyone was watching them. They weren't. Under the table she kicked off her right stiletto and let her very well pedicured foot settle into his crotch. "What is it you need, Curt?"

He flinched, but her powers of persuasion were too great, and his resistance was fleeting. *This isn't happening...is it?* "I'm sorry, I uh...I'm..." he managed, squirming in his seat.

"Don't you find me attractive, Curt?" she asked, pouting for effect as she continued the massage. She didn't need him to answer, as her toes had already gotten his nonverbal response, loud and clear. "Mm...I'll take that as a big *yes* then," she said lasciviously, her eyes closing as she smiled. She raked her tongue across her strawberry lips once more, the snake going for the kill.

"But I can't—"

"What do you say we get out of here, Curt? Out of this noisy, crowded place?" she asked, interrupting his train of thought. "Here, let me help you up," she said, standing, steadying him by his elbow as he slowly rose from his seat.

"I...need to...call..."

"It's okay. We can do that once we're outside...I've got you, Curt. Come on, easy does it," she said, her snake eyes scanning the crowd for any alerts. Other than a few sideways glances from other guys who probably wished it was they being led out by her instead, nobody seemed to be paying too much attention. At least she hadn't aroused any suspicion.

Curt was leaning into her a bit more as they shuffled through the exit and out into the parking lot. As the door closed behind them the jukebox could be heard cuing up the next selection: Patsy Cline's "Crazy."

POP POP'S PATIO
FRIDAY, 6:40 PM

Smoke billowed from the four-burner Weber grill as Pop Pop lifted the lid and shut down the burners. He looked at his watch. Curt should've been home twenty minutes ago, according to Phoenix, and he was the most punctual person he knew.

"Chicken's coming off, can't wait," he called out to the kitchen.

Phoenix was standing at the sink, watching from the window, as she washed and dried her hands for probably the fourth time. They weren't dirty.

She picked up her phone and dialed the number again. Straight to voicemail.

"Honey, it's me again," she said, her concern evident. "Call me as soon as you get this; let me know you're all right. Starting to worry a little..." she added, pausing as she heard a vehicle out front. "Maybe that's you...hope so," she said as she briskly walked over to the kitchen door. She stepped out into the driveway just as another truck continued past the house. "Call me, baby. Love you." She hung up the phone and stuffed it in her hip pocket as she re-entered the house. *Please, God.*

"Where's Daddy?" Rose asked, sensing her mother's worry.

"Daddy's probably stuck in traffic, honey. He should be here any minute," she answered with more confidence than she was feeling. "Go wash your hands, baby. Dinner's ready."

"'Kay..." she replied, scampering off to the bathroom.

Pop Pop entered the kitchen, holding an enormous steel platter laden with steaming chicken pieces and a half dozen grilled brats. He gently kicked the patio door closed behind him and set the platter down on the counter, next to Phoenix's grilled veggies. "He here?" he asked.

Phoenix shook her head, her eyes meeting his. "Probably stuck in traffic," he offered.

"Yeah. Doesn't explain why he hasn't answered my calls though. Goes straight to voicemail." She lowered her voice so as not to concern Rose in case she was within earshot. "I'm worried, Pop Pop. It's not like him."

Pop Pop wiped his hands on the towel and replaced it on the oven's door handle. "I know, sweetie. It's not...he said he was stopping for a drink at Rocky's?"

She nodded. "One drink, he said. With a couple of fellow teachers. He promised."

"I know...listen, why don't you and Rose go ahead and start. Okay? I'm gonna run by there. I'll find him, bring him home. Phone might be dead. Flat tire's likely what happened. I'll follow the route he would take. Okay? I'll call you when I get there," he said, putting on his game face. "He's a big boy and can take care of himself; I'm sure he's fine." He kissed the top of her head and grabbed his keys.

She stared back at her giant adoptive father. He'd always come through for her, as had her other giant protector, the man who was now missing.

"In the meantime, call me if he gets here. Capiche?"

"Capiche," she answered. She didn't want to worry Rose. "Thank you, Pop Pop."

As he stepped out the door, he turned back to her and winked. "Save us each a couple drumsticks and a brat. Be right back."

CHAPTER SEVEN

ROCKY'S TAVERN
APACHE JUNCTION, ARIZONA
FRIDAY, 7:05 PM

P OP POP HAD retraced Curt's likely route, in reverse, taking the couple of miles of surface streets leading away from his house to the highway, with no sign of Curt's truck. If Curt had experienced any car trouble, it would have happened on the US-60, he decided.

Pop Pop had scanned every inch of highway over the thirteen-mile span, including the westbound side. Not seeing any police activity or vehicles stuck on the shoulders, he headed straight to the tavern.

As he pulled his truck into the parking lot, he found it to be almost completely full, which came as no surprise on a Friday. He'd passed by this place countless times over the years, never paying it much attention. All he knew was that it had previously been known as Buzzard's Tavern before changing hands a few years before. Other than the signage, it looked exactly the same from the outside.

He crept along slowly through the main lot, his eyes scanning for any activity or the familiar two-toned, dark chestnut metallic F-150. He glanced at his watch and rubbed his face as he followed the lot around to the south side of the building, where more customers had parked. The lot's lighting was spottier on this side, so he took his time. He was about to continue around to the back when his headlights raked across a familiar looking tailgate and, below it, an even more familiar license plate. *He's still here?*

With no available parking spaces, Pop Pop parked against the Dumpsters, hopped out, and strode with purpose as he made his way to the tavern. The music was loud enough to be heard outside, and as he got to the entrance, the door flew open, and a young couple spilled outside. Johnny Lee's "Lookin' for Love" smacked Pop Pop in the face as he made his way inside.

Pop Pop's height came in handy as he scanned over the top the crowd without a problem. The tallest guy in the room searching for the other tallest guy. But not seeing him. *Got to be somewhere...truck's still here.* He navigated his large frame through the crowd, his eyes locking on to the small sign at the far wall: *RESTROOMS.*

The hallway was tight, and as he navigated to the men's room, a man stepped out, still zipping himself. They had just enough room to pass each other.

"Excuse me," Pop Pop said.

"No problem, man."

"Hey, was there anybody else in there...a big guy?"

"No, man. Just me. It's a one-hole shitter," the man said, stifling a belch.

"Thanks," Pop Pop said, stepping inside to see for himself. It was indeed a spartan facility. Just the single toilet with the seat still down. The guy had had bad aim, he noted, and a few paper towels were strewn about the floor, nowhere near the trash can.

Pop Pop exited to the main room and approached the very busy bar. His height also gave him the advantage of being impossible to miss. He made eye contact with the gal behind the counter, and she wiped her hands on a bar towel.

"What can I get you, hon?" she called out.

"Hi, um, nothing, thanks. Looking for somebody though; maybe you've seen him?"

"Seen a lot of guys here tonight but...might have. Who are we looking for?" she asked with a friendly smile.

"Tall guy. Like me, but younger. About six-four, mid-thirties. Attractive..." Pop Pop replied, hoping to be heard above the jukebox assault.

"Well, that certainly narrows it down," she said, scanning the patrons. "I did see one guy matching that description earlier. He was sitting right here, in fact," she said, indicating the occupied stool in front of him. "Nice guy. Had one drink, paid cash. Friendly sort. Hadn't seen him in here before," she added.

"Definitely sounds like Curt," Pop Pop replied, mostly to himself. He looked at her more earnestly. "Was he here with anyone? I ask because he was supposed to be coming straight home, and his truck's still outside."

"Now that you mention it, yeah. I think I remember him with a group, at first anyway, at that table," she said, pointing.

"But he got his drink at the bar, from me. Margarita with a floater. Was chatting it up with the gal seated next to him here. Seemed to know each other, but who knows?" She was reading his face as she continued. "He paid for her drink as well. Just the one."

Pop Pop furrowed his brow. "Did you happen to see him leave?"

The barkeep hesitated a moment and nodded. "Yeah...I did. I remember the two of them had moved from the bar and finished their drink at the table there."

"Are you saying, the two of them left...together?" Pop Pop asked, measuring his tone. None of this was making any sense to him. Curt would have some explaining to do.

She nodded. "Seemed like he was a little unsteady. The girl—real tall, by the way—looked like she was kind of helping him. Like I said, he just had the one drink here."

Pop Pop surveyed the bar again. "Look, I know you're busy, and I don't want to take all your time," he said, placing a twenty on the bar. "But do you think you could describe this girl?"

"That I can do."

POP POP'S
7:25 PM

Phoenix's phone jumped to life and, noting the caller ID, so did she. She answered on the first ring.

"You find him, Pop Pop?"

"No...can't say as I have, but I found his truck," Pop Pop replied delicately.

"Where? On the freeway, or...?"

"Not on the freeway, and not car trouble, so you can relax about that."

"Okay...where then? Where's the truck? Let's not play twenty questions, Pop Pop. Please...I'm just a little freaked out here."

"Sorry, honey; I know. His truck's still in the parking lot. At Rocky's. But he's not here; I checked around inside already."

"You check—"

"—the restroom, yeah, I did. Also asked the bartender if she remembered seeing him."

"And?"

"She remembered serving him. Said he only had one drink while he was there—a margarita," he replied, dreading the question that would be coming next.

"Did she see him leave?" Phoenix asked, her tone measured, her pulse beginning to ramp up.

"Yes, she saw him leave," he said, pausing to choose his words. "She said, despite having had just one drink, he appeared a little unsteady upon getting up to leave. Needed a little help."

"*Curt...?* Were his teacher friends still there? Did they help him?"

"They'd apparently already left, before him."

"Darn it, Pop Pop. What aren't you telling me? Who helped him then?" Phoenix replied, more upset at her husband than her adoptive father right now.

"Bartender remembers Curt chatting with another person at the bar. It was a woman, Phoenix, and not one of his teacher friends. I got a description of her, and an estimated time for when they left, but...."

Phoenix tried to catch her breath during this exchange but interrupted him with a blurted response, in a hushed tone as not to have Rose hear her alarm. "They fucking left *together,* Pop Pop? Is that what you're trying to tell me?"

The few seconds of silence at the other end of the line confirmed this. Phoenix put her free hand to her mouth, her wide eyes scanning the kitchen. Thankfully, Rose was down the hall and out of earshot.

"Okay..." she began, choosing to know there must be some reasonable explanation. "Okay, so apparently, he was at least slightly inebriated. He was helped outside by some mystery woman...and forgive me for asking for her description, but what the fuck did she look like, Pop Pop? Please tell me it wasn't a hooker...because I'm about ready to completely lose my shit here."

Phoenix looked around to make sure her daughter hadn't heard her expletives. She hated using foul language and tried to reserve it for the rare moment that called for it. Like this one.

"There's a lot we don't know, honey, so let's not jump to conclusions. You're concerned. I get it. Hell, so am I! None of this makes any sense. Curt isn't that kind of guy, and it sounds like he only had the one drink, according to the bartender. Let's give him the benefit of the doubt, please."

"I'm...trying to."

"Mama?" the little voice asked from the kitchen doorway. "Is Daddy home?"

"Mm...not yet, sweetheart. Hopefully soon," Phoenix answered, a forced smile as she held her hand over the mouthpiece. "Did you brush your teeth, baby?"

"No. I was waiting for dessert. You said we'd have it when Daddy got home," Rose said, her disappointment evident.

"We'll have dessert in a few minutes, okay?"

"Promise?"

"Promise, honey. I'll come get you."

"'Kay," Rose said, temporarily satisfied. Phoenix watched as she disappeared down the hall.

"Sorry...where are you now?" Phoenix asked, redirecting her focus to the phone.

"I'm still at Rocky's. In the lot. I'm standing next to Curt's truck right now. It's locked."

"Is there enough light to be able to see inside the cab, Pop Pop? Everything look okay?"

"As far as I can see...wait...it...looks like his cellphone is still in the cupholder. Probably explains why your calls weren't returned."

"Okay..." Phoenix muttered as she closed her eyes and tried to process the scene and the events that had transpired since she'd talked with her husband. It had only been a couple of hours, but it seemed like an eternity now. She opened her eyes as a thought came to her. "Do you have one of those Slim

Jims by any chance, Pop Pop? Not the sausage...the thing you open a car door with?"

"I know exactly what you're talking about, and...yeah, I think so. Used to, anyway. I'm walking to my truck now... might still have one in the glove box, but not sure. Been a long while since I've needed one," he replied, sounding slightly out of breath.

Even through the phone, Phoenix could tell he was walking briskly.

"Got to be some logical explanation for this whole deal, Phoenix," he offered. "Hopefully, this time tomorrow, we'll all be laughing about this whole deal."

"Somehow, I don't see that happening," she replied resolutely. She, probably more than anybody, had long ago stopped seeing any humor in being terrified.

Through the phone, Phoenix could hear Pop Pop's creaky truck door open, followed by his grunts as he climbed inside the cab and began rifling through the glove box. "Still there, kiddo?"

"Yeah, Pop Pop," she replied softly, closing her eyes and praying he'd find the tool.

"Sorry, it's a mess in here; bear with me," he said with a groan. A few moments went by before she heard him declare, "Eureka!"

"Found one?" she asked, hopefully.

"Yeah...buried beneath a pile of napkins. Man, I thought I'd lost that thing. Okay!" he said, slamming the glove box shut and exiting the truck. "Hoofing it back to Curt's rig."

"Thanks, Pop Pop." A moment later she asked, "Think I should call the police?"

"What...you mean, *now?*" he replied, a bit winded. "Too

early for that, Phoenix. It's only been...what...an hour," he added as he reached Curt's vehicle and gently inserted the Slim Jim into the driver's window molding. "Come on, you rascal," he muttered. "Did you and Rose eat, I hope?" he asked, making conversation as he slowly swept the tool left and right, fishing for the door's locking mechanism.

"Lost my appetite, Pop Pop. Rose had some of your chicken though," Phoenix replied. "How's it going there?"

"Almost...all...most..." he muttered as he pulled up the device, unlatching the door lock. "Got ya!! I'm in, Phoenix!" he declared as he removed the device and opened the truck's door. "Still got the touch," he said to himself, squinting from the bright light coming from the overhead fixture. "Yep, his phone's where he left it, in the cupholder," he said, liberating it and stabbing the power button with his thumb. "It'll take a minute to fire up."

"I wish he would've just kept it in his pocket like usual. He's never without that thing," Phoenix said, her worry evident.

"Well, if it were me, just going in for one quick drink with friends, I probably would've left mine in the truck too, truth be told," Pop Pop said. "But, yeah, I wish he would've carried it. Okay, she's powered up, batteries a little low, but we can remedy that. I see what looks like three missed calls from you and a couple of voicemails."

"Sounds about right," she said softly.

"Not seeing anything else, really. Want me to take it with me?"

Phoenix bit her lip, feeling at a loss. "No, Pop Pop. Let's leave it where you found it. Like you said, maybe—*hopefully*—he'll return to the truck soon and will friggin' call me... he'd better."

"Roger that, kiddo. Putting it back now. This lot's kind of dark, so it should probably be okay."

"'Kay," Phoenix said, letting out a huge sigh.

"Want me to stick around a while? Watch for him? Happy to do so, Phoenix."

"Nah, Pop Pop. Thanks. Tell you what, though. If you could go back inside, ask for a pen and paper. Write a note for him, please, and make it abundantly clear he needs to call me immediately."

"I'll do it."

"Okay. Then, come on home. There's a mountain of chicken on the counter here."

"Love you, kiddo. See you soon," Pop Pop replied. "And don't forget Rose's dessert."

"'Kay. Love you too, Pop Pop. And thanks," Phoenix said.

"Meantime, if you hear from your wayward hubby before I get there, let me know. And try to go easy on him. He may've had a rough night."

JUST OUTSIDE LOST DUTCHMAN STATE PARK
APACHE JUNCTION, ARIZONA
FRIDAY, 9:25 PM

Tempest hadn't really thought her plan through; she knew she was winging it, and although that seemed to be her specialty, it was fraught with risk.

From Rocky's, she hadn't travelled far. Not at all. A short jaunt northeast on AZ-88 into north Pinal County, it was under ten miles drive. Even strictly adhering to the posted speed limits on this Friday night, the place she'd chosen was a scant twenty minutes away from the scene of the crime.

Had it been a crime? Probably.

Okay, definitely. The van was parked in an isolated area, about two miles beyond the actual state park entrance and hidden behind a scrub-covered hill that made her vehicle impossible to spot from the North Apache Trail.

There were a billion stars out here and not much in the way of light pollution coming from Phoenix. The Superstition Mountains were close. Real close. Their unique silhouette was framed by a starfield that would put any planetarium to shame.

She'd hiked out here a few times years back, and she believed the superstitions this range had been named for.

Having not made a reservation at the state park, and risking a potentially crowded campsite, she'd chosen this as her stop for the night. Come morning, all bets were off. She'd figure it out. She always did.

Tempest's companion groaned, stirring slightly, and she raised her head off his massive chest to assess the situation. She scanned his strong face. It was a gentle face, even with his five o'clock shadow, and she was reminded of Paul Bunyan.

Curt was still lights out, and the tie-down restraints—all at floor level—were holding him just fine. There were the two leather-cuffed wrist restraints, along with one for each ankle, and their steel cabling was secured by carabiners attached to the metal hoops bolted along the edges of the floor.

These weren't factory-installed options.

He laid there atop the inflatable mattress, tied down as if by Lilliputians, her Gulliver.

Tempest had already changed out of her party dress and thrown on a pair of sweats, an Arizona State tee, and warm socks. She laid her head back down upon his chest, listening to his slow, rhythmic breathing and his strong heart. She imagined this must be what it would be like to spoon with a buffalo. God, he smelled good too.

She settled back in for more snuggle time, but her eyes sprang open as her thoughts decided there were a million things that needed addressing. None of them easy.

Among them:

After tonight, what???
What if Curt doesn't like me?
What about Abby??? Will she even talk to me after this?
How do I make this right with Mom? Do I even need to?
Where do we go??? Where can we settle down?

Shit.

She'd have to sleep on it because nothing was getting figured out tonight. *Let go, Let God.* She took a sip from her water bottle, tossed back three Wellbutrin, and pulled the blanket up over the two of them, knowing this buffalo was sufficiently tranquilized for now.

Goodnight, my yummy man.
Somewhere, someone.

POP POP'S
FRIDAY, 10:15 PM

Pop Pop stacked his sixth naked drumstick bone atop the others. He looked at the structure of the pile, just now noticing it looked like the foundation of something he'd built with his Lincoln Logs, back in the day. He pushed aside the otherwise empty plate and looked across the kitchen table at Phoenix.

She hadn't touched one bite of his specialty grilled vegetables, and those were her very favorite thing in the world. A quick glance at his watch confirmed they were going on four hours past the time Curt had promised to be home. C+4, his military mind thought. *Curt, missing. Four hours elapsed.*

Pop Pop had relinquished Phoenix of her parenting duties for the night and tucked little Rose into her guest bed down the hall an hour before. He had found it difficult to answer her twenty questions about why her daddy wasn't home. Probably because he didn't have any answers.

"I know you don't feel like eating, but you've got to keep your strength up, Phoenix. Here, let me heat this up," he said, reaching for her plate.

"Don't," she said quietly. "I couldn't eat anything right now." She looked up at him. "Thank you, though." She attempted a flicker of a smile, but her facial muscles had gone slack hours ago, making her appear twenty years older than she was. Her eyes telegraphed a combination of worry, anger, and regret. Pop Pop hadn't looked in a mirror recently, but he was sure his did as well.

"I know it's only been four hours, but we haven't heard anything, and I'm worried as hell, Pop Pop. I can't just sit here and do nothing. I literally *can't*. I *won't*. I mean, what if he's hurt? What if he can't call because he's not near a phone? What if—?"

"I know, sweetheart," he interjected, touching her on the arm. "There are a million *what-ifs*, and it's not my style to sit idly, either. You, better than anyone, know that."

She searched his face, knowing this to be true. Pop Pop had risen to the occasion when she'd needed him most, taking command as they navigated the family's worst nightmare, during Christmas week a year and a half ago. Both he and Curt had been her strength, and together they had championed the mission that helped rescue their precious Rose from the clutches of evil. She loved her two men for that, and they were her protectors.

But one of her protectors was unaccounted for. *He* might need protection right now, and from what—or whom—they had no clue.

"Got to call it in, Pop Pop," she said with complete certainty. "We've waited long enough," she added, grabbing her phone. "If it were me that had gone missing, I know you would do the same."

Pop Pop nodded his agreement and studied her as she punched in a number and raised the phone to her ear.

"Yes, my name is Phoenix Martinsen," she said. "I need to...I need to file a missing person report." She rubbed her eyes as she answered the officer's question. "A family member, yes. It's my husband. Curtis—with one ess—Martinsen, M-A-R-T-I-N-S-E-N, *Martinsen*."

POP POP'S
FRIDAY, 11:20 PM
AN HOUR LATER, C+5

As to not add any clatter to an already stressful call, Pop Pop had waited to clear the table until Phoenix hung up the phone. He'd managed to wash half of the dishes before the patrolman's arrival, a scant ten minutes later.

He and Phoenix sat across the table from a young Hispanic officer by the name of Uribe. He'd been with the force for three years and seen a few missing persons cases. He took another sip of the coffee Pop Pop had served him and was on his second cup. With several hours still to go on his shift, he appreciated the boost.

"So, you say your husband has no identifying marks? No tattoos...piercings?"

"He teaches second grade, officer. Nothing like that, no," Phoenix replied. Under other circumstances she might've found humor in the question, but not now. "The photo there is current and is what he looks like. Clean cut, dark hair...and like I said, he's tall: six-foot-four."

"Six-four...okay. What would you say his weight is? Approximate is okay."

"He's...kind of husky. Not fat, and not a bodybuilder. More lumberjack-y if you know what I mean. I'd guess he's probably around two hundred twenty pounds. Maybe two thirty, now that he's got a more sedentary job."

Pop Pop nodded in agreement with her assessment, as he was built similarly.

"Thank you for that, Mrs. Martinsen," Officer Uribe said,

taking another look at the color photo and jotting a note into his report. "Like I said, this is only the initial report, so the case will be assigned to a detective who will further investigate if need be. Hopefully your husband walks in the door tonight and has a good explanation, but in the event he's still unaccounted for, you'll likely be hearing from the lead investigator within the next couple of days."

"What about his truck?" she asked.

"You said the vehicle was still onsite at..." he murmured, pausing to check his notes, "...where he was last seen, at Rocky's Tavern...over in Apache Junction?"

"That's right," Phoenix replied.

"I did a cursory looksie there a couple of hours ago, Officer. The truck was left parked along the south side of the building. Spoke with the bartender while I was there. Name's Amy," Pop Pop said. "Curt's phone was still sitting in the truck's cupholder."

"Got it," Uribe said, jotting another note and, taking a last sip of his coffee, stood. "We'll check things out over there tonight. Thank you for the coffee, and we hope to find your husband soon," he added, initiating handshakes to both. "And, if he walks in the door before we get back to you, please advise. I hope that he does."

"Thank you, Officer," Pop Pop said, reciprocating with his firmest handshake.

"Yes, thank you, Officer," Phoenix said, wiping away a tear. "I know it's late...we appreciate your coming out."

"Don't mention it," he replied. "You folks have a good evening."

Phoenix and Pop Pop watched as he walked back down the long drive toward his patrol car. Once he was out of sight,

Phoenix closed and locked the door. Her stomach growled in protest, and she turned to Pop Pop.

"Guess those veggies aren't gonna eat themselves," she said softly.

"Atta girl. You sit; I'll heat 'em up."

CHAPTER EIGHT

POP POP'S
SATURDAY, APRIL 4
6:12 AM

SUNRISE ANNOUNCED ITSELF with bright shafts of light sneaking through the plantation shutters in Pop Pop's living room. Phoenix's eyes fluttered open, squinting at the beam that had been trained on her. It took a moment to get her bearings. She was still on the loveseat, where she'd waited all night for Curt to walk through the door.

She uncrooked her neck and looked at her watch. She figured she must have fallen asleep after the last in a series of calls to area hospitals, and that was around 2:00 a.m. Before she could register another thought, she could hear the impending stampede coming down the hall toward her.

As they rounded the corner, leading the pack was Sidney, running at full tilt. When she got within four feet of the loveseat, the little furball leapt, sailing the distance before landing in Phoenix's lap and smothering her with puppy kisses.

"Oomph! Hey, you little monster!"

Luke arrived two seconds later, and he too jumped atop her. "Hey! Guys! Wait—"

Prick joined the pile a second later. "Hey, babies...good morning...oomph!"

Pop Pop entered from the kitchen and approached with two coffee mugs. He set one on the coffee table in front of Phoenix as he settled into his favorite easy chair. "Mornin', kiddo."

"Mmm...mornin', Pop Pop," Phoenix answered through tight lips as Sidney continued the kiss fest. "Okay, guys...c'mon... off...all of you..." she said as she nudged them off the furniture. "How long you been up, Pop Pop?" she managed through a yawn.

"Not long. You fell asleep a little before me and I put the blanket on you. I was toast shortly after that," he said, taking a sip from his mug. He looked at his watch: 6:15.

Curt was due home twelve hours ago.

Phoenix's phone both rang and vibrated on the coffee table, and she grabbed it on the second ring. "Hello?" she answered, fully awake now. She put it on speaker.

"May I speak with Phoenix Martinsen, please?"

"This is she," she said, squinting at the caller ID: Gilbert Police Department.

"Good morning, Mrs. Martinsen. This is Officer Uribe; I took your report last night."

"Yes, of course. Sorry, I'm a little out of it," she replied.

"Sorry to be calling so early. Two reasons for my call. First, I wanted to know if your husband's returned home or if you've heard from him?"

"No...and it's been...what...twelve hours now. Not a word," she said, her concern evident.

"Okay, I'm sorry to hear that. Which brings me to the other purpose of my call. I wanted to let you know we went over to Rocky's Tavern after our meeting with you last night. Spoke at length with the gal tending the bar, Amy, as well as the owner of the establishment. Amy recounted the events of last night and it didn't deviate from what she had told your father."

"Hello, Officer Uribe. I'm here...sorry, the phone's on speaker. I'm listening."

"Hello, Mr. LaFlamme. As I said, Amy reiterated her recollection of the timeframe and there weren't any inconsistencies with what she'd told you."

"Roger that," Pop Pop replied.

"Mrs. Martinsen, we have a pretty good description of a person of interest last seen leaving at the same time as your husband."

"The woman...the tall woman," Phoenix interjected, trying to contain her upset.

"Yes, ma'am. We are circulating that information and hope to get a hit soon. As for your husband's vehicle, it was still parked in the lot..." he said, trailing off.

"You saw his phone there, right? Still in the cupholder where—"

"That's the thing...the truck was locked, but when we gained access and did our search, there was no phone in the vehicle, ma'am."

LOST DUTCHMAN STATE PARK
APACHE JUNCTION, ARIZONA
SATURDAY, 6:45 AM

The van quietly crept along the circuitous roads that serpentine the one hundred thirty-four campsites. Tempest thanked her lucky stars that she had managed to score a site, let alone one with electric and water. She followed the signage that directed her toward Sites 75-104.

The Superstition Mountains were striking, surreal—stereoscopic even, and like something from a View-Master slide. They looked almost close enough to touch, and the early morning sun showcased them beautifully.

She remembered hearing of the legend associated with this range, of the Superstition Mountains having got their name from the stories of the Lost Dutchman's $200 million in gold supposed to be hidden somewhere up there.

The gold had eluded thousands of treasure hunters over the years, and it was probably just an old wives' tale anyway, she decided. Besides, the "Dutchman" was actually a German dude, so the whole "legend" thing had lost a bit of credibility as far as she was concerned.

As she passed various campsites, she noticed some already had their firepits going, and plumes of smoke indicated the early risers were heating their coffee, frying their eggs, and probably burning their bacon. Her stomach growled.

It was a mix of RVs and tent campers here, and she'd been advised by the park ranger that her campsite would be the furthest from the restrooms, as well as the showers. She was fine with that. Better than fine. There would be fewer people traipsing around. A hot shower would be on the program once she settled in at her site. *Their* site.

Tempest glanced at the rearview and confirmed that her lumberjack was still asleep. She'd plied him with enough tranquilizer to knock out an elephant, but she'd heard a few groans. *Poor boy probably needs to go potty.* She'd have time for a quick shower, brush her teeth, and make herself pretty for her man, she figured.

She'd purchased some breakfast staples as well as a loaf of bread, lunchmeats, and four large cans of Dinty Moore stew. She hoped he liked that; she hadn't asked him. This was enough to get through the next couple of days and nights, she decided, and that's how long she had the campsite reservation for, but after that all bets were off. This was an evolving plan if you could even call it a plan.

She shook three bupropion from their bottle and swallowed them dry as she rounded the corner, keeping her speed as close to five miles per hour as possible so as not to disturb anyone. She spotted the gray building that housed the restrooms and showers and as advertised, and her designated campsite number was posted, indicating it was some two hundred yards beyond it.

She smiled as she backed into the campsite and cut the engine. It was quiet. Semi-private compared to the other sites. Serene even. With a ninety-nine-foot pad, it was designed as a pull-through site for large RVs, but a family's last-minute cancellation had been her good fortune.

She surveyed the site and smiled. *Water. Power. Firepit. Picnic Table. Grill. Our first place together.*

PARADISE FOUND MOBILE ESTATES
SUPERSTITION SPRINGS/EAST MESA, ARIZONA
SATURDAY, 7:05 AM

Abby was still asleep down the hall, so Vicky made herself a half-pot of coffee, fired up her third cigarette of the morning, and opened the slider before settling into her easy chair. The TV was on, but muted, and tuned to the one local news station she got on her decades-old set.

She took another drag off her Pall Mall and shook her head as she reread the note that had been left on the kitchen counter for her. She wasn't too happy about it either.

Mom,

Sorry to burden you. Please don't be too upset with me.

I'll be back in a couple of days probably. Just need time to figure a couple of things out, find a place, etc.

Abby's out of school this week for Easter. It's not much, but I'm leaving you $40 for Abby's food (she likes Wiley's) and maybe you can get her an Easter basket?

Thanks. T.

Vicky ground her ciggie into the ashtray and set the note, along with the two twenties, next to it. "God help you, Tempest," she muttered to herself as she turned her attention to the TV and an atypically grim-faced female news anchor, Molly Metz.

Vicky unmuted the TV as Molly began to chronicle a local news story.

"We're live now with Felix Gomez, who's on the scene at Coyote Gulch Golf Club, in Gilbert, with more. Felix, what's the latest?"

The studio shot switched to a split-screen of the anchor and a male field reporter standing outdoors and holding a microphone with the NEWS 3 flag on it. Behind him, a smattering of trees and what looked like a lush green fairway. He was nodding as she finished his introduction, and then the image switched to Felix as he began his walk-and-talk along the tree line.

"Thanks, Molly. Yes, well, as we'd reported previously, it was indeed a grim scene here Thursday morning with the discovery of deceased tree maintenance worker Richard Franco. Mr. Franco, an experienced arborist, had been working here on Wednesday, thinning parts of the tree line you see behind me. As part of his job, he was tasked with operating the wood-chipper machinery, whereby he'd feed the fallen tree branches and foliage into the machine and in turn it would be ground to a pulp and collected in an attached dump truck."

Felix stopped at a clearing that still had yellow tape cordoning it off from its surroundings.

"And it was right here, where I'm standing now, where Mr. Franco's remains were found. Still lodged in the machine."

The image switched back to a split-screen to include Molly in the studio.

"That is such a terrible tragedy, Felix," Molly said, shaking her head. "Has this officially been ruled an accident? Has foul play been ruled out?"

"Molly, I've spoken with several people, including the manager of the course, the owner of the business that employed Mr. Franco, as well as two detectives with Gilbert PD who were on the scene Thursday morning. As I mentioned—and this was strongly reiterated by Mr. Franco's employer—the deceased had several years of experience with this machinery as well as an exemplary safety record. Still, nothing has been ruled out, as investigators wish to exhaust every avenue before closing this one out, Molly."

"Can you tell me anything more about Mr. Franco?" Molly asked.

"Only that he doesn't seem to have any next of kin in the area, but he had been living in Surprise for some time. Authorities are still trying to locate an alleged roommate of his, in hopes of talking to her, but have been unsuccessful so far. That's it from here, Molly," Felix said, tossing back to the studio.

"Goodness...thanks for that report, Felix," Molly said, turning directly into the lens. Her expression snapped back a little too quickly to her typical bubbly persona as she segued into the next story fed into her teleprompter.

"In other news, the Easter Bunny will be coming to Discovery Park next Sunday, and children of all ages are invited to join in the Easter egg hunt! Bring your baskets!" she said, giddy with excitement.

Vicky grabbed the remote and stabbed the OFF button

with her thumb as she stared into nothing. It was then she recalled what Tempest had mentioned the day before about having to leave Surprise. *Not the best situation, I'm afraid.*

She chewed on that for a moment before turning toward her stacked books by the slider. The scrapbook was gone.

GILBERT POLICE DEPARTMENT
RAMAGE'S OFFICE
SATURDAY, 8:05 AM

Detective Moser sat at the round conference table, enjoying the first sip of her venti soy mocha sans whip latte, as she watched her partner's expression. Ramage hadn't touched the tall coffee with an espresso add shot she brought him. Instead, he sat behind his desk, his brow furrowed, as he immersed himself in the case file that had just come across his desk. She hadn't seen him look this intense in a while.

"Not possible," he muttered to himself. "No way."

Moser kept her gaze on him, waiting for some elaboration. When none seemed to be coming, she ventured facetiously, "UFO sighting over Gilbert?"

Ramage grunted as he looked up from the file. "What?"

"Nothing," Moser replied. "Are you going to share this *impossible/no way* report with me at some point? My curiosity is piqued."

He looked back down to the file, flipping back to its first

page. "It's a missing person report from last night. But get this," he said, looking her in the eye now. "Tell me if any of these names seem familiar to you."

"Okay, shoot. How about starting with who filed the report?"

"This was filed last night. Late. Here...in Gilbert. Patrolman Officer Uribe responded to the call, met with the family at their residence. Here's where it gets interesting...residence address was that of one David LaFlamme," he said, letting that juicy nugget hang in the air. "Ring any bells?"

"No way."

"*Way.*"

"Jesus...please tell me Rose didn't go missing again. She's been—"

"Nope. Thank God. Not Rose."

"Don't leave me hanging, Jeff. I haven't even had my coffee yet. Cut to the chase," Moser begged, sitting forward in her chair now.

"Sorry. Okay. So, Phoenix Martinsen was the party that called it in. Uribe met with both her and her dad— LaFlamme—around 11:30. Mrs. Martinsen reported that her *husband* didn't show up at home after work."

"Wait...*Curt?* You're talking about Curt Martinsen...*he's* the missing person?" she asked, her expression mirroring how incredulous this was. "Sweet mother of God."

"I know. Like *that* family hasn't been through enough already." Ramage flipped back to the second page and paraphrased. "Says he had left his workplace, La Joya Elementary, a little before five, called home, told his wife he was going to have a quick drink with a couple of teacher friends, then come straight home. He was due back home for dinner by 6:30. Never showed."

"Do we know where he was supposed to have gone? For drinks, I mean?"

"Says here he went to that tavern in Apache Junction... the one that used to be a biker bar but changed owners..." he said, pausing to confirm the name. "Rocky's Tavern is what they call it now."

"Never been...not my crowd...but I've driven by it a million times. Okay, what else? Any confirmation he made it there?"

"Yeah. After Mr. Martinsen didn't show up for a family barbecue, LaFlamme apparently took a drive out there to see if Curt had experienced car trouble—or whatever. Spoke with a gal tending the bar there and she said she'd seen him. Served him one drink, at the bar, and he left shortly afterward. *Gawd...*" he said, rubbing his face.

"Wait...what else did she say?"

"Curt left the bar accompanied by a woman."

"Could've been one of his teacher friends, right?" Moser asked, trying to give him the benefit of the doubt.

"Not unless one of his teacher friends likes to dress like a high-priced call girl."

Moser let the imagery gel in her mind before she responded. "Nah. Not buying the hooker angle. This is Curt Martinsen we're talking about. Teaches first grade. Has a loving family he'd do anything for. Hell, he *has* done every-thing for his family and more than once."

"Truth," Ramage muttered. "Doesn't sound like some-thing our guy would even consider."

"Tell me, did the gal LaFlamme talked to—the

bartender—did she provide a description of the woman he left with?"

"Apparently Officer Uribe also talked with the bartender and the account she gave him matched the one she gave Mr. LaFlamme. Says here she hadn't seen the gal there before. Real looker, glam makeup, dressed to the nines...in a minidress, slit up the side. Described her as brunette, quite tall. Maybe *six-feet* tall...."

Ramage's voice trailed off and as he looked up, he could tell his partner was thinking the exact same thing he was. He closed the folder, grabbed his coffee, and stood.

Moser clutched her latte and stood as well. "I'll drive."

LOST DUTCHMAN STATE PARK
SAME TIME

Tempest sat cross-legged on the beanbag chair she'd positioned behind the van's driver seat as she fiddled with the Samsung cell phone. The position also afforded her the best vantage point to keep tabs on her prize, whose gag she'd removed.

She thanked her stars she'd had the presence of mind to double back to Rocky's, and to Curt's truck, halfway into her drive the night before to retrieve the item she held in her hand.

She hadn't had to search too hard as he'd left it right out in the open. In a matter of seconds, she'd made off with the phone, as well as its charging cable. Nobody had seen her and, armed with Curt's full ring of keys, she'd accessed the vehicle without having to break in. He hadn't set an alarm anyway.

Her own device of choice was an Apple iPhone, and she was quite fond of it. She wondered how the Android system would be on this one. She had to unlock the damn thing first.

She was pretty sure she'd memorized Curt's birth month and year from her search of the database at work. Still, she cross-referenced it against the driver's license that lay in her lap. Other than the state issued license and his school ID card—with the *adorable photo*—there hadn't been too much else of interest in his wallet. There was forty-two dollars in cash, which she'd pocketed. *Expenses.*

She tried the four digits from his birth month/year, hoping he'd chosen something obvious for his phone's unlock password. Nope. Next, she tried his birth month and day. When that didn't work, she began rattling her brain for some other choices he might have gone with. She had also managed to memorize Phoenix's birth date, but that too was met with an annoying error message: *Incorrect PIN entered.*

The house number in Gilbert? Again, no cigar. Realizing she probably had, at most, ten chances to get it right before being completely locked out and risking losing the device's stored information, she threw up a Hail Mary and punched in a code she knew would be wrong, because only an idiot would use it. It was a longshot: 1 2 3 4. Bingo!

Really, Curt?

A ginormous grin spread across her face as she watched the phone's locking screen switch to the home screen and its smattering of app icons appear. The battery indicator in the top right corner was flashing, indicating there was only 5%

power, so she climbed back into the driver's seat and inserted its cord's adapter into the cigarette lighter. *Charging.*

"*Ummph! Arrgh!*" came from the cargo area.

Tempest spun around to look at her hunk of a man. He grimaced, squeezing his eyes tightly shut and, after several attempts, managed to blink them open a little. He remained clearly disoriented as he squinted at his surroundings.

"Mm..." he grunted, licking his dry lips. "Gawd...where am I?" he asked, his voice raspy. As he went to rub his face, his right arm stopped short of its target, jerking back against the noisy metal cable. He turned his head to survey the problem and noticed the leather cuff restraining his wrist. "What the hell?"

"Good morning, sleepyhead," Tempest said cheerfully as she beamed a smile. "How did we sleep?"

Curt's synapses weren't yet fully firing. He tried his other hand and was met with the same restriction. Summoning up more force, he yanked both arms toward him simultaneously, but the cables held strong. The same with his legs as he kicked.

"What the fuck?!" he barked, his eyes wide now. Cursing wasn't typically in his repertoire, but he didn't think twice. "What's going on...and who the hell are you?!!"

"Now...now, Curt. What kind of greeting is that? Are you trying to hurt my feelings?" Tempest replied. Her smile was still there, adding another layer of weirdness—and terror—to his predicament. He tried to prop himself up on an elbow but wasn't completely successful.

"Where am I? Why am I chained up like...like a...fucking animal? And who—?"

"You don't remember?" Tempest responded, adding a pout

for effect. "After our lovely evening together, you've already forgotten my name? I must say, I'm hurt, Mr. Martinsen."

Curt was trying his damnedest to shake the fog and the mention of his last name shook away a few cobwebs. The last person to call him by that name—other than his students— had been..."Wait... You're not...from the *bar*? That was...*you*?!"

"C'est moi!" Tempest said, an impish smile returning. "Though I may have presented a little differently in my dress-up clothes. You seemed to like me enough last night," she added with a naughty giggle.

Curt yanked on his restraints again, trying to channel some Herculean powers, but he was securely locked in place. He shook his head, trying to clarify his thoughts, anything to help remember the previous night and why he was here. Wherever *here* was.

"I had one drink last night. That was it. With friends. Don't try and tell me otherwise!"

"Are you sure about that, Curt?"

He pursed his lips tightly as he searched his memory. He was still foggy, but his recollection of events at Rocky's seemed to end with having had one margarita. The flirty girl at the bar had initiated a conversation, but things were blurry after that. Worse than blurry. He was drawing a big blank.

"I only had one drink because I was on my way home... for dinner!" he barked. He scowled as he regarded his strange captor. Even dressed down in sweats and a tee, she was disarmingly attractive. This added to the threat he felt. Still, he was confident he'd done nothing wrong. "Nothing happened! You must have me confused with somebody else because there is no way I would ever—!"

"Would never *what*?!" Tempest replied, interrupting

him. "What, pray tell, would you never do, Curtis Martinsen, mister holier than thou?" She scrunched her face into something he couldn't read. The fact that she'd just addressed him by his full name, along with her tone, was enough to clue him into the probability of another layer of danger, just below the surface.

"I would never...pick up a woman in a bar," he answered resolutely.

"Is that the way you see it?" Tempest replied, climbing from between the front seats and plopping into the beanbag. "You picked me up, did you?" she added with a seductive smile. "You horndog...you just couldn't resist me, could you? *Curt.* I haven't met a man yet who could," she added with a naughty laugh. He watched her closely, her gaze shifting down to the crotch of his Dockers now. "You seemed pretty happy to see me last night, believe me."

"It's not like that, and you know it. I'm a—"

"Married man!?" she interjected, her eyes bearing into his now. "Mister faithful. Loving father, committed husband."

"That's right."

"To a friggin' midget," she muttered, adding to her mocking assessment.

Curt's expression indicated she'd hit a nerve, so she continued. "Oh, I've seen your little...wife...or was that your daughter? Pretty tiny, that Phoenix. That's her name, right? Phoenix? You even have that on your license plate if I recall. *LVG PHX? Leaving Phoenix*, I assume. Cute. Maybe even a bold double-entendre if you're thinking on leaving *Phoenix*. Who would make that their license plate if they had plans to leave their wife? Tell me, am I close?"

"I'm sorry...whoever you are...but you're obviously off

your rocker. You know nothing about me but pretend that you do. You have no idea about what goes on in my personal life! Who the hell do you think you are? My license plate—" he said, pausing at the absurdity of her assumptions. "Leaving Phoenix? Is that what you think that means? You jump to some bizarre conclusion that I'd...announce to the world... that I was leaving my *wife*?! That's a stretch!!"

"Okay, then, you're leaving Phoenix. Arizona. This place. Is that it?" she replied smugly. She resented being told she was wrong. About anything.

Curt's thoughts flashed to his urgent need to pee, but he stuffed it down long enough to reply to this obviously crazy person. "I don't suppose it ever crossed your mind that maybe you've misinterpreted things? Not that I'm compelled to tell you—of all people—but, for your information, my license plate translates to my *love* for my spouse, okay? How do you like that? *LVG PHX* equals *Loving Phoenix*! Okay?! Yes, I love my wife."

"Shh...don't spoil it," she replied softly.

"I *love*, and will continue to love, my loving *wife, Phoenix*!" he managed before hearing a belly laugh in response to his distress. "You clearly need help," he added, shaking his shackled feet.

Tempest's smug expression disappeared as if her face was an Etch a Sketch that had been shaken too hard. She stared at Curt, her expression blank, but something behind her eyes told him she was processing what he'd said.

"We'll see about that," she said, reaching forward to stuff the cloth gag back in his mouth. Satisfied, and with an eerie calm, she climbed back into the driver's seat and picked up the phone.

"How about we send your precious Phoenix a little love message, shall we?"

POP POP'S HOME
SATURDAY, SAME TIME
8:35 AM

Phoenix and Pop Pop sat at the kitchen table while Rose watched her Saturday morning cartoons. They were both weary and on their third cups of coffee. Phoenix was already dressed.

"Mama, can I have French toast?"

"Just a second, honey," Phoenix replied, loud enough to compete with *Bert and Ernie's Great Adventures* coming from the next room.

"What?" Rose called out.

"Please turn down your show so you can hear me, Rose."

"'Kay," she said as she reached for the remote and dialed the volume down.

"Thank you," Phoenix responded, rolling her eyes at Pop Pop. She turned back to her little elf in the living room. "Now, please ask your question again."

"I want French toast."

"Well, I want a million dollars. Was there a question you wanted to ask?"

"May I have French toast, please, mama?" Rose asked, selling it with an impish smile.

"That's better. And, yes. You may have French toast." Phoenix said. She took a quick sip of her coffee and turned to Pop Pop. "Would you mind terribly if I asked you to make Rose some breakfast? I've got to get going if I want to be there in time to open the shop."

Pop Pop gently laid his huge hand on Phoenix's arm. "You don't have to go in today, kiddo. There's nothing the guys can't handle in your absence if you want to just stay home and be with Rose. She's asked me twice about her daddy this morning already. Maybe it would be a good—"

A knock on the door interrupted the conversation.

"I'll get it. Just a second, Pop Pop," Phoenix said as she got up from the table. A moment later the doorbell rang as well, indicating new urgency, and making all three dogs go ballistic from down the hall.

"Hush! All of you!" Pop Pop bellowed in the hounds' direction before joining Phoenix at the door as she opened it. They both registered complete surprise when they saw who was standing there.

"Sorry to come unannounced. Especially on a Saturday morning," Detective Ramage said.

"Good morning, Mr. LaFlamme. Mrs. Martinsen," Detective Moser said, mustering a half-smile as she initiated handshakes.

"Goodness...it's been a long time, Detectives," Pop Pop said, shaking hands with both. "Nothing personal, but we never thought we'd see you two again," he added. "I mean, after all that—"

"I know," Ramage interjected. "We're as surprised to be here as you are."

Phoenix stood there; her hand remained on the doorknob

as she searched both detectives' faces. Just seeing the two of them again—especially having gone through so much together as they'd collectively tried to rescue her kidnapped daughter—made Phoenix catch her breath.

Neither detective's expression seemed to telegraph impending bad news about her missing husband. Not yet anyway. She was blindsided, but she wasn't rude.

"I'm sorry...good morning, detectives. I, uh...like Pop Pop said, this is a surprise. Forgive me, we've had a...a rough night. But you probably already know that. Please, come in," Phoenix said, stepping to the side to allow them room.

Sidney was still barking up a storm and the detectives telegraphed some apprehension.

"Sorry...the dogs are all in their crates, down the hall. It's okay," Phoenix assured them before turning toward the source or the mayhem. "Shut uuuuuppp!!"

Satisfied Sidney's whimpers of distress were ramping down, Phoenix sighed. "There."

"We've made coffee, if you'd like some," Pop Pop offered.

As they entered, the detectives both took pause as they saw the young girl laying on the couch, innocently watching television, not a care in the world. Neither had seen Rose, nor her family, in nearly a year and a half, and it had been under the worst of circumstances. It was heartening to see her.

"Please, come, have a seat in the kitchen," Pop Pop said, gesturing for them to follow. Ramage proceeded while Moser paused just long enough to study Rose, and to allow a brief memory of events to run their course. As the mother of a young daughter herself, the Christmas-week kidnapping of Rose had been especially nerve-wracking. It remained Moser's greatest fear that anything might ever happen to her precious Darla, and it would forever be her life's mission to prevent that.

She made a mental note to try and find an opportune time to introduce Rose to her Darla. It had been her daughter who had made those saguaro Christmas cookies for their family after all. She smiled to herself and, as if on cue, Rose looked up from her program just long enough to return the smile.

The scooting of wooden chair legs across linoleum floor redirected Moser's attention and she made her way to the kitchen to join the others.

Pop Pop brought a mug of coffee to Ramage and set the sugar bowl next to it.

"You have an outstanding memory, Mr. LaFlamme," Ramage said with a smile as he began shoveling multiple spoonfuls. "Thank you, sir."

"None for me, thank you," Moser said, sliding in her chair.

When they had all been seated, Ramage took a sip, then ceremoniously set down his mug, looking Phoenix and her Pop Pop in the eye. "As you may have gathered, Detective Moser and I have been assigned to your missing person report, Mrs. Martinsen." His mouth was a tight line, and he shook his head slightly. He couldn't believe it either.

"I figured as much when I saw you on the porch," Phoenix replied softly. "I assume you've read what we told Officer Uribe."

"We have, ma'am," Ramage replied.

"That's why we're here," Moser added as gently as possible. "I wish we were seeing you under better circumstances."

"Yeah, well, the circumstances do suck," Phoenix said softly, keeping her volume below that of the television. "Officer Uribe called us with a follow-up a couple hours ago—about the missing phone—but that's the last thing we've heard. Am I to assume there's nothing new at your end?"

"No, ma'am. Except we're looking for a person of interest who may've been the last person to—"

"The tall chick. From the bar. Sorry, I assume that's who you're referring to," Phoenix interjected, pushing her mug away. She shook her head. "That's a person of *interest* all right."

Moser and Ramage exchanged glances and Pop Pop rubbed his face. Nobody spoke for a moment, then Ramage broke the silence. "Yes, Mrs. Martinsen. That's who I'm referring to, and we're diligently looking for this individual."

Phoenix's emotions were stirring, a cocktail of anger with a generous splash of fear. She fixed the officers with a penetrating stare as she spoke. "Please believe me when I tell you how I'm trying to process this whole thing...objectively... without...without jumping to conclusions. I mean, I think you both know my husband pretty well—better than most people, even. And, well...do you think Curt—we're talking *Curt* here—would ever be involved with someone like that? Hell, forget that. Do you think he would ever stray from his family...with *anyone*!? Because I don't. Not in my wildest dreams."

Before Moser could consider her reply, Phoenix's phone interrupted her with a chirp.

"Excuse me," Phoenix said as she snapped up the phone and looked at the display, the number beyond familiar. Her eyes went wide as her face grew long. "Oh, my God," she muttered as she stared at the screen: 1 New Message.

TEN MINUTES LATER...

Rose continued to enjoy her cartoon marathon in the living room as she devoured the two pieces of French toast Pop Pop had whipped up for her. He'd drowned them in syrup and liberally dusted them with a snowfall of extra powdered sugar; it was their little secret.

Pop Pop hung up the dish towel and returned to his place at the table. Phoenix was still staring at the phone's display, her brow deeply furrowed, and her eyes moist with the tears that had left tracks down her cheeks. Nobody had said so much as a word for several minutes.

"Mind if I see it, honey?" Pop Pop asked gently.

Phoenix nodded almost imperceptibly as she handed him the phone and stared into space. Moser and Ramage exchanged a glance as they shifted their attention to monitoring LaFlamme's reaction to the incoming missive.

Pop Pop silently read the text message for a third time, trying to make sense of what he was seeing. He bit his lip as he shook his head.

"May I ask...what does it say?" Moser said, willing him to make eye contact. He looked up from the device, first to the detectives and then to Phoenix, as if asking her permission to speak. She nodded very subtly, indicating approval. She couldn't bring herself to utter the words on the screen. She'd read them twenty times.

Pop Pop cleared his throat, pausing to get a grip. The words he was about to speak were beyond troubling. He stared at the communique and, considering its source, felt his chest tighten.

"Sorry," he said, shaking his head. "It's from Curt," he

began, buying a moment's more time, "but you already know that. Okay...it says, 'Phoenix...I am sorry to have to tell you this, especially this way, but I cannot keep it a secret any longer. I have met someone.'"

Phoenix's shoulders were shaking now, and she buried her face in her hands. Hearing the words read aloud was even more painful and, picturing their author, his words were samurai swords, mercilessly slashing her to the bone.

Pop Pop rested his free hand on her shoulder to comfort her. "We could stop and—"

Phoenix shook her head.

"Want me to—?"

She nodded sharply.

Pop Pop looked across the table at the detectives. Ramage's expression was tight. Moser's was as well but with an additional layer of dread, her memory recalling a *Dear Beth* letter she'd received from her then-fiancée nearly two decades before. Moser and Ramage both nodded for him to continue. Pop Pop returned his gaze to the tiny display as he found where he had left off.

"'I have met someone,'" he repeated for continuity's sake.

"Go on," Ramage said.

Pop Pop scrolled down to the next line. "It...it is not you; it is me. I have found someone special, and my feelings have become very strong for her. I know this is hard to hear and our daughter will not understand but she will eventually, with time. Please just let me go and try to find a way to move on without me. There is nothing to discuss. I have made my decision. You will not see or hear from me again. This is goodbye. Thanks for understanding."

Moser closed her eyes, trying to process the communique.

"Is there more?" Ramage asked directly.

"Only his sign off: 'Curt,'" Pop Pop said softly, setting the phone back on the table, screen side down.

"May I?" Ramage asked, indicating the phone.

"Sure," Pop Pop replied vacantly, sliding the device across the table.

Ramage picked it up and stared at the dark screen. "Powered down. Mind punching in the password so—?"

"Five-six-seven-eight," came the answer from Phoenix as she pulled her hands away from her face. "That's the password."

Ramage powered up the phone and punched in the four digits. "You might wanna consider changing—"

"I know," Phoenix interjected, not needing a lecture on password security right now. Ramage didn't pursue it. He studied the message's timestamp, then read the words on the screen silently, studying them, scrutinizing them.

"If you don't mind me asking," Ramage began, looking across the table at Phoenix, "were there any problems or arguments leading up to this?"

She shook her head slowly, deliberately, her eyes boring back at him to punctuate her conviction. "No...nothing... not *even*...."

"Okay. Thank you for your answer," he said as sensitively as he could before returning his attention to the device in his hand. A moment later he looked up again. "It just seems— and correct me if I'm wrong—the wording...did anybody else sense anything...I dunno... *odd* about it?"

"How do you mean?" Pop Pop replied.

"I mean, you both know Curt much better than we do, but hearing it read out loud, it seemed to me it was—"

"Cold?" Moser cut in. "Not only from the standpoint of

delivering such news, but the *way* it was said. Oddly robotic if you ask me."

Phoenix looked the female detective directly in the eye, replaying Curt's words in her head before replying. A nod followed, her thoughts crystalizing.

"First, Curt would never do anything like this...not to me, not to anyone. He's simply incapable of being unkind, of inflicting pain on another, unless they had it coming. And, to your point," she said, looking at Ramage now, "yes, I find it odd. After listening to Pop Pop read it aloud, something clicked: Curt doesn't talk that way! I should know. There wasn't a single...*contraction*...used in that whole message. He's way more casual than that. If anything, he's the king of using contractions, okay? This couldn't have been a weirder message had the letters been cut out of a magazine and pasted into a fucking ransom note."

Ramage considered Phoenix's response, then turned to Moser, seeking input.

"That's what I meant by robotic. You would know better than anyone, Mrs. Martinsen, and maybe—"

"Please...call me Phoenix. And I can tell you right now, with complete certainty: even though it was sent from his phone, this message wasn't from my husband."

A moment went by before a light bulb lit behind Phoenix's eyes. It didn't go unnoticed.

"Something else come to you?" Moser asked.

"I don't know...maybe...I'm not sure...be right back," Phoenix replied before disappearing down the hall. She was back in her seat inside of thirty seconds. "Might be nothing, but I found this in Curt's shirt pocket yesterday. Struck me as odd," she added, handing the strip of paper to Detective Moser.

"What is it, honey?" Pop Pop asked, leaning in.

"A receipt?" Ramage asked.

"Yeah...from Wiley's," Moser answered as she studied the specifics. "Wednesday, timestamp says 3:40 p.m."

"That would've been after school, on their way to Rose's therapist appointment in Mesa," Phoenix said.

"What'd you find out of the ordinary, Phoenix?" Ramage asked.

"The order. First, there's enough food and drink for a small army. But it's more the *stuff* that was ordered. Neither Curt nor Rose would ever order fried zucchini. Heck, I'm a vegetarian, and *I* don't even like it. Then there's an extra Big Wiley Burger listed there, as well as an order of nuggets, not to mention the two iced coffees. Curt *detests* cold coffee," Phoenix said, watching for a reaction.

Moser and Ramage eyes met at the mention of the iced coffees, and it didn't go unnoticed by Phoenix. "What?" she asked.

"We'll need to take this with us, ma'am. It may prove important," Ramage answered.

"Think we should take a run out there?" Moser asked her partner under her breath.

"Yeah, once we're done here," he said, turning back to Phoenix. "Now, where were we?"

THE VAN
MOMENTS LATER

Tempest stared at the display, satisfied that her missive had been sent. *She's read it by now.*

From the cargo area, Curt stared at his psychotic captor; his rage and fear mounting. How had he managed to get himself into this mess? He tugged on his restraints again but only managed to further chafe his wrists. He'd have to find another way out of this. He mumbled a complaint against the gag.

Tempest turned away from the phone and regarded her prize as he glared at her. "I'm sorry; did you want to say something, sweetie?"

He nodded. Tempest climbed between the seats and squatted next to him as she began loosening his gag. "You're not going to yell, or scream, are you? Because if you try any of that, I'll just put a Depends on you and put you back to sleep for a while."

Curt shook his head emphatically.

"No? You're going to be a good boy?"

He closed his eyes and nodded. A moment went by while Tempest tried to gauge his sincerity, then she removed the gag. "There, that's got to feel better."

He nodded, licked his dry lips, and found his indoor voice. "You think you could at least let me go pee? Pretty sure there's something in the Geneva Convention about that."

"Hm, I don't think I heard the magic word."

"I have to pee...*please*," he said, catching himself. "It's an emergency. I'd hate to have to soil these lovely accommodations."

"Well, now, we wouldn't want that...Curtis," she replied,

her odd smile off-putting. "I understand you have needs, and we'll have to find a way to address them, won't we?"

"Thank you," he said, hoping for an opportunity to improve relations, better his odds, and relieve his bladder of last night's margarita.

Tempest studied him for a moment before climbing back into the driver's seat. She scanned the entire area through the windshield, her carefully chosen vantage point affording her a hundred-eighty-degree view of the campground areas. As she had backed the van into her end spot, away from the other sites, she knew it would allow for unseen comings and goings from the van's cargo area, should they arise. And they had.

"Okay, Curtis. Here's the deal."

MEANWHILE...
POP POP'S KITCHEN
SATURDAY, 9:45 AM

The detectives were still seated across the table from Phoenix while Pop Pop busied himself at the sink, tending to Rose's syrup-laden plate.

Moser studied the text for what must be the tenth time, as if solving a particularly challenging algebraic equation. Her partner's expression was hidden behind his steepled fingers, but his wheels were turning.

The more they each analyzed the incoming text from Curt's

phone, Moser and Ramage, along with Pop Pop, all agreed with Phoenix's assessment: the structure of the message didn't sit right.

"I don't pretend to be a linguistics expert, but I was an English major before switching to criminology. This just hits me as odd. We can't say with certainty that he didn't send it—not yet anyway, but I'm with you, Mrs. Mart—*Phoenix*," Moser said, catching herself as she handed the phone back to Phoenix.

Detective Ramage stared at the phone for another moment before turning his gaze to Phoenix. He collapsed his steepled digits and spoke. "Before we submit a formal request to ping the location of your husband's phone, perhaps we should try a round of authentication, the old-fashioned way."

Pop Pop set down the dishtowel and resumed his place at the table.

"By that, what do you mean exactly?" Phoenix asked.

Ramage exchanged a glance with Moser, who nodded. "By that, I mean we should come up with a good reply."

Phoenix slowly nodded before jumping up from the table and disappearing down the hall.

"I'm sorry, did we say something…?" Moser asked, looking to Pop Pop.

He looked back at the detective and shrugged. Before he could come up with a response, Phoenix returned to the table and plopped herself into her seat. She set a lined yellow tablet in front of her and clicked her ballpoint pen.

"Okay…I think my husband would expect me to start off my reply to such bullshit with something like this: '*Curt, What the fucking fuck*?!'" She scribbled it down and looked up at them for feedback. Both detectives and Pop Pop nodded thoughtfully.

"Sounds reasonable," Moser said.

PARADISE FOUND MOBILE ESTATES
SUPERSTITION SPRINGS/EAST MESA, ARIZONA
SATURDAY, 10:05 AM

Vicky stood at the kitchen counter measuring water into a bowl of pre-measured Krusteaz pancake mix. "Dammit," she muttered, realizing she'd added too much liquid to the powder. She shook some more mix from the box and did the back-and-forth ingredients ratio dance until the batter was the right consistency. Looked like she'd be making a buttload of pancakes this morning.

The television was muted and switched to a cartoon program she hoped Abby might enjoy. She didn't need her granddaughter watching the morning news bulletins.

As Vicky whisked the batter into submission, she could hear the shower water turning off, signaling Abby should be emerging from down the hall shortly. She had let her sleep in and knew her granddaughter would have more questions about her mother's whereabouts.

Vicky had her own questions about that but couldn't yet answer them. All she knew was the feeling in her gut, and upon seeing the news story earlier, she was all but certain that Tempest was in trouble again. She grabbed the crumpled cigarette pack from her robe pocket and shook one out, firing it up.

"Grandma?" the voice called out from the bathroom.

"What is it, sweetheart?"

"Do you have a hairdryer?"

"Check the bottom drawer, honey. Should be there," Vicky called out, pausing to cough.

"Found it."

Vicky knew it would be there; she had put it back in its place after Tempest had lazily left it on the counter, along with a pile of her used towels. She shook her head as she set out two place settings and a bottle of Mrs. Butterworth's syrup.

She honestly couldn't remember the last time she had breakfast company. She took a drag of her cigarette, put out two of the "good" paper napkins, and sprayed some Pam onto her griddle.

As Vicky fired up the front burner, she remembered Tempest's note and the Wiley's cash she'd left. After breakfast she'd put some gas in the Maverick, take Abby for a drive to buy the boilerplate makings of an Easter basket, then visit the Wiley's drive thru. It's what grandmas do.

THE VAN
LOST DUTCHMAN STATE PARK
SATURDAY, 10:15 AM

It had been several years since Tempest had been tasked with assisting her then toddler with a potty break, and it had been nothing compared to the challenge of a helping a very large adult male whose feet were cabled together and wrists in restraints.

It had taken considerable fenagling.

The rear cargo doors were opened wide. Curt had to be spun around a hundred-eighty degrees so that his legs faced the right direction, and he could be scooched into position with his bum sitting on the lip of the cargo floor and his feet dangling out, facing her.

She was thankful that he'd only requested to pee, but all bets were off later when he might have to do anything more.

Still cabled like a prisoner-of-war marionette, Curt groaned a complaint against his gag.

"Shh...come on now, Curtis. I know it's not ideal, but it's better than having an accident, right?" Tempest said, checking the security of his wrist restraints. His arms were strung at just above shoulder height now, the cables affixed to two steel ring hooks, and it looked like he was being readied for crucifixion.

She began fumbling with the belt of his trousers.

"Mmfff...."

"It's fine, I'm just going to...loosen your belt...and...we'll slide your pants down a little so you can do your business."

"*Mmmffff!*"

"I'm only trying to help. You've got to work with me a little...there we are," she said, lowering his trousers until they rested, bunched just above his ankles. She peeked around the two open rear doors to make sure they weren't being seen. "Okay, now...we'll have to do the same with your skivvies...."

Curt's arms ached as he yanked at his bonds. He was a trapped animal and about to become a naked one. He had decided his captor was clearly certifiable, and in his helpless state, he realized she was capable of anything.

Her fingers found the elastic band of his Fruit of the Looms and began slowly nudging them south. He realized there was nothing he could do and a moment later he felt a sudden breeze of cooler air against his groin.

"Well...hello there!" Tempest said in a singsong-y voice. "Mm...look who's come out to play!"

Curt bucked but to no avail; she had secured him tightly. He looked her in the eye, defiantly, burning her with contempt.

"Now, now. You said you had to pee, so this is how we have to do it. For now, anyway. Don't worry; I won't watch," she said. A pinging alert sound came from inside the van. "Go ahead...do your business...I'll be right back."

Tempest walked around to the driver's door and climbed into the seat. She picked up her phone from the cupholder and inspected it, but it didn't show any alerts. Also within arm's reach was Curt's phone, which sat atop the dashboard. She grabbed it, removed its charging cable, and noticed an alert on the display:

1 New Message.

Tempest clicked on the icon and the message app revealed its new missive, and that it was in response to her own:

>*Curt, What the fucking fuck?! Where are you and what the hell are you talking about?? You're not making any sense and we're all worried about you! Did you not get all the voicemails I left last night? Are you hurt? Tell me where you are, honey. Please. Tell me you're ok. What-ever's going on, we can work it out. Together. That's what couples who love each other do... You need to call me as soon as you get this message! Call me, honey. I'm worried sick and Rose needs her daddy.*

I love you!

Tempest read the message to herself several times,

processing the emotions behind it, before peeking over her shoulder to monitor Curt's progress. "How're we doin' back there?"

Getting no response beyond a grunt, she started to put the phone back on the dash when another pinging notification popped onto the screen:

1 New Message

She re-opened the folder and was met with a follow-up text. Same sender, Phoenix, which she expected, but this one's brevity indicated it was an afterthought, having meant to be part of the first:

>S M F

Tempest's features scrunched as she stared at the new text and muttered it aloud.

"*S-M-F*...what the hell's that? Obviously, a typo."

At the sound of his phone's notification beep, Curt had turned his head toward his right shoulder, allowing him to overhear his captor's last utterance. He immediately turned back away, feigning ignorance.

He still had no idea why he was here, or what this unhinged person's plans were, but he did know one thing:

That was no typo!

POP POP'S KITCHEN
SATURDAY, 11:02 AM

Pop Pop, Phoenix, and both detectives were still seated at the table when Rose came padding in from the living room. Their expressions were glum, especially Phoenix's.

"What are you doing?" Rose asked her mommy.

"Hey, honey," she replied, trying to summon up a happy face for her child. "Are you done with your cartoons, baby?"

"Yeah. The good ones are over. I'm bored."

"The adults are just talking, honey," Phoenix said, giving her a peck on the forehead.

"About what?" Rose said. She wasn't one to be easily dismissed.

"Oh, we're just trying to figure out some stuff, baby. Okay?"

"Are you talking about Daddy?"

Moser and Ramage exchanged glances, deferring to Phoenix.

"Well...yes, honey, we are. These nice people are helping us to find Daddy and make sure he's okay and gets back home safe. That's what we all want, right?" Phoenix managed, trying not to fall apart herself.

"Yes...I miss Daddy," Rose muttered, her bottom lip beginning to quiver.

"How about we get you dressed and your teeth brushed, Rosebud?" Pop Pop said, selling it with a grandfatherly smile as he got up from the table. "Then maybe we can—"

"Maybe we can...what?" Rose asked, her curiosity piqued.

"How about I tell you once we get ourselves ready, okay, Peanut?"

"Hey!" she giggled. "Okay," she added as she followed him down the hall.

Phoenix let a moment go by to make sure her daughter was out of earshot. She turned to the detectives. "This is so hard...."

"I know it's very difficult. I'm a parent of a young daughter, too. I get it," Moser replied.

"We've probably taken up enough of your time this morning, Mrs. Mart—" Ramage said, catching himself. "—er, Phoenix. We'll let you get back to your routine, to the best of your ability anyway."

Ramage and Moser stood, prompting Phoenix to as well. "Thank you. Not knowing where he is is tearing me apart," Phoenix said, glancing back at the silent phone.

"Let us know the second you hear anything. If you get a reply text, we need to know about it," Ramage reminded her.

"We'll be running down some leads and you can reach us at either of our phone numbers," Moser said, handing her both their cards. "If you hear back, call us, and we'll figure out a reply message together, okay? We need to keep the dialogue going, then we have a better chance to determine the location...and the situation."

"'Kay," Phoenix said softly. "I will."

"We can let ourselves out," Ramage said as he exited the kitchen.

Moser stood there a moment longer and offered her best half smile. "Keep the faith," she said, which got a weak nod and a reciprocal half smile from Phoenix.

Keep the faith.

WILEY'S BURGER
MESA, ARIZONA
SATURDAY, 11:40 AM

The line of cars in the drive-thru queue was impressive. Moser pulled into the one empty spot in the parking lot and cut the ignition. She turned to her partner and heard his tummy growl.

"Saturday...lunch time," Ramage muttered.

"Yeah. This place must have a license to print money... unbelievable."

"Yep. So's the food. Ever tried it?"

"Darla loves it. And, yes, it's pretty incredible," she conceded.

"Beats beets, that's for damn sure!" Ramage replied with a knowing chuckle.

"Did you want to order something?"

"Mm...maybe...but it can wait till after our chat. Let's head inside," Ramage replied, opening the car door. He sat in his seat as his olfactory senses were swamped with the righteous smells of flame-grilled burger patties and freshly cut French fries, their fragrances deliberately pumped outside courtesy of strategically placed exhaust fans. It was impossible to resist, and—based on the volume of cars—business was amazing.

He'd be changing his response from *maybe* to *definitely* once they were done.

The detectives approached the front counter and waited for the family in front of them to complete their sizeable order.

The inside of the restaurant was packed, and a half dozen young teens could be seen scurrying around the kitchen. Though the pace was a bit hectic, all of the employees managed smiles as they hustled, retrieving baskets of fries from the bins of hot oil, tending to the assembly line of burger orders, and attending to the busy shake machines. It was an impressive operation to behold and didn't go unnoticed by the detectives.

"Kudos to the management team," Moser said softly to her partner.

"Gotta hand it to 'em."

The family stepped away from the counter and headed toward the soda machines with their drink cups. Two seconds later, a charming cheerleader type addressed the next customers with her blinding smile.

"Good morning, and welcome to Wiley's! What may I get for your today?"

Realizing the order taker was addressing them, Moser returned the smile as Ramage responded. "Yes, good morning," he said, pausing to read her nametag. "Thank you, Tambi. Actually, we'd like to speak with the manager, please."

"Um, sure. Yes, sir," she said, her smile hiccupping for the briefest of moments. "Was there a problem I could help you with, or...?"

"No, nothing like that," Ramage assured her. "We'll be eating later, but first we just wanted to ask your boss a few questions, if we may. Can you please let him—I'm sorry, is it a him or her, your boss? I assumed it was *Wiley.*"

"A her. My boss. Mrs. Oliver," Tambi said. "I'll let her know. May I tell her who…?"

"Detectives Moser and Ramage," Moser interjected with a friendly-enough smile. "Just take a few minutes. Nobody's in trouble."

"Okay, I'll just let her know you're here. Excuse me," the girl said politely, flashing a professional smile, before turning away toward the kitchen.

"Guest number seventy-one, your order's ready!" a male employee called out from his station, a few feet down the counter. Clean cut and maybe sixteen, he looked like he was straight out of Central Casting, Moser noted. *Probably on the same cheer squad.*

Ramage and Moser stepped aside to allow room for the next customer to step up. Moser reached into her pocket and retrieved her notepad, pulling out the receipt Phoenix had provided them. She studied its details again. "Tambi," she said, looking at Ramage.

"Yeah, the manager's obviously assembled a great team."

"That's true…but…her *name*. Ring a bell? Tambi's the name listed on the receipt as the drive-thru person for Curt's order.

"Good observation there, partner. Let's see how well—"

"Good morning!" came the cheery voice from behind them. They turned to see an amiable woman who'd just materialized through the employees-only door that connected the kitchen to the lobby. She was in her mid-forties, with a short brunette bob tucked beneath her Wiley's cap. She extended her hand along with a smile as she approached.

"Welcome to Wiley's. Missty Oliver. I'm the manager here. I understand you wanted to speak with me?"

"Thank you for taking the time, ma'am. *Missty*...with two eses...unusual spelling; I like it." Moser said, as she noted the manager's name tag. We know you're slammed," Moser said.

"Thanks...my parents used to call me their 'little miss.' Took me a little while, but I've come to like the spelling of my name," she replied. "And...yep, we're slammed. But we're fine."

"Thank you, ma'am. I'm Detective Ramage, and this is Detective Moser," gesturing politely to his partner. "This shouldn't take more than a few minutes. Just a few routine questions," he added, surveying the busy restaurant. "Might there be a place we could talk?"

"Sure. If you'll please follow me."

The detectives settled in around a small round table in Missty's tiny office, just off the rear of the kitchen area. As Missty closed the door behind her, the din of kitchen activities diminished by half. She sat into her computer chair and wheeled it up to join them.

"Forgive me if I get called out for an emergency, but I think we should be able to talk uninterrupted for a few minutes," she said, again with a warm smile. She was clearly a managerial rock star. "Busy shift...Saturday."

"We can see that, and you have a terrific staff," Moser said. "In fact, there's one in particular we'd like to single out for her professionalism and personality."

"I'll bet that's Tambi you're referring to," Missty answered proudly. "She's only been with us three months, but she's proved to be an outstanding asset to our team here."

"Yes, Tambi..." Moser said. "In fact, we were hoping you

might be able to help us decipher an order that was placed here a few days ago...on Wednesday afternoon?"

Moser handed the receipt to the manager whose trained eye quickly scanned every detail. "Drive-thru order...3:40 p.m....and looks like Tambi was working the window," Missty said. Not seeing any obvious anomaly, she looked back up at the detectives. "Was there a problem with the order?"

"No. Nothing like that, ma'am," Ramage interjected. "It's just that we were provided this receipt from a woman who's reported her husband missing. We're investigating."

"Oh, dear...."

"This order was placed by her husband, who went through the drive-thru with his young daughter on Wednesday afternoon. His wife found it curious that he had ordered several items he wouldn't typically have ordered. We know how busy you are and how many customers your employees interact with, but we were wondering if perhaps the drive-thru attendant on that shift—Tambi—might've remembered anything out of the ordinary. Anything at all."

"If you'll excuse me a moment," Missy said, rising from her chair and opening her door, which afforded a view of the inner sanctum. Another young girl had just entered the kitchen and was putting on her apron. Missty called her over and spoke loud enough to be heard over the beeps of the French fry machines and to be overheard by the detectives.

"Sandy, you're back from lunch?"

"Yes, ma'am."

"Good. Would you please relieve Tambi at the front counter for a few minutes and ask her to come to my office?"

"Sure," Sandy replied with a smile.

"Thanks, doll."

Missty reentered the office and closed the door behind her. She brought over another chair. "Now...where were we?"

A knock on the door signaled Tambi's arrival. "Come in, honey!" Missty called out.

Tambi poked her head inside and saw her manager at the table with the two she'd talked with minutes before. "Am I...?"

"No, please come in, Tambi. Take a seat next to me. These people are here from..."

"Gilbert Police Department," Moser answered. She and Ramage both smiled as Tambi settled into the empty chair. "Hello, Tambi. We were wondering if you might be able to help us remember an order you helped a customer with on Wednesday?"

"The drive-thru," Missty added for clarification.

"Um, sure. Did I get something wrong? A complaint?" she asked shyly, wondering if she might be fired or, worse, arrested.

Ramage jumped in. "No, Tambi. You were perfect. What we need help with is if you might remember anything unusual during your shift that day." He summoned up a non-threatening smile as he handed her the receipt. "Any special customer requests, or anything...different...you might recall?"

"I'll try...I take a lot of orders," she said, smiling nervously before surveying the tally in her hand. She confirmed her own name and looked at the time. "Three forty..." she said aloud.

As Tambi verbalized that, her boss spun around in her chair and scooted it up to her desk. Mounted just above it were a handful of black & white computer monitors with feeds of the security cameras. Her eyes went to the monitor that afforded the best view of the vehicles at the drive-thru window. "Wednesday...three forty..." she muttered to herself as she found the corresponding video file. "Let's see what we've got."

Tambi looked up from the receipt as she began wracking her brain for any memories of the order. She looked from Ramage to Moser. "I didn't get anybody complaining; I would've remembered that. Nobody rude or anything."

Behind her, Missty Oliver was scanning the timecode window at the corner of the frame as the images and numbers flew by in a blur. Until she got to a section that might shed some light on the matter. "Three thirty five..." she muttered. "Looks like four vehicles in the queue. A dark Honda CRV...a...*what is that*...a Plymouth PT Cruiser...then we have a Ford F-150 truck."

This got the detectives' attention. "Did you say a Ford F-150?" Ramage asked.

"Yes. Might be light brown...placing an order at the menu board. We'll have a better look when he pulls up closer," Missty said. Both detectives were now standing behind her as she jockeyed the controls. "Okay...here it comes. Male driver and looks like a young child—a girl—in the booster seat."

"I remember that man," Tambi said, watching the screen now as well.

"What do you recall? What about him made you remember?" Moser asked. "Anything might help, honey."

"I remember he was very nice. Not just polite to me, but... now I remember: when he got to the window to *pay* for his order, he asked if it would be okay to pay for the order of the car behind him in line. He said something like he thought the lady might be having a hard time...something like that... and he asked me if he could...*pay it forward.*"

"Pay it forward," Ramage said. "Did you know what he meant by that?"

"Yes. The man asked if I could add the other car's order onto his and he wanted to pay for both. It seemed like a nice thing to do."

"This is very helpful, Tambi," Moser said, adding a comforting smile and nod.

"Okay...here we are," Missty said as the image clearly showed a view of Curt and Rose as Curt paid Tambi at the window and received their small order. Curt smiled at Tambi and pulled ahead, revealing a better look at the next vehicle.

"Hellooooo..." Ramage muttered as an off-white Dodge Tradesman 300 cargo van approached the window. "Can you pause it here, please?"

Missty punched a button, and the screen froze, revealing a young woman looking toward the drive-thru window. She appeared frazzled and was accompanied by a young female child as well. "We're going to need this footage, ma'am," Ramage said, still staring at the monitor.

"Not a problem. I can provide you with still screenshots as well if you'd like."

"We would like," Moser replied softly, as she studied the image. She turned to her partner. "Sits pretty tall in the seat, don't you think?"

"Yeah. She's a tall drink of water, all right. Could well be a six-footer. Uh, Mrs. Oliver, could you please mark this frame number and shuttle forward a little—just to where she receives her order from Tambi?"

"Sure thing," Missty said as the images slowly progressed to the point where Tambi's arms emerged through the window, stretched out toward the vehicle, and handed the driver two food bags and a cardboard drink holder with what looked like two tall, iced coffees.

"Right there. Freeze it, please." Ramage slowly turned to his partner. "Bingo!"

"She's a blond," Moser said.

"True, as per Franco's apartment manager's description, but like you said, she's likely a brunette now. And if that's the case, she's just become a person of interest in *two* cases."

"I'll run her plates and get forensics to take another look at the partial they found on the coffee lid from the golf course," she said.

"Is there anything else I can assist you with, detectives?" Missty asked, turning her chair to face them.

"No, ma'am. Just the footage, please. You've been most helpful," Moser said.

"Tambi has as well," Ramage said, giving the girl an appreciative wink. "We'll let you get back to your day, Mrs. Oliver."

Moser turned to her partner as they reached the door. "Did you still want to—?"

"Absolutely. We'll get it to go."

LOST DUTCHMAN STATE PARK
SITE 88
SATURDAY, 12:20 PM

Rick Moe poked at the remainder of the embers in the firepit. He and his family had enjoyed the first of what he hoped would be three relatively blissful nights here, and so far, this was turning out to be a great shakedown trip with their new, thirty-four-foot Forest River fifth-wheel trailer.

His wife, Liz, had made her first breakfast of pancakes for him and their twin nine-year-old boys, but she was compelled to use the shiny, new RV kitchen as opposed to roughing it. This was her idea of camping: a walk-around king bed, two color TVs, and a living room with faux fireplace.

Liz had outright forbidden him from preparing his beloved applewood-smoked bacon indoors, however, as it would be smelly, so he'd been relegated to using the outdoor firepit. Which was fine with him. Hell, they were camping, for Chrissake.

Rick glanced over at what was left of his meager wood pile. Two logs weren't going to cut it, especially if they were doing s'mores again tonight. He stood, brushed some ash from his jeans, and walked over to the big whale.

The trailer door was closed, and upon opening it, he could immediately hear cartoons blaring from the living room's flatscreen. The boys were stretched out, still in their jammies, and taking up both couches. "Is this what you have planned for the whole day?" he asked, shaking his head. Just outside there was this amazing mountain range, almost close enough to touch, but they weren't having it.

Rich could hear the shower running from down the short

hallway. He tried the pocket door, but it was locked, so he called out to his wife, hoping to be heard above the stream of water splashing against the molded plastic enclosure.

"Hon, I'm gonna go see if I can scrounge up some more firewood. We're almost out. Back in a little while."

"'Kay."

"Boys are watching TV still. Uh, you might want to remind them that we're...camping."

"'Kay."

"Yeah..." he muttered to himself as he headed outside and slammed the trailer door. He grabbed an empty cardboard box and headed off in search of some burnable scraps of wood.

MEANWHILE...
WILEY'S DRIVE-THRU

Grandma Vicky pulled the dilapidated Ford Maverick ahead, slowly, until her window was perfectly aligned up with the order pickup one. She'd inched closer to the building than most customers, as she had to factor in her short arms, and she hated dealing with dropped change.

She looked over at her granddaughter, who seemed a little nonplussed with her Easter candy basket. It was light on the chocolates and lousy with black jellybeans.

The window slid open, and the attendant greeted them with a smile. "Okay, that will be twelve fifty-five, please,"

Tambi said. She was much happier working the window than the front counter and was glad she'd been moved here for the remainder of her shift.

"Sure," Vicky said, fumbling with a coin purse she kept in the console. She retrieved two quarters and five pennies and handed them, along with twelve singles, to Tambi. "Got exact change for you today, honey."

"Perfect. Thank you, ma'am," Tambi said. As she completed the transaction, she couldn't help but do a doubletake upon seeing the young passenger. She looked just like the child whose face she'd watched several times on the video that morning.

As Tambi handed Vicki the food bag and two milkshakes, her wheels started turning. "There you go," she said, pulling the ballpoint pen from her uniform pocket. "Thank you for choosing Wiley's," she added as the car pulled away, and she scribbled down the license plate on a napkin.

GILBERT POLICE DEPARTMENT
RAMAGE'S OFFICE
SATURDAY, 12:45 PM

Detective Ramage regarded the edible work of art he held in his hands. It was nothing short of a masterpiece with its perfect ratio of fresh-not-frozen beef patties, melty cheese, onions, and condiments. Even the bun was noteworthy.

In his estimation, it probably should have its own display atop a pedestal in the Fast Food Hall of Fame, if there was such a place, with special signage and a halogen light trained on it.

He almost hated to spoil it but was only too happy to ruin it as he sunk his teeth into the concoction and rolled his eyes back into his head like a great white shark.

"Mmmm...my...gawd..." was the mumbled praise that emanated from his very full mouth.

Moser was still unwrapping hers, and she had to smile at her partner's unbridled enthusiasm, especially since he'd been a trooper at the juice bar recently. "Don't sugarcoat it; tell us how you really feel about that burger," she said with a chuckle and genuine happiness for the man. She took a bite, and her reaction almost echoed his. "Oh, my...."

"See?"

"Good call, partner...oh, my goodness. Now I see why Darla loves this place so much. Holy cow...no pun intended."

"Pass me my fries, would ya?" Ramage asked. "Please."

Moser handed him the bag and continued with her burger. Ramage's cellphone rang, and he wiped his mouth before answering.

"Yeah. What ya got?" he responded. Moser watched his expression as he listened to the call from the Police Services technician. "Uh-huh," he interjected as he considered taking another bite. But his eyes opened wide, and he trained all his attention on the call. He set down his burger. "No kidding? You've confirmed this? Great work, Martina! Thank you!"

He hung up the phone and popped a fry into his mouth.

"The plates?" Moser asked, setting down her food.

"Yes, indeed-y!" he said, a smile on his now catsup-stained face. "Our person of interest has a name. Get this: Tempest Cage!"

"I'll run that against the partial print they found on the drink lid," Moser said, smiling. "Wouldn't that be something if—?"

Her phone chirped, interrupting her thought. "Moser."

Ramage snuck in another big bite as he watched his partner field her call. She was nodding as she listened, scribbling onto her napkin. "Absolutely. You did the right thing, Missty! And I hope Tambi gets a big fat raise when the time comes! Thank you so much for calling us with that. Yes...yes...thank you, ma'am. And please thank Tambi. Okay."

Moser punched the off button and looked up at her partner with an even broader smile. "Looks like this may be our lucky day!"

"Tambi? Like, from Wiley's Tambi?"

Moser's expression conveyed the obvious. "No...my brother, Tambi," she answered, dripping with sarcasm. "Yes... our favorite server should be promoted to detective, I think. Turns out she was working the drive-thru just now and another customer placed an order at the window—an older woman with a young female passenger in tow—and the girl was an exact match for the one in the video!"

"She's sure."

"Yeah, Missty said Tambi told her she's certain it was the girl, and she managed to get the vehicle's plate. Ford Maverick. Aren't many of those still on the road. Let's see if Martina in Records can make lightning strike twice!"

"Roger that!"

CHAPTER NINE

LOST DUTCHMAN STATE PARK
THE VAN, SITE 91
SATURDAY, 12:57 PM

C URT'S POTTY BREAK had proved rather exhausting for them both, but Tempest finally managed to get Curt re-configured to a prone position deeper inside the van. She'd re-cabled his wrist restraints to the lower hooks along the floorboard so his arms wouldn't go completely numb. The rear cargo doors remained open, allowing a view of the tree line as well as sunlight to see what she was doing.

The sips of Gatorade she'd rewarded him with had been laced with just enough tranquilizer to induce a short nap while she inventoried her camping supplies and other belongings. It was a hodgepodge of plastic bins and cardboard boxes, and it represented all her worldly belongings, save the boxes of eight-track tapes that remained at Vicky's.

Tempest moved the sleeping bags off to the side, revealing the scrapbook she'd lifted from her mother's place. She picked it up and regarded first the front cover, then the spine. There were no annotations to provide a clue as to its contents, so she cracked it open, settled into a comfortable position against the sleeping bags, and was immediately transported to an unplanned journey down bad-memory lane.

Her reaction was immediate as her jaw slackened and eyes widened. This was a true Pandora's box of memories going back many years, and it promised to be both twisted and terrifying.

Page one delivered the opening salvo as a series of weathered color photographs established her as a young child. The margin surrounding the few baby pictures had been labeled in her mother's hand: *Tempest, age 1*

"My God..." she muttered to herself. Several of the photos she'd never seen before.

The old Kentucky house...the storm cellar...where I was born. Jeezus. She turned the page and her brow furrowed, her face tightening at seeing the images of her father. Standing on the front porch. A tall, lean man with a seemingly ever-present smile. By outward appearances, he seemed respectable enough—even friendly—but she knew another side to him.

A secret side. An evil one.

"You effing bastard," she muttered softly. Her hatred was resurfacing, and neurotransmitters began to surge, firing and misfiring. Her brain chemistry was simmering, stirring, and sloshing a weird, unbalanced cocktail of serotonin and dopamine.

Just seeing his grin, and the evil she knew lurked behind it, began to rekindle a host of memories she thought were long behind her.

She paused, not sure if she wanted to turn to the next

page, but she felt compelled. She reached into her pocket and fished out a couple more bupropion, sending them home with a gulp of Mountain Dew.

"Okay, you fuck, let's see what you've got," she whispered, flipping the page.

Her mother had written a label for her first school photo: *Tempest, age 6. First grade.*

By anyone's standard, Tempest had been a stunning child. Even at a tender age, her cheekbones and perfect features announced her as a beauty. A smattering of youthful freckles gave way to short, unfortunate bangs her father had unevenly chopped because the family was on a budget and the barber in town charged eight bucks.

Six-year-old Tempest looked straight into the lens, her expression neutral, yet something behind her eyes hinted at an inner trouble nobody could possibly know about.

Yet.

Tempest's fingers touched the photo, as if she could somehow reach back in time and protect the innocent child staring back at her, but the damage had been done. She let out a sigh and blinked away a tear, willing her hatred to quash any feelings of sadness.

The next photo was of her father, Donald Cage, in a long-sleeved, white dress shirt with a thin black tie. He was leaning against the family station wagon. It was a secondhand Oldsmobile and its whitewall tires seemed out of place, as if trying to impress their nearest neighbors, two miles down the road. *Again, with the grin.*

In the photo, through the opened rear-seat window, Tempest was visible, in what looked like church attire, and discernably sad.

Tempest (7) and Dad. Easter Sunday

"Fuck."

She shuddered as more unsolicited memories started to trickle in and, like unwelcomed visitors, knocking loudly on her amygdala, the complex area of nervous tissue in the middle of her brain that processed threat scenarios.

One of the therapists she'd seen in her twenties had explained that the amygdala was the part of the brain associated with a person's response to fight-or-flight stimuli. He'd also told her that it was thought the amygdala's development can be adversely affected in a trauma-inflicting environment, such as abuse, particularly in childhood and adolescence.

Thoughts of her therapist and the bullshit he'd made her endure as he analyzed her—*labeled* her—conjured up a tightness in Tempest's neck and shoulders. She tossed back the last sip of the Dew and slowly tilted her head to the right, forcing her neck almost forty-five degrees until she got the desired pop of release. *Fucker.*

"Borderline Personality Disorder...what do *you* know?" she murmured softly. *BPD*...bullshit. More like B-*F*-D...big fuckin' deal, dickhead," she whispered to herself.

As if it wasn't bad enough having a shrink hang that acronym on you, having her mood swings misdiagnosed as bipolar disorder for several years prior had been even worse.

"What do *any* of you know?" she hissed quietly, banging her clenched fist against her knee. "You don't know *me!*"

The so-called symptoms and markers had been drilled into her in an effort to arrive at what the therapist decided was her proper clinical diagnosis of BPD. She had exhibited a mandated five of the nine traits to arrive at the diagnosis, he'd told her, but she refused to accept the label...even though she was an overachiever, having checked every one of the nine boxes.

She lost count as she rattled off the traits in her head as if it were a grocery list:

Fear of Abandonment? Yep.

Unstable Relationships? Absolutely.

Identity Disturbance? Sure.

Impulsivity? Fuck yeah.

Suicidal Thoughts or Behavior? Not so much recently, but years ago it was rampant.

Affective Instability? Not convinced I did, but dickhead said I did.

Feelings of Emptiness? Dude...

Inappropriate/Intense Displays of Anger? Big time...

It all didn't matter.

Much to the frustration of her then-therapist, Tempest had glommed onto what she thought was the operative word in that diagnosis: *Borderline*...as in *not quite* a personality disorder. There was no arguing with her, and soon after, the sessions had ended.

Tempest crushed the empty soda can in her hand and as she turned to the next page, she was immediately sucked in a vortex of madness and pain, triggered by a photo from the same period, when she was seven or eight and her sorry excuse for a father had drifted into another in a series of dead-end career moves, none of which seeming to last more than a few months.

She remembered him being gone long hours, sometimes working shifts at two jobs back to back, only to walk in the door in time for his evening meal, a whiskey sour, and maybe serving up a beating for her mother, or herself.

A merciless mental slideshow of greatest-hit images flashed before her: Donald Cage, security guard at the department store in town; pumping gas at the Sinclair station; the crossing guard at her elementary school, which was beyond embarrassing for her; the apathetic door-to-door Kirby vacuum salesman, which her father really sucked at.

And then, the vocation portrayed in the photo she now stared at, her hatred burning even hotter as she thought about it. Donald Cage, driver. Not just your run-of-the-mill driver gig, like a cab driver or a school bus. No, her dad had landed a plum job with the local sausage company, and it was a position he relished.

Frank's Brats & Wursts wasn't a national brand, not yet anyway, but the namesake owner had designs on expanding his business, for better or wurst. And, following the cue within Oscar Wilde's declaration, "Imitation is the sincerest form of flattery," Frank schemed to create his own version of the wildly popular phallic-shaped weenie wagon. On a budget.

It was a cheap knockoff, crudely constructed of chicken wire and fiberglass and mounted atop an old motorhome chassis with a Chevy V8 engine. It got people's attention when it rolled into the neighboring towns, offering up Frank's own brand of steamed sausages.

Unlike the more well-known original he'd bastardized, Frank's machine had particularly poor visibility, offering the driver a decent-sized windshield and two small door windows, but little else. When it rained, water might seep into the cab through the ill-fitting windshield moldings.

The air-conditioning, when it worked, was laughable, and the vehicle had been designed solely as a traveling billboard, a ginormous hot dog cart on wheels with a cooler, two steamers, and lots of room in the back for inventory. And, because Frank was too cheap to pay for a motel for out-of-town trips, the driver slept on a cheap single mattress in the rear of the monstrosity.

Its paint job was poorly executed and more in the brown tones than red, and he'd unapologetically plastered his name on both sides in a mustard yellow.

Tempest stared at the image, taking in every detail, comparing it against what had been savagely etched on her memory. Her father standing by the wagon's open door, wearing his company apron and his shit-eating grin.

She looked up from the book and shuddered, shaking her head as if to make the thoughts go away, but they remained. She turned her attention outside the van's open cargo doors but not really focusing on what she saw. It was just the blurry image of sunlight washing across the rustling leaves of the green trees.

A soft snoring sound next to her brought her back to the present. Tempest let her eyes focus again as she retrained them on the image in the book.

Her mother didn't know about what went on. At least she never indicated that she did. It didn't make it okay with Tempest, however. Not by a long shot. Fearing her own beatings by her husband, Vicky had chosen the bliss of ignorance, or at least feigning such, as she enabled the years of abuse of their daughter.

Tempest's father's grin taunted her, as did the imagined sound of his voice now, asking his then seven-year-old daughter the seemingly innocent question that became code for her unwitting involvement. An invitation to visit a very real Hell.

As she further surrendered to the thoughts, Tempest's toes began curling involuntarily open and closed; while her face started to flush, her hands became clammy as she heard her father ask the dreaded question:

"Hey, Tempest...want to go for a weenie ride?"

It would prove to be the first of many...and this, she realized, had been the start of her undoing.

After an unscheduled fit of crying, Tempest had soldiered on, navigating the collection of photos and clippings her dear mother had included in the album. She was still pissed at herself for allowing emotions to get the best of her, but the album was a lot to absorb.

Subsequent pages gave way to photos portraying a seemingly happy family of three, doing seemingly normal things, but it was all a façade and a lie. Tempest had always loathed the very-occasional backyard get-togethers with the nearest neighbor family.

Mercifully, they were annual events, usually falling on the Fourth of July because good ol' Frank gave Donald Cage the day off to be with family. Besides, and the real reason, people had already bought their celebratory grilling meats and rolling the giant weenie into town was a huge waste of gas.

The neighbor family were Frenchies, the DeForests—or as Tempest secretly referred to them, the Doofuses. Henri and Claire DeForest were nice enough, but they had lame accents Tempest struggled not to laugh at, and an even lamer daughter, Suzette, who was Tempest's age.

Daddy dearest, Donald, would invariably grill up a platter high with Frank's finest sausages, while her dear mama Vicky would spend two hours constructing a potato salad that was too heavy on the mayo. In Tempest's estimation, the DeForests were only invited because they owned the French bakery in town and would always bring a fluffy version of their signature raspberry cheesecake.

Suzette, she assumed, was only brought along because she was outwardly awkward and lacked any social skills whatsoever. Her folks hoped she and Tempest might strike up a friendship. But it would never happen.

From the age of seven going forward, Donald had ruined Tempest from ever again consuming a hot dog. And over the course of years, he'd blazed the trail for his daughter's lifelong struggle with the mental illness that would plague her.

A few more random telephoto pictures she'd never seen had also found their way into the book, moments of Tempest captured by her mother from around the same period: Tempest chewing on a long shaft of grass; Tempest reading a book under the dead tree; Tempest whittling pieces of wood with the folding pocket knife her father had given her for her birthday.

As she continued flipping pages, Tempest found some of them particularly alarming, mainly because Vicky had chosen to do some digging into areas Tempest had no idea she'd been privy to. Dangerous territory.

A subsequent page was filled with local newspaper clippings about a suspicious fire that had destroyed the elementary school Tempest attended. Another page featured a collection of her school portrait photos, annotated accordingly: *Tempest, age 9... Tempest, age 10... Tempest, age 11.*

The age 11 photo portrayed hints of trouble if you knew how to look for it. A self-induced chopped haircut, her intensely sad eyes that belied her age, and an absolute refusal to smile. It was at age eleven, in sixth grade, that the school had been torched. Nobody seemed to know how it had happened. Except Tempest.

And maybe Vicky. Tempest didn't think it coincidental that her mother had saved this clipping, let alone pasted it next to her school photo in this album. *What else does she think she knows?*

She turned a few more pages, mostly benign images of the family lie they had lived. Other than one photo of her mother wearing her robe and a towel turban, there weren't any others of her in the album. Maybe it was because in this one shot, she was sporting the remnants of a recent black eye, plus she had apparently taken on the role of family photographer and preferred to be behind the camera.

Tempest paused and managed a half-smile as she looked at the few pictures of herself with her beloved dog, Rufus. A loveable and atypically gentle lab mix, Rufus had been the closest thing to a childhood friend she'd ever had, and there was a sweetness shared between them, well captured in a half dozen candid shots.

Tempest's mood turned on a dime as she remembered

coming home from middle school only to find her sweet dog had been taken to the pound without so much as a discussion about it.

Fuck you, Donald.

She bit her lip and turned the pages, landing on a pictorial of her turbulent high school years. Her sophomore and junior year school photos weren't particularly noteworthy as, by this time, Tempest had at least tried to fit in. She'd kept to herself, for the most part, making few friends—none of them close. *Tempest, age 14... Tempest, age 15... Tempest, age 16.*

She turned the page. Her mother had glued her eight by ten-inch senior portrait onto its own page, on the left side of the fold, labeling it accordingly: *Tempest, age 17.* It was noteworthy because she'd been allowed to style her hair, and it merited a rare half-smile.

On the right page, facing it, was another local newspaper clipping, and it had been given a prominent place in the album. Its headline read, CLAYTON HOLT, FOOTBALL HERO, DEAD.

Tempest's heart began to race as she looked at the clipping. *What do you think you know about it, Mother?*

The accompanying story told of the high school varsity quarterback's unfortunate demise at the tender age of eighteen. He'd been found dead in a secluded orchard area adjoining the campus, having succumbed to a particularly vicious series of stab wounds. The coroner had concluded that the first knife wound had been fatal. The subsequent fifty-six stab wounds had been carried out in a crime of passion, "a beyond-evil display of anger," the police chief had called it.

Tempest looked at the grainy news photo of Clayton, which showed a clean-cut blond athlete with chiseled features, a bright smile, and a promising future. Being Clayton's girl-friend had been the dream of every one of the cheerleaders, and it was rumored that he'd sampled them all. But unbe-knownst to anyone, he'd had designs on another girl. One who was off everybody's radar. And it would be his secret.

As much as she tried to stop them, scenes of her senior year began to flash back into Tempest's head. It was a rush of imagery, even sounds, all distorted and competing for her attention:

Clayton turning to her and making deliberate eye contact in their shared World History class. The smile flashing briefly, just for Tempest. Clayton during football practice, pausing to pull off his helmet and smile at her when she walked by. Clayton being in the right place at the right time as Tempest's math book fell from her arms, only to pick it up and hand it to her. Service with *the smile.* Those images faded, giving way to another memory of herself walking away from campus, on her way home, cutting through the wooded area as she often did because it was a more direct route for her. And Clayton materializing out of nowhere with a smile and an offer to carry her heavy backpack.

Tempest's initial thought was that he was just another bully toying with her, because she couldn't imagine how somebody like the homecoming king football hero would possibly pay her any attention.

Much to her surprise, and for the first time in her young life, somebody had shown a genuine interest in her.

Clayton Holt had been courteous, kind, and a gentle-man, and exhibited a sense of humor that even got Tempest to giggle more than once on the walk home to her driveway.

After giving her the backpack, he'd smiled once more as

he walked away. He had presented as a genuinely good guy, and with no expectations.

Over the course of the next several days, Clayton had continued to walk Tempest home. It was the following week when he had paused during their walk to proffer the idea of her joining him at a party happening later that evening at a friend's house.

Tempest, not knowing how to respond, had simply flashed an awkward smile, and nodded. "I'll try," she'd said, knowing she'd have to run the gauntlet with her loving parents being home.

Family dinner had been a particularly strange one, with Tempest ruminating on thoughts of what could be construed as her first-ever date. She had silently gone about eating the meal of KFC's finest her father brought home. Donald and Vicky exchanged glances throughout the dinner, while her father threw back a couple of whiskey sours.

She knew there was no way they would allow her to go out at night, let alone to a party. With a boy. No, she'd have to sneak out, which is what she did.

Tempest rubbed the grimace from her face as she let the flood of memories carry her downstream. This was a particularly troublesome patch she was navigating, and she already knew the outcome. She surrendered to it...experiencing it in what almost felt like real time. And without a lifejacket.

She remembered putting on a flattering enough pair of jeans and her best comfortable shoes. The sweater was clingy for her and form fitting. Her bedroom window opened out on to the back of the house, and she'd made her escape after feigning an illness and telling her parents she wanted to go to bed early.

The party had been a loud affair. Two-kegs-and-a-live-band kind of loud. The host, Jimmy Xua, was a former teammate of Clayton's, and his wealthy Chinese parents had left him alone to "watch the house" for the weekend.

Clayton had paid Tempest little mind at the party and, as a result, so had everybody else. Her hair was hiked up into an atypical bun, and she didn't make eye contact or talk with anyone. She didn't even know why she was there. She knew nobody and nobody chose to know her. It was like she was invisible.

She wished she'd stayed home.

It was a sea of hormonal teenagers, blowing off steam, making moves, and refilling their red Solo cups with what-ever mystery concoction had been thrown into the punch bowls. At one point Clayton had walked by, offering Tempest a cupful but after one sip, she'd declined. Whatever it had been was probably best left for stripping hardwood floors. That hadn't stopped Clayton from throwing back a few.

By the time Clayton suggested they leave the party, he was exhibiting an until now unseen side. And she wasn't altogether sure she liked it.

They'd walked a country mile to the party together and were retracing their path through the orchard in hopes she could sneak back in through her window before her parents found out. But Clayton, mister All American, had other plans.

He'd paused on the trail as the moon snuck behind a cloud. Turning to her, he forcibly kissed Tempest. It was devoid of any pretense at romance. It was aggressive, a *You know you want me; I'm the team captain* kind of gesture that made it clear he was one who was used to getting what he asked for.

And he wasn't asking. He was taking. And going for the touchdown.

As Tempest tried to pull away, Clayton's strong grip tightened around her waist, his other hand thrusting its way under her sweater as he began roughly groping her.

"Stop!" Tempest had managed before he slapped her. Her cheek stung, and she tasted a drop of blood in the corner of her mouth.

"Shut up. You know you want it," he hissed back with a slur before silencing her with his nasty lips upon hers. His lips tasted bitter; his breath smelled like floor cleaner and nachos. His eyes had a feral wildness she'd never seen in him—or anyone else—before. Except for her father, during a painful romp in the back of his weenie chariot.

She brought her knee into his groin but that only emboldened his resolve as he tossed her onto her back; she landed atop a shallow pile of leaves and twigs. He was breathing more heavily now, pulling at the buttons of her jeans.

As he stood over her, his eyes wide and a crazed expression on his face, the moon re-emerged. He clumsily unzipped his fly and before she knew it, he had forced himself on her.

And *in* her.

He'd held Tempest tightly by the wrists as he had his way with her, grunting like a maniac for the seemingly endless three minutes it took him to achieve his goal. Her cries of protest were unheard by anyone save the neighboring owl, and she was flush with tears.

As Clayton rolled off her and begun reaching for his undies, Tempest had made her move, catching him completely off guard as the four-inch blade of her pocketknife thrust through his neck. A geyser of blood was shooting out in long spurts as his hands clutched his ruined throat. As Clayton tried to survive this mortal wound, Tempest's next volley of stabs repeatedly found many of his major organs, including his lungs, heart, kidneys.

He had long expired before she made her final statement. She knelt there and paused to catch her breath, wiping blood from her eyes as she readied herself for the extra point.

Clayton Holt's genitals were never found. Nor was his murderer.

Tempest had carefully cleaned most of the blood and soil from her hair and body with the garden hose before quietly reentering her bedroom through the window. Her clothes, shoes, and favorite whittling tool she'd buried at the base of an old dead tree stump a block away, having run home completely naked.

There'd been no school the next day, being a Saturday, so Tempest had stayed in bed, continuing to feign her illness through the weekend.

It was also her alibi.

Tempest looked back at the news clipping and noticed what had to be her mother's annotation in red ink in the margin. It was a big red question mark, and it was circled.

Tempest took pause and noticed her pulse had begun to race. Her unbalanced brain chemistry was signaling overload, and flashing lights seemed to penetrate her closed eyelids. Her thoughts and emotions noisily bounced around like so many ball bearings in a pinball game about to go full *TILT*.

She shook her head in an effort to quiet the machinery, taking a long moment before willing herself to peel back one more torturous page.

And there it was: her so-called father's obituary clipping from the local paper.

It was glued on to the center of its own page. No annotations. But her mother's placement of it here spoke volumes.

Tempest stared into the fine dot matrix of the newsprint photo's grain. A photo taken of the late Donald Cage, then fortyish and wearing that half-grin, as if he were in sole possession of a joke. To Tempest, the joke was that this was a church photo taken at the Presbyterian church in the neighboring town, where he was a deacon.

He had them all fooled. All except Tempest.

Tempest read the obituary copy that accompanied the photo and slowly shook her head as she read the account of this man. Her father. Her monster. It was fiction, almost all of it.

A well-respected family man, Donald was a loving husband to Victoria and doting father to their daughter, Tempest.

A dedicated and distinguished three-time Employee of the Month recipient with his current employer, Frank's Brats & Wursts.

A deacon in his church.

Blah...blah...fucking blah. She didn't need to read about his cause of death. Mainly because she had been the instrument of it. She was sure that was why Vicky had included the clipping with the other items in her hall of shame.

Not that her mother could prove anything, but she was signaling that she knew just the same. This thought triggered another flashback of events long buried in Tempest and she allowed it to play out.

Donald Cage had been determined to cut down or, at the very least, severely prune the mess of a dead tree in the yard. Its only purpose in recent years had been to provide meager support for Tempest's tire swing, as well as a place of refuge where she could spend time in her blackened branches.

But Donald Cage got a wild hair, and one Sunday afternoon, when they got back from church, he'd taken his tallest fruit-picking ladder and the chainsaw from the garage and decided he was now Donald Cage, Arborist.

The tree was a dead maple. Tempest remembered how it, not unlike herself, had once been beautiful, leafy, colorful. She'd watched it grow over the years and thought maybe it too had finally grown tired of its exposure to its hellish patriarch and slowly committed some kind of tree suicide. If there was such a thing. God knows Tempest had thought about it herself. Many times.

Her father had been working the uppermost branches and was alternating his footing between the ladder's top step and the nearby branches, all while wielding the whirring instrument of destruction.

Tiny twigs gave way to small branches, then larger ones, all cascading down to the ground in a heap. It was while negotiating a particularly stubborn branch that Donald lost his balance, the ladder kicking away from him and landing with a thud amongst the debris. Seconds later, the chainsaw joined it, followed by Donald, who crashed down to earth from his lofty perch.

Vicky had been doing laundry and wasn't privy to this development. But Tempest had been watching it all from the bench seat by her bedroom window. She heard her father's cry as he lay on his back, half his body sprawled awkwardly atop the legs of the fallen ladder and the other half amongst the foliage.

She had come outside and casually made her way toward the mayhem, her father's pain more than evident. As she approached him, it appeared that he'd broken a leg, and maybe more. All she knew was that it was distended at a weird angle that couldn't be good. He had scratches on his face and hands, and he had the wind knocked out of him. Still, to the best of his ability, he pleaded for Tempest to go get her mother and call for help.

Tempest looked down at the pathetic man, her expression devoid of any emotion. She rather enjoyed seeing him lying there, helpless, in pain, and completely unable to help himself. She had plenty of experience with those feelings, thanks to this pathetic monster, and she decided she'd taken her last "weenie ride."

Looking back toward the house, then out past the edge of the property toward the street, she had seen that nobody was looking, no cars were around. Satisfied, she picked up the chainsaw and gave the starter a good rip.

The coroner had ruled it a freak accident as it appeared he'd fallen atop the chainsaw when he landed, mortally cutting through his crotch and the femoral artery.

Too bad...so sad. Tempest slammed the album shut. She'd seen enough, and it was becoming clear that her mother had long been harboring suspicions about her. This was a very loose end that could not be ignored, and she would have to figure out how best to deal with it.

Shy of killing her, ideally.

A stirring sound seized her attention as Curt shifted slightly, his cabling limiting his range of movement and rattling in the process. He was propped up into a kind of seated position and she could sense his discomfort. She knew she couldn't keep him this way forever and she'd have to change things up a little.

First things first. Breakfast...er, brunch.

CHAPTER TEN

THE VAN
SATURDAY, 2:11 PM
FIFTEEN MINUTES LATER

CURT'S NOSTRILS FLARED as the aroma of a campfire woke him. The smells began coaxing him out of his fog, and it was the unmistakable scent of bacon that got his stomach gurgling. His eyes blinked open. He vaguely remembered having eaten his sack lunch the day before at school and was pretty sure he hadn't had a scrap of nutrition since.

"Good morning, sleepyhead! Or I guess I should say, good afternoon," Tempest said, looking up from the cast iron skillet and smiling that disarming smile of hers.

Her rare, flawless rack of teeth was framed by wide, perfect lips that, together, formed a smile that was impossible to resist. It was an incredible weapon and on the same level as one of his eighties-era musician fixations: the singer from the girl band, the Bangles, whom he'd had a crush on ever since the late eighties.

Yeah, that was what her smile reminded him of, and this crazy chick seemed to be able to deploy it on and off like a switch. He was sure it was visible from space.

Damn. Careful. "Mm...." He tested his lips. She'd removed his gag.

"Have a good nap?"

"What...what time is it?" Curt asked, trying to sit up and suddenly remembering his plight. "Are you going to unchain me at some point? My shoulders are killing me, and this isn't fun anymore."

Tempest carefully turned the eight slices of sizzling applewood bacon, one by one, and looked up at Curt. "What's the matter? You don't like me anymore?" she said with a cutesy pout for effect.

Curt wasn't buying into it. At all. He was too busy assessing his situation and it was now abundantly clear that he was at the mercy of a very unstable person; his situation was dire. She had the upper hand, and he was immobilized. He had no choice but to not further antagonize her. He had to figure out an angle, find his chance, and take it.

"Nobody said anything about not liking anyone," he murmured, looking away.

"Maybe you'll be in a better mood after some bacon and eggs. How do you take them?" she asked, liberating two eggs from their brown shells. They hit the flat griddle and started hopping against the heat. One of the yolks had broken and was spreading across the surface. "Mm, well, I guess we'll be having scrambled," she said with a light chuckle as she began stirring them, adding two more to the goopy mess.

Curt was salivating a river. He needed to get some sustenance into him to keep his strength up and his mind sharp.

Whatever drugs she'd been doping him with had left him feeling foggy, and he hated it. As a result, he'd have to play nice in the meantime. He was at her mercy.

"Scrambled's fine," he said softly.

"Okay then," she said as she finished them. She grabbed the handle with a potholder mitt and removed the griddle from the grate of the firepit. The bacon was beyond crispy, and she set the cast iron skillet atop a cement block. "There we go," she said, all Susie Homemaker as she blotted up the grease with paper towels.

Her back-and-forth shifts in demeanor were giving Curt a serious case of the creeps. He shuddered as she prepared a Melmac plate for each of them. She put the lion's share of the eggs on Curt's plate and piled on six of the eight pieces of bacon.

Without so much as a thought, she went to hand him a plate, having momentarily forgotten that he couldn't grab it. "Oopsie....sorry...forgot," she said, climbing back into the van. She took a seated cross-legged position near his shoulders and dangled a piece of bacon near his mouth. "Here comes the choo-choo...."

Curt dutifully opened his mouth like a baby bird, closing his eyes as she fed him a slice. He threw embarrassment to the wind. He was ravenous and couldn't help but chew it quickly. It tasted so damn good. It was bordering on orgasmic.

"Hey...hey...slow down, big guy. Can't have you choking to death now, do we?"

He swallowed and opened his eyes, looking at her now.

"Okay, let's take it easy...and if you play your cards right you might even get some pancakes."

He desperately needed fuel in his tank, so he had no

choice but to play along by the rules. "Thank you," he whispered, chomping into another slice.

Tempest couldn't help but be reminded of how she used to feed her little one in the highchair. Baby Abby had always had a messy face and invariably tossed handfuls of food onto the floor. That wouldn't be an issue here, especially since Curt had no use of his hands.

Tempest took a moment for a couple of bites from her own plate before delivering his eggs in three successive spoonfuls.

As Curt swallowed the final bite, he realized—and he knew it was entirely based on the fact he'd been starving—this was probably the best breakfast he could remember ever having. But he sure as hell wasn't going to tell her that.

"Good job, big boy." She waited for him to finish swallowing, then slipped the gag back into Curt's mouth. He watched as Tempest climbed back outside, cleared the plates, and dropped the dishes into a large plastic bucket of soapy water to soak.

So much for pancakes.

Tempest noticed the logs in the firepit were sputtering and needed some encouragement. With an impressive series of swings, she set about splitting a few logs and parked the long-handled axe's blade deep into the nearby stump.

Definitely don't want to be pissing her off.

She placed a few pieces of wadded-up paper and some dry kindling into the firepit and began layering a teepee of the logs atop it. It took three long matchsticks to get it all to light, but it had begun to flame and looked like it might amount to something.

Curt watched her, and his brow furrowed as she then ripped several pages from what looked like a scrapbook album and ceremoniously fed them, one at a time, into the appreciative fire. As she did so, her expression, he noted, took on a rather maniacal quality. Tribal, maybe.

After a few minutes, she walked over to the back of the van. The two rear cargo doors were still propped open, facing out into great wide open, affording Curt a view as well as some fresh air. She poked her head back inside.

"Got the fire re-started," she said, smiling as if they were happy newlyweds about to enjoy their honeymoon vacay together, and not in some twisted hostage scenario.

Curt stared back at her in disbelief. His mind was racing with thoughts about how to get the hell out of there. "Mmph..." he mumbled against the gag.

Tempest grabbed the bath towel hanging from the van's open door, draping it over her shoulder as she pulled a bar of Irish Spring and her years-old, nearly empty bottle of Herbal Essence shampoo from the plastic bin near Curt's foot.

"Hey, I'm going up to the restrooms. Freshen up a little. Maybe we can give you a sponge bath later. Back in a few, hon," she said. She walked a couple of steps and turned back toward him. "Don't go anywhere," she added in a singsong-y tone, smiling that smile, before heading off for the restroom building at the far side of the campgrounds.

Curt listened to the crunch of her steps as she disappeared. He rattled against his restraints, assessing the strength of the hoops the carabiners were fastened to. He wasn't going anywhere.

God, please...help me.

It was proving to be slim pickings for Rick Moe as he finished foraging amongst the brush behind Site 89. The area behind the three sites he'd visited had already been picked over.

Sorry, boys…looks like there won't be any s'mores tonight.

So far, he'd only managed to compile a few small kindling-sized scraps of dry wood and he was momentarily tempted by the open box of commercial firewood sitting adjacent to this site's pit. With nobody around, it was seemingly there for the taking, but he shook his head no. He wasn't that guy.

About a hundred yards ahead, at the end of the campground loop, he noticed another sizeable pull-through site: 91. There was smoke coming from the firepit area, beyond the van parked there. This would be this hunter-gatherer's last try before heading back to his own site, he decided, as he made his way toward the site.

Can't hurt to ask if they can spare a couple of logs…you don't ask, you don't get.

POP POP'S KITCHEN
SATURDAY, 2:44 PM
SAME TIME

Phoenix finished off her tumbler of Sunny D and stared at the long-silent cell phone on the table in front of her. Its blank screen taunted her, and she didn't do well with being taunted.

She heard the door open and the unmistakable sound of tiny human feet scurrying toward her. She spun in her chair just in time to grab her little monkey. "Hey, honey!"

"Mommy! Pop Pop took me to get a new Easter basket!"
"Really! Wow…can I see?"

Rose was over the moon, grinning little ear to little ear as she held it up. "Pop Pop said the Easter Bunny has lots of room to put jellybeans and candies in it. But not the black jellybeans; those are yucky."

"Those aren't my favorite ones either, sweetie. Maybe we'll leave a note for the bunny to not leave those ones. How does that sound?

"Yeah! We should probably say *please*."

"You're right. We should always say please."

"And thank you!" Rose added with an impish smile.

"That's what's up, buttercup!" Phoenix said, mustering her best upbeat response even though she felt like sitting in the corner for a good cry.

The door slammed and Pop Pop materialized, carrying in two bags of their favorite go-to Mexican takeout. "Hey, kiddo. Brought dinner for later."

"Thanks, Pop Pop," Phoenix said, already salivating from the aromas sneaking through the containers. Her thoughts went to Curt. This was his favorite food in the entire world.

"Anything?" he asked, indicating the phone on the table. Phoenix shook her head.

"Hmm...hey, if you're okay for the moment, I thought I'd run by the shop and see how the crew's doing. Anything you need while I'm out?"

"Nah. Thanks, though."

"Okay...call me if you hear anything or need anything."

"Will do, Pop Pop," Phoenix said, offering a weak smile as he kissed the top of her head.

"Won't be long."

"Bye, Pop Pop," Rose said, skipping away down the hall.

"See you later, jellybean!" he called out, pausing as he awaited her response.

"Hey!" Rose called out with a chuckle from the office/guest room. "I'm not a jellybean!"

"Oh, that's right! I forgot!" he replied, loud enough for Rose to hear. It was still their little back-and-forth game, and he hoped it would never end. But, like all good things, he knew it would someday.

He turned to Phoenix and winked. "See ya, hon," he said as he closed the kitchen door behind him. Moments later she heard his truck backing away.

Phoenix picked up the device, powered it up, and stared at the last message she'd sent. The one she hadn't received a reply to. She had to know, with complete certainty, whether she was in contact with her husband or, she shuddered, some troll. She punched in a follow-up text:

> *Curt. If you're getting my messages, show me it's you. Convince me. Assure me you're okay at least! Where the hell are you? You're worrying the shit out of me, and you owe me a response. Hurry home. We have enchiladas!*
>
> *SMF*

She read it twice, then hit send.

CHAPTER ELEVEN

THE VAN
SITE 91
SATURDAY, 2:51 PM
MOMENTS LATER

URT WAS CONTINUING his visual survey of the van's interior, and assessing his fate, when he heard his phone chiming from the front of the cab. It was the tone notifying him of a new message.

He turned his head toward the sound and could see his device sitting atop the dashboard. He cursed his restraints. It had to be Phoenix. His anger at his predicament was peaking now.

As the phone finished its alert Curt heard another sound piercing the eerie silence. It sounded like footsteps on gravel, and they were coming closer.

There's no way she can be back already!

Curt turned his attention to the limited view the open rear cargo doors provided. He braced himself for whatever version of his psycho captor would show up. His level of terror was ratcheting up as the footsteps slowed, nearing the van.

"Hello?" a man's voice called out. "Anyone here?"

Curt yanked on his cabling, hoping it could be heard. *For the love of God...please!!*Then Curt saw a stranger's face peek inside and the look of shock it displayed.

Rick Moe's eyes went wide upon seeing what amounted to what was either a bound and gagged prisoner or some twisted sadomasochist staring back at him. He dropped his cardboard box and was momentarily unable to speak.

Curt attempted to scream through his gag and the wild-eyed expression of fear and horror on his face told the visitor that he was in genuine peril.

"Good Lord almighty," Rick muttered, looking to his left then his right, then back at the shackled man. "Sir, what the hell's happening here?" he asked, stepping closer and peering inside.

"Mmmfffff!!!" Curt managed, turning his head from side to side to indicate his carabiner restraints. He rattled his feet as well.

"Holy Mother of God," Rick said, hastening to climb inside far enough to reach and unbuckle one of the arm restraints. With its release, Curt's right arm pulled away, gravity doing its job and blood beginning to circulate in his limb.

Rick slid backward toward the open doors and fumbled with the carabiner attached to Curt's shackled feet. As he unhooked it, freeing his lower limbs, he looked back at the poor man's face. Curt's eyes were wide with alarm now, and he was shaking his head violently, trying desperately to warn the man to an unseen threat.

"Sir, what kind of trouble are you in? Who the hell did

this to—?" Rick managed before a sickening thud could be heard and his own eyes went wide, his face frozen in an open-mouthed, death-mask expression of pain.

Curt stared back as the man stood there for a couple of seconds, his would-be rescuer's face mirroring the horror of the unfortunate soul in Edvard Munch's painting, *The Scream*.

A deathly gasp escaped the man before his lifeless body collapsed to the side and another person came into full view.

And it was the most terrifying site Curt had ever seen.

Tempest pulled back the axe and delivered a second fierce blow to the base of the now-limp man's neck, severing his spinal cord completely, and nearly his head with it.

She tossed the axe to the side and stared back at Curt with a ferocity that gave him chills. Her hair was wet from the showers, blown into a Medusa-like tangle of snaky strands from the gusts of breeze, and her contorted face was speckled with blood spatter.

She leaned in closer, hissing now. "Now look what you've done."

Curt nearly lost bladder control as he stared into the eyes of this seemingly rabid creature and his impulses rapidly returned to him. He'd only have one shot.

She began to climb in. "I leave you alone for a few minutes and you've managed to—"

With urgency and an economy of motion, Curt brought his knees in towards his chest and planted his feet against Tempest's chest, interrupting her sentence while launching her into orbit, toward the firepit.

Tempest's head violently glanced against the upper lip of the door jamb on the way out, her back making contact as she crashed down awkwardly against the cement block and brick structure. Her right hand had upset the pit's grate and landed in the red-hot embers.

She screamed as she yanked her arm away from the heat and grimaced at her new, very real complaints as she lay there, dazed, her back and her head now writhing in pain.

It took all of five seconds for Curt's free hand to unbuckle his other wrist and yank the gag from his mouth; his first free-speech utterance declaring it was *GO* time.

"Fuck! Fuck! *Fuck!*" he screamed, willing the blood to renourish his limbs. He scooted his butt towards the back of the van and looked out toward the firepit, assessing the new situation. She was still sprawled out on her back, and he could tell she was temporarily immobilized.

Curt hastily scrambled to get to his feet. Upon jumping to the ground, his left foot awkwardly found the edge of a large, protruding tree root. He'd already committed his whole weight to the maneuver and as he stood, he received simultaneous alerts to his senses.

His ankle had cruelly folded inward nearly ninety degrees, in a direction it was never designed for, accompanied by a loud popping sound and a wave of sudden, excruciating pain he'd never experienced.

A howl escaped him as he fell back onto his butt. He tried to stifle a wave of nausea as he regarded his rapidly swelling ankle. This was more than a basic sprain; he'd had an ankle sprain when he played high school football. That had hurt. But not like this. This was worse. Way worse.

He wasn't sure, but he thought he'd probably broken it, and possibly in more than one place.

He rolled over onto his side and surveyed his surroundings. To his left lay his wholly unstable, axe-wielding captor.

She was temporarily stunned by her own fall, and it was anyone's guess for how long. Next to Lizzie Borden, the dead, nearly decapitated man who had found himself in the wrong place at the wrong time.

She could get up at any second and chop him into pieces if he didn't get out of there. The dead guy was all the confirmation he needed.

He groaned in pain as he rolled over to his other side, providing a wide view of the distant campsites, all of which seemed a million miles away. He didn't see anyone milling around the other sites, and based on his bad wheel there was absolutely no way he'd be able to close that distance to find assistance over there.

It was the sound of distant laughter that got his attention, and it was coming from somewhere deep in the thick tree line behind the site. He had to establish contact, and fast.

A thought came rushing to him, and with great effort, he pulled himself to his feet, leaning heavily on the van's rear door. He limped his way along the side of the van and threw open the driver's door. A quick scan of the cabin revealed his cell phone on the dash and his ring of keys in the cupholder. There was no sign of his wallet, and he didn't care. He didn't have the luxury of time; he'd have to check messages later. He pocketed both items with the haste of a subway pickpocket.

He climbed back out, careful to avoid putting any pressure on his left foot. The laughter got his attention again. It sounded like a man's laugh, and it was definitely coming from somewhere deep in the trees behind the campsite.

Each step was brutal, sending signals of fire through his nervous system. He gritted his teeth and grunted as he hobbled his way back down the side of the van. He paused as he heard another sound. Much closer. He looked over to see the crazy woman still on her back. Her eyes were closed, yet he knew she could regain consciousness at any moment. The sound of the sigh that escaped her was all it took to light a fire under him.

Seeing his options were few, Curt made his decision without hesitation.

Seconds later, he gimped away like a lame kid playing hopscotch and disappeared into the woods.

CHAPTER TWELVE

GILBERT POLICE DEPARTMENT

RAMAGE'S OFFICE

SATURDAY, 3:20 PM

MOSER WAS READING an incoming report on her laptop as Ramage finished his call with his favorite Records clerk, Martina. She was somebody who always gave a hundred ten percent, and that went a long way with him.

"Her mother? Seriously? Wow, great work, Martina. That's the solid lead we were looking for." He paused to listen to her response, making eye contact with Moser, then added, "Until you're better paid, please accept my huge thank you. Yeah...I owe you a veggie burger."

He hung up the phone and looked at his partner, nodding slowly.

"Her mother? Like, Tempest-with-the-dark-hair's mother?" Moser said, looking up from her report. "Do we have an address?"

"Yep. Let's see if we can add some brushstrokes to this little picture we're painting."

"Okay, I'm done here," Moser said, closing the laptop a moment later and fixing him with a look that said she had some news as well.

"What? What's going on?"

"Another brushstroke for you. Forensics was able to match the partial off the iced coffee lid we found at the golf course. Turns out the print's a match to those from the driver's license report we got from the Department of Transportation," Moser said with a smile.

"Wow."

"Yeah, wow...and get this. The agency's also where Tempest Cage is employed."

"No shit."

"Her address on file with the department is an older Post Office box in Surprise, but the pieces are starting to come together, I'd say."

"Yippie ki-yay, partner," Ramage replied with a wide grin. "How 'bout we take a run out to East Mesa, talk with mom, and see—" he said, the ring from his desk phone interrupting. He held up his finger in a "wait one" gesture as he picked up. "Ramage."

Moser watched him closely. Her partner's eyes were darting around the room as he processed what he was hearing, his face growing taut. "Yeah, yeah. We'll need to talk to him. Yeah...on our way," he said and slowly replaced the receiver into its base. *"Fuck!"*

Moser just looked at him. She knew her partner well enough to let him process his thoughts before interjecting.

Ramage rubbed his face and turned to her, his expression dead earnest.

"The chat with mom will have to wait."

"Yeah? Why, pray tell?"

"Looks like we've got another body."

POP POP'S KITCHEN
SATURDAY, 3:42 PM

It was becoming painfully clear to Phoenix that simply willing a return message to appear on her phone wasn't working. Either Curt was getting her messages and—for some reason God only knew—was truly pissed at her, or he was in some kind of genuine peril.

She decided it had to be the latter. And a new wave of fear came with that determination.

She set the phone on the table and decided it better to direct her obsessive thoughts to her daughter, who was now sitting next to her at the table, in the early stages of crafting another crayon masterpiece.

"Would you like a snack, sugar pie? Some juice maybe?"

"No thank you, mama," Rose replied, her concentration focused on her work in progress.

"Okay. You let me know if you change your mind, baby. Mama's got to finish folding the laundry and make a quick call, okay?"

"'Kay."

"What are you drawing, honey? May I see?"

"Not yet," Rose said, covering her eleven by fourteen drawing paper with her left arm. "It's a surprise."

"Okay, I'll be down the hall if you need anything," Phoenix said, kissing the top of her mini-me's noggin. She picked up her phone and carried it down to the laundry room.

Come on, Curt. Answer me. Give me a sign, baby.

She emptied the lint trap and began removing the items from the dryer one at a time, folding them neatly and placing them in the rectangular laundry basket.

The last thing she retrieved was Curt's favorite button work shirt—the same one whose pocket she'd discovered the Wiley's receipt in. She picked up the shirt and held it to her face, inhaling its aroma, hoping it might still offer a hint of Curt's masculine scent. The fabric softener sheet had done its job because the shirt only smelled of Hawaiian Breeze, or whatever they marketed its artificial fragrance as.

She took extra time folding it, a few tears welling up as she did. She wiped them away and placed the shirt atop the rest of the family laundry.

She shook her head and picked up the phone, calling Detective Moser on speed dial. She tucked the phone under her chin as she carried the basket back toward the kitchen.

It rang several times, and she set the basket down next to the fridge. Moser picked up as Phoenix reached the table.

"Detective Moser," she heard her answer.

"Hey, Detective Moser, sorry to interrupt you, but I just needed to check in to see if there were any new developments you can share with me," Phoenix said, her eyes scanning the room, the ceiling, and little peeks at the edges of Rose's artwork. It was starting to look like something. A landscape of some sort.

"Mrs. Mart—er, Phoenix, hi. I was going to call you later this afternoon. We're running down a couple of leads right now and we have to check them out before we can tell if they're any good. Anything new at your end?"

"Okay...no, nothing. Sounds like you're in the car."

"We are. We're actually...where are we? Wait one."

Phoenix could hear that Moser had covered her mouthpiece as she consulted with her partner. "Just entering Pinal County," Phoenix heard Ramage's muffled voice answer in the background.

"Just entering—" Moser began to parrot.

"I heard," Phoenix interjected. "Anything I need to know about? Where in Pinal County?"

"We're just checking on something out in the Sonoran Desert. Superstition Mountains area. Might be nothing, but you never know. You familiar with it?" Moser replied.

"Superstitions? Yeah. Pop Pop—er, David and I used to go hiking in there sometimes. Been a few—"

"Look, mama!" Rose said, pulling on Phoenix's arm as she smiled proudly.

"Excuse me, Detective. Just a sec—sorry, it's my daughter," Phoenix said before turning to see what so urgently needed her attention.

"I'm on the phone, honey, can it—?"

Several seconds of silence went by while Phoenix processed what she was seeing. Rose turned the art tablet so that her mother could better see her masterpiece.

"You like it?" Rose squealed.

The room disappeared as Phoenix's vision narrowed down to an area eleven by fourteen inches in size, her entire world view a vignette as she now focused on the imagery her daughter had created with her jumbo box of Crayolas.

Moser's voice interjected through her device's earpiece. "Phoenix? Are you still there?"

"Uh, yes, Detective. Sorry, I'm going to have to call you back," she replied, clearly distracted as she ended the call and picked up the artwork.

It was an incredible rendering—especially considering a seven-year-old had created it—and she knew at once what she was seeing. A stretch of desert highway, exhibiting a keen sense of perspective, stretching away toward a distant range of mountains.

Their outline was unmistakable, as if copied from a photograph, and Rose's use of both the gray and navy-blue crayons had provided uncanny detail of the rugged nooks and crannies. It was in every way incredible. Almost like looking at a giant postcard, but with the requisite little kid's embellishment of a gigantic sun, smiling down from the corner of the paper.

"That's very nice, Rose! It's so good, honey! Wow..." Phoenix said, both proud and perplexed. She didn't remember having ever taken her daughter on this road.

"How did you choose this to draw, sweetheart?"

Rose looked at the drawing, pointing to the mountain range, then back up to her mother as she answered. "It's where Daddy is."

"What?" Phoenix couldn't believe what she was hearing. "Wait...what do you mean? Why do you think...that's where... your daddy is?" she dared, biting her lip.

"Because Willie told me!"

CHAPTER THIRTEEN

LOST DUTCHMAN STATE PARK
CAMPGROUND LOOP, SITES 75-104
SATURDAY, 3:57 PM

THE FAR END of the campground loop was cordoned off, keeping nonessential eyes from seeing a very fluid crime scene. A smattering of orange cones, sawhorses, and police cars were in place on both sides of the road, forbidding access beyond Sites 94 and 95.

A couple dozen curious campers were assembled behind the barricade near Site 86, hoping to get a sense of the emergency. Two State park rangers were monitoring the crowd, their radios occasionally squawking out unintelligible sounds.

There was no disguising the fact that an ambulance was parked at the very end of the loop. Detectives Ramage and Moser were on site, assessing the scene as they spoke with a very seasoned park ranger.

Moser stepped around the bloody patch of ground, careful not to disturb the scene as she joined her partner. Twenty yards away, the gurney containing the victim's body was being loaded into the back of the ambulance by a couple of grim-faced first responders.

Ramage briefly glanced at the ranger's name tag: *Rick Danger*. He chose not to address him by that, opting for something more generic, because he knew it would sound funny to address him as Ranger Danger.

"You say the victim was deceased when you found him, sir?"

"Yes. Like I said, I was the first on the scene," Ranger Danger replied, pausing as he looked off in the direction of a woman and two boys huddled together about a hundred yards away, sobbing.

Ramage followed his gaze, then renewed eye contact as the man continued.

"Mrs. Moe, there, contacted our ranger's office, express-ing concern that her husband hadn't returned after having gone looking for firewood. She sounded panicky; I told her I'd look around, and..."

The ranger paused, collecting himself and letting out a deep sigh. In his twenty-six years in the State Park system, he'd never encountered anything like he'd stumbled upon today.

"Sorry..."

"Take your time, sir."

"Yeah, well, I found the man lying right there. He was face down, and there was a lot of blood. Sorry, that's obvious, I guess. His neck wounds were quite severe, and at first glance, it looked like maybe he'd been mauled by a bear."

"You have bears here?" Ramage asked.

"Quite a few animals make their home in these moun-tains. More common to see desert cottontail rabbits, coyotes, the occasional desert mule deer. Some big cats—the bobcats and mountain lions—are out there too but rarely come into the campgrounds. As far as bears go, there are the occasional black bears, but, like the cats, they're more elusive."

"When did you know it might be something else?"

"When I saw..." the ranger managed before clearing his throat. "When I saw the huge gashes at the base of the man's neck, and the angle of his head, I realized it didn't fit the profile. The bloody axe lying there. That clued me in to what must've gone down here."

Moser finished jotting a note into her notebook. "Were there any other witnesses, sir?"

"Not that have come forward, no. I don't think he'd been there awfully long before I got there. The family is having a real tough time, as you can imagine. This is a peaceful place. Families come here almost year-round. We don't have trouble like this. Not here."

Moser nodded, her eyes surveying the site. Ashes from a recent fire, a bucket with kitchen utensils and a couple of camping plates soaking in it. The axe. And fresh tire prints.

"The guest who'd reserved this spot. Can you tell us the name on the reservation, sir?"

Danger consulted his clipboard. "Says here it was a woman. Last name Cage, first name Tempest."

The detectives exchanged knowing glances.

"No other name on the reservation, sir?" Ramage asked.

"That's the thing. It wasn't really a reservation. There'd been a last-minute cancellation. A family had to change their plans after a kidney stone emergency. This woman was lucky to get this site. She wanted something secluded, and this was the only one open. Paid for two nights."

"Who was she with, sir?" Moser asked.

"Just her," the ranger replied, consulting his clipboard. "Tempest Cage, driving a van, Dodge Tradesman. One of the long ones. You want the license number?"

"Yes, please," Moser said, copying the information into her note pad. She knew it to be the same one they already had.

"You've been a big help, sir. We appreciate it," Ramage said, handing him his card. "If you think of anything else, Ranger Danger, please don't hesitate to call."

As the detectives walked back to their vehicle, Moser gave her partner a gentle elbow to the ribs. "Oh, my God. Ranger Danger? You just couldn't resist, could you?"

Ramage's sly grin was all the answer she needed.

As they climbed in, Moser powered up her phone. "Looks like we missed a call from Phoenix. Should we fill her in on this?"

"Mm...not just yet. Don't want to send her into full panic mode. The prints on the drink cup, the drive-thru footage, the daughter's school verifying her hasty removal, and now this."

Moser nodded. "It's coming together quickly, but we don't have anything on Tempest Cage's whereabouts. Curt could still be with her, and, if so, we don't know how much danger he's in. I agree."

"Roger that. The all-points bulletin is out there. Let's pay that little visit to mom."

PARADISE FOUND MOBILE ESTATES
SUPERSTITION SPRINGS/EAST MESA, ARIZONA
SATURDAY, 4:22 PM

The sky-high clump of palm trees came into view, and a block later, Ramage turned left at the sign, indicating they'd found Paradise. He pulled into the entrance of the property and began the five-mile-per-hour crawl along the loop as he strained his neck to find unit numbers.

"Jeezus...they could film a zombie movie here."

"C'mon. It's not that bad," Moser lied as she regarded the slow shuffle of octogenarian residents huffing their way toward their respective hovels. "Please tell me you'll never allow anyone to put me in one of these places," she muttered, having changed her mind.

They proceeded past the pool, which was teeming with reptilian creatures and one youngster. "Should be up ahead on the right," Moser said.

Ramage got a few suspicious stares from a couple as he pulled alongside them. He just nodded and smiled as they continued along the loop.

"There. Number 88," Moser said, pointing to the numbered parking space across from the unit registered to Vicki Cage. "Looks like her car's gone. Guest spot next to hers is open."

"Roger that," Ramage said, consulting his mirror and activating his blinker before making the turn into the narrow space. He didn't need to add to the body count by running over any of the desert tortoises.

Moser grabbed her notebook and phone off the dash as

they exited the car. They made their way across the drive to the double-wide, and as they reached the dreary porch, Ramage cricked his neck.

"Plants are pretty hammered," Moser muttered softly.

"You have my solemn oath I won't let anyone put you in one of these places," Ramage promised under his breath. He knocked on the frame of the meager screen door. It bounced back against his knock, flying further open, revealing that the front door was also slightly ajar.

He exchanged glances with his partner then knocked on the door's frame. "Hello! Mrs. Cage? Vicki Cage?" he called out, not loud enough to garner attention from other residents but enough to be heard by anyone inside the mobile home. "Ma'am, it's Detectives Ramage and Moser, Gilbert Police Department, ma'am."

They stood on the porch anticipating the occupant to come to the door, but after several moments of complete silence, they exchanged glances again.

"Ma'am, it's Detective Moser, we'd like to ask you a few questions if we may. Would it be all right if we—?"

"Look," Ramage said, interrupting his partner as he pointed to what looked like a couple drops of blood smeared near the doorknob. "Ma'am!" he called out with more urgency, nodding to Moser. "Gilbert PD, ma'am. We're coming inside," he added as he pulled his Glock from the holster. Moser did the same and nodded.

Ramage gave the front door a slight push and it creaked open noisily. The interior was dark, as the lights were off, and the blinds closed. The smell of secondhand smoke was pungent.

"Mrs. Cage?" he called out to the hallway. "Ma'am, are you okay?"

Using the side on her free hand, Moser flipped on a light switch in the living room, which powered up all three bulbs of the goose-necked reading lamp extending above the recliner.

"Jeezus," she uttered at seeing the diminutive woman slumped over in the chair. "Jeff, in here!"

Ramage emerged from the hall and followed Moser's gaze. "Holy mother...."

Vicki's chin was limply resting against her bloodied chest. Vast amounts of blood had also soaked her lap, the chair cushions, and the area of the floor by her feet. An expired cigarette butt was still wedged between the index and middle finger of her right hand.

"What the hell happened here?" Moser asked.

"Definitely no needlepoint accident," Ramage muttered as he knelt alongside the victim, without touching her, and assessed her wound. "Looks like her throat was slit. Ear to ear. Jeezus...gawd...."

"I'll call it in," Moser said, stepping back out onto the porch, fighting back the nausea.

Ramage slowly rose to his feet, stepping back from the victim's chair, as to not contaminate an obvious crime scene. His weapon still drawn, his eyes swept the room and he glanced into the small kitchen area, then made his way back down the hallway.

Poking his head into the first doorway, he could see the bathroom wasn't in disarray. The door to the room at the end of the hall was open. The master. It too didn't appear to be disturbed.

Moser materialized behind him. "Anything?"

"Not yet," he replied, his features tightly drawn. "One more room," he said, gesturing to the last door, which was ajar. He pushed the door open, ready to respond to anyone who might be waiting, but was met with nothing but old exercise equipment and a few boxes.

Moser flipped on the wall switch, bathing the storage room in soft overhead light. Two of the cardboard boxes were off to the side, away from the rest of the stack, and appeared to have been hastily opened. One of them had been left on its side and spilled some of its contents onto the shag carpeting.

Without touching anything, he crouched down for closer inspection. It looked like a failed garage sale with all the eight-track tapes strewn about.

"Robbery?" Moser asked.

"Not unless the perp's a collector of old...what are these? Not cassettes."

"Looks like eight-tracks. My father used to have a bunch of those. Old technology; died like the dinosaurs. Cassettes were destined to outlast them," Moser said.

Ramage stood. "Everything else appears to be in order," he said, mostly to himself.

"Backup unit and coroner should be here momentarily," his partner said, shaking her head. "What are you thinking?" she asked as they made their way back down the hall and onto the porch.

Ramage glanced back down to the smear of blood adjacent to the front doorknob. "I'm not a hundred percent sure, but my gut—which is about ninety-nine percent sure—tells me this is the work of a tall, brunette axe-murderer. And I think we just missed her."

CIRCLE K
SUPERSTITION SPRINGS
SATURDAY, 4:55 PM

They hadn't had her first choice of color at the drug store, but it really didn't matter much at this point. As long as it wasn't her current dark brown. She had to change it up, and in a hurry.

Tempest didn't have time to do the typical leave-in-for-thirty-minutes job either. She'd grabbed the first box of Just for Men she saw on the shelf because of its advertised claim, and they were fresh out of Just for Maniacs.

She didn't consult her watch but figured it had probably been about ten minutes, which seemed like an eternity to be locked up in the gas station restroom. There had been a few knocks on the door, but her barked complaints of worst-case diarrhea had chased the people away.

She hoped the sandy blond shade would be enough of a change as she rinsed the residual product into the rust-stained sink.

She regarded her new look in the graffiti-carved metal mirror. It was a bit lighter but nowhere near what her previous blond shade had been before this whole nightmare started. It was fine. She wasn't entering a beauty contest.

Tempest pulled out her pocketknife and noticed there were still a few drops of blood on the blade. She gave it a quick rinse and began haphazardly carving away handfuls of her locks, dropping the clumps of hair onto the floor.

The restroom had a sketchy, air-blowing hand dryer, and she stooped down to its level as she let the lukewarm air wick away some of the moisture. She let the machine run three cycles.

A minute later she stood and gave herself another look. Her hair was chopped unevenly, as if by an unsupervised blind child with a pair of school scissors, but she didn't give a rat's ass. She had a couple of hours before the park closed, and she had to find her man.

Somewhere, someone. He couldn't have gotten too far.

Tempest jumped in the pathetic Ford Maverick and got back onto AZ-88. She hated this car. Both the legroom and headroom were inadequate, plus the stereo system was a crap-sounding aftermarket Radio Shack cassette deck with one tape, and it was frigging showtunes.

Any port in the storm, though. She'd had to ditch her van a block away from the trailer park and she'd managed to stealthily walk into the property without garnering much attention. The Maverick, with all its faults, was hers for the taking.

She stomped on the accelerator.

LOST DUTCHMAN STATE PARK
SIPHON DRAW TRAILHEAD
SATURDAY, 5:10 PM

Curt hobbled up to the sign marking the entrance to the trailhead and, wiping the sweat from his brow, parked himself against the post and sat.

It hadn't been a hot day, not enough to justify his profuse sweating, but the trip through the wooded area with one good leg had pretty much kicked his ass. It had been slow going, and he never did find the source of the mystery laughter he'd heard from the forest behind the firepit.

It wasn't like he had a map. He'd followed a sound into the nearest woods out of desperation to get away from his captor, who had just demonstrated her lethal abilities. He didn't know how long she'd been incapacitated but his guess was it hadn't been long enough.

She was bipedal, athletic, and had an axe to grind. He, on the other foot, had a busted wheel, a lack of familiarity with the terrain, and no bars showing on his phone.

He reasoned that any other hikers had already completed this hiking loop previously in the day, as they would have gotten earlier starts and weren't similarly handicapped.

The trailhead sign provided clues to the challenge ahead. It stated the end elevation of 1,030 feet, with Siphon Draw's three-mile circuit taking about two and a half hours. An icon of a stick figure hiker on a slight grade indicated it was an "easy trail," provided they turned around at the Flatiron.

Those who dared to go farther, however, experienced a marked increase in elevation to nearly 2,800 feet, which was represented accordingly by another stick figure hiker hoofing it up a steep grade. *Difficult.*

From the diagram on the sign, he knew that even the lower circuit was all uphill. Not much of an option in his case.

Curt's left ankle was shooting out sharp pains and it throbbed in protest as he labored to get back to his feet. He licked his lips. He was parched and hadn't had the luxury of preparing a daypack with water. Or beef jerky. He tried not to think about it, but he knew his blood sugar was tanking.

He looked up at the sun. It was getting lower in the sky, and once it disappeared behind the mountain range, the temperatures would drop considerably. His short-sleeved shirt wasn't going to cut it.

God, if you're monitoring this, I could use your help right about now!

CHAPTER FOURTEEN

LOST DUTCHMAN STATE PARK
CAMPGROUND LOOP, SITES 75-104
SATURDAY, 5:35 PM

TEMPEST, NEWLY SHORN, was hiding the trainwreck under her Arizona State ball cap and wearing the fresh red flannel shirt from the plastic bin she'd managed to grab before abandoning the van.

She pulled up alongside the ranger kiosk window.

Unrecognizable enough, she figured, but wore dark sunglasses just the same. And her height wasn't quite so obvious from the Maverick's low perch.

"Good afternoon, ma'am."

"Hi. I'm joining some friends for dinner at their campsite," she lied through her smile.

Tempest took slight comfort in seeing that this junior ranger was young, and thus a newbie. He looked to be early twenties, so she dialed up the charm a notch to expedite things.

"I'm running a little bit late...I was supposed to be there at

5:15 for a surprise birthday," she said, lowering her sunglasses as she treated him with a broader smile.

The young man smiled nervously. "Oh. Uh, do you know the way to their campsite, ma'am?"

"Oh, yes, thank you. I've been there many times and, like I said, they're expecting me."

"Okay, ma'am. Just in case, here's a map of the grounds, and if you'd please hang this pass from your—"

"Certainly," she said, taking the items and hanging the pass from her mirror. "Thank you so much," she said, pausing to look at his badge. "Mark," she purred.

"Yes, ma'am," he replied, trying not to blush. "And, uh, just a reminder that the gates lock at 8:00 p.m., so...."

"No problem. You've been very helpful, Mark. Have a good evening," Tempest said, weaponizing her smile as she rolled up the window and slowly pulled away.

Ranger Mark compliantly jotted down the license number on to his clipboard log.

As Tempest made her way down the campsite loop, she noticed several gawking looky-loos gathered around the saw-horses and taped-off areas near Site 86. She knew exactly why it was cordoned off.

Slowly pulling off the pavement and looking around for a place to stash the Maverick, she saw her best option presenting itself: a seemingly unoccupied fifth wheel trailer. She pulled around the back, grabbed her daypack and a five-cell beast of a flashlight from the rear seat, and locked the vehicle.

The looky-loos paid her no mind; they were too busy drinking beers and solving crimes. Now on foot, she circumvented the populace and the loop as she found her way to the tree line behind her old site.

Law enforcement personnel had already left the scene, which left a couple of junior ranger types to keep out any curious campers. Tempest, from her vantage point thirty yards away, could tell that the man's body had been removed, as had the few camping items she'd left behind in her hurry to vacate the premises.

She quickly looked over both shoulders to make sure she wasn't being watched.

Seeing the firepit and its displaced grate reminded her of what had transpired earlier. She rubbed the bump on the back of her head and winced. She'd been temporarily incapacitated by the fall, but she wasn't entirely sure for how long. She thought she remembered seeing, through the slits of her eyes, Curt, free of his restraints, hobbling away.

He hurt himself!

And she recalled the direction she'd seen him hobble away in.

She pulled her canteen from the daypack, took a swig, and closed the lid, then swapped it out for her long flashlight. It would be getting dark soon, she knew, as she dashed off into the tree line.

You couldn't have gotten too far. Don't worry; I'll find you, my love.

POP POP'S
SATURDAY, 6:22 PM

Phoenix poked at her cheese enchiladas.

It didn't matter that they were her favorite food in the entire world, and from her favorite place. The thought of enjoying this feast—or anything for that matter—while Curt was still out there, somewhere, had completely killed her appetite.

"You need to eat something, kiddo," Pop Pop said, walking the talk by scooping a generous forkful of the spicy entree into his mouth. "Mmm."

"Not hungry, Pop Pop," Phoenix replied, corralling the beans into their corner of the plate.

"I know, but still..." he said with his mouthful. "Gotta keep your strength up."

Phoenix looked away, her gaze going to the kitchen window. It was getting dark, and her man was out there. Somewhere. Probably cold. Probably scared. Possibly hurt.

She pushed her plate away and stood from the table. "Sorry, I can't."

Rose put down her taco and looked up at her. "I miss Daddy too," she said, tears forming in the corner of her doll eyes.

"I know, baby," Phoenix said, kneeling and giving her cherub a long hug. "I know."

A minute went by before Rose broke the silence.

"Pop Pop...."

"Yeah, sweetie pie?"

"Just a minute," Rose said, as she got up from her chair and scurried down the hall.

Pop Pop exchanged looks with Phoenix, and a moment later the little minion returned to the table with a broad smile and carrying her art paper. "Look what I drawed today!"

"I definitely want to see what you *drew* today, cupcake! Will you show me?"

Rose came around alongside his chair and proudly handed it to him.

Pop Pop pushed his plate off to the side; he didn't want to get any chili sauce on it. With great ceremony he laid the paper flat in front of him. "Let's see what we've got, lollypop!"

"Hey!" she giggled.

Pop Pop wiped his mouth with his napkin and looked down upon the art paper. Phoenix watched his expression as he took in what he was seeing, his jaw going slowly slack, his eyes seemingly unbelieving. He scanned the image his granddaughter had created, taking in its details, and saying nothing for several seconds before turning to her.

"Did somebody help you with this, Rosebud? It's an amazing picture, honey!" He looked up at Phoenix, who was still processing what she'd seen hours before. It was incredible.

"I drawed it!"

"You *drew* it? he said, again with the subtle correction. "All by yourself!?"

"Yes!"

"What is this picture of?" he asked, hoisting her up onto his lap. He knew full well that it was a nearly perfect rendering of an all-too-familiar landmark that had fascinated him for decades.

Phoenix's cheeks were puffed out fully. She was close to blowing a gasket.

"It's where my daddy is!" Rose said, pointing to the Superstitions.

Pop Pop blinked several times, then his eyes slowly took in the room, landing on Phoenix, whose tightlipped expression telegraphed her growing unease.

"Really...you think so, do you?" he asked, turning back to Rose.

"Yes."

"And why do you think that?" he responded, genuinely curious.

Phoenix braced for the answer she knew was coming. She watched for Pop Pop's reaction.

Rose leaned over and whispered in his ear. A moment later his smile disappeared, and his eyes went wide.

Pop Pop finished washing the last of the dishes and placed it in the rack with the others, then wiped his hands on the dishtowel. With Rose freshly tucked into bed down the hall, the house was deathly still.

Rose's artwork was now prominently displayed on the fridge, held in place by four Hello Kitty magnets. All it needed was some museum glass.

Pop Pop picked up his half-empty glass of Guinness from the counter, and on the way to the table Phoenix was sitting at, lost in her own world of pain, he paused for another look at the rendering. He shook his head. Rose's portrayal and sense of perspective was uncanny.

"I'm still lost for words, honey," he said, sliding into his chair and taking a pull from the glass of ale.

"Same..." Phoenix managed. Through unfocused eyes,

she was staring at an invisible pile of nothing in the middle of the table.

"I mean, what should we make of it? In all my time reading with Rose, and our time together on the computer, this image has never, ever come up. Do you think she may've seen it at school?"

"Don't think so. I...I dunno..." she said. "I have a couple of her other drawings to show the therapist, but nothing like this one. And that'll have to wait. I'm not going to keep our appointment for this coming week. Not with all—"

"I know," Pop Pop said, gently touching her arm. "Remember the times we hiked there? You and me?"

Phoenix nodded as the memories returned. "Long time ago...what was I, fifteen?"

"Probably so. All I remember is I couldn't keep up with you. You were a regular billy goat," he said, winking.

"You mean nanny goat." Phoenix smiled weakly as she looked up at the kitchen wall clock: 7:55.

"Suppose you're right."

"I've got nothing left in the tank, Pop Pop. I'm going to bed. I'm leaving my ringer on in case we get a call."

"I will too, Feebs," he said, his old nickname for her slipping out. "Get some rest, honey. Rose is sound asleep, and I'll be here if she needs to get up for anything during the night. Capiche?"

"Capiche," Phoenix said, sighing as she stood. She came around and gave Pop Pop a hug. "'Night...love you," she added as she made her way to the kitchen door.

"Love you more, kiddo..." he replied. "So much, forever."

MOSER RESIDENCE
GILBERT, ARIZONA
SATURDAY, 7:55 PM

Bethany Moser finished tucking in her daughter, Darla, capped the routine with their nightly prayer, and gave her a kiss on the forehead.

"Sweet dreams, honey," she said as she turned off the nightstand lamp.

"Goodnight, Mommy," her almost six-year-old princess replied, clutching her stuffed doggie. Beth had been putting off getting her daughter a real dog for nearly two years, but maybe that would change soon.

Standing in the hallway, Beth smiled, sighed, then gently closed the door, leaning against it with her back. It had been a brutal day, steeped in mayhem and death, and she couldn't help but think about the trauma young Abigail Cage must be going through tonight.

Abby's only parent was a murderous fugitive from justice, and her only other relative was on a slab at the morgue. There would be nobody to properly tuck her in for the night, aside from a counselor and somebody from Child Protective Services. It wasn't quite the same.

She shook her head and made her way to the kitchen and her phone.

One New Message.

RAMAGE'S HOVEL
A MINUTE LATER

Jeffrey Ramage was sitting at the kitchen counter when his phone rang.

"Hey," he said, swallowing an enormous bite of his meat-lovers' combo pizza. He wiped his hands on a paper towel and pushed away the untouched, premade salad. It's the thought that counts sometimes. "You got my message."

"Yeah, just now. So, the ranger's log entry was a match for the Maverick license plate of the deceased?"

"Indeed, it was. I just got off the phone with Ranger Danger," he said, a half-smirk momentarily returning to his face. He couldn't help it.

"And...?"

"And the junior ranger on duty provided his best recollection of the driver: Female, seemed to be on the tall side, late twenties to early thirties, short hair—she was wearing a ball cap—and a noteworthy smile. Not his exact words, but that was the general description."

"Pretty ballsy choice to return to the scene of the crime, don't you think?" Moser opined.

"Yeah, I'd say so. Especially having just come from murdering her own mother at the trailer park. A two-fer...loose end, maybe...who knows."

"This ranger, did he describe any conversation they may've had?"

"He did. It was a brief exchange, but she sold him a story about meeting up with some friends for a surprise party, or some shit. The Maverick was found by park staff during a routine patrol of the camping areas. Stashed behind a trailer. She must be on foot."

"Jeezus."

"Yeah, Jeezus...factoring in her track record of dealing with loose ends, I'd say she's probably on the hunt for the one who got away. If he indeed did."

"Yeah. I mean, why else would she return to a still-hot crime scene unless that was the deal?"

"My thinking exactly, partner."

"So...Tempest Cage, fugitive from justice, may be out there somewhere, on foot, looking for Curt Martinsen. Do we think she's armed? I mean, other than her knife or whatever?"

"Martina in Records ran a firearms check; nothing registered to Cage, but we can't assume she isn't carrying. The APB lists her as armed and dangerous, and she's definitely fucking dangerous," he said, catching himself. "Sorry for the language. It's been a fucked-up day, but you already knew that," he added, wolfing down another sausage-laden bite.

"Roger that. So, do we share this new intel with Mrs. Martinsen—Phoenix? If so, how much?"

Ramage finished chewing and looked at his wristwatch. "I say let's not throw her into a further panic tonight. Nothing good can come from that. She and her family have had the day from hell and they're probably—hopefully—asleep. I'm gonna take a drive out there when I'm done eating," he said, stifling a belch.

"To the house? You just said they were—"

"No. The park. Probably leaving in about ten minutes. See if there are any more rocks to turn over."

"Really? Tonight? Want me to come with? I might be able to get the babysitter back—"

"Nah. I shouldn't have even said anything. You and Darla need to be together tonight. It's just me and my friggin' fish, so I don't mind making a run out there. Nice night for a drive, actually. Did you see the moon?"

"Yeah, I did... okay, well, I'll leave my phone on if anything comes up, okay? Be safe out there, Jeff."

"Roger that, Beth. I'll call you in the morning. And, depending on what the status is at that point, we'll give Phoenix an update as well. She deserves that much."

CHAPTER FIFTEEN

WITH A GREAT deal of effort, Curt had managed to gimp along the first mile of the rock-strewn trailhead, hobbling, sometimes hopping, with one good leg.

As much as he loved his New Balance sneakers, the biggest challenge they'd faced prior to this adventure had been navigating the classroom, or the playground area during yard duty. They weren't rated for this.

The incline had been relatively gradual thus far, but he knew the sign he'd earlier seen regarding the elevation change had noted it was around the two-mile mark. Wherever that was.

One thing that was becoming painfully obvious: there was no way he could continue on to the Flatiron. Not without a rocket pack.

As he huffed along, he noticed something lying on the ground, just off the edge of the trail, to his left. It appeared to be a piece of wood, probably from one of the surrounding trees, which were becoming much sparser out here.

Curt hopped over and bent down to pick up the piece of wood. It was indeed a tree branch, maybe four feet long and not terribly girthy, but relatively strong. He guessed it to be from a dead mesquite and gave it a quick assessment, hoping to God it might help somehow.

It was straight enough for his purposes, and it was the only game in town. Gripping it in his left hand, he hesitantly tested is against his body weight. It flexed some, but didn't immediately snap, which was good. It was better than nothing.

Thank you!

Curt paused, out of breath, plopping down on his fanny in an effort to recharge his meager batteries. He wiped away the sweat and knew, shy of a sudden miracle monsoon, there weren't going to be many, if any, opportunities to quench his intense thirst.

His stint in the Boy Scouts many years before had taught him that without water he was hosed. Without food, he wouldn't have the energy to keep going for long. And without those, his hope would soon be depleted.

It was dark as hell out here, but he was grateful for the brilliant moon tonight. It was his only flashlight. He looked up at it, amazed by its brightness. He studied its face, its features, and wondered if Phoenix could see this.

As he thought of her, of his daughter, of Pop Pop, he lowered his head. He'd never felt so helpless, so humbled, and so utterly emasculated. He was supposed to be the strong one, the protector, and somehow, he'd surrendered his power to a complete stranger—a woman—who had already demonstrated she was very capable of killing him.

He knew that she would, too, once she found him, and for the sake of his family he would do everything in his power to prevent that from happening.

He pictured Phoenix's face, her smile, her otherworldly mane of fiery hair. Rose's impish grin, her giggles, and the smell of her hair…all the senses were heightened, and they all came rushing back at him, mercilessly.

And as he sat there, before God and the man in the moon, he felt broken, exhausted, hungry, and on the verge of dehydration. He hadn't had time for tears since this all began, what, twenty-four hours before, but he surrendered to the enormity of it all.

And the waterworks began.

God, help me.

THE GRANNY UNIT
SAME TIME

As emotionally exhausted as she was, Phoenix had found it impossible to fall asleep. The moonlight was streaming in through the blinds, and all she could think about was her husband. Her gaze went to the window and the sheer enormity of Earth's only natural satellite. It was blinding.

Could Curt see this moon right now?

She began to cry as she pictured him. A flood of images, flashes of a Curt Martinsen highlight reel streaming across her consciousness.

There was their first meeting, out on the porch at Liam's home. He'd come through the door, all Paul Bunyan-like and flashing that perfect megawatt smile of his. Their first date-that-really-wasn't-a-date dinner at Fandango! The fireside table, their drive along 17-Mile Drive. The first, accidental kiss. Curt coming to her rescue and the perilous car chase that ensued as they tried to evade the murderous "Pirate." Their simple but magical wedding on the beach in Maui. The proud new daddy holding his newborn child for the first time in the recovery room. And their young family's trials rescuing their precious Rose from a den of evildoers.

"Oh, my God," she gasped to herself. They had been through so, so much, and they'd already experienced more challenges than anyone should face in ten lifetimes.

Phoenix turned onto her back and closed her eyes. "Please, Lord, I beg of you," she sobbed. "Please watch over my Curt right now. Wherever he is and whatever he's facing. I can't live without him, and my daughter needs her daddy back. Keep him safe, please, and return him home to us. Help me help him, Lord. I swear I'll never ask you for another thing. You've been so good to us...so many times...please, in Jesus's name, just...one more time. Amen."

Phoenix lay there several moments, her eyes shut, the tears streaming down her cheeks. When she finally opened them, she looked up at the ceiling through her blurry tears. She blinked them away, and as her vision cleared she saw, staring back down at her, the biggest, blackest spider in the history of arachnids, hovering directly above the bed.

And nobody there to save her.

LOST DUTCHMAN STATE PARK
SIPHON DRAW TRAIL
MILE 1.5 MARKER
SATURDAY, 9:05 PM

The moon disappeared behind some clouds, and darkness again obscured the rocky trail.

Tempest pulled the heavy, heavy-duty Maglite from her daypack. Its five lithium D-cells provided ample power not only to light the trail, but also its super long beam throw was adjustable.

She switched it on and adjusted its beam from spot to flood focusing. *That's better.*

As she looked down at her feet, she could better see what looked like a set of fresh footprints, and they appeared to be about Curt's size. Funny thing was, they were mostly prints of the right foot, with tiny divots in the soil where a left toe may have lightly touched down. Those, along with another, more pointy indentation, confirmed this hiker was favoring one foot and was probably utilizing a walking stick of some kind.

The trails had been officially closed for over an hour and this was the only set of prints going up the trail. They were his; she knew it.

He's hurt. He can't be too far ahead.

With her free hand, she pulled out a fresh piece of

Pemmican jerky and brought it to her mouth, tearing off a huge chunk, like the lioness she was. Her prey had to be just ahead.

LOST DUTCHMAN STATE PARK
RANGER STATION
SATURDAY, 9:15 PM

Ramage had called ahead of his visit and Danger was awaiting him.

The ranger poured two coffees from the decanter and handed one to the detective.

"Take anything in it?"

"Just sugar, if you've got it," Ramage replied.

"Sweet & Low's all I've got," Ranger Danger said, placing the small basket of coffee additives on the desk in front of his guest. Ramage gave them a quick scan. It was all powdered creamer and sugar substitutes.

"Black's fine, thanks," he said politely.

The ranger walked behind his desk, pushing in his metal chair as he gestured to a detailed, plexiglass-covered wall chart of the park. "So, we're here," he said, tapping a tiny icon on the sprawling map. He traced his finger over to another feature, emphasizing, "The campground loop, where we found the victim...and...the Ford Maverick."

Ramage took a sip of his coffee. It was bitter and tasted like it had been reheated several times over on the hot plate and filtered through an old boot. He set it down on the corner of the desk, shook out a handful of Tic Tacs, and crunched them as he came in for a closer look.

"This area here," Ramage said, pointing to the tree line extending beyond the end of the loop. "Where does this go? I mean, I see a whole bunch of wilderness, but let's say our missing person got away from the perp, our suspect, and he's on foot. Do you think he may've gone in there?"

"Well, being as there haven't been any other campers in the loop who've reported seeing him, that would be my guess. And, if the suspect, the woman, came back looking for him, my best guess says she probably went in there after him. Especially if he may've been a witness to a murder, right? It gets pretty rugged back there, and it sounds like neither party may be properly equipped to deal with the conditions."

"Yeah," Ramage said softly. He was feeling a whole new level of worry for finding Curt.

"I have an inbound police chopper equipped with spotlights and heat-seeking technology. I'd like to make a few passes in this area, extending away from the campsites so as not to disturb anyone, and up toward the trailheads there."

Ranger Danger looked at his wristwatch. Most campers would likely still be sitting around their respective firepits, enjoying s'mores and Budweisers. They were night owls.

"Should be okay. Plenty of moonlight tonight. I've got a pretty robust Jeep we can take a ride in while the flyboys do their thing. If you want, that is."

"You're speaking my language, sir. The copter's about twenty minutes out, and I'll be in radio communication with the pilot, so the sooner we're wheels up, the better."

"Let me grab my jacket," the ranger said, retrieving it from the back of his chair. He grabbed a second one off the hook and handed it to Ramage. "Here. Gets cold out there after dark."

LOST DUTCHMAN STATE PARK
SIPHON DRAW TRAIL
SATURDAY, 9:35 PM

Curt limped up to a rock facing. He figured he must be close to the two-mile marker, but he hadn't seen it. It didn't matter. He'd be up shit's creek once the elevation started climbing abruptly, and that would be right about now.

With one good foot, no water, no food, and zero options, he explored the wall before him. It might as well have been a brick one. The temperature was dropping, the wind was starting to gust harder, and he had to find a place to hunker down.

The moon had disappeared a little while back, and it was difficult to see anything. His fingers gripped the rock, brushing against clumps of dry vegetation as he moved along the rugged surface. His ankle was experiencing a whole new level of hurt, and he grimaced in pain.

God, help me out here, please.

He continued to his right, hopping on his good foot and gimping along with his makeshift cane. As he reached out, stroking the rockface, he felt his hand disappear into a void of some sort. It might only be a tiny recess, so he didn't want to get his hopes up, but he hopped toward it and, as if on cue, the moon came out to play again.

Suddenly, the area was flooded with light, and it immediately became evident that he'd found a cave-like recess, one that might even be big enough to climb into. Curt looked over his shoulder and up at the moon.

"Thank you!" he said before turning back to the matter at hand. He wasn't sure how long the moon would cooperate, so he quickly studied the opening. It was narrow, less than the width of his shoulders, and the wash of moonlight spilling across it didn't offer any clues beyond showing him the opening. To anything. It was pitch dark beyond that.

Would it be big enough to climb into? At least enough to get him out of the elements? He had to at least try. *Better than nothing.*

Curt turned to the side, took a deep breath, and slipped his right shoulder into the narrow opening. His head followed and, as it did, the gusts of wind that had been beating him up went almost silent.

He could see nothing now. He reached his right arm into the void, touching nothing. Slightly encouraged, he hopped up a step further, his left shoulder and hip now clearing the opening as well.

As he brought his left leg in, his ankle bumped against a protruding rock and sent an excruciating wave of pain with it. He gritted his teeth, hissing like a wounded opossum, as he suppressed the urge to scream out. He didn't know if he had company out here, animal or human, and he had to play it safe with announcing his presence.

As the stab of pain diminished to a dull throbbing, he brought his mesquite stick out and slowly waved it about in front of him, then to his sides. Reaching out at full extension now, he realized he hadn't touched anything, which meant he had at least six feet of space on all sides. And he hadn't bumped his head.

"Thank you...thank you...thank you..." he whispered, then he stopped to listen. He thought he heard something small scurry away into the pitch dark, but it was otherwise quiet as a tomb. Hell, it was a tomb.

Curt felt the ground underneath his feet and found a flat surface to squat down onto. He was out of the elements. *Check.*

He was still out of every other manner of life support. He might die of starvation and dehydration, but at least his cause of death might not be hypothermia. He closed his eyes and listened. Again, he heard what sounded like a possible mystery rodent scurrying about. It wasn't far away, he determined, and in the absence of any proper foodstuffs he might just eat the damned thing if he could spear it with his stick. In the pitch dark. *Yeah, that'll happen.*

His thoughts returned to the big picture. He was pretty sure his captor—*what was her name? Tempest!*—was still out there looking for him. She'd proven beyond the shadow of a doubt that she was resourceful, mean as a snake, and used to getting what she wanted.

And she wanted him. *Fuck me.*

He suddenly remembered that he had his phone! As he fumbled to remove it from his pocket, it slipped out of his grasp, tumbling into the black hole that was his surroundings. *Shit!!*

His hands swept the area near his feet, and he felt the edge of his hand bump against the device, pushing it further away. *No! No! No! No! Nooooo!*

Wincing in pain, he got down on his hands and knees, a blind man carefully sweeping the ground in slow, arcing motions like he was searching for beach treasure with a metal detector. It was his left hand that hit paydirt and he grabbed the phone, clutching it carefully as he awkwardly returned to the seated position.

In his haste to escape, he'd only pocketed the device and since ignored it. He hadn't, until now, thought to power it up, and he hoped it might still have some juice. Had she charged it? He didn't remember in all the chaos.

Curt hit the power button and waited an eternity, silently praying as it slowly booted up. After a few moments, the home screen came to life and a host of familiar icons populated it. He didn't care about any of those. Only two indicators were important right now: *Signal* and *Battery*. As his gaze focused on the top right corner of the screen, one of his worst fears was realized. There were zero bars of reception out here. He wasn't completely surprised by this, only severely disappointed. The other indicator showed that he had 54% battery remaining, which was, in itself, amazing.

He had never had cause to use it, but he remembered having seen a flashlight icon amongst the myriad of other features he'd never bothered to open since getting the phone.

Perhaps, if he used it very conservatively, he might be able to briefly get a lay of the land. He knew he'd have to be very mindful of the fact it was the mother of all power-sucking apps and would be a battery killer. But he had to know what his situation was.

He searched the screen for the icon, tapped it, and squinted as the cave was immediately bathed in a bright light not seen since the Hiroshima event. "Jeezus!" It took a few seconds for his pupils to adjust, and he took the next ten seconds to give his new digs a visual scan.

It appeared that this hole in the rock was about eight,

maybe ten, feet across and about as deep. In the far corner there was what looked like evidence of another hiker's abandoned single-burner propane kitchen. Next to it, a couple of feet away, something shiny.

With the phone flashlight in his left hand, he got back into the crawling position and, doing the best to keep his left foot elevated, made his way over to the object. He wouldn't have much time before the phone battery faltered and plunged him back into the abyss.

As he got to within a couple of feet, Curt realized what he was seeing, and it wasn't just one shiny object, but two. And one looked to be an unopened food can!

He picked it up and was truly excited to see that it was twelve ounces of corned beef hash, and not a can of Rodent Helper. And, God be praised, it had a pull-top opener!

Yes!! Thank you!!

The other shiny object turned out to be something else entirely. It wasn't another can of foodstuffs at all, but instead a partially consumed plastic water bottle, laying on its side. Upon closer inspection he figured it probably had close to ten ounces of purified water remaining in it.

"Thank you, God," he whispered excitedly as he unscrewed the cap, smelled it, and took his first measured sip of lifegiving hydration. "Ahhh!"

Curt replaced the cap and turned his attention to the food tin, pulling back on the ring and tossing the sharp lid into the far corner. Without any hesitation, he embraced his inner Neanderthal, thrusting his middle and index fingers into the meaty, potato-y goo. As he delivered the finger scoop of hash to his mouth, he switched off the flashlight and closed his eyes, reveling in what had to be the *new* best meal he'd ever had in his life.

As he continued eating, he counted his blessings. He had a meal, a little bit of water, and crude temporary shelter, none of it expected. He wanted for nothing. Except maybe a pair of crutches, but he didn't want to push his luck.

He finished the can and was about to toss it into the corner when he thought better of it. No sense making any loud noises when she could still be out there, looking for him.

He allowed himself another tiny sip from the bottle. *Cooties be damned.*

Curt replaced the cap, took inventory of his phone and walking stick, and sat in the darkness. Listening.

Hearing nothing but the occasional gust of wind outside the cave opening, he moved his hand along the dirt-covered rock floor of his cave. It seemed flat enough. Pushing aside a few pebbles and small rocks, he created what was to be his bed for the night.

Curt turned on the phone's flashlight one more time to inspect his work, and as he was about to power the device down, a thought came to him. Switching off the flashlight, he began composing what might be his final text message to his wife in the event he didn't make it out of here alive.

The device's battery indicator was flashing, confirming its remaining power level mirrored his own, so he quickly launched into tapping the keys, and with little expectation it would be delivered.

>S.M.F.

Curt's thumb errantly hit Send, and his entirely-too-brief partial message was on its way.

"What the—?! Oh, *shit*!" he barked, admonishing himself for his clumsiness. "Not quite enough information there, Curt...might want to at least tell her where you are!" *Fuck!*

He reopened the message thread and began typing in some key supporting facts:

>*Phoenix! I'm so sorry!! I'm alive! Some crazy psycho woman drugged me, kidnapped me, and I saw her KILL a man! I got away but she's still trying to find me! I'm in the Lost Dutchman range. Siphon Draw trail...found a cave...but not sure how long I can*

And...the screen went black.

"*Fuck! Fuck!! Fuck!!! FUCKKKK!!!!*" he whisper-screamed. "Please no...please no...come on...*pleeeease*!!!" he begged the electronics as he repeatedly tried to restart the now-dead device. It was no use.

The message had not been sent and he cursed himself for having blown his one chance through a moment of carelessness. The reality of the situation was the kick to the gut he didn't need on top of everything else, and as he let the useless device drop from his fingers, he leaned against the wall, shoulders heaving as he wept a death row cry.

Ten minutes later, and feeling utterly defeated, Curt retrieved his dead phone, and gathered what was left of his worldly belongings. He tucked them in close as he lowered himself to the ground, lying down on his right side to keep pressure off his left ankle. The hard ground was unforgiving, but he managed to remain grateful for his bounty.

And he allowed himself to drift off to sleep.

Even if it was fitful and short-lived.

"Come out, come out, wherever you are!" the haunting voice called out, all sing-song-y like kids in a game of hide and seek.

Curt's eyes blinked open but he found he was blind. It took him a few seconds for his senses to return to him and he sat up quickly, suddenly remembering where he was, and why. *How long was I out?*

Had he really heard a voice or was it just a dream?

"Olly olly oxen free!!" the catchphrase echoed loudly from somewhere outside his cocoon. And not far away. It was a woman's voice and one he immediately recognized. It was her.

This was no dream.

"Come on now, Curt...maybe we got off on the wrong foot here. Don't spoil it!"

Curt shivered, a new chill running up his spine, while the hair on his arms stood on end. His thoughts raced as his pulse quickened.

"I know you're out here..." the voice sang out. It sounded like child's play, which only made it more terrifying. "I won't bite! Much."

Curt stuffed his now-useless phone into his pocket and got a firm grasp on his walking stick as he scooted himself to the edge of the cave near the opening. Clenching his teeth, he got to his one good foot and hugged the wall.

A minute went by, then another, as he listened. He had no idea how close she might be. Hearing nothing, he got closer to the cave's entrance, and sticking his head halfway outside, he saw that the moon was behind the clouds.

He looked to his left, then to his right and in the direction of the area where he thought he'd left the trail. He didn't see anyone, and the voice had gone quiet.

Maybe she went in a different direction.

Before he could get his hopes too high, they were immediately dashed by new visual information as he saw a long, bright beam of light dancing across the trail in a back-and-forth sweeping motion. And it was slowly coming his way.

Curt tucked his head back inside, his back hugging the wall, as he tried not to hyperventilate. His heart was beating like a sledgehammer, and he clutched his wannabe spear tightly. It might as well be a Tyrannosaurus Rex just outside.

"Y'know what?! I'm fucking tired of this, Curt!! Just come out where I can see you and nobody gets hurt! Scouts honor!" she yelled, louder now.

She was getting closer, and with a little help from the moon, and/or her torch, she'd soon discover his hiding place, and it'd be game over.

From just outside, he heard a stumbling sound, accompanied by a cry of momentary pain, before she began cursing like a drunken sailor. "Fuuuuuck!! Curt Martinsen, goddammit! Get your pansy ass out here and show yourself! You're starting to really piss me off, darlin', and you don't want to be doing that!"

Curt's eyes were wide, useless in the black void of what was now his cage. He could hear the approaching sound of boots scuffing the ground. His best guess was that she was, maybe, twenty-five yards away and closing. He'd be no match for her now, he knew.

So, this is how it ends.

The crunching sound of boots on gravel was getting louder, deafening...almost like a thumping now. Curt readied his stick, knowing the gig was up. He closed his eyes and listened.

The thumping sound was getting exponentially louder... nearer...but different...almost like...

...a helicopter!!!

He risked peeking outside, and the whooping sound of the blades filled his ears, becoming deafeningly loud. A moment later, the craft's aptly named NightSun 60,000-lumens searchlight slashed through the dark, spilling across the hillside, then the trail.

"There! Port side—on the trail—near the rockface! I think I saw something!" the co-pilot barked through his mouthpiece.

"Roger that!" the pilot acknowledged, coming in closer and pivoting the helicopter left. The searchlight swept across the area near the trail, and the aircraft's blades buffeted the dead vegetation while kicking up dust as it began to slowly descend.

A couple of muzzle flashes came from the vegetation below and were synchronous with two loud plunks against the helicopter's fuselage.

"Shit! They're fucking shooting at us!" the pilot yelled, initiating a sharp arc in the opposite direction, and a climb. "You have eyes on 'em?"

"Negative!" the co-pilot answered. "Wait one!! There! Nine o'clock!" he added, pointing to their left. "Someone just jumped off the trail!"

"Affirmative!" the pilot said, gaining a little altitude as he turned toward the sighting. The NightSun's beam swung around, washing the trail and the surrounding area in artificial daylight.

"Shots fired!" Ramage relayed to Ranger Danger, who had been guiding the Jeep along the trail toward the light source. Despite his awesome name, Danger hadn't seen much of it in all his years in the park system. Until tonight. He was rather enjoying the rush from it, and he stepped down harder on the accelerator.

Ramage keyed his radio, "We're probably a hundred yards out, on your trail. I repeat. We are on the trail, coming your way. Will watch for any movement down here, over."

"Roger that, Jeep. We see your position. Keep your lights on, please, over."

"Roger, over," Ramage acknowledged. He turned to his driver. "You doin' okay?"

"Me? Yeah," Danger replied. He gripped the wheel tightly as he negotiated a twist in the trail. "Beats sitting in the office and watching some cop show!" he added, making brief eye contact. Ramage couldn't help but notice the man's smile. This guy was living up to his nametag tonight.

At the initial sound of gunfire, Curt had ducked his head back inside. The stakes had been raised. The psycho was packing heat, and she wasn't afraid to use it.

Any thoughts of running to the helicopter were shot down now that he realized she was armed. Besides, he'd be hobbling, at best, in his effort to reach presumed safety, and being out in the open, fully exposed and bathed in spotlight, would make it too easy for her. It'd be like shooting fish in a barrel.

The police officers didn't even know he was there; they were fully engaged with his pursuer.

What a shit show!

Tempest rolled into some tall, dead grass and ducked down. She checked her weapon and peeked out from behind a rock to get a better read on the helicopter's position. She knew she'd hit it, but she hadn't damaged any vital systems. *Dammit. They must've found the Maverick. Which means...they found Mom.*

None of this was supposed to go down like this. *If Curt had just played nice.*

Her Glock 17 still had fifteen rounds, and she had another full clip in the pack. But they had a fucking helicopter and its searchlight put her Maglite to shame. She could try bringing down the chopper with her available thirty-two rounds, but she didn't relish getting herself into a full-on firefight.

She ducked her head down into the brush as the searchlight's beam raked across the ground. The spot was trained on the area just in front of her as the chopper hovered in place. Had they seen her? She thought not.

She waited a few moments, squinting up at her adversary. She had to risk it.

Fuck it!

She raised the Glock, training its sights, and squeezed the trigger.

A third muzzle flash came from below, and this one hit its mark, snuffing out the copter's spotlight and completely returning the scene to its natural state of near pitch black.

"Shit!! We just took another hit!" the pilot yelled into his mic. "We've lost our NightSun! Repeat, we've lost NightSun! Over!"

"Fuck! Roger that!" Ramage barked back into his radio. "Are you guys okay? Over."

"Affirmative, but we no longer have eyes on 'em, over," the pilot admitted, pulling out from his hover. He turned to his partner. "Anything?"

"Negative. Might've rolled down into those rocks, but can't say for sure," his co-pilot said, grasping the long gun on his lap. They'd been rendered blind and were now sitting ducks. "Better take her up!!"

"Roger. Initiating climb!" the pilot said.

The Jeep crested a small hill and stopped as they saw the chopper gaining altitude, only its running lights visible as its beam was now extinguished.

Ramage keyed his radio. "Roger. We're right below you, crest of the hill. What'd you see, over?"

"Jeep, we no longer have eyes, but we had a brief visual of one suspect. Tall, slender build, wearing a ball cap. Disappeared into some brush near this position, over."

"Were you able to make out the gender, over?"

"That's a negative. Slender build, appeared to have short hair, but can't confirm either way, over."

"Roger," Ramage said, unkeying his mic. "Dammit," he said to the ranger. "I know it's her. She's here somewhere, right under our noses."

"What do we do? She's got a gun, right?" Danger asked, starting to feel more uneasy.

"Unfortunately, yes," Ramage said, looking him in the eye. "Listen. I know you didn't sign up for this kind of shit when you took the park ranger oath. I mean, I don't want you being in harm's way here."

"I'm good, Detective. You just tell me what you want me to do, and I'm down. If this person is responsible for—for what I found at that campsite this afternoon—I wanna take 'em out just as much as you. Before someone else gets hurt... or worse." His expression was dead earnest. He wasn't turning around and driving back to the ranger shack.

"Okay. Okay," Ramage said, his mind racing. "For now, let's find a place to stash the Jeep where we're not out here in the open. You know this park probably better than anybody. This trail...is there more than one way out?"

"Only two ways they can go. One's heading back the way we came. The other's up to the next level of the trail, the Flatiron, but it's almost triple the incline, nearing 3,000-foot elevation. I'll speak for myself, but you'll probably agree with me on this: neither one of us is a billy goat anymore. It can be a tough hike in the daytime. At night, I wouldn't want to try it."

Ramage gave this some thought. He could dispatch resources toward the Flatiron, but that would have to wait until daylight if they couldn't get another NightSun-equipped chopper out there. Alternatively....

"First things first. Let's stash the Jeep. Then we'll fan out, you and me, keep a close eye out for any movement along the trail while the chopper bugs out of here."

"Roger that," the ranger said, shifting the Jeep into drive. He knew just the place.

As they bounced along the rocky path, Ramage pushed the light button on his wristwatch:

11:35
I'm too old for this shit.

Curt clenched his eyes shut and his head sunk into his chest. As he listened to the whup-whup-whup of the helicopter blades, the doppler effect told him the chopper was pulling away.

Leaving him behind.

CHAPTER SIXTEEN

LOST DUTCHMAN STATE PARK
SIPHON DRAW TRAIL
SATURDAY, 11:40 PM

T EMPEST HADN'T MOVED a muscle. Still laying low, and hidden amongst the clumps of dead vegetation, she was poised against the berm of the main trail and what looked like a gentle but rocky slope down.

With the Glock firmly in her grip, she regulated her breathing, listening, as the now-distant helicopter disappeared into the night. The whoop of its blades was replaced with the occasional gusts of wind. Other than that, the only sound on her radar was the howl of a pissed-off coyote and the nearby jackrabbit hightailing it to safer ground.

She gave herself a silent cheer, knowing she'd managed to send the chopper away with only three shots fired. But she couldn't take too much comfort in that knowledge, as there was a very good chance that another similarly equipped aircraft might be on its way to pick up the search.

She'd have to get off this trail.

The moon was starting to emerge from its hiding place, which afforded her a better look at the off-trail terrain below.

It also meant she was far more exposed now.

From what she could see, the slope appeared to be strewn with more rocks and clumps of vegetation, but the grade appeared manageable. She hadn't planned to go off the trail—hell, she hadn't planned for any of this shit—but the camping shovel in her daypack might come in handy in the absence of a pick or any climbing gear.

She'd have to chance it, and it would have to be right now.

She tucked the Glock into her hip holster and double-checked the Velcro fastener. The Maglite was stuffed into the daypack—or, in this case, the *night* pack—and she zipped it tight, squaring it between her shoulders as she began the slow, silent descent, hugging her chest against the hill as she went. She spit out a puff of bitter soil as she whispered her declaration:

"You haven't seen the last of me, Curtis."

Ramage and Ranger Danger had, several minutes before, parked the Jeep off the trail, killed the ignition and extinguished its lights. Now that the chopper had left, any noise would be amplified, and they hoped they hadn't made their presence known. They too listened to the sounds of the night.

"How long's it been?" Danger whispered, his eyes glued to his binoculars.

"Ten, fifteen minutes, maybe," Ramage whispered back. He glanced at his watch.

"Think she could be injured?"

"Anything's possible, but I think she's probably doing what we're doing. Listening."

"Mm-hmm," Danger grunted quietly. "Now that the moon's out, she might tip her hand."

"Yeah, but she's been smart enough not to use her flash-light, and she has one. Lemme see those for a second," Ramage said, taking the binoculars for a spin. He raised them to his eyes and scanned the trail, then handed them back.

"What's the play? Stay here a while longer, or…?"

Ramage looked him in the eye. "I'm gettin' out, gonna try to get closer to where she was last reported," he said, checking his firearm. "Probably safest if you remain in the Jeep, being as you're unarmed."

Danger reached over and popped open the glovebox, bumping Ramage's knee in the process. The compartment's pale light bulb was enough to illuminate his .38mm revolver.

"Who said anything about being unarmed? I'm coming with you."

"Aw, now you don't have to put yourself in—"

"Danger?" the man interjected. "Last I checked that's my friggin' name."

Ramage took five seconds to process the development before responding.

"Cool."

CHAPTER SEVENTEEN

POP POP'S
THE GRANNY UNIT
PALM SUNDAY, EARLY

P HOENIX LAY ON her back, staring at the dark ceiling. Any semblance of restful sleep continued to elude her with noisy competing thoughts of her missing husband, all while vigilantly monitoring the movements of the monstrous spider.

The moonlight returned, sneaking through her blinds, and raking its beam across the ceiling. It was enough to confirm her immediate concern: the spider was no longer where it had been.

Shit.

Her eyes widened as she scanned the rest of the ceiling, then each wall. No sign of it.

Shit!

Phoenix's next course of action was arguably a bit dramatic, and probably more appropriate for a missing scorpion scenario, but she violently kicked the blankets and sheets away and hopped off the bed.

She turned on the nightstand lamp and scoured the bed for any anomalies. Finding none, she woke her phone to find out what time it was:

3:55 a.m. "What the hell? Jeez," she muttered. She needed to pee like a racehorse and, phone in hand, beelined it to the bathroom, scratching a spot on her chest with her nails along the way.

She *had* drifted off to sleep, which explained the spider escaping her radar. It also explained the ginormous, very-itchy bite on her chest, just below her left clavicle.

As she sat on the potty, she found herself scratching it raw. She finished, flushed, and fumed as she got her first look at it in the mirror. An angry red and white bump, right in the middle of her phoenix tattoo.

"Holy crap!" came the panicky blurt. "You bastard...better not be a brown recluse, fucker."

Phoenix set the phone on the over-sink shelf while she washed her hands and splashed water on her face. As she finished patting her face dry, her gaze went from her now-violated tat to the phone's display and the flashing icon:

1 New Message.

Setting the towel down on the sink, she picked up the device and opened the messaging app. Any thoughts of the arachnid attack faded away as she furrowed her brow and tapped the icon.

Brief as it was, it took Phoenix several seconds to register what she was reading before she let out a gasp. The phone tumbled from her hands, and her legs turned to jelly as she folded to the floor like a cheap tent.

>S.M.F.

CURT'S CAVE
PALM SUNDAY, EARLY

His kingdom for a mattress. And maybe a blanket. *First world problem, Curt.*

Not only was the hard, pebble-strewn ground unforgiving, but also Curt awoke to find himself laying in a tight fetal position and freezing. Not literally *freezing*, but it sure felt like it.

How long have I been out?

His eyes were wide, their pupils completely dilated and rendered useless as they tried to grab onto some kind of visual information—anything—but failing in this black void. With the absence of light on this level, it was surreal just how deep absolute darkness could be.

He figured he'd probably managed to maintain an alert status for an hour or so after the helicopter left the mountain. Had he heard a vehicle as well in all that commotion? He wasn't sure but, if so, it too was long gone.

Since then, he hadn't heard anything else from his new biggest "fan" either, which was a relief. Still, she was probably out there somewhere.

He wondered what time it was. *What's-her-face* had taken his wristwatch...not that he'd be able to read it anyway; he was an analog guy, and in a black hole.

His phone would tell him, if it still had any juice, but he held little confidence it would even fire up after last night's failed texting session. He would only need a second, if it would spot him a large favor. *C'mon....*

He closed his eyes as he pushed in the power button, willing it to life like it was Frankenstein's monster. He waited nearly a minute, praying for it to return from the dead. The screen finally flickered on with dim glow; its battery indicator rapidly flashing, showing it had a whopping 2% of juice left, and that the time was...

4:20

The screen went dark, meaning the phone was now completely toast. And now, maybe he would be too. He released a massive sigh.

Sunrise won't be for another couple of hours, at least. Still dark out.

Curt ached all over, and as he got to his feet, his swollen ankle sent an excruciating reminder that it wasn't at all happy. In fact, it was downright pissed.

He brushed off the dirt from his clothes, as well as from his hair and face.

He hopped over to the narrow cave opening and listened. The nighttime wind gusts had moved on, leaving behind a deafening quiet. In the distance, a coyote was ordering room service, and what sounded like its meal of choice scampered away into a nearby shrub.

The whirlwind of events that had transpired since stopping off for "one drink" on his way home had Curt questioning everything. It had all started off so innocently, and it should have been good, clean, celebratory fun with his cohorts. How downright rude it must have felt to Margie and the others, as he'd seemingly ignored them, bailing without a word, when he'd actually just disappeared into the restroom. *If only... dammit.*

But that wasn't the worst of it. Not by a long shot.

Being taken hostage, witnessing a savage murder, severely injuring himself while escaping his captor, being shut off from everyone he loved and not being able to contact them...plus complete sensory deprivation. Combined, it all had a way of clouding things a bit.

None of this was covered in the *Boy Scouts Handbook*. And as a former Eagle scout, he should know.

One thing he *did* know, however, was that he had to pee, and not wishing to lose the deposit on his cave rental, he'd have to chance venturing outside.

OUTSKIRTS
SIPHON DRAW TRAIL
PALM SUNDAY, 4:30-ISH AM

Ramage switched off his flashlight. It wasn't doing much good anymore as several hours of scouring the trailhead, and its offshoots, had depleted its batteries. It had also depleted his own reserves.

Ranger Danger extinguished his own weakened beam as he walked over to the detective. Shuffling slowly, he wasn't used to this kind of exertion—especially in the middle of the night—and he'd long before burned off the super burrito he'd scarfed down for his lunch.

They had split up upon leaving the Jeep hours before, and they were now reconverged on the slope edge of the trail, not far from where Tempest Cage had last been reported by the air crew.

The moon was out again now, spilling its light across everything.

"She couldn't have gotten past us, not going down the way we came up," the ranger said, wiping his brow with the back of his hand. He holstered his revolver. "There's not much else we can do out here. Park reopens at six, and that's when a lot of the hikers like to hit the trails."

Ramage nodded. "I suggest you direct your staff to put up some Trail Closed signs at the entrance to this trailhead before letting anyone come up here. Until further notice. Advise all hikers verbally as well. We don't have to give them a specific reason. Make something up. Bobcat sighting...whatever. But if this suspect is still up here somewhere, we know she's armed and dangerous, and we don't want to put any civilians at risk."

Danger removed his ball cap and rubbed the short bristles of his military style buzzcut. "Agreed. I'll put that in motion. Listen, I don't know about you, but my feet are feelin' about three sizes too big for these boots right now. I say we get some fresh eyes—and fresh legs—up here once the sun comes up."

"Yeah," Ramage said with a sigh as he kicked at the dirt.

"Dammit, we had her. She was right...*here*," he added, his voice trailing off as he studied a break in the berm near his feet.

"What is it?"

"Not sure. You have any juice left in your torch?"

"Maybe a little," the ranger replied, handing it to him.

"Here," Ramage said, aiming the flashlight's beam onto the dark side of the slope, a few feet away from the berm. "What do you make of this?"

The ranger stooped closer and saw the anomaly. Something—or some*one* had slid off the trail at this juncture, and the evidence could be seen for a few feet before extending beyond the light's beam and into the darkness.

"Well, I'll be damned," Danger muttered. He stood and looked the detective in the eye. "This creates a whole different scenario."

"Where's this slope end up?"

"C'mon," Danger replied, fishing out the Jeep's keys. "I'll show ya."

JUST OUTSIDE THE CAVE
MOMENTS LATER

Curt was finishing his business, having nearly recreated the iconic "mural" from the Who's *Who's Next* album cover, as his stream completed its graffiti of the rock wall. *Ahhhh.*

He was in the process of zipping his fly when he heard the distinct sound of a vehicle's engine.

A rescue party! Yes!!

In all the excitement, he managed to catch a piece of himself in a tooth of the zipper and he let go a yelp of pain. "Yeeowwww! *Mutha*—!!!"

Dammit. He gritted his teeth as he lowered the zipper a notch and freed himself. *Phew....really!?* Trying not to cry, he carefully finished zipping and paused to listen. He had indeed heard a vehicle.

"Heeeyyyyy!! Over here!!!" he called out with everything he had. "I'm over here!!!!"

But his excitement was short-lived as he listened more closely, and he could clearly hear the vehicle heading away from him, down the mountain, and leaving him in the frigging dust.

MAIN CAMPGROUND
SITE 44
PALM SUNDAY, 5:02 AM

The Revere family was at their respective stations, working as quietly as possible at this hour. Their tasks were varied, and the foursome were veterans of many RV adventures.

While Mary Revere attended to battening down the kitchen area of their forty-foot Holiday Rambler, their twelve-year-old twin daughters, Carol and Eva, securely stowed the family's belongings for the next leg of their trip. The girls were all too ready to get moving. They hadn't met any cute boys here. Hopefully, there'd be some in Palm Springs; they'd heard California had the cute guys.

Mary's husband, Michael, was outside, port side, affixing the twenty-five-foot flexible hose to the black water tank. He put on his latex gloves, turned the valve, and sent three days' worth of toilet waste gurgling toward the camp's designated dumping area.

He'd been doing this for years, so the smell didn't bother him. He'd gotten past it. It was the same for employees in a florist shop; they probably didn't even smell the lovely fragrances after a while.

They had a long drive ahead today, and as captain of this ship, he'd endeavored to be anchors aweigh at 05:30. Being retired Navy, he was the only one in the family who spoke in military time, and his crew of three indulged him.

From a hundred yards away, Tempest Cage studied the goings on at Site 44.

The large clusters of campsites were quiet at this hour, with most people still asleep in their rigs. But not the folks currently attending to their Class A whale. They were getting ready to shove off and this might just be her ticket out of here.

It would have to be.

The slide down the hill hadn't been pretty and the

scratches to her chest and arms confirmed that fact. Her face and clothing were covered in dirt, her arms bloodied, and her ego bruised.

She'd left Curt up there, and she was royally pissed at herself for that.

She'd have to deal with that later. Right now, she had to get the hell out of there.

Off in the distance, another sound got her attention. It sounded like a vehicle coming from the direction of the trailheads. She turned toward the sound, confirming it as a Jeep, a couple hundred yards away, and making its way toward the main campground loops.

Fuck!

Michael Revere had finished dumping the tanks and was spooling up the rest of the hoses, as well as the electrical. After securing the rig's dump station gear, he closed the hatch and made his way to the front of the forty-footer for a quick look under the hood.

Inside, Mary tucked their tiny coffee maker into its designated corner of an under-sink cabinet, bungeed the cabinet doors closed for travel, and decided to make a quick visit to the rig's restroom before getting trapped on the long, meandering highway.

As she sat on the porcelain loo, she could hear her husband thirty feet away, futzing under the hood, inspecting the hoses, checking the levels. He was awesome that way, and they'd managed to enjoy a trouble-free trip since leaving their home in Albuquerque. They hoped to keep it that way.

After stepping on the flushing pedal, she washed her hands and checked herself in the mirror. *Not bad for five-fifteen.*

Another sound got her attention; this wasn't from the front of the rig. She opened the bathroom door and stood in the tiny hallway that separated the rear bedroom from the kitchen and living areas, listening.

The only sound she was hearing now was the whirring of the living room's slide motor. Eva was standing at the switch panel, retracting both front slides. That was one of her duties.

"Hey, honey, did you hear that just now?" Mary asked.

"Hear what?"

"I don't know. Maybe I'm imagining things. Did you get the camping chairs stowed?"

"Yeah, mom."

"Okay, thanks, honey. Where's your sister?"

"I think she's holding a wrench or something for Dad. Back slides are already in."

"You're awesome," Mary said, smiling.

"I know!" Eva smiled back.

Despite the urgency of the situation, Ranger Danger did his best to maintain a safe—and quiet—approach to the campground area. It wasn't even 5:30, so he didn't want to cause a major disturbance. After all, they were working on a hunch and not verifiable intel at this point.

He'd already made a couple of radio calls to his staff on the way, instructing them about the trail closure protocol and necessary signage.

There were several dozen sites here in what was known as the Main Campground, and they were a mixture of those they called "rustic" and the larger, pull-through sites with water and 20/30/50-amp hookup options for the bigger rigs.

It was still quiet time here and the only activity whatsoever was coming from one of the big pull-through campsites up ahead, Site 44.

"What time do people typically start their day around here?" Ramage asked, his eyes scanning the area.

"That's the beauty of camping, Detective. Most folks leave their alarm clocks at home. You wake up when you wake up. Savor your coffee. Maybe cook some bacon and eggs—everything tastes better out here—and everything tends to move a little slower," Danger replied.

"What about them?" Ramage asked, pointing to the big rig up ahead.

"They're the early birds. Probably have a long travel leg ahead of 'em and looking to get a jump on the traffic. Wanna talk to 'em? Ask 'em if they've seen anything?"

"Yeah...please."

"Good, me too."

Danger maneuvered the Jeep along the loop, pulling to a quiet stop in front of the behemoth motorhome parked behind the Site 44 marker. The owner of the rig closed the hood and wiped his hands on a towel as a girl who appeared to be his daughter hopped inside the rig.

"Mornin'," Danger said in a muted tone as he and Ramage approached the man.

"Morning to you, Ranger," Mike Revere replied. "Help you?"

"Not sure. Looks like you're ready to head out so we won't keep you but just wanted to ask if you—or anyone in your family—might've seen anything, or anyone, unusual this morning?"

"Unusual, like...??"

"Just..." Danger turned to the detective.

"Good morning, sir," Ramage said, flashing a friendly, non-threatening smile to the man. "I think the ranger means, uh, anything out of the ordinary. Anybody who looked out of place...in distress even?"

Mike Revere scratched his stubbled chin and shook his head. "No, can't say we have. Just finished three great days here, no problems. Heading out in a few minutes, actually. Anything to be concerned about?"

"If you haven't seen anything, probably not, sir. Just making sure everyone's having a safe and enjoyable visit to the park," Danger interjected.

"Okay."

"So, you haven't seen a young woman walking around, sir? Tall side, short hair?" Ramage asked.

"Can't say as I have."

"Okay, sorry to bother you, sir," Danger said, quelching any awkwardness. "We wish you and your family a safe and pleasant trip," he added, using his best park ranger smile.

"Thanks," Revere said before checking his watch and climbing inside the rig.

A few seconds later, the whirring of hydraulic levelling jacks could be heard as they stowed themselves into the chassis, and the motorhome's 40,000 pounds of weight returned to its wheels.

"Gotta get me one of those when I retire," the detective said to the ranger.

"Forty foot Class-A is a lot of rig. How big's your family?" Ranger asked.

"Just me...and my fish."

Tempest Cage had heard the entire exchange from her vantage point atop the roof of the rig. Lying on her belly and hugging the crowned, nonskid fiberglass surface, she was obscured behind the air-conditioning units and the satellite dish. And the cloak of darkness didn't hurt.

She could feel the giant rig settle into travel mode and, moments later, she heard the wheel chocks get tossed into their compartment and the entry steps retract.

The motorhome's four hundred-horsepower Cummins diesel engine roared to life and idled for a few minutes before the sound of its brakes releasing signaled its departure. The neighboring campers, jarred from their collective slumber, would all be enjoying this right about now.

Tempest checked her fingers' grip along the edges of the rooftop appliances and peeked at her Timex as the vehicle commenced its slow exit from its berth.

5:30

POP POP'S
PALM SUNDAY, 5:35 AM

It was still dark out and Pop Pop hadn't set his alarm, but something jarred him awake.

Lying on his side, he opened his eyes to make sure his CPAP machine wasn't acting up. No, it wasn't that; it was just making its typical Darth Vadar-like sounds. Still, something had awakened him.

He reached down toward the floor, fumbling in the darkened bedroom for his breathing machine's power button. He stabbed the big button with his finger and rolled onto his back, peeling off the octopus-like mask he was destined to wear at bedtime for the rest of his life.

Pop Pop listened. All was quiet now apart from the low rumble of what sounded like a muscle car's engine as it pulled away down the street. *Phoenix?*

He was still a little foggy, but he knew it was Sunday. *Shop's closed today.*

Shuffling to the bathroom, he peed, then washed his hands, staring at himself in the mirror and inspecting the impressive collection of strap marks embedded in his face. He hated that, but he knew it was part and parcel with wearing the frigging thing. They usually disappeared in a couple of hours.

As he made his way toward the kitchen, he paused outside the office/guest room's closed door. Not a peep, which meant little Rose was still asleep.

Pop Pop sleepily assembled a pot of drip coffee, not exactly sure how many cups to make but he decided on eight.

As he watched the coffee pot slowly fill with the magic, lifegiving nectar, his gaze went to the refrigerator as he anticipated the need for Half & Half.

What caught his eye, however, was the big expanse of gleaming white surface on the fridge's door. The magnets were still there, but the gallery's central display piece wasn't.

Rose's drawing was gone.

STATE ROUTE AZ-88
NORTH APACHE TRAIL
PALM SUNDAY, 5:55 AM

Other than a certain dayglo Hemi Orange 1970 Road Runner, there were very few cars on this stretch of road this time of morning, save a few diehard, gotta-catch-the-sunrise-from-the-Superstitions folks.

Phoenix had reached Pinal County, having left Apache Junction and the Superstition Freeway in her wake. She drove in silence, lost in her thoughts, lulled by the throaty sound that could only come from one of Detroit's finest creations: the six-barrel Mopar 440, with its available 375 horsepower. It was her music of choice this morning.

For an almost-thirty-nine year-old muscle car, this impeccably maintained beauty still had it, and for the eight or so years since she'd been blessed with this gift from Pop Pop, she smiled just about every time she turned the key.

But smiles were in short supply at the moment.

Phoenix had vague recollections of the namesake stories and myths the Superstition Mountains were known for. Something about lost gold and a crazy Dutchman, or something. But she wasn't searching for gold. The only treasure she was seeking was the return of her husband, and there was a chance he might be lost...somewhere...and possibly in that vast range.

As she barreled down the road, the moon illuminated the silhouette of the Superstition mountain range. It was unmistakable. It was intimidating and huge. Its rugged terrain had a million nooks and crannies, like something out of a western.

She was driving straight into her daughter's crayon drawing—the one that now lay upon her dashboard.

This mission was clearly a Hail Mary, needle-in-a-haystack undertaking, but she was undeterred. She had to find him, her precious Curt. Failure was not an option, and it seemed like the detectives weren't being entirely frank in sharing recent developments.

Since last night, her calls to Detective Ramage had gone straight to voicemail, which seemed odd and bordering on unprofessional. He and Detective Moser had been on their way to this area last time they'd talked. *What aren't they telling me?*

She kept her eyes on the road and the growing mountain range as she closed in on it. Its scope began to fill her windshield.

Her left hand solidly gripped the wheel as she turned her attention to the Mickie D's breakfast she'd all but forgotten about on the passenger seat. She reached into the bag and made short work of the two cookie cutter sleeves of hashbrowns, the ones she still referred to as "Barbie Potatoes."

Next on the menu were the two egg and muffin sandwiches she'd ordered, without the meat. Her eyes were fixed on the mountain, and her thoughts went to Curt as she unwrapped the first one and chomped into it.

"Jeez-o-Pete!!" she cried out as the undercooked egg ejaculated its yolky orange goo onto her chin and down the front of her ASU sweatshirt. "Dammit..." she hissed as she fished around in the bag for some napkins to mop it up.

"What the hell?" she said, finding it hard to believe the drive-thru dude hadn't given her any napkins. Not even one.

"First day on the friggin' job, dude...?" she muttered, seething as she reached over and popped open the glovebox. She always tried to keep some extras in there.

With her eyes straight ahead, she watched as a Subaru passed her while she rummaged amongst the glovebox's contents with her free hand. *Maps...the road flare...and... what's this?*

She grabbed the mystery object and glanced at it. A cassette tape, which wasn't at all unusual considering her preference for the vintage technology.

But this one she didn't recognize.

She turned on the dome light and chanced a closer glance at the annotations and track listings, gasping when she identified the penmanship. This wasn't a tape of her creation.

It was Curt's handwriting! *He* had made a mixtape for *her*, which was a first! *Dear Jesus.*

Phoenix glanced back at the road which was, thankfully, a straightaway. She liberated the tape from its box and inserted it into the cassette deck. As it cued up, she grabbed a handful of napkins and mopped up the sauce. Satisfied, she tossed the soiled napkins onto the floorboard and anxiously awaited the first song. She honestly had no idea what to expect.

Then it began.

The opening guitar chords had an immediate soothing effect and, moments later, were accompanied by the honey-smooth vocals of an artist she at once recognized. This was a song from Dan Fogelberg's *Phoenix* album, and the fact that Curt had chosen to surprise her with this as a special lead-in tune began to bring tears to her eyes.

She absorbed the emotions of every lyric as they washed over her, her vision made blurry by the tears. To the best of her ability, she focused on the mountainous shape ahead but, even though it wasn't raining, it felt like she was looking through a wet shower door.

She let the song wash over her:

Joy at the start

Fear in the journey

Joy in the coming home

A part of the heart

Gets lost in the learning

Somewhere along the road

Along the road

Your path may wander

A pilgrim's faith may fail

Absence makes the heart grow fonder

Darkness obscures the trail

Cursing the quest

Courting disaster

Measureless nights forebode

Moments of rest

Glimpses of laughter

Are treasured along the road

Along the road

Your steps may stumble

Your thoughts may start to stray
But through it all a heart held humble
Levels and lights your way
Ahhh…Ahhh
Joy at the start
Fear in the journey
Joy in the coming home
A part of the heart gets lost in the learning
Somewhere along the road
Somewhere along the road
Somewhere along the road

The song faded out in much the same manner as it had faded in minutes before. This was a direct message from her man. He was lost and darkness had indeed obscured the trail. The song's lyrics couldn't have been more poignant.

Phoenix couldn't go any farther without processing this in the only way she knew how. She pulled over to the shoulder of the road and engaged her hazard lights. Her shoulders heaved as she stared at the mountain ahead of her, trying to picture her man somewhere within them.

She allowed herself a ten-minute ugly cry before wiping her eyes and declaring to the universe: "I will find you, Curt! I'm coming for you, baby!"

CHAPTER EIGHTEEN

THE HOLIDAY RAMBLER
STATE ROUTE AZ-88, SOUTH
PALM SUNDAY, 6:05 AM

MIKE REVERE GRABBED his thermal travel mug from the oversized cupholder on the center console and was just now taking his first sip of coffee.

"Finally..." he muttered, taking a second sip while he was at it. "That took forever."

"We've never had security like that when leaving a state park," Mary concurred. "Weird."

"Yeah...that line put us a half hour behind where we wanted to be, but we'll be fine. We'll make up some time once we hit the interstate," he said, coming out of a turn and enjoying the straightaway.

"And their questions...anyway, I'm looking forward to California, honey," she said, smiling at him before returning to her *People* magazine.

Mike was thinking back now to his brief conversation with the ranger and the other man, the one who hadn't identified himself. *Seen anything unusual this morning?*

Unbeknownst to the Revere family, "something unusual" was indeed hanging on for dear life just above their heads.

Rooftop, Tempest still lay prone, her fingers feeling stress fatigue from gripping the inadequate edge of the AC unit. She didn't know these people, or where they were heading, but she knew she'd have to find an opportune moment to safely execute her dismount before the huge RV reached freeway speeds.

She turned her head to the left and, from her lofty vantage point, could see the morning park visitors streaming toward the mountain. *Y'all missed all the excitement!*

To take her mind off the pain in her fingers, she began counting the approaching cars. *Subaru. Subaru. Subaru... 4Runner... Jeep... Road Runner...Road Runner? Nah!*

And just that quickly, the orange muscle car disappeared from view. Tempest tried rolling slightly onto her right side but couldn't chance a glance back over her shoulder to confirm the sighting without falling off her chariot.

As she rolled back onto her belly, she felt a little clunk as something fell from her right hip.

Jesus! The Glock!!

In an instant the pistol had slipped out from its ill-fitting holster. It evaded her flailing attempts to grasp it and, despite her best efforts, continued further, past her feet as it slid down the entire length of the RV's roof and onto the highway below.

FUUUCKKK!!

Tempest dug her fingers in and turned her wide eyes front as they approached Apache Junction, just ahead. She shook her head and cursed her luck as she shivered from her perch in the mercilessly brisk morning air.

It's cold as fuck up here!

Inside the rig, the climate control was optimal, and the whale's smooth ride was like floating on air. Mike and Mary had made the right choice, trading up their Class C Minnie Winnie for the Holiday Rambler. There was no going back.

"Did you hear that?" Mike asked, turning to his wife with a look of concern.

"Nuh-uh. What'd it sound like?"

"I don't know. Like a clunk. Up top?"

"Hmm...nope. Maybe a bird?"

"Don't think so. I'll check it out next opportunity."

"'Kay...it's going to be another amazing day, hon," Mary replied, looking over her shoulder as Eva arrived, hunched over between their front seats.

"Don't kill me, but can we make a quick stop before we get on the freeway?"

Mary replied to their daughter before her husband could. "If you need to, you can use the restroom in back, honey."

"Umm...I don't think so, Mom. I think that chili we had last night isn't agreeing with me. It's...kind of an emergency. Can we stop when we get to that town up there, Dad... please?" she asked, bordering on a beg. "Just for a minute?"

Mike briefly considered making this a teachable moment, making her tough it out for a while—especially since he'd told everyone to be "wheels-up ready" at 05:30. That meant restroom breaks too. But he figured he could top off the tank at the Circle K in Apache Junction. Besides, he wanted to make sure everything was okay with the rig.

"Just this one time," he said in an attempt to sound stern, his half grin only visible to his wife.

"Thanks, Dad!" Eva said, kissing his cheek before returning to the couch and buckling herself back in.

"You can be such a hard ass," Mary whispered kiddingly to her husband.

CIRCLE K STATION
APACHE JUNCTION, ARIZONA
PALM SUNDAY, 6:20 AM

Mike navigated the family bus into the driveway of the Circle K gas station and convenience store, waiting for a minivan to finish their fill-up so he could assume their prime position at the pump.

The minivan pulled away and none too soon as Eva found herself dancing in anxious circles inside the RV.

There were few cars at this hour, which provided a convenient pull-through opportunity as well an easy exit. The forty-footer needed the entire row, taking up the curb along all three pumps at the island.

Mike switched on the rearview camera's monitor and maneuvered the beast into position. As he killed the engine,

Eva wasted no time flying out the exit door and running toward the convenience store's indoor restrooms.

"You need to use the restrooms too, honey?" Mary asked Carol.

"Nah, I'm good," she replied, not looking up from her phone. "I didn't have the chili."

"Okay, as long as you're sure, because we'll be on the highway until lunchtime, and we don't plan to make any stops till then," Mike interjected, exiting his captain's chair and RV.

"Would you please get me the new *People* magazine, hon?" Mary asked him.

"Sure."

Mary cracked her neck and her eyes drifted across the myriad of switches, indicators, and displays on the dashboard. She was glad her husband was up to speed on this stuff, because it was all black magic to her.

The RV's rear camera was still on, and its 7-inch color monitor afforded a wide view of the parking lot behind the unit. As Mary returned her gaze to her magazine, something caught her attention out of the corner of her eye. A momentary streak of movement on the monitor.

She furrowed her brow as she trained her eyes on it. *Nothing. Must be imagining things.*

Tempest had done her level best to slide silently on her belly toward the back of the motorhome's roof, carefully descending the RV's ladder in the process. As she reached the ground, she avoided the side of the vehicle where she knew the owner was quenching the massive diesel's thirst and, a second later, with her daypack squared between her shoulders, she disappeared into the dark, predawn morning.

THE CAVE
SIPHON DRAW TRAIL
PALM SUNDAY, 6:25 AM

The rattling of the discarded food can served as Curt's wake-up call.

The mystery rodent—at least Curt hoped it was only a rodent—was stirring, and it seemed to be pissed he hadn't been left more of a portion.

"Yeah...you and me both, pal," Curt muttered to the critter.

He rolled from his side onto his back, wincing at the multiple points of pain he was experiencing. His ankle continued to scream its well-founded complaints while various pressure points vied for attention as well.

He'd all but given up any hope after being abandoned by both the helicopter and potential ground rescue team hours before, sending him into a deep funk and tail-spinning into a comalike sleep. There was no need for blackout curtains in this room, and the place had ruined him for ever wanting to have a "man cave" of his own.

Curt licked his dry lips, his tongue feeling like it was coated with sand in his arid mouth. He remembered he still had a couple ounces of water left in the bottle and, shaking the vessel to confirm its measure, he allowed himself half of it.

He lumbered to his good foot and hopped over to the cave opening. The morning sky was starting to wake up, and he figured sunrise would be imminent.

Will they return to look for me here? Have they abandoned this area and moved on?

The prospects depressed him even more.

He wasn't up for any more hiking, not with his bad wheel. His wannabe walking stick was no crutch, that was for sure.

With only enough remaining water to wet his lips once more, and no known source to replenish it, he dreaded the coming sun's appearance, as it would quickly bake him into submission. His carcass would be a welcome brunch for a wake of vultures.

Curt shook away the thought, trying to get his mental bearings:

What day is it? Sunday!

Is the park even open on Sundays?

The trails...?

God...is this...really...how it all ends?

Don't answer!

CHAPTER NINETEEN

SUPERSTITION WILDERNESS
LOST DUTCHMAN STATE PARK
PALM SUNDAY, SUNRISE

PHOENIX PULLED OFF the road and entered the queue of vehicles in line for admittance to the park.

Her Road Runner's throaty idle got the attention of more than a few of the Subaru owners. She couldn't help but feel their looks were less in admiration for her muscle car than judgment for her vehicle's carbon footprint.

Phoenix paid them no mind as she inched forward toward the ranger kiosk. One vehicle that caught her eye, however, was a non-official looking sedan with a blond woman at the wheel, just a couple of cars ahead of hers.

The blond woman seemed to be aware of her as well, based on the repeated looks via the rearview mirror.

Phoenix squinted...the driver looked familiar.

Then it clicked. For both of them.

Phoenix.

Detective Moser!

Phoenix waved her right hand in recognition. It wasn't a happy wave, just letting her know she saw her.

The detective's car was next in line as it pulled up to the kiosk. Phoenix watched as Moser flashed her badge, exchanged a few words, and was handed a piece of paper. Phoenix saw Moser proceed ahead before pulling off to the side. She appeared to be waiting for her.

She's got some splainin' to do... Phoenix thought, channeling her inner Ricky Ricardo.

The next car pulled up and Phoenix again watched as the ranger handed the driver a printed flyer of some sort. And they were on their merry way.

As Phoenix pulled up the tiny kiosk, she rolled her window down and was greeted with a smile by a young female ranger cadet. Phoenix figured she was maybe nineteen.

"Good morning, ma'am. That'll be ten dollars, please," the girl said.

"'Morning...sure thing," Phoenix replied, handing her two fives. The ranger handed her a printed receipt as well as one of the flyers.

"Just so you know, ma'am, the Siphon Draw trailhead is closed till further notice."

Phoenix stared at the flyer, which confirmed this fact. "Oh, okay. Good to know. Thanks. Um, any particular reason why?"

The girl lowered her voice a notch. "Report of a bobcat in the area, I believe."

"Ooh...also good to know. Any other interesting developments?"

The ranger seemed to be a bit thrown by this unscheduled

game of Twenty Questions. "Um, not that I know of ma'am," she said, recovering slightly. "Enjoy your day in the park. And please observe the posted speed limit."

"Absolutely," Phoenix said, feathering the throttle as she pulled ahead fifty feet and parked alongside Moser's vehicle. Phoenix got out and walked over to the detective's driver side window. Moser, who had been staring straight ahead, turned as Phoenix approached and rolled down her window.

"Mornin', Detective," Phoenix said. "What a coinkidink... going for an early morning hike, are you?"

The detective suddenly felt like a teenager who'd been pulled over for exceeding the speed limit. She knew Phoenix had every reason to be upset.

"Mrs.—Phoenix. Good morning..." she said, mustering an awkward smile in return. "I'm sorry, I'm afraid we have a little catching up to do," she added, motioning for Phoenix to come around and climb in.

"Ya think?" Phoenix replied, slipping into the passenger seat of Moser's rather messy, years-old Ford Taurus. This was obviously her personal vehicle and not a department one.

"Sorry," Moser said, clearing away some old Wiley's wrappers and a few girly toys from the seat. "My daughter's still learning to clean up after herself."

"No problem. So's mine," Phoenix said, looking her in the eye now.

Moser dropped any official pretense and flashed a genuine, mother-to-mother smile. "How *is* Rose doing with all this?"

"Oh, you know...just...not real well, truth be told," Phoenix replied. "That goes for the whole family, as you can probably imagine."

Moser nodded. She looked away, watching a couple of

cars go by as she formulated a proper response. So much had happened in the past twenty-four hours, and she'd only herself learned of the latest developments when her partner had called her a little over an hour before.

"Phoenix, I'd like to apologize for the lack of transparency. Detective Ramage and I have been working several new leads, at all hours and in real time and, well...let me just say that a lot has gone down since we last talked."

Phoenix considered this, nodded in response to this attempt at apology, and turned to better face Moser as she settled in, crossed her arms, and rest her back against the window.

"You have my undivided attention, Detective."

LOST DUTCHMAN STATE PARK
RANGER STATION
TWENTY MINUTES LATER

Ranger Danger walked over to his two new guests, placing steaming mugs of coffee on the table near their chairs.

Phoenix immediately began dumping in copious amounts of sweetener from the packets that he had provided. She took a moment's pause when she saw the faux creamer packets but shrugged it off as she went about dumping in three packets of the off-white powder.

Moser gave the ranger an appreciative half-smile but

ignored her mug. Instead, she exchanged knowing glances with her partner, who, after his all-nighter, looked like he'd been eaten by a coyote and shit off a cliff.

The ranger's space heater was glowing red in the corner. It kept the room plenty warm, yet the atmosphere remained frosty.

Phoenix's conversation with Moser, along with what Ramage had just added to fill in the blanks, meant she was now up to speed. But it didn't mean she was okay with having been kept out of the loop.

"So," she began, setting down the mug very ceremoniously. She turned to Ramage and spoke in a measured tone as to not lose a gasket. "If I understand this correctly, it sounds like, after all of yesterday's mayhem, the *killings*, and the shootout with the friggin' helicopter, this Tempest chick is still unaccounted for."

"That's affirmative," Ramage replied. His level of fatigue was painfully obvious. It was probably good he didn't have a flight to catch because the airline would have to charge him for each of the bags under his eyes. "We believe she came back down off the trail, but her whereabouts are not presently known."

"I see," Phoenix said. "And you say there were no sightings of my husband?"

"No, there were not. But the suspect's presence on the trail indicates she had to be searching for him at the time we encountered her," Ramage replied, trying to blink away his fog.

"Okay. Well, I have a bit of a news flash for you all," Phoenix said, pulling the phone from her hip pocket. "My husband, Curt—you remember him—the one who was kidnapped a few days ago by this psycho, managed to send off a message to me sometime during the night."

She pulled up the message stream and held out the phone at arm's length for them to see, before handing it to Moser.

"I know cell service sucks out here, but this arrived early this morning. It's brief, but I can tell you with absolute certainty, this one's definitely from Curt. And, goddammit, he's still alive!"

Moser inspected the message stream, making note of the time the last one had been sent. "Looks like it was sent at 10:18 p.m.," she said.

She handed the phone to her partner, who directed his burning eyes on the tiny screen.

"10:18 p.m.," Phoenix said. "Which I believe is when you guys were up there on the trail."

Phoenix's features were chiseled in stone as she fixed each of the detectives with a look that told them, in no uncertain terms, she wasn't leaving here without him.

Detectives Ramage and Moser had stepped outside onto the porch for a partner briefing, during which Moser put her foot down, strongly emphasizing her need to take the baton for a while, as the all-nighter had left her partner a shell of himself.

Phoenix watched the two of them from the window, getting a good sense of their conversation. As Moser made her closing argument and patted Ramage on the shoulder, the gesture was reminiscent of a coach sending his starting pitcher to the locker room in the ninth inning due to his pitch count.

It was clear she was sending him home for some

much-needed shuteye. As Ramage shuffled off to his car, Moser answered her phone.

It was now or never.

Ranger Danger grabbed a handful of the trail closure flyers from his desk, powered down the coffee maker's heating element, and grabbed his hat.

"I've got to go and get the rest of these posted, so if you'll excuse me, I'll—"

"I can do it. Just tell me where," Phoenix interjected, seizing the moment.

"That's okay, ma'am, I've got some cadets who can put them up. You've got enough on your mind right now."

"No, I mean it. The trailheads, right? You said Siphon Draw in particular?"

"Siphon Draw, yes. You know the park?"

"Some of it, yes," she answered, glancing out the window to monitor Moser's whereabouts. "Hiked some of the lower trails when I was younger. Been a while, but yeah."

"You're sure about this? I've got other staff who—"

"No, I want to. Hell, I *need* to. Please," Phoenix replied, holding out her hand. Her look told him she was resolute.

"If you insist." Danger handed her the stack of flyers and a heavy-duty stapler.

"Thank you," she said. "Oh, and you don't need to mention this to the detective. She's got a lot going on."

"Indeed, she does," the ranger acknowledged. "Seems we all do right now."

The walkie on his desk squawked. "If you'll excuse me, I've got to take this." He picked it up and keyed the talk button. "Go for Danger."

As Phoenix slipped out onto the porch, she closed the

door quietly and disappeared around the back of the building, where her car was.

Being as the Road Runner was the throatiest, most badass 440 Hemi engine in these parts, she wouldn't be taking it. Instead, she tucked the flyers under her arm, reached in through the open window and grabbed the daypack—and her extra bottle of Sunny D.

POP POP'S STREET
A HALF-BLOCK FROM HOME
PALM SUNDAY, 8:05 AM

Prick, er, *Rick*, led the charge as the pack rounded the corner and headed for home. At sixteen years old, the little chihuahua still enjoyed his walks and almost always set the pace, even if it had slowed a smidge.

While he held the reins on Rick and Luke, Pop Pop monitored little Rose as she maintained a firm grip on the pink leash tethered to Sidney's matching harness.

"You doing okay, Peanut?"

"Yes! And I'm not a peanut!" she answered with a smile. "*Sidney* is the peanut!"

"Oh, that's right!" Pop Pop replied with a grandfatherly giggle. They were almost home, and Luke was being a bit squirrely, which meant he was ready for his breakfast. In fact, there was rarely a moment when the goofy German Shepherd wasn't jonesing for a meal.

Pop Pop's phone rang, and he switched the leashes to his other hand to answer it. It was Phoenix. "Hey," he answered, keeping his voice low. "Good morning...where are you? I woke up and you were gone. Everything okay?"

Phoenix had the phone tucked under her chin as she finished stapling a flyer to a trailhead marker. "Yeah, mostly. I'm...I went for a drive...ended up at the Lost Dutchman."

Pop Pop motioned for Rose to tighten the leash a little, then replied to his daughter on the other end of the line. "I kind of figured as much when I saw the drawing was gone from the fridge door. Is that where you are now?"

Phoenix set the few remaining flyers atop the marker post, using the stapler as a paperweight with the slight breeze that had come up.

"Yeah. Hey, I don't have a ton of time to fill you in on everything, but the detectives are up here too. Well, one of 'em...Ramage spent a crazy night and morning up here and he just went home. Moser's here, coordinating some stuff with the rangers and other officers."

"And you're...."

"Helping out in my own way..." she said.

"Okay."

"Listen, Pop Pop. Here's the skinny: Curt sent me a text last night—late—and I just received it early this morning!"

"Wow...seriously, that's great, honey! What'd he say?"

"It was brief, Pop Pop. But I know this one was from

him—not like the other ones. And I just found out there was a crazy pursuit up here last night. The mystery psycho, a shootout with a police helicopter, and a couple of murders they figure her for. It's turned into some serious shit, Pop Pop, and I'm worried half to death."

"Listen, honey. We're just finishing up our dog walk—I have Rose with me. After I feed everybody, I can put the pooches in their crates and come out there. I'd have Rose with me, but I—"

"No need, Pop Pop," Phoenix said, cutting him off. "They've got another police copter in route and there's a bunch of park staff keeping an eye out. I...I'm gonna...go for a little hike."

"Phoenix, if things are as volatile as you say, that's way too dangerous to be traipsing around in that wilderness. Let's not forget what happened the last time we got involved in something. I suggest you leave things to the professionals. Wait for the helicopter. Please tell me you'll—"

"Sure, Pop Pop. Hey, my battery's dying. I'll have to call you back," she lied, as she ended the call.

Phoenix took a swig of her Sunny D and, leaving the leftover flyers atop the trailhead's signpost, climbed through the less-than-effective yellow caution tape that had been put there to cordon off the Siphon Draw.

CHAPTER TWENTY

CIRCLE K GAS STATION
GLENDALE, ARIZONA
PALM SUNDAY, 8:40 AM

THE CANDY-APPLE RED Kawasaki Vulcan 1600 Mean Streak roared toward the station; its four-stroke, V-Twin, 1552cc engine purring as it downshifted and entered the driveway, sidling up to an empty pump.

The driver engaged the kickstand, climbed off, and removed his matching helmet. This afforded his passenger a first real look at the twenty-year-old blond surfer type who'd responded to her hitcher's thumb.

Tempest removed the helmet he'd provided, shook her head, and smiled at him.

"Thanks for the ride," she said, flashing an appreciative enough smile. She didn't want anything to do with him beyond this brief but exhilarating ride. She had other fish to fry.

"No worries," the guy said, flashing his own smile. "So, you wanna grab some breakfast? Or something?"

"Mmm...nice thought, but I just needed the ride, thanks. I really appreciate it," she replied. "Oh, here," she said, handing him the helmet.

He stashed the helmet in his saddlebag and began the flow of fuel to his four and a half gallon tank. He looked back up and squinted at the backlit beauty he'd just shared a seat with. He'd liked the way she hugged his waist when he cranked it up to ninety miles per hour on the straightaway, and he hoped this one wouldn't get away.

"Maybe some other time," he said, trying on his cute rejection smile. "Can I call you, then?"

"Sure. That'd be nice," Tempest lied, cinching her daypack strap and wanting this conversation to end right now. "Got something to write on?"

The fuel nozzle clicked, signaling his tiny tank was topped off. He replaced the nozzle and fished around in his pockets, coming up empty. "Just a pen...no paper," he said, a combination of embarrassed and disappointed.

"Here," she said, taking the pen. "Give me your hand."

"Yeah?"

"Yeah," she replied as she wrote down seven digits on the back of his hand to placate him. She added a small heart and wrote her name, albeit a fake one. "Call me."

"I will...8-6-7-5-3-0-9...nice number," he said, his clueless face lighting up as he read what she'd written. "Tiffany, nice!"

"Thanks again!" she said as she walked away, commencing her hike down the long stretch of roadside sidewalk.

She only had about four blocks to go, she figured, and her arrival would be a complete surprise.

THE SIPHON DRAW
MILE 1 MARKER
PALM SUNDAY, 8:50 AM

Phoenix paused as she reached the sign. She pulled her Sunny D bottle from the daypack and took a swig, following it up with a Necco wafer. She placed the confection on her tongue.

"Body of Christ," she muttered to herself.

She had taken her time, her keen eyes watchful for anything that might provide a clue as to her husband's whereabouts, and his condition.

Curt had rather ginormous feet, and he wouldn't have had the benefit of proper hiking boots, she knew. She tried to envision what he'd been wearing when she last saw him on Friday morning—a long time ago—before he'd left for school.

He'd be wearing his New Balances.

Phoenix replaced her snacks in the pack and, eyes to the ground, continued along the trail. In search of her own personal "Bigfoot."

Fifty yards ahead, she stopped at a clearing. A large, single footprint, and not from a boot. Phoenix kneeled to better inspect it. The size was right, as was the tread. But there was only the right foot's print. She touched it with her fingers. *He was here!*

As she stood to track them, she noticed something odd. There wasn't a corresponding left shoeprint to be found, only the right, then a pointy divot, as if from a stick, where the left foot should've touched down. Then another right one.

Then her heart skipped a beat. "Oh, my God."

Curt's injured!

KOKOPELLI APARTMENTS
GLENDALE, ARIZONA
PALM SUNDAY, 9:11 AM

Tempest stood on the sidewalk in front of the rather run-down, two-story apartment building and wolfed down the remainder of the breakfast sandwich she'd grabbed along the way. She was ravenous and a little burned out on the teriyaki jerky she'd had for dinner on the trail.

Tempest knew she was at the right place because she'd committed the address to memory a while back. Plus, there was that goofy looking humpbacked flute player dude on the signage. Yes, this was the place.

She glanced at her watch and nodded. *Probably not a churchgoer. Should be home.* There wasn't a parking garage, only two adjacent carport lots with assigned parking. Each space had a modest, lockable, wooden storage cabinet mounted above it for personal items.

Tempest walked the course of the first lot before cluing into the fact that each parking space had a corresponding number, which meant she was in the wrong lot.

The other group of carports proved to be more promising. Tempest scanned the space numbers and the vehicles assigned to them, stopping as she arrived at the desired spot: 202. Yes, this was the one, confirming the space number against its occupant: a beater Ford Fiesta.

Finding the corresponding staircase, she slinked up the steps, two at a time, her long legs making quick work of them.

She arrived at the second floor landing and paused outside the door of apartment 210. The place looked more like an old motel than an apartment complex, mainly because of the open-air hallway and the faded red paint on the door facings. This side of the building took the brunt of the afternoon sun and it showed.

Tempest scanned the area. There was zero activity and everyone's blinds appeared to still be drawn.

She slipped off her daypack, stuck her hand inside and retrieved the necessary item, stuffing it in the right rear pocket of her jeans. She rezipped the pack and squared it between her shoulders as she quietly made her way down the landing.

As Tempest reached the halfway point, the door to apartment 206 opened and a large woman wearing a bright floral muumuu stepped out to grab her newspaper. A lit cigarette dangled from the woman's lips, and she appeared to be just as startled as Tempest was.

In a bid to diffuse the situation, Tempest flashed a smile. "Good morning," she whispered.

The woman cleared the frog in her throat, and as she responded, her deep voice indicated she was probably a three-pack-a-day gal. "'Mornin'..." she managed, not altogether unfriendly, as she ducked back inside her unit and closed the door. A second later, her air conditioning wall unit began to hum loudly.

Tempest resumed breathing, and as she counted down the room numbers, she stopped outside apartment 202. The one with the Marilyn Manson door mat. *Of course.*

She listened. It sounded like a TV was on in the living room. Not cartoons. News, maybe.

She didn't huff, or puff, or blow the door down. She simply knocked with the knuckle of her middle finger. Hopefully loud enough for the occupant, but not the neighbors.

"Just a minute," the voice she'd hoped to hear said from somewhere beyond the door. "Be right there."

Tempest tilted her head to the side, cracking her neck and getting the desired popping sound. She took inventory of the bulge in her back pocket. She closed her eyes and breathed in.

Half a minute went by before the sound of a security chain being dragged along its track announced the occupant's arrival. Next was the turning of the deadbolt, after which the door slowly swung open.

They stood there, taking each other in. Tempest was the first to smile because the other gazed back through red-rimmed eyes, open-mouthed, thunderstruck.

"Good morning, Paige."

"Oh, my God."

"Sorry to arrive unannounced, is this a bad time?"

"No...no, not at all. I was just having some cereal and watching some TV. Oh, my God!"

"May I come in?"

"Of course, yes! Wow, I never thought—"

"Well, when you asked the other day if maybe we could hang out some time, I thought, yeah! Let's see what Paige is doing. Should've called first..." Tempest said, stepping inside the hovel. It was as bad as she had imagined. A little worse, even. It smelled heavily of pot.

Several goth and metal band posters were thumbtacked to the walls, and at odd angles. Bauhaus, Christian Death, Killing Joke...it was a dark palace she kept, this little wannabe goth chick.

"Here," Paige said, closing the door and clearing an empty pizza box off the thrift store sofa. "Sorry about the mess. Have a seat," she clucked, turning down the volume on the TV as she went to the kitchenette. "Can I get you something? Had breakfast? Some coffee?"

Tempest gestured a polite stop with her hand. "Nothing, thanks. I'm fine," she replied, her eyes settling on the flickering images on the TV screen.

She'd been right; it was the news she'd heard, and a story about a missile strike somewhere in Pakistan, killing at least sixteen. Even with the sound off, the pain and anger of local tribesmen was evident as they blamed the United States army.

Paige came back into the living room with two glasses of apple juice and a couple of eclairs on paper plates. "Nothing fancy," she said sheepishly as she set the pastries down on top of the pizza box she'd previously relocated, and next to the recently used bong, which didn't go unnoticed by her guest. *Paige, you naughty girl...*she hoped she didn't get a contact high.

"You really don't need to feed me, Paige," Tempest said with a half-smile. This wasn't a social call, and she wasn't interested in getting stoned with her.

"Well, I don't get a lot of visitors, so it's the least I can do. Oh, my God..." she said, almost squealing. "So..."

The news story finished, and the screen now flashed a BREAKING NEWS graphic, which got the attention of both women. The image switched to a split-screen shot of the local Phoenix-area news anchor, Molly Metz, as she tossed to the station's lead field reporter, Felix Gomez.

The chyron graphics at the bottom of the screen provided all the information one needed as Felix stood, stone-faced, in front of the main entrance to the Lost Dutchman State Park.

As he addressed the camera, the video feed cut to B-roll footage of a campsite draped in yellow Crime Scene tape, a police helicopter buzzing the mountain range, a covered body on a gurney being wheeled out of a trailer park, and then back to the studio as Molly Metz now occupied half the screen and a WANTED graphic accompanying an enlarged driver's license photo. The chyron text warning dominated the screen: ARMED AND DANGEROUS.

And a name: TEMPEST CAGE.

Paige's jaw slacked as she stared at the screen. She slowly turned her head toward the couch and the lady she'd just seen on TV.

The lady looking back at her, her coworker, looked completely different to her now. A stranger...dangerous. Tempest's eyes were cold, her expression neutral, and she now held a large knife in her right hand.

Tempest spoke three words to her host, the last she'd ever hear:

"I'm sorry, Paige."

CHAPTER TWENTY-ONE

SIPHON TRAIL
1.5 MILE MARKER
PALM SUNDAY, 9:55 AM

P HOENIX HAD FOLLOWED the series of hopscotched footprints, and as she paused at the 1.5-mile marker, she noticed some others now, entirely different from those left by her husband.

These new prints were smaller than Curt's, certainly, but also several sizes larger than her own, and left by someone wearing a narrow hiking boot. *A woman.*

A quick swig from her bottle and Phoenix was back on her way along the next leg, toward the next marker, and hopefully her injured husband. She wondered if he had any water. Any food. These questions drove her legs and her resolve.

The woman's boot prints seemed to be tracking the intermittent ones left by Curt and about two hundred yards later, the pursuer's prints abruptly stopped.

Phoenix adjusted her ball cap and kneeled, inspecting the

ground. There were two additional sets of footprints evident here, relatively fresh ones, and they stopped here as well. As if the people who'd left them had been mulling around.

She determined these had to be from the ranger and Detective Ramage during their search the previous night. *Right here, which means....*

That's when she saw the break in the berm, its dirt having given way to what looked like evidence of someone having slid down the hill.

This, she now realized, was where the psycho had abandoned the trail during the incident with the police helicopter the night before.

She hadn't found Curt...which means he may still be up ahead.

Phoenix stood, looked at her watch, and slowly forged ahead.

"Curt!!" she yelled out to the mountain. "Currrrrt!!!" she screamed again, now competing with what sounded like a helicopter searching another part of the mountain.

Phoenix pulled out her phone to check the signal. Coverage was meager at best out here, which explained the delay in receiving Curt's message. She didn't know if he even had an operational phone at this point, but she had to try. She composed a brief text and hit send:

>*I'm coming for you. Stay strong, baby. S.M.F.*

Phoenix stuffed the device back in her pocket and continued up the trail.

Unbeknownst to her, another set of eyes had been watching her closely for a while now, and they weren't her husband's.

THE CAVE

MOMENTS LATER

The pain and swelling in Curt's ankle were getting worse by the hour, and the injured appendage screamed in protest. Was that what he'd just heard? He no longer trusted his senses, or his mind.

A trifecta of fears competed for his attention: *Will the maniac come back to hunt me down and kill me? Will I die of dehydration? If I somehow survive this, will I lose my leg?*

Curt's energy reserves were almost completely tapped, and he'd already had his final drops of water hours ago. He lay on the bumpy cave floor, feeling utterly despondent, depleted, and defeated.

He had no idea what time it was, and he wasn't entirely sure of the day. It was all a blur. The pitch darkness of the cave offered a state of near-complete sensory deprivation, with no visual references to hang on to. He'd always hated going to casinos for this reason, as they designed the gambling spaces to be devoid of clocks, and the windows were blocked out to snuff out any reference to the outside world. Only this was a thousand times worse. This was a life-and-death gamble, and the chips were stacked against him.

Curled into a big ball, he had succumbed to exhaustion— both physical and mental. He knew he couldn't walk out of here, so he hoped his Hail Mary prayers would be heard. In recent years he'd come to believe in miracles, and with good reason. As he lay there, he allowed himself to take inventory of a few of his miraculous greatest hits:

Meeting Phoenix (then-Phoebe). Miracle? Yeah.

Rescuing Phoenix and surviving the "Pirate" in California. Miracle? Hell, yeah.

Becoming a daddy to Rose. Miracle? Absolutely.

Saving Rose from the clutches of human traffickers. Miracle? There can be no doubt.

Miracles were everywhere if we took time to reflect on them, he knew. And with nothing but his ankle to distract him, he had plenty to reflect on.

Please, God...deliver me from this place. Return me to my family. Curt rolled over onto his back and listened for a response from the Almighty. Maybe he'd already called in his last favor; he'd been blessed many times before, but maybe you were allowed, like, maybe five in your lifetime and then it was somebody else's turn.

It felt like he was in a vacuum chamber and his fate had been hermetically sealed. The dark thought returned. *This is how it ends.*

He thought he was hallucinating now as a low, very faint droning sound vied for his attention. It sounded almost like... he wasn't sure. It got quieter, and he dismissed it as a delusion, until a few moments later, the sound came back, just a little louder, slightly more prominent, and almost like a...

...helicopter? Helicopter?! A helicopter !!

Curt propped himself up on his right elbow and cocked his head to the side, not unlike Luke did at home when he was trying to understand something. Curt was trying to understand if this was something real or just an example of his deteriorating senses playing a particularly cruel joke on him. *Please be real!*

With every fiber of his being, he summoned what little

remaining energy he had and directed it all to his sense of hearing. There it was. *Whoop, whoop, whoop.*

As Curt's mind seized on the fact that this was indeed the sound of helicopter blades, his facial muscles slowly began to arrange themselves into an enormous, involuntary smile. He was too tired to laugh. His eyes began to pool with tears as he processed the event.

He listened to the melodic sounds, whirring closer. Then, something new to the mix?

Whoop, whoop, whoop...Currrt...whoop, whoop, whoop... Currrt!!

There was no way he was hearing that correctly. His name? And the *voice*...it had sounded almost like...

...*Phoenix*!!?

SIPHON DRAW TRAIL
10:20 AM
MOMENTS LATER

Phoenix called out Curt's name twice more before pausing for a swig of *the D*, her nickname for her beverage of choice. She was now starting into her second bottle, and she wanted to save the lion's share of it for Curt when she found him.

After a very conservative sip, she recapped the bottle and put it back in her daypack. The terrain was beginning to hint at a sharp increase in elevation just ahead, so she took out her collapsible walking stick, just in case.

It had been a just-because gift from Pop Pop a couple of years back and it was, until now, untested. He'd gotten it for her for protection—something to keep in the car—more than for hiking, as its overall length made it more of a long baton than a true hiking stick. Still, it might come in handy on this part of the trail.

Phoenix slipped it from its nylon sheath. It felt heftier than she recalled, especially for something with a closed length of only twelve inches. Its rubber handle provided a solid grip, and the black stainless-steel housing was impressive. Its build quality was obvious, and she made sure to hold it out to the side, heeding Pop Pop's advisory of never pointing it at yourself.

Using her thumb, she slipped the safety switch to the off position and shrugged. *Let's see what you've got.* She activated the button on the handle and—*schwing!! Instant stainless steel wannabe lightsaber!*

The internal spring mechanism had instantaneously rocketed the footlong baton's second and third stages into what had now become a thirty-one inch-long tactical weapon. *That's one helluva a hiking stick! Thanks, Pop Pop!*

She rezipped her daypack and, satisfied with the solid purchase her new toy made as she jabbed it into the rocky trail dirt, she continued toward the rock face up ahead.

Her watcher maintained a stealthy distance as he observed the lone hiker move further up the trail. He'd stalked her for a while now from the cover of dead foliage that paralleled the trail, and wobbly on his feet, he quietly emerged, taking a position fifty yards behind Phoenix.

THE CAVE
MINUTES LATER

Curt now understood a little better how a wolf must feel as it unsuccessfully tries to free its bloody, mangled foot from the cruel steel jaws of a hunter's trap.

His severely swollen lower leg felt like that now, and if he had the wherewithal, and the means to do so, he might just chew the damned ankle off to alleviate the pain a little and take his chances gimping down the hill with one leg.

He hadn't heard the voice again, but he'd determined the helicopter must be making a series of passes in the area because it had gotten a little louder. He had to try to get to his feet. If he didn't, the search team would abandon him a second time, and he wouldn't be around to see a third.

Curt gritted his teeth and clamped his eyes shut as he scooted himself on his butt, closer to the wall nearest the narrow cave opening. His useless foot dragged along the ground despite his best efforts to lift it. He grabbed his mesquite stick in his left hand. With his right, he felt along the cave wall until he found a protrusion, a handhold he could grab on to. He needed all the leverage he could find right now.

He counted down from five and, on zero, grunted loudly

as he used every morsel of his strength to get himself to the standing position on his one good foot. *Lord, have mercy!*

It took him three hops, but he aligned himself with the narrow opening, and having turned himself sideways, his head and right shoulder emerged into the supernova of daylight he wasn't prepared for. If he were a vampire, he would have been instantly reduced to dust.

Curt clamped his eyes shut for several seconds, shifting his sensory power to his ears as he listened to the sound of the helicopter's blades buffeting the canyon. They had turned away from his position and seemed to be making another elliptical pass over the trail area.

He opened his eyes slightly, squinting to get a visual, but the aircraft had disappeared behind the hillside again. *Come back...please, come back!*

Standing with his back against the rocky face, he hung his head in despair, staring down at his ball-and-chain of an ankle. He wasn't going back inside the cave. Not now. It had served him well, and it had bought him a little time. But his only chance now, slim as it might be, was to stay out in the open. To be found.

Or die trying.

100 YARDS AWAY

Phoenix approached a crest in the trail. She hadn't seen any more footprints—at least not any human ones. Other than a few fresh tracks that looked like they might have been from rabbits, the trail had grown cold.

She stopped, and as she stood there, listening and watching, she saw the craggy face of a rock formation up ahead. It seemed to have just violently jutted out of the earth, and it probably had about eighteen million years before.

With no more useable tracks to follow, she dug in her heels, and her walking stick, and forged ahead. It sounded like the helicopter was still circling around on the backside of the hill, so she set her course accordingly.

"Currrrt!!" she yelled out. A few moments later, she tried again. "Curt Martinsen!!"

The thick cobwebs that had all but choked off Curt's remaining cognitive powers instantly disappeared upon hearing the voice again. He cocked his head to make sure he could trust his own senses.

"Currrt!!" the voice had called out. It sounded like it had come from somewhere down the trail, and not too far away. "Curt Martinsen!!"

There it was again! The female voice, an unmistakable one!

"Phoenix!" he managed, his weak, gravelly response only loud enough for the nearest lizard to hear. His throat was dry as sandpaper and he hadn't used his voice in what seemed like forever.

His saliva was depleted, and he made several attempts to clear his throat before trying his response again. If this was to be the last utterance he ever made, he had to make it a good one. He took in a deep breath and gave it his best shot.

"PHOE-NIIIIIIIIX!!!" he bellowed.

Had she heard it? He waited several seconds, then cleared his throat to try again.

"CURT!!!" came the response, followed by the visual of a tiny human hiker coming into view. It was better than any mirage could aspire to, and he waved his arms in the air as his beautiful, diminutive wife began running toward him.

"CURT!!" Phoenix cried out again. She appeared tired, but seemed to find new life as she began to close the distance. "Oh, my God!"

Curt had nothing left in the tank, but he knew his prayer had been answered. He smiled broadly, his dry lips cracking in the process.

As Phoenix got to within about thirty yards of him, Curt saw something else on the trail that was at once unsettling, and a very real danger, closing in behind her.

His long-dormant Boy Scout training from twenty years before came rushing back to him in a flash of recognition as he assessed the threat.

As Phoenix came to within twenty yards, he saw her eyes examine him in concern, and he imagined how she saw him. On his butt with an injured leg. He began to wave his arms erratically as he felt his smile disappear, replaced by a look of sheer panic.

"PHOENIX! STOP! RIGHT! THERE!" Curt yelled out coarsely, his eyes laser-focused entirely on the large adult bobcat now circling his wife's left flank.

The animal, he determined, was probably a male as it was on the larger side and appeared to be about thirty pounds.

Wobbly on its feet, agitated, and foaming at the mouth, this bobcat was obviously rabid, which made it the most dangerous and unpredictable kind.

"Phoenix...try not to move, honey!"

"Wha—?" she replied, as she complied with his order. He knew she was close enough now to see that Curt wasn't looking at her anymore but, instead, at something behind her.

"Honey," Curt said, trying to instill greater calm than he was feeling. "Try to stay still while I look for a rock." He scanned the area around him and saw that the nearest suitable rock was some twenty feet away. He scooted slowly on his butt toward the crude weapon. "Just keep calm while I—"

For Phoenix, the next few moments passed as if in slow motion. She stood absolutely still, her heart pounding loudly in her chest, her eyes trying to search her periphery, and her ears listening for any clue as to whatever unseen horror was behind her.

From Curt's reaction, it could be a king cobra...a charging hippo...a Tyrannosaurus Rex. But they weren't indigenous to these parts. Whatever it was, she had to know.

Phoenix tightened her grip on the rubberized, ridged handle of her walking stick/baton as she slowly began her one hundred eighty-degree pivot to her left. As she'd almost completed the arc, something at ground level got her attention as it growled and lunged through the air directly at her.

"PHOENIX!!" she heard Curt scream out, powerless to act other than to shimmy on his belly toward the previously observed jagged, baseball-sized rock. In a blur of motion, the three-foot-long bobcat's razor-sharp claws had shot out from its foot pads and found purchase in Phoenix's left calf and thigh, while its long, equally-sharp canine teeth dug into the fleshy part of her hip.

Phoenix screamed out from the excruciating pain as she tried to shake the maniacal predator free. She reached for its tail, but it was only six inches long and, with the flurry of chaotic motion, impossible to grab.

She shook again, violently punching the animal in the side of the head. It growled, undeterred, the dark, pointy tufts of hair on its ears flopping as it shook. Another punch to the jowl. The bobcat momentarily fell to the ground and Phoenix, now hyperventilating, turned away to her right, but the rabid creature lunged for her again, landing on her back, inflicting another slash across her torso and a savage bite to her shoulder.

With the animal firmly latched on to her back, she was further disadvantaged. Her only means of defense, the tactical baton, was useless if she couldn't hit the creature with it. No amount of shaking seemed to free the beast so, without hesitation, Phoenix resorted to what she saw as her only hope. If she failed, her defenseless husband would also be ripped to shreds.

She pushed off with her feet, as if entering into a backflip into the pool, only with a shallower arc. Her feet shot into the air and, in the tenth of a second it took, she prepped for what she knew would be a hard landing. A deliberate back flop.

Phoenix crashed down hard, as she had hoped, directly onto her back, which got a loud roar from the dazed, thoroughly pissed off bobcat, who had taken the brunt of the landing.

The cat's grip went slack as Phoenix rolled to her side, freeing herself from the creature's claws and, in a fluid motion, raising the heavy steel rod over her head.

Bleeding from several places and with shocks of extreme pain surging from several places on her battered torso, she summoned all of her might as she fiercely brought the baton down on the animal, making contact first with its ribs, then its hip and, a split second later, delivering a blow to the creature's cheek bone.

The animal twitched, snarling and hissing in pain. Its front legs scratched at thin air as Phoenix lowered the hammer for a fourth time, the instrument's tempered steel trumping the strength of the animal's skull.

Phoenix managed to raise herself and stepped back a few feet. She let the shredded daypack slip from her shoulder and hit the ground. With the club at the ready, if need be, she looked down at her crazed adversary. Rabies foam and blood were bubbling from the bobcat's mouth as it lay there, still alive, but barely.

Phoenix had no merit badge in such things, but based on the bobcat's appearance and erratic behavior, even she could tell that this cat had to be carrying rabies.

Which meant she too had likely been infected. *Fuck!*

Lying on its side now, the bobcat trained its wide-open eye on Phoenix. Immobilized, bloodied, and batshit crazy with advanced-stage disease, it looked up at her. There was no denying its deadly intent, but it almost seemed to be pleading with her. *Kill me.*

With the last of her remaining strength, Phoenix raised the bat high overhead, took one step toward the beast, and drove home the winning run, crushing the life from it.

The severely wounded warrior Phoenix tipped her head back to the sky and let loose a primal victory scream that could likely be heard in the three neighboring states, and probably Mexico.

Curt finally had the rock in his grip and at the ready, but in the several seconds it took for the exchange to play out before him, he realized he was a day late and a rock short.

Phoenix had handled it. She had saved both of them.

And now that the brief but deadly fight was over, he could see that the victor—his wife—was severely injured. Their only hope was getting her to a hospital immediately. His injury no longer mattered to him.

Phoenix was in bad shape. She sunk down to her knees, moaning as the blood slowly oozed from her wounds. She let the baton slip from her bloodied fingers and into the dirt.

Curt was frantically crawling toward her, sobbing as he groveled across the ground, his heart breaking at the sight of his critically injured wife.

"Please, God! Save my girl!!" he cried out.

As he got to within a few feet of Phoenix, something else got Curt's attention in a big way. A deafening sound that got exponentially louder as the loose clumps of vegetation and dust started kicking up around them.

He craned his neck to the sky to get a read on the copter's location. Seconds later, the fuselage revealed itself, backlit by the sun as it emerged from behind the cliff face. With one hand he shielded his eyes from the invading dirt; he waved his other arm wildly toward the sky.

"They're here, baby! Hold on! They've seen us!" Curt cried out.

OVERHEAD
THE CHOPPER

"There!!" the officer in the second seat barked into his microphone as he pointed below them.

"I see him!!" the pilot replied, pivoting the aircraft with surgical precision. "Big guy...matches the description. Wait... are there two of them?!"

"Roger that! One male...the other...female, I think. Smaller. Might be a child. Can't tell!"

"Okay, call it in! I'll look for a spot to set her down!"

RANGER STATION
SECONDS LATER

Detective Moser was staring out the back window of the ranger shack. The Road Runner was still parked there, and nobody had eyes on Phoenix. Fuming, she resumed pacing the cheap linoleum floor, threatening to wear a hole through it, when she heard the squawk come from the ranger's radio. She stopped in her tracks as he answered it.

"This is Dutchman Ranger Station. Please repeat, over," Ranger Danger said, releasing the talk button. His eyes met Moser's as they awaited a response.

"Dutchman, this is Police Helicopter Charlie One. We've established a visual on what appears to be your missing person, male, thirties, matches your description. Over."

Danger's grip tightened on the walkie, and both his and Moser's faces lit up.

"Roger that, Charlie One! Fantastic job, officers! What vicinity? Over."

The response from the chopper was replete with the roar of the aircraft's blades in the background, which meant they were still airborne. "We're currently hovering, near the Mile 2 marker of Siphon Draw Trail. He appears to be injured. Over."

"That's a roger, Charlie One! Will notify the local hospital and have them on standby to receive the patient. Over," Danger said, already looking up the emergency number on his cellphone.

"Dutchman, be advised we have eyes on a second hiker in distress, same location. Over."

"Second hiker?" Moser muttered.

"Hiker appears to be female—can't determine age, but smaller. Advise emergency personnel to also prep for arrival of a victim of animal attack. Bobcat. Likely rabid. Over!"

POP POP'S
FIVE MINUTES LATER

"Sweet Jesus," Pop Pop said softly, his expression a mix of fear, concern, and relief.

He held the phone to his ear as he paced the kitchen, trying to remain calm for little Rose's sake, as he bussed Rose's pancake plate to the sink.

The ranger's assessment of new developments was grim,

even more so now that Phoenix was being rushed to the hospital as well. Curt had been found, thank God, but they certainly weren't out of the woods yet. Not by a long shot.

"Yes, Ranger. Thank you, sir...yes...I'll notify him. Bless you. We're on our way. Roger that," Pop Pop said, signing off, his own military training kicking in as he ended the call.

He counted to five, re-checked his facial expression, and turned to Rose.

"C'mon, honey. Let's get your teeth brushed. You and Pop Pop are going for a little ride."

"Roger that," she parroted, giggling as she bounded down the hall to the bathroom. Pop Pop waited until he heard the bathroom door close behind her, then he burst into tears.

"Thank you, Lord! Please...watch over my family."

CHAPTER TWENTY-TWO

RAMAGE'S HOVEL
GILBERT, ARIZONA
PALM SUNDAY, 11:45 AM

T HE TWO HOURS of sleep Detective Ramage had managed had been on and off and fitful at best.

He had, minutes before, given up hope on getting any more as it was doomed by his active mind. He finished rinsing the shampoo lather from his crewcut and turned off the shower spigot. A sound was coming from outside the enclosure: his phone, vibrating on the bathroom counter.

The shower door slid open as he grabbed the towel from the rod and picked up the device. He put it on speaker and set it back on the counter as he continued drying himself.

"Beth. Hey, what's going on?"

"Sorry to wake you, Jeff," Moser said. Her tone indicated her stress.

"No, you didn't. Couldn't sleep anyway. What's the latest? I can hear it in your voice."

"Lots. Curt Martinsen's been found! Chopper team located him on the Siphon. He's been medevacked to the emergency room. Dehydration and what looks like might be a busted ankle. Maybe more. Not sure yet."

"Great news that he's been found! Has his family been notified? Phoenix?"

"There's more, Jeff. They've *both* been medevacked off the hill!"

"What do you mean, both? Phoenix?"

"Yes. She went up the closed trail looking for him—unbeknownst to me or anyone else—and got into a bad fight with a bobcat. She's got an emergency team waiting for her as well. Severe lacerations and bites. Rabies, almost certainly."

"Jeez-o-Pete...gawd."

"Yeah, pretty much."

"How bad? And how sure are they it was rabid? Did the cat get away?"

"They sounded pretty sure about it. The cat didn't get away. Phoenix saw to that."

"What do you mean? Sorry, I'm still a little foggy. What happened?" Ramage replied, toweling himself off quickly.

"Phoenix kicked the bobcat's ass is what happened. She killed the damned thing, but it kicked her ass first."

"Jeezus...I'd almost forgotten how scrappy—and fucking stubborn—she can be. Pardon my French."

"No worries. Listen, I just wanted to give you the heads-up from here. It's been quite the morning. Hell, it's been quite the frigging week. Oh, and our guy, Ranger Danger? He's earned his stripes—and his name—if you ask me," Moser said.

"Concur, partner. Concur," Ramage said, picking up the

phone and taking it off speaker. "You need me up there for anything? If not, I might head back to the office."

"Nah. I'm driving to the hospital now. I'll let you know more once I—just a second, Jeff, I've got another call coming in. I'll call you back."

"Roger that, partner. I'll have my ringer on. Hey, thanks for directing traffic up there this morning. You—" he replied before realizing the call had already ended.

As soon as he'd set the phone back down next to the sink, its display lit up again, the device both vibrating and ringing, vying for his attention. But this one wasn't from Moser.

KOKOPELLI APARTMENTS
GLENDALE, ARIZONA
PALM SUNDAY, 1:10 PM

Ramage had hastily dressed, fired down a banana, and jumped in the car upon getting the call. It had taken him forty minutes to make the fifty-minute drive.

He stood on the landing outside the door of apartment 202, along with several other officers and medical personnel, as he waited for the forensics team to finish processing the scene. His head was splitting because he'd neglected to have his requisite cup of coffee. He wouldn't make that mistake again. Ever.

"You can come in now, Detective," the officer in charge

said, handing him a pair of paper booties and a pair of latex gloves.

"Thank you, Officer. What do we know?" Ramage asked, stepping into the unit, careful to avoid the two large pools of blood that had soaked into the cheap, years-old Berber carpet. The mini blinds had been opened, allowing the early afternoon sun to illuminate the otherwise dark, one-bedroom apartment.

"Single victim. Female, twenties. Positively identified as Paige Peterson, renter of the unit. Cause of death, stabbing. Slit throat," the officer replied, pulling back the sheet draping the gurney. Paige's eyes were open, staring up at them. "Defensive wound on her left hand. Looks like she tried to resist her attacker but...."

"Any determination on what type of weapon was used?" Ramage asked, pulling on his second glove.

"Judging from the depth of the cuts and the clean slash across the neck, we're looking at a larger locking-blade knife, possibly hunting style, but not serrated," he answered. "All of the kitchen knives in the knife block are accounted for. The assailant was carrying his own," the officer added, replacing the drape on the victim.

Ramage nodded, turning his attention to the front door. "Or her own..no sign of forced entry?"

"Negative. The victim knew her killer. She'd let them in, offered snacks...and boom."

Ramage rubbed the top of his head as he processed things. "So, it all happened here. In the living room. Nowhere else? The bedroom?"

"Right here. Blood spatter across the TV there indicates it went down where we stand."

"I'm gonna take a quick peek down the hall," he said, holding up his gloved hands in a show of compliance. It was a quick trip as he reached the first of two doors: the tiny bathroom. Poking his head through the door, he saw that it was devoid of blood or obvious sign of further struggle, but his attention went immediately to the open door of the over-sink medicine cabinet.

It had not just been casually left ajar; it was wide open, and the three glass shelves appeared to have been ransacked. A few plastic bottles were lying in the sink, seemingly discarded in a hasty search for something else. Aspirin. Some Pepto tablets. Also, a jar of Ben Gay.

Ramage looked at the remaining items on the shelves. It was a veritable pharmacy of prescription antidepressants and over-the-counter mood enhancer supplements. There were several gaps in the rows, indicating the perp had made a desperate med grab before leaving the crime scene.

He stepped out into the hallway and got the attention of the officer in charge.

"What can I help you with, Detective?"

"Just wondering. Besides pilfering the medicine cabinet, anything else the suspect took?"

"Just one thing," the officer replied, confirming with his notepad before elaborating.

"The victim's car keys."

WILLOW CAMPGROUND
WADDELL, ARIZONA
PALM SUNDAY, 1:40 PM

Tempest pulled the beater Fiesta into a shady area off the beaten path and killed the ignition. Obeying the posted speed limits along the way, the drive due west had taken her thirty-five minutes.

She'd had a fleeting thought along the way, along with a guilty chuckle, being as tomorrow was Monday. She felt slightly bad for her supervisor, Allison Peck, as she'd be short two employees in the morning. *I quit.*

She pulled the gas-station tuna sandwich from the paper bag on the passenger seat, peeled back the plastic seal of its container, and wondered how many days before this odd-smelling monstrosity had been prepared. And by whom. *No friggin' pickles!*

The white bread still had the crusts on it, but she didn't bother to cut them off. Her recently soiled knife still needed a proper cleaning before she'd consider that, and besides, she was starving. She held her breath, sunk her teeth into it, and almost gagged at the fishy overload.

She'd paired her meal with a tall can of Modelo Especial, and upon taking a swig to wash down the sammich nastiness, she found the awkward control handle for the recliner and eased the seat back with a clunk.

At least she was off the main roads, and she hoped she'd bought a little time before anyone found Paige—or discovered her vehicle missing.

As she suffered through her meal, she chewed on some hard truths as well.

Abby. She'd completely abandoned her daughter and with no regard as to her well-being. *Who does that?! Only the world's worst mom!!*

As she waited for the bolt of lightning to strike her dead, Tempest took stock in the knowledge she couldn't completely blame the series of recent manic decisions on her brain chemistry. Not entirely, anyway. She had abandoned her young daughter—her one connection to something...good. She had killed her own mother. And...there were the others she'd left in her wake.

She was even more damaged than she'd ever let herself believe. A tear rolled down her cheek.

It wasn't like Abby could go to live with her dad. Hell, Tempest wasn't even entirely sure who that was, considering she'd been impregnated by one of the nameless, drunken redneck foursome who'd raped her atop the pool table at Jimmy's Bar back in Louisville that night.

The four men had been transient truckers, making it difficult to identify them. To track them down. And to kill them. They'd left her lying there on the pool table, unconscious, her un-Lucky jeans gathered around her ankles. She been drenched in their semen, along with the beers they'd poured on her.

Tempest threw the remains of her heinous tuna-on-white back into the bag and, to expunge it from her memory, made short work of a whole box of Milk Duds.

She flashed back to the present, to her predicament, and her unfinished business.

She had some shit to figure out.

BANNER GOLDFIELD MEDICAL CENTER
APACHE JUNCTION, ARIZONA
PALM SUNDAY, 3:20 PM

The medical center was relatively small as hospitals go, but its proximity to the Lost Dutchman State Park had made it the emergency medical techs' default location today, as time was of the essence with rabies exposure.

It was a fifteen-minute drive, and two of the facility's twenty beds had been prioritized for the new emergency arrivals.

Curt was in the recovery room, still quite foggy after the emergency surgery to repair what X-rays had determined to be an ankle broken in three places. He didn't know it yet, but he would soon enough: he was now the recipient of a titanium plate, along with enough screws to stock an aisle at the hardware store.

Three rooms over, and unbeknownst to Curt, Phoenix had been undergoing a series of treatments for her injuries.

Detective Moser had observed the comings and goings of doctors and nurses attending to Phoenix and she couldn't help but think the poor girl looked like she'd been hit by a truck.

She had stayed well out of the way as they attended to all of Phoenix's lacerations and the vicious bites the bobcat had inflicted. It had been a flurry of activity with the medical staff thoroughly washing the all of the wounds with soap and water, as well as irrigation with a virucidal agent: povidone-iodine solution.

Immunoglobulin had been administered as a passive immunization at a dosage of twenty international units per kilograms of Phoenix's body weight, which, in her case, was ninety-five pounds.

Pop Pop now joined Detective Moser in the waiting area while a staff member supervised the little girls, Darla and Rose, in a well-equipped children's activity room nearby. The youngsters sure didn't need to see the goings-on here.

As the doctor approached, Pop Pop stopped rubbing his hands and jumped to his feet.

"How's she doing, Doctor?" he asked, barely able to contain his anxiety.

"Mr. LaFlamme, I can assure you that Phoenix is being well attended to. If there's a silver lining, it's the fact that she was admitted for care immediately after exposure and without delay. As Phoenix had not previously been vaccinated for viral rabies, I ordered post exposure rabies prophylaxis."

"Which—" Pop Pop began to ask.

"She received a tetanus shot. And the rabies vaccine to induce an active immune response with neutralizing antibodies was injected into the deltoid muscle at a dosage of one ml, as this was day zero—the first day of vaccination. Additional injections will be necessary on days three, seven, fourteen, and—possibly—day twenty-eight, but only if her immune system is found to still be compromised."

"Sweet Lord."

"It's not an easy fix with an animal attack such as this. The wounds were many, with multiple lacerations to her torso as well as deep bite sites. These have all been irrigated and cleansed to prevent infection and they'll be sutured shortly."

"Poor girl. She fought bravely," Moser said softly.

"Yes, she did. That's another silver lining. In most cases, the attacking animal gets away, making it more difficult to determine if rabies was present. In this case, the animal was found on site, deceased, and with a very clear case of late-stage rabies infection. Your daughter is a warrior, Mr. LaFlamme. She likely saved not only herself, but also her husband, and possibly others, from potential infection and even death."

"A warrior," Pop Pop replied, absorbing the doctor's assessment. "I can tell you, she is definitely that. Thank you, Doctor."

"You're welcome. Phoenix will need some time off from work while she recovers. We'll provide a doctor's letter; perhaps you can notify her employer."

"Well, that would be me," Pop Pop chuckled. "No problem there."

"Oh, and her husband, in Room Six—Curtis. He's still in recovery, but I understand his surgery went well."

"Yes, thank you. His doctor briefed us twenty minutes ago. We're grateful to you both, and your excellent staff."

The doctor smiled and shook both of their hands. "If you'll excuse me," he said as he briskly made his way over to the nurses' station.

Pop Pop slowly let out a measured breath from his ballooned cheeks. "Thank God."

"Yes, thank God," Moser replied.

CHAPTER TWENTY-THREE

BANNER GOLDFIELD MEDICAL CENTER
ROOM 6
PALM SUNDAY, 3:45 PM

CURT SLOWLY CAME out of the fog.

He blinked away some of the cloudiness, but he thought he was still dreaming when his gaze settled in on the incredible beauty standing bedside.

"Daddy!!" Rose squealed, stopping shy of jumping onto the hospital bed. It helped that Pop Pop was holding her, as he'd made sure she knew her daddy was hurt and that she could kiss him, but that was it. Pop Pop leaned forward, dipping Rose in for a shared kiss with her papa.

"Rosebud!" Curt answered in scratchy reply, his face rediscovering something to smile about. "How's my baby girl?"

"I'm not a baby! Silly!" she laughed. She studied his face, now seeing that he looked quite worse for wear. "Are you okay, Daddy?"

"I will be, sugar. I will be." Curt turned, looking up to Pop

Pop. "Hey, Pop Pop," he said, smiling weakly. His expression clearly telegraphed his need to know how his other half was.

"Good to see you, champ. The doc says your surgery went well and you'll be wearing the cast for a few weeks."

"The...cast?" Curt murmured, trying to lift his head to see the far end of the bed.

"Hey...hey. Easy," Pop Pop said, guiding his head back to the pillow. "The ankle suffered breaks in three places, so you won't be running any marathons anytime soon."

"Jeez...and Phoenix?" he whispered.

"Recovering. The cat had rabies...."

"A cat had babies?" Rose interjected. "Where are they? Can I see 'em?"

"No, honey. No kitties here," Pop Pop assured her.

"Is she...?" Curt began, his eyes pleading for elaboration.

"They got her here—got you both here—quickly, which helps. Her wounds have been cleaned, treated, and sutured. She's pretty carved up and will have to get several more shots over the next two to three weeks to ward off any complications of the infection. Your wife's a trooper, Curt. And her doctor called her a warrior, no less."

"Yeah...man, if he only knew how much of one," Curt replied, adjusting his position to see the new arrival who'd stepped into the room. "Detective Moser," he said. "A sight for sore eyes."

"That's a two-way street, Mr. Martinsen. There have been a lot of people looking for you, and we're all very relieved to have you back with your family."

"I couldn't be more grateful. Thank you, Detective," he said, his gratitude evident through his smiling eyes.

"Mr. Martinsen," the attending nurse said as she entered

the room. "How are you feeling, sir? Any pain?" she asked, smiling as her eyes scanned the monitors and the levels of the bags providing him fluids.

"I'm...mostly good, I think. This bed feels really nice right now."

"I'll bet. Better than a cave floor at least, right?"

"Way better," he replied. "And the food is too," he quipped, nodding at the lime green Jell-O cup on his tray.

"Yeah, well, we try...so, the doctor will be in shortly to explain what's next for you. And you'll be happy to know we'll been sending you home, probably in a couple of hours."

"And my wife?"

"Her doctor will be making that determination shortly, I'm sure. In the meantime, you just relax, and we'll take good care of you both.

Rose looked up at Pop Pop, signaling she'd like some more kissy time with her daddy. He smiled at her and dipped her in. "I love you, Daddy."

"So much forever, baby girl..." Curt replied softly, his tear ducts no longer able to hold back the waterworks.

BANNER GOLDFIELD MEDICAL CENTER
ROOM 3
PALM SUNDAY, 4:10 PM

Phoenix opened her eyes and surveyed her surroundings.

Her gaze traveled from the overhead fluid bags and down her drip hoses, then scanned the impressive array of gadgets constantly updating her medical stats. There was even the gizmo clipped to her index finger, plus an oxygen line to her nostrils.

What the heck happened here?

She shifted her body slightly and the multiple gauze-and-surgical-tape bandaged sites reminded her of the reality of what she'd just been through on the mountain. It hadn't been a dream.

"You've had quite a day, Phoenix," the man's voice said. She turned her head toward the source and saw a rather handsome young man in a lab coat smiling at her from beside the bed. He looked to be a few years younger than herself even, and appeared to be of Middle Eastern descent.

"Are you—"

"I'm Doctor Ansari," he said, confirming the fact that he was indeed her attending physician and not a first-year intern. "How are we feeling?"

"All things considered?"

"All things considered, yes."

"I kind of feel like I should've gotten the license number on that truck that hit me," she said, attempting a laugh, but it was accompanied by a grimace of pain.

The doctor leaned in, checking on the condition of her dressings. "I'm afraid it wasn't a truck, Miss—"

"Phoenix."

"Phoenix. I must say, you are one very lucky lady. And a very brave one. You're not the first person I've treated for an altercation with a bobcat, but you're the first one to emerge victorious. That was some cage fight, from the looks of it."

"I kind of wish I'd taken a selfie with it," she replied with a pained chuckle. "Ooooch...bragging rights and all."

"Yes, well, you suffered several lacerations—rather deep ones—and a couple of deep bites as well. They've been cleaned and sutured. They will heal."

"Scarring?" she asked, looking him in the eye.

"Likely, yes. We'll make every effort to reduce that, but... yes. Bragging rights, right?" he replied with a tight smile.

"When can I—?"

"Go home? Sorry. Didn't mean to interrupt. We will monitor you for the next couple of hours, and if all's looking well, we hope to let you return home tonight."

"When can I—?"

"We'll bring your family in shortly. I'm sure you're all anxious to see each other," he said.

"You're psychic, aren't you, Doctor?" Phoenix replied with a tiny smile.

"I'm not sure about that, but...I'll be back in to check on you again in about thirty minutes. Your nurse will help you manage any pain, and if you play your cards right, she might even bring you a gelatin cup," he said with a wink as he turned for the door.

"Don't you tease me," she replied, her ill-advised chuckle eliciting another warning. "Yowch! Holy mother—!!"

Phoenix slept fitfully for the next two hours, replaying the day's encounter in her subconscious on what seemed like a loop.

She would moan in her sleep, tossing back and forth on occasion, while her rapid eye movements indicated she was in the heat of battle with the crazed beast.

The evening attending nurse had just started her shift and noticed this as she worked quietly, monitoring her patient's fluids and vitals, and updating the chart. She was in her early forties and had a smooth, plumpish face, not unlike one of the Campbell's Soup kids.

"You poor girl," she whispered. "We've got you."

As the nurse reached up to open the privacy curtain so she could continue her rounds, a raspy utterance stopped her. She turned back to the bed and saw Phoenix looking back at her, blinking away her nightmare, and getting her bearings again. Beads of perspiration were on her brow, which the nurse wicked away with a tissue.

"What time is it?" Phoenix asked groggily.

"A little after six, hon. How're you feeling? Any pain?"

"Some, but it's okay I guess," Phoenix replied, licking her dry lips. "Thirsty."

"Here, let me help you with that," the nurse said, grabbing the water bottle from the tray and adjusting its straw as she handed it to her.

"Mmm..." Phoenix hummed her thanks as she took a swig. Then another.

"I just came on a little while ago. I'm your shift nurse, Nancy."

Phoenix handed her back the bottle. "Thank you, Nancy."

"From what I've heard, you've had quite a day," Nancy said, adding a matronly smile.

"You could say that," Phoenix said, hardly believing it herself. "Umm, I know your shift just started, but do you know when I might be able to see my husband? He's another patient here...broken ankle?"

"Ah, Curt! He's been asking about you as well, hon. Sweet man."

"Yes. He's okay, right?"

"Well, perhaps you should ask him yourself," Nancy said, flashing a toothy smile.

"Yeah?"

"If you're ready...yeah."

A knuckle rap on the door frame announced an arrival, and the sweet music of a very familiar voice accompanied it.

"Knock-knock..." Curt said from the other side of the privacy curtain.

"Oh, my God...Nancy would you please...?"

Nancy was way ahead of her, drawing the curtain's rings across the curved metal railing, revealing Phoenix's prize.

"Curt! Curt! Sweetheart...oh, my God..." Phoenix gushed, wishing she could jump out of the bed. But there was no need; Curt hobbled over with the assistance of a pair of crutches.

"I thought I'd never see you again!" Curt managed between sobs.

"Me too, baby! I knew you had to be okay! I prayed so hard!" Phoenix cried, barely getting the words out.

Curt's vision was blurry from the fountain of tears, and unable to utter anything intelligible at this point, he leaned into Phoenix and kissed her forehead and her cheeks, then rested his head against her chest as they both heaved big tears of joy.

A few seconds went by before Phoenix opened her teary eyes. Standing there, behind Curt, were her two other favorite people in the world.

"Mommy!!!" Rose squealed as Pop Pop released her hand.

"Rose! Hey, lovey! I'm so glad to see you, sweetie! Mommy missed you...and Pop Pop!" Phoenix cried out through her tears.

Rose wasn't quite sure what to make of the sight of her mama bandaged, battered, and connected to tubes. Her concern was evident. "What happened to you, Mommy?"

"Oh...I'll be okay, sweetie. Mama just got scratched up by a cat," she replied, a wink to Pop Pop who returned one.

"A cat?" Rose replied, her face scrunched up as she tried to process that scenario.

"Uh-huh...big one," Phoenix replied. "Come give your mama a kiss, baby."

Rose wasn't quite tall enough to reach, so Pop Pop lifted her closer, into the kissing zone.

"How're you feeling, champ?" he asked, trying his best to maintain his composure. It killed him to see her this way and his eyes were starting to moisten.

"Okay, all things considered, Pop Pop. Doc said I'll be getting, like, a gazillion shots, and my battle scars will take a little time to heal up. Might have to take a couple of days off work though, sorry."

"Already handled. I've got things covered. You're not going anywhere near the shop for at least the next two weeks. With pay, mind you," Pop Pop said with a reassuring smile that also said this was non-negotiable.

Nancy, who had taken a step back outside the ring, smiled, and drew the privacy curtain closed around them.

She had rounds to make and these lovely people had some catching up to do.

POP POP'S RESIDENCE
GILBERT, ARIZONA
SAME TIME

Phoenix's Road Runner had a habit of making its presence known, its throaty Hemi engine happily purring as it made its way down the block and paused at the entrance to the driveway of the LaFlamme/Martinsen residence.

The driver made the turn, slowly bringing the beast to a stop at the end of the long driveway, nearest the garage. One final rev of the engine signaled the eagle had landed, and he turned off the ignition.

The car door swung open, and Ranger Danger emerged. He closed the door, locked the vehicle with its key, and smiled as broadly as a teenage boy who'd just lost his virginity.

"My kingdom for one of these..." he muttered to himself as he patted the car's roof affectionately. He walked over to the mailbox on the porch, dropped the keys into it, and pulled out his phone. Thankfully, he lived in Gilbert, as did his twenty-year-old daughter. She picked up on the third ring.

"Hey, honey. Think you could give me a ride home?"

POP POP'S RESIDENCE
PALM SUNDAY, 8:40 PM

"Wait here. I'll be back to help you guys in a minute," Pop Pop said to the battle-scarred and weary passengers.

Phoenix and Curt remained in the truck while Pop Pop unlocked the front door to the house and brought Rose inside. The first thing Phoenix noticed as they'd pulled into the drive was that her precious Road Runner had been parked there. And, parked off to the side, was Curt's F-150.

"How—?" she started to ask before Curt interjected.

"And my truck!"

As promised, Pop Pop re-emerged from the house and made his way over to them. He opened the passenger door and assisted Curt as he labored to swing his bulky, cast-encased leg out of the cab. Pop Pop grabbed the crutches from the back and helped Curt settle into them.

"Got it?"

"Yeah...think so."

"Okay, next," he said, offering his hand and an arm for Phoenix to grab on to as she slid across the seat to its edge. "Take my arm, Feebs. I don't know where to grab you without popping your stitches...easy does it."

"'Kay...just help me down to the ground and I'll be good," she said, her tiny feet dangling over what seemed like an abyss down to the driveway.

"On three," Pop Pop said. He didn't bother counting to one and two. "Three!"

"Oof!"

"Good?"

"Mmm...yeah. Good," she said, her feet touching down on the precious, familiar pavement of home. She gestured to the cars. "How'd—?"

"Curt's truck? I got it out of impound," Pop Pop replied.

"Thank you," Curt said. "By any chance was my—?"

"Computer? Yep, it was under the seat. I brought it inside."

"Cool."

"What about my car?" Phoenix asked, clearly puzzled. "How'd it get here?"

"No idea, kiddo. Good Samaritan, I guess. C'mon. Let's get you both inside."

MOSER RESIDENCE
GILBERT, ARIZONA
PALM SUNDAY, 9:20 PM

Detective Moser picked at the vestiges of her chicken pot pie as she compared notes with her partner via speaker phone.

"And no sightings on the Fiesta?" she asked, her fork spearing a paltry piece of poultry.

"Not yet. APBs are out for her, plus the TV news stations are all over it. Not a lot of Ford Fiestas on the road, and the suspect's got to be feeling the heat. My money says she's probably skipped the state," Ramage replied. "Helluva fucking day," he added through a yawn before remembering Beth had a young daughter at home. "Sorry, you on speaker?"

"It's okay, I tucked Darla in an hour ago," Moser said, pouring a second glass from the four-dollar bottle of chardonnay she'd paired with her wannabe Hungry Detective dinner.

"Yep...a banner day."

"What about the Martinsens? They're back home?"

"Yeah, both patients were discharged a couple hours ago. No need to burden that family with buzzkill news of another victim. I'll check in with them in the morning on my way to the station. If they're not already privy to the latest development from the TV news, I'll fill them in tomorrow. In the meantime, I got assurances from their Pop Pop that they'd keep all the doors and windows locked until further notice.

"Roger that."

"Okay...unless there's anything else, I'll see you tomorrow, Jeff," she said, rubbing the day from her tired eyes.

"Get some sleep, partner. 'Night."

"Mmm...'night," she managed through a cavernous yawn as she ended the call, switched off the kitchen light, and carried her wine glass down the hall.

CHAPTER TWENTY-FOUR

POP POP'S RESIDENCE
MONDAY, 7:59 AM

POP POP STEPPED out onto the porch and fetched the newspaper, tucking it under his arm.

As he turned to go back inside, he remembered he hadn't checked the mail the day before. Opening the lid, he saw none so he reached inside the box, his fingers brushing against something. He pulled out Phoenix's keyring and smiled. Somebody deserved a big thank you.

Setting the keyring on its wall hook in the kitchen, Pop Pop made his way through the living room to make sure his little princess was making progress on her scrambled eggs and that she had a kid-friendly cartoon on.

Satisfied, he went back into the kitchen and put the finishing touches on the large breakfast tray he'd been working on. Two mugs of hot coffee, a small pitcher of creamer, a dozen sugar packets. *Check.* A plate of dry sourdough toast, assorted marmalades, two glasses of orange juice. *Check.*

A bowl of Lucky Charms for Phoenix, milk, a spoon. *Check.* Two eggs over easy, six crispy pieces of bacon, and a fork for Curt. *Check.* Marmalade knife. *Check.* Pop Pop inserted the short-stemmed rose bud into its dainty vase and smiled. *Now...don't drop the friggin' tray!*

THE GRANNY UNIT
FIVE MINUTES LATER

A light knuckle rap on the door hadn't been enough to rouse them, so a more robust one followed, accompanied by a low, deep voice, emulating a train-car porter.

"Breakfast service."

"Mmm..." came the foggy groan from Phoenix.

Another knock from the porter. "Breakfast!"

"Honey?" Phoenix said, nudging her still-snoring husband. "Curt?"

"Yeah...huh...what?" he mumbled.

"Never mind," she said, remembering he had a gimpy leg.

Phoenix pulled back the covers and slowly swung her legs over the side of the bed, eliciting complaints from several stitched-up parts of her body. "Jeez, Louise," she moaned, eventually getting to her feet and shuffling the few steps to the door. "Just a sec."

She swung the door open slowly, a broad smile stretching across her face at the sight of Pop Pop and the cornucopia of breakfast treats on the tray he was holding.

"Holy cow!"

"Breakfast for the lady and gentleman in first class," Pop Pop said, employing the porter gag for a last time.

"Pop Pop...you're the best," she said, raking her fingers through her considerable mane.

"What is it, hon?" Curt mumbled, pulling himself into a sitting position. A second later his olfactory system clued him in. "Bacon...."

"Good morning, handsome," Pop Pop said. "Time to rise and—to the best of your ability—shine. I've got *stuff*." He stepped in with the impressive spread and turned to Phoenix. "Where would you like it?"

Phoenix looked around the tiny space, which was mostly taken up by packing boxes. There was no free counter space to be had, nor even a place to sit. "How 'bout on the bed?" she shrugged with a smile.

"Breakfast in bed. When's the last time you kids had that?"

"Gawd...Hawaii...our honeymoon? A hundred years ago. Right, there's great, Pop Pop. Thanks."

Pop Pop set the tray down carefully, right next to Curt, allowing room for Phoenix to join him. "I'll just let you two enjoy a little breakfast in peace. Rose is finishing up her breakfast. I've got her entertained. Just...take the time you need. No agenda today. Okay?"

"Sounds amazing, Pop Pop. Thank you so much," Phoenix said, giving him a peck on the cheek.

"And don't forget to tip your server," Pop Pop said with a chuckle. "Oh, and almost forgot: your morning paper, miss" he said, pulling the folded newspaper from where he'd tucked it and laying it next to the tray.

Phoenix blew Pop Pop a kiss as she watched him close the door behind him, her eyes traveling back to their bounty, and to the headline above the fold:

ANOTHER SLASHING VICTIM KILLED AT HOME

WILLOW CAMPGROUND
WADDELL, ARIZONA
MONDAY, 9:05 AM

The morning was shaping up to be a beautiful one as the young park attendant whirred down the trail in the city-owned golf cart, humming to herself as she made her morning rounds along the edge of the campgrounds, her blond pony-tail flopping in the breeze.

As a first-year theatre arts/music major at Arizona State, Caitlin loved her part-time gig here. The hours were perfect, it was a zero-stress gig, and she could practice singing showtunes as she rode the paths, being mindful to keep the volume in check. You couldn't do that working at Wiley's.

Some tent campers were still sleeping, so she kept her speed—and her voice—down as she traversed the loop on her way to the off-limits tree line area, where teenagers were known to party from time to time.

The cart bounced a little as she left the main path and made her way toward the tree line. She hoped she didn't have a ton of beer bottles to pick up like she did with last week's clean-up effort. At a mere nineteen years old, she was only a year or two older than them and, having never consumed alcohol herself, she had zero empathy for partying teenagers.

*Kids.*She saw some litter up ahead and pulled to a stop alongside it. Grabbing her trash bag, she climbed out of the cart, put on her latex gloves, and picked up three items: a Modelo beer can, an empty Milk Duds box, and a half-eaten tuna sandwich in a bag.

"Not much of a party," she murmured as she bagged the items and placed them in the cart. She was just glad there weren't any spent condoms lying in the grass, like she'd found the previous weekend.

As she climbed back in, she noticed a more egregious anomaly ahead: a parked vehicle, up against the tree line, meaning the kids had not only disobeyed the posted No Parking signs, but also may have been too buzzed to drive home.

"Stoners," she sighed as she put the cart in motion, whirring toward the car. As she reached the vehicle, Caitlin hopped out and approached, fully prepared to give some hungover youngsters a good talking to, as well as issuing a very real threat of notifying their parents.

She cleared her throat loudly, announcing her arrival as she walked up to the driver's side door. The window was down, and it was immediately discernable that nobody was inside.

As she pulled out her tablet to issue a violation, something else caught her eye. On the passenger seat: smears of blood. Not a lot of it, but enough to tell something wasn't right. She reached for her radio and called it in.

POP POP'S RESIDENCE
MONDAY, 9:20 AM

Detectives Moser and Ramage were seated at the kitchen table, joined by Phoenix, Curt, and Pop Pop. The morning newspaper was sitting in the middle of the table, next to a tub of cream cheese and a plate of bagels, of which only Ramage was partaking.

Sidney was raising holy hell from her crate, down the hall where she and her four-legged siblings were sequestered.

"Sidney! Hush!" Phoenix called out. "Sorry...our terrier... you were saying?"

"We have an all-points bulletin out for the victim's car, a Ford Fiesta. As you've probably seen, both the print news and broadcast stations have run with it as well. No reported sightings as yet, but we're—"

Ramage's phone interrupted Moser's statements, getting everyone's attention as it loudly vibrated on the table. He set down his cream cheese-laden bagel to answer it. "Yeah."

Moser watched Ramage closely, as did the others, as he listened, processing the information coming in. "Waddell?" he responded, grabbing the pen from pocket and scribbling something onto his napkin. "No...yeah, that's... absolutely... yep, thanks," he said, ending the call and looking around the table. "We have the Fiesta."

CVS PHARMACY
SUN CITY, ARIZONA
MONDAY, 9:32 AM

A rather decrepit red Plymouth Voyager van entered the parking lot, drove the length of it and, its driver not seeing any law enforcement vehicles, doubled back, pulling into a spot near the entrance.

Tempest checked the rearview, surveyed her surroundings one more time, and climbed out. She didn't bother locking it, and it was her good fortune that its owner at the campsite hadn't bothered to either. The keys had even been left in the ignition. *Very thoughtful.*

A quick glance through the Plexiglas window of the newspaper dispenser confirmed her suspicions: Paige had been found. The photo of herself, alongside another of the stolen Fiesta, didn't help matters.

She pulled down on the bill of her ballcap, shielding her face from the store's cameras to the extent possible, as she entered the store. Aside from a young mom picking out Easter candy with her daughter, and a disheveled guy perusing the wine aisle, the store was devoid of customers. The bored teenage girl at the register paid her no mind.

Tempest looked at her watch. *They've probably found the car.* She planned to make this a very quick in-and-out stop. She was on a mission, and things were really heating up for her.

Tempest grabbed a red basket and, acting casually, went down the snack aisle, tossing in a few packages of Corn Nuts, several boxes of Milk Duds, and a large bag of gummi worms. From the cold case, she grabbed four tall cans of Arizona Iced Tea.

She looked down at her ratty tee-shirt with its telltale dirt stains running down its front. The small display rack of low-thread-count touristy tees provided her with her new wardrobe. They were the only XLs on the rack, and each of the three was emblazoned with I ♥ ARIZONA, which, in addition to being tacky, was a blatant lie. Didn't matter. Into the basket they went.

The end cap display of Pringles resulted in an impulse buy of four cans as she made her way to the hair color aisle. That's what she had come in for, and it took her all of fifteen seconds to make her selection from L'Oreal Paris's "Power Reds" collection:

Multi-Faceted Shimmering R57 Cherry Crush

The checker didn't even bother to make eye contact with Tempest as she mindlessly scanned the items. As the clerk scanned and bagged the final can of Pringles, Tempest handed her exact change before being asked if it would be cash or credit. She'd correctly tabulated the total in her head, even factoring the tax. She didn't like using credit, and she sure as hell didn't have a Rewards number on file.

The clerk didn't often handle cash transactions, which momentarily stumped her. She took her time sorting the bills and coins into their rightful slots in the register tray and proceeded to churn out a receipt long enough to wallpaper a room with.

By the time the receipt finished printing, Tempest was long gone.

POP'S AUTOMOTIVE
GILBERT, ARIZONA
MONDAY, 12:10 PM

Pop Pop slid the Visa card back into its slot in his wallet and hung up the phone in his office. He checked off another box on the list he'd been working on and returned the tiny note pad to his work shirt's pocket.

A quick glance at the clock told him he had five minutes to power down the foot-long turkey & avocado sandwich sitting on his desk. With Phoenix out of the line-up, Pop Pop had committed to rolling up his sleeves for the next couple of weeks. The Chrysler Imperial's brake job was all his today.

IMPOUND
GILBERT POLICE STATION
MONDAY, 12:40 PM

Detective Moser observed the forensics team as they went over the Fiesta with a fine-tooth comb. A couple of hair strands had been found on the driver's seat, and they weren't even close to matching the victim's. Prints had been lifted and blood evidence was being gathered from the fabric of the passenger seat.

Moser knew in her gut that the blood would surely be an exact match for the recently deceased Paige Peterson. The hair and fingerprints, her killer's.

Her phone vibrated and she answered on the second ring.

RAMAGE'S OFFICE
GILBERT POLICE STATION
MONDAY, 12:42 PM

"Hey, partner. How's it going over there? Any results yet?" he asked, removing the phone from the crook of his neck as he scribbled a note. "Just a sec, putting you on speaker...okay," he said, setting the phone down.

"Forensics just finished retrieving blood evidence from the

one seat. Trace hair evidence that's entirely foreign. Prints are being processed. Not expecting any surprises but doing due diligence. How about you? Anything?" Moser asked.

"Yeah. Possible. Maybe...can't be sure yet, but I think so."

"Oh?"

"The park in Waddell. What was it...?" he said, consulting his chicken scratch notes. "Willow...where they found the Fiesta."

"Yeah, what about it?"

"Might be something, might be nothing, but my ample gut tells me there's a connection. A vehicle was reported stolen there this morning. A family of campers is missing their soccer mom van, told the park staff they'd left keys in the ignition, thinking nobody would bother it."

"And we think this might be our suspect's new ride?"

"Thinking exactly that, Beth. Feeling the heat, our perp must've needed new wheels. The timing of the Fiesta dump and the van heist seems more than coincidental."

"Agreed...what're we looking for now? Wait one...got a text coming in."

"Probably the APB I issued."

"Indeed, it is. A 1989 Plymouth Voyager, red. Another in a series of sexy rides."

"Any port in the storm at this point, partner. Let me know if you get any updates. In the meantime, I'm gonna duck out and grab some Wiley's. What can I grab you?"

"Against better judgment, just get me the same as what you're having."

"Be careful what you ask for," Ramage replied with a chuckle.

RAMAGE'S OFFICE
GILBERT POLICE STATION
MONDAY, 1:25 PM

Detective Ramage was clearing a stack of file folders from his side table and pulling up a chair for his partner when she entered the room.

"Perfect timing," he said. "Getting you set up over here, so you'll have room to spread your stuff out."

"Whatever you ordered, it smells pretty great," Moser said as she closed the door behind her and watched as he set two food bags at her table and another two on his desk for himself. He handed her one of the two large chocolate milkshakes, each with an inordinate amount of whipped cream peeking through the top of its clear domed lid.

"Good lord, how much food did you order?"

"Mmm...I was starved, and, well, I duplicated my order per your request. Sit."

As she took her seat, Ramage handed her an impressive stack of napkins. "Gonna need these."

Ramage sunk into his chair, methodically spread four napkins across his desk, and with the lustful look of a junkie prepping a speedball, he retrieved four items from his to-go bags and laid them out before him. He looked up and saw his partner watching him, her jaw slightly open.

"What?"

"Not to sound unappreciative, but for the love of God, please tell me you didn't get me all of...that," she said. Ramage's sheepish expression confirmed that he had done just that.

"Double-double Wiley, extra cheese, extra spread, extra

grilled onions—on yours—two tacos, which were only a buck, and large Wiley fries," he clarified. "Please, just do the best you can," he said, sinking his teeth deep into his burger.

Moser shook her head slightly as she unwrapped her burger, unsure just how she was expected to get her mouth around it. "Thanks, Jeff," she said appreciatively, knowing her diet had just been run off the rails.

"Mmm..whadjufindowtfromfrenzix?" came his completely unintelligible query.

Moser took a dainty bite and looked at her partner with amazement, and not the good kind. While she waited for him to finish masticating, she savored her own bite and managed to eat two fries before he came up for air.

"Sorry...what did you find out from forensics?" he said, wiping his mouth.

"Waiting on hair analysis, but blood's confirmed as the victim's. Prints, our perp's.

"Mmm."

"Like I said, no surprises there," she replied, attempting to suck the mud-like shake through its inadequate straw. "Any sightings on the soccer van?"

"Uh-uh, but we've cast the net wide. She might be laying low...or might be getting the hell out of Dodge." He grabbed three fries and made short work of them. "If she's smart," he continued, "and thus far she has been, she probably wants to leave the Grand Canyon State in her rearview. Alerts are up for Nevada, Utah, New Mexico. Sonora, Mexico too."

Moser nodded as she set down the burger. It tasted great, but there was no way she'd be able to put a dent in it without dislocating her jaw. She wasn't a python. Instead, the tacos were calling, and she poked one of them halfway out of its grease-soaked sleeve.

"Remind me again. Any other known family?" she asked, taking her first crunchy bite.

"Not anymore. I mean, we know about Mom...killed her. Dad died years ago. Daughter...abandoned her. Boyfriend...likely mulched him. Don't think there's anybody left. Which doesn't help us anticipate her likely next move," Ramage replied, taking a loud slurp.

"Think she'd stick around here?"

Ramage popped a fry and considered his answer.

"Let me just say this," he began. "Based on the empty pill bottles and random assortment of meds found in her abandoned van—plus those she may've pilfered from Miss Peterson's apartment—our perp's self-medicating. Desperately. She's probably popping this shit like SweeTarts. Her irrational decisions and manic behavior seem to be fueled by whatever's coursing through her veins at any given moment. It makes her that much more unpredictable."

Moser wiped greasy fingers on a napkin and looked her partner in the eye as she replied.

"And that much more dangerous."

CHAPTER TWENTY-FIVE

POP POP'S RESIDENCE
THE GRANNY UNIT
MONDAY, 5:45 PM

PHOENIX FINISHED PUTTING the lion's share of her impressive cassette tape collection into the second of two medium-sized packing boxes and folded the four flaps closed on each.

The collection represented the soundtrack of her life so far. She'd been creating her own mix tapes since she was in the sixth grade, which was when Pop Pop had first shared his passion, and taught her the mastery of the cassette recorder's pause button.

Save the two mix tapes she still had in the car, this was all of them.

Reaching for the packing tape dispenser, another twinge of sharp pain told her she was definitely violating the abundantly clear doctor's orders she'd been issued. *No physical activity.*

Not wanting to risk popping her stitches, or worse, she decided to call it a day. She'd managed to pack almost all her clothes, save what she'd need to keep out for the rest of the week. And she'd done the same for Curt's.

She'd bagged and tossed both hers and Curt's "adventure" clothes in the outdoor bins. Hers were torn to ribbons, and she didn't need any reminders of how they'd gotten that way. That's what scars were for.

Curt was lying on the bed, where he'd been catching zees for the past couple of hours. Based on how loudly he was snoring, she knew the extra-strength Vicodin he'd been prescribed for pain was knocking him out pretty good.

His massive arm was draped across their tiny daughter, who had tucked herself into his armpit for a nap with her daddy. Phoenix smiled at the sight of the two of them lying together.

Phoenix wiped some perspiration from her brow as she padded over to the bathroom. She stood at the sink, staring into the mirror, as she psyched herself up for changing out of her sweaty ASU tee shirt. She figured now was as good a time as any, since Rose was crashed out, and she didn't want her daughter further traumatized by the extent of her mommy's injuries.

The thought served to remind her she needed to check in with Rose's therapist later in the week. Phoenix had had to cancel Rose's last appointment with zero notice, but she figured she would understand. A few things had come up.

Setting her fresh change of clothes atop the toilet tank in the tiny bathroom, Phoenix counted down from five and it was all she could do not to scream out from the pain as she pulled the tee over her head.

She let it fall to the ground. As painful as that maneuver had been, it paled in comparison to seeing the multiple gauze-covered sites of her sutured lacerations and bites.

The bruising was intense as well, the carnage extensive, and the sum effect made it look like she'd been hit by a frigging semi and spit out from its rear wheels.

It was at-once shocking, and a gut punch to see the amount of devastation her tiny body had endured. She gasped to catch her breath, then immediately spun toward the toilet, getting the bowl's lid open just in time.

Curt was still sawing logs and, amazingly, Rose was still asleep, undisturbed by his chainsaw.

Phoenix seized the moment to give herself a quick sponge bath at the sink and checked her gauze dressings. She was scheduled for her second rabies shot on Wednesday, which would be "Day 3" of the regimen. They would also assess the status of her wounds then, she figured.

As she counted forward to what would be the follow-up vaccine shot on "Day 7," her shoulders sunk a little at the thought it would fall on Easter Sunday. Rose had been looking forward to the community Easter Egg Hunt that morning and, come hell or high water, Phoenix was determined to be there with her, along with Pop Pop and hop-along Curt.

The display on her phone lit up, signaling an incoming call, and she picked it up off the counter. She'd had the ringer off so as to not disturb Curt.

"Hey, Pop Pop," she answered in a soft voice.

"Hey, hon. Everything okay there?" he replied.

"Yeah. Mostly. Curt and your little Rosebud have been

lights-out for most of the afternoon and I'm gonna wake them here in a minute," Phoenix said, grimacing as she slipped on a fresh shirt. "Cleaning myself up a little and wishing I'd gotten the license number on that frigging sabretooth tiger. It ain't pretty, Pop Pop."

"Aw, I'm sure it isn't, sweetie. But we'll get you healed up; I promise. Plan on me taking you for your shot on Wednesday, okay?"

"'Kay. Thanks, Pop Pop."

"Say...I hope you guys have an appetite because I'm bringing home some righteous chow. Leaving the shop now and have one other stop to make along the way. Should be home around seven."

"'Kay. Another stop?"

"Yeah, but it'll be brief. Oh, and do me a favor: set another place at the table, okay?"

"Wait...who—?" she'd started to ask, but the call had already ended.

POP POP'S RESIDENCE
MONDAY, 7:10 PM

Pop Pop pulled his truck into the driveway, coming to a stop at the halfway point. Curt's F-150 was parked on the cement pad to the side of the garage, which was usually his place, but he'd forgotten Phoenix's Road Runner was still parked outside of the garage. At seventeen feet long, it didn't leave him much room. He tucked in close behind her bumper.

Pop Pop killed the ignition and turned to his passenger, gesturing for the three large plastic take-out bags.

"I'll take those. Thanks. Mind waiting here for a second?"

"Not at all," the passenger replied.

"Be right back," Pop Pop said, smiling through the window as he closed the driver's door and proceeded toward the house. With a little effort, he managed the screen door's handle and squeezed through, bags and all, before it lazily closed behind him.

Phoenix was placing a fifth set of utensils at the kitchen table as Pop Pop entered.

"Hey, Pop Pop," she said, smiling as she watched him lay the bags of culinary treasures on the counter by the sink. "Table for five...I brought in the office chair, hope that's okay."

"Hey, kiddo. That's perfect," he replied, returning the smile as he did a quick inventory of the bags' contents. "It's all here. Got some extra too. Umm, be right back," he said as he disappeared through the screen door.

Phoenix cocked her head to the side as she saw him scurry back outside.

Did you get a keg of beer too?

She shrugged and made her way down the hall to check on her little munchkin's progress with the toothbrush.

"How're we doing, honey?" Phoenix called out as she neared the bathroom.

"Gooww," Curt answered through a mouthful of toothpaste foam. He spat into the sink and scooped up a handful of water from the running spigot, rinsing with it. "Good."

"Rose already brushed?" she asked from the doorway.

"Yeah. She's playing with her dolls. Pop Pop back?"

"Just got here. Food's gonna get cold. I'll get Rose...meet you in the kitchen in a minute, okay?"

"Okay. Maybe two minutes...mind grabbing me those?" Curt asked, pointing to the crutches propped up in the corner, next to the toilet.

"Here," Phoenix said, handing them over and smiling as she gave him a kiss and exited.

Curt tucked one crutch under each armpit and, grabbing their handles firmly, began gimping his way, bumping his injured leg on the doorjamb in the process.

"Jeeeezzusssholymotherofcries!" he hissed through clenched teeth, trying not to cry.

Phoenix was holding Rose by the hand as they rendez-voused with Curt in the hallway.

"You okay, Daddy?"

"Never better, baby girl," he lied through a strained smile.

As the three of them entered the kitchen, they saw Pop Pop standing there with a goofy grin, his hand resting on the screen door's latch handle.

"What's going on, Pop Pop?" Phoenix asked, trying to read his expression. "You hire a mariachi band or something?"

"Not quite." Pop Pop chuckled, nodding a signal outside.

Phoenix and Rose tucked in next to Curt as they all watched the screen door slowly open and a very familiar visitor step into the kitchen. Their three jaws slacked as Rose ran to him.

"Grandpa!!!" she shrieked as she jumped up into his waiting arms. "Grandpa!!"

"My dear, dear Rose," Len Martinsen said, embracing his granddaughter warmly. "It is so good to see you, angel. And look how big you're getting!" he added, smiling warmly as he gently set her back down to earth. "Goodness!"

From her crate down the hall, Sidney was already barking bloody murder at the sound of a stranger.

"Sidney, hush!" Phoenix called out to her. "Sorry...our resident rug rat."

Len's gaze swept across the kitchen, his smiling eyes settling on both Phoenix and his son.

"Oh, my God," Phoenix said in disbelief, her hand covering a huge smile.

"Phoenix," Len responded warmly, his arms held wide to receive her hug. "Phoenix, my dear," he gushed, mindful not to hug her too hard. Pop Pop had clued him in to her injuries. "When I heard what happened...I've been on pins and needles," he managed, near tears.

Pop Pop watched the reunion from his spot by the door; his own tears welling up.

"Dad!" Curt chimed in, hobbling over. Tears were already forming, and he was unapologetic for them as they rolled down his cheeks. "Dad."

"Curt...how's my favorite son?" Len replied, robustly hugging the clone of himself.

"Your only son," Curt said through a chuckle. He closed his eyes, experiencing the moment for all that it offered. Which was a lot. This was another face Curt thought he'd never get a chance to see again, as he'd contemplated his cruel fate in that dark cave.

Len came out of the hug and gently cradled his son's face in his hands. He looked deep into his eyes, kissed his cheek, and whispered, "I love you, son."

"I love you too, Dad."

A group hug ensued, with Pop Pop joining in. The last—and only—time this group had been fully assembled had been that Christmas, nearly a year and a half before, as Len had surprised them all with his visit here.

It had served as his introduction to his new daughter-in-law and had reestablished his long-dormant relationship with his then-estranged son. Not to mention their then-six-year-old daughter, Rose, and Phoenix's Pop Pop.

Being here again with everybody was nothing short of magic for Len. For everyone.

It wasn't the time, or the place to mention it—nor did they need to. They all felt it as they held the hug, their appreciation for each other, and the moment, unspoken.

Len hadn't been a part of it, but he knew all too well that the team assembled here, assisted by Pop Pop's old Navy buddy, Murf, had narrowly rescued young Rose from the clutches of monsters who had only the worst intentions for her.

Rose, and the dozen other young girls whose rescue they'd helped facilitate, were victims of trafficking, and had been assembled for the selfish, perverted, and evil gratification of sexual deviants. It was nothing short of a miracle that she'd been saved before her innocence and purity could be forever spoiled, and these four adults each recognized it as such as they finished the hug.

"Let's eat!" Rose chirped a moment later, her innocent statement serving as the group's transition. "Grandpa gets to sit next to me!! Okay, Mommy?"

"Of course, sweetie," Phoenix nodded, wiping away a tear.

"I'd like that very much, sweetheart!" Len said, as they shuffled over to their spots at the table.

"Is it okay if Daddy sits on your grandpa's other side?"

Curt asked, letting go of his crutch's handle long enough to pat Rose's head.

"I guess so," she replied with a chuckle.

"Good," he said, pulling out the chair and awkwardly settling into it. Phoenix collected his crutches and propped them up in the corner.

"This is such an amazing surprise!" Phoenix said, smiling as she took a seat across from Len. "It seems the only time we get our dearest people together is when we've been faced with a tragedy of some sort. Goodness."

"Well, you folks are obviously just starved for attention," Len said, adding a wink.

"Clearly," Curt said with a chuckle.

Pop Pop was at the counter, organizing the food orders but listening to the conversation. He looked over his shoulder to Len. "Want to tell 'em what you told me on the way over?"

Len nodded, cleared his throat, and looked around the table.

"What is it, Dad?"

"Don't keep us in suspense, Len," Phoenix said.

"Okay then," he began. "Well, I've come to the conclusion that we don't see nearly enough of each other."

"That's for sure," Phoenix said.

"And, well...."

"And...?" Curt quipped.

"I've decided to list the condo in Castle Rock and see about finding a place that's closer to family. Closer to you all," Len said, searching their faces for any hints of disapproval.

"Are you kidding?!" Phoenix almost squealed. "That would be amazing!"

"We'd love that, Dad," Curt said. "Wouldn't we, Sunshine?" he added, a big smile for Rose.

"Grandpa, I want you to move here and stay with us and live with us and sleep with us and do fun things with us and take me to the park and eat with us and stay with us!" Rose said, weighing in with an enthusiastic run-on reply.

"Wow...that sounds like a very nice invitation, Rose! Thank you. I think your grandpa will start looking to see if there's a house he can live in that's near to your house. Would that be okay?"

"Yeah!" came the choral response.

"All for it," Pop Pop said as he began distributing the entrees. Phoenix was ecstatic for her cheese enchiladas with green sauce, as was Rose with her two tacos. Len, not being familiar with the food, had requested an order of "whatever Curt's having," and he already knew he was going to love it.

"Hey, people, there's extra rice and beans on the counter. Help yourselves to the pitcher of margaritas on the table," the host offered.

"Yay!" Rose chirped.

"All except you, squirrelly girl," he replied with a laugh.

"Hey!"

"I'll get you some lemonade, honey," Phoenix said, grabbing a carton from the fridge. "That other juice is for grownups."

"It's grownup juice?"

"Yes, honey. When you're a grownup, someday, you can try some...maybe...when you're about forty," Phoenix said, which got a laugh from Len.

Curt eagerly watched as Pop Pop carried over a heaping plate that he hoped was his. As it was set in front of him, Curt's senses went into overload.

The aromas were otherworldly, and the sight of his favorite dinner in the world, the adovada rib flautas, brought a tear to his eye. Only he knew just how important this meal was to him tonight, as he'd obsessively thought of it during his stint in the cave. Other than his family, it was one of the few things he'd held out hope for, and it had helped see him through.

Pop Pop brought over his own plate of carnitas and took a seat. "Okay, who'd like to say grace?"

"Me! Me!" Rose declared, her hand shooting up like she'd been asked to solve a math problem.

"That would be very nice, honey," Pop Pop said, holding out his hands to initiate a circle. When all hands were joined, he cued her. "Whenever you're ready, sweetie."

Rose closed her eyes, cleared her throat, and launched into her best run-on prayer ever.

"Thank you, God, for bringing Grandpa here so he can live here and play here with me and for bringing Daddy back to us, and, and please make his foot feel better, and thank you for Pop Pop, and for helping Mommy win the fight with the mean cat...and for this food. And for Grandpa. Amen.

"Amen," came the choral response as they shared winks.

CHAPTER TWENTY-SIX

POP POP'S RESIDENCE
THE GRANNY UNIT
TUESDAY, 8:05 AM

PHOENIX STIRRED, HAVING slept fitfully.

She blinked her eyes open, confirming that it was Rose's hand lying across her face. With Len spending the night in Pop Pop's office/guest room, Rose had slept here, sandwiched between her and Curt.

It was a tight fit, but Phoenix could see light at the end of the tunnel when Rose had her own bedroom and she and Curt had their own room with a locking door. *This week!*

Phoenix handed Rose's arm back to her and swung her legs over the side of the bed as she psyched herself up for what she expected would be a painful exit. *Three...two...one...*

"Oooch..." she whisper-screamed. She thought she heard voices outside and got confirmation as she peeked through the miniblinds. Pop Pop and Len were filling the back of his truck with packing boxes.

Phoenix smiled and walked out to the driveway as she tousled her hair and pulled up the waist of her Scooby jammies. "Wow, you guys," she said, punctuating with a yawn. "Sorry..."

"'Mornin', kiddo," Pop Pop said, adding another box to the load and stepping down from the bumper. "Hope we didn't wake you."

"Nuh-uh, you didn't."

"Good morning, Phoenix," Len said with a smile as he initiated a hug.

"Good morning. Gosh, thank you both so much for doing this. Len, we didn't mean to put you to work while you're here."

"It was Len's idea, honey," Pop Pop said, grabbing what might be the last box to fit this load. "Besides, neither you nor Curt are supposed to be lifting anything heavier than your toothbrushes, so we're happy to help."

"That's right," Len said. "Least we can do. And after all that's happened, I'm never letting you three out of my sight again." He winked at her, but his expression made it clear that he meant it.

"You're the best," she replied to both. "You going in today, Pop Pop?"

"Yeah, we're going to drop these things off at your apartment. Then I want to treat Len to a proper pancake breakfast afterward. He wanted to see the shop, so we'll probably be gone for a few hours," he said, draping a rope across the boxes and securely cinching it to a cleat.

"Anything you need while we're out?"

"Mmm. Maybe a couple bottles of Sunny D. If you don't mind," she said, selling it with a smile.

"Roger that," Pop Pop said before turning to Len. "Ready, Freddie?"

"I was born ready."

"Okay then. Oh, and Phoenix...meant to ask..."

"Yeah, what is it Pop Pop?"

He gestured for her to come over to where he was. As she came alongside, she noticed the Road Runner was listing slightly.

"Did you know you've got a deep slash in your right rear tire?"

"What?"

"See for yourself," he said, squatting down as he pointed to the terminal gash in the sidewall.

"*What. The. Hell...?*"

QUAIL RUN APARTMENTS
APARTMENT 133
GILBERT, ARIZONA
TUESDAY, 8:50 AM

Pop Pop and Len hefted the final two packing boxes from the bed of the truck and made their way around the corner to the open apartment door. Thankfully, they'd scored an end spot in the parking garage, nearest the unit, and it was even better that it didn't involve any schleps up the stairs.

"Where you want this one? See a marking anywhere?" Len asked, trying not to sound winded.

Pop Pop set his own box down in the kitchen area and scanned the one Len was holding. Phoenix had marked them pretty clearly thus far.

"Let's see...looks like you got the heavy one. Turn the box for me?"

Len spun the box ninety degrees to the left. Still no marking.

"One more time." Pop Pop said as Len complied. A neat annotation in felt tip marker appeared. "There: 'Rose's Room.' Second room there. Thanks, buddy."

"Thanks," Len replied, placing the box on the floor next to what would be Rose's closet. There were two sealed, oversized cardboard cartons already there, both with the manufacturers' markings on them. One contained a Weber three-burner gas grill and the other a tabletop pizza oven.

"Looks like the kids'll be eating well," Len said, stepping back out into the living room area.

"Yeah...that is, once I find time to assemble the barbecue. Lord knows it'll have a gazillion pieces. It's a surprise—as is the pizza oven—so mum's the word on those, por favor."

"My lips are sealed, my friend. Hey, if you want, after work, we can swing back by here and I'll help you bang that out. I'm pretty handy with instruction manuals. Got tools?"

"Tools, I've got plenty of. Time, not so much. That's a hell of an offer, Len. May just take you up on that. You're sure...?" Pop Pop asked.

"I've never been so sure in my life, buddy. It'll make a helluva housewarming gift. Speaking of which, I'd love to chip in. Can I at least reimburse you for the pizza oven?"

"Aw, that's a nice offer but you don't—"

"No. I insist," Len cut in. "Please. I feel strongly about it. I'd like nothing better, and I'll get them some pizza-making tools to go with it. Deal?" Len pressed, his smile impossible to resist.

"Roger that," Pop Pop said, patting his new BFF on the shoulder as they walked out and locked the door.

POP POP'S RESIDENCE
TUESDAY, 7:55 PM

Phoenix was standing at the kitchen sink when she saw Pop Pop's headlights enter the driveway and the truck pulling forward all the way to the garage door. There was room now that the Road Runner wasn't parked there.

In between his other duties, Pop Pop had made a few calls from the shop: one to his favorite tire supplier, another to a tow truck owner who owed him a favor, and the last to Phoenix asking her to make her keys available to the guy when he showed up.

Pop Pop, bless him, had ordered her not one, but a whole set of four new tires for her ride, and it wasn't anywhere near her birthday.

Phoenix finished drying the last of the dishes the three of them had used and would've literally skipped out the door to meet him if she wasn't all banged up.

Len was with him, as he'd accepted the gracious invitation to stay there the rest of the week in the office/guestroom while he researched some properties. Longer, if needed, as there would be ample room in the soon-to-be-vacated granny unit.

"Pop Pop!"

"Hey, kiddo! Sorry we're later than I said. I hope you guys worked the leftovers," he said, giving her a gentle hug.

"We did. Hey, Len!" Phoenix said as he came up to join them.

"How're you three getting along, sweetie?" Len asked, his expression showing genuine concern.

"We're limping along but, you know, one day at a time. Tomorrow's my next shot, and I'm all about having doctors sticking needles into me," she said with a chuckle as she hugged him. As they all walked to the door, Phoenix turned her attention back to Pop Pop, unable to contain her enthusiasm as she slipped into shop talk.

"Pop Pop, you are the best! Oh, my God, I can't believe you got me a set of 235/60/15s all around, and with the white lettering. I'll pay you back, I promise," she said as they entered the kitchen.

"I wouldn't think of it, kiddo. Tread was marginal on the two front ones anyway, so it made sense to put new shoes on all of 'em at the same time. Decided you needed a front alignment too, so...Merry Christmas!"

"Love you!" Phoenix beamed.

"Love you more," Pop Pop said, and he was confident in that fact.

"Hey, Dad," Curt said from his place at the table. "Excuse me if I don't jump up," he added, gesturing to the massive cast on his outstretched leg. "I'm a bit gimpy."

"No need, son," Len said, coming over and leaning into a hug. "How's the pain?"

"Mmm..Vicodin makes me groggy as all get out, but I could swear it was a sugar pill. Ankle still hurts like hell, and—"

"Hey!" Rose yelled out from down the hall.

"Sorry, honey. I meant to say *heck*," Curt called back to her, giving his father a wink.

"She is something, I'll tell ya what," Len replied warmly.

"Dogs been out for a potty break recently?" Pop Pop asked as he finished washing his hands.

"Been a couple hours. You mind taking 'em?" Phoenix said, employing an impish smile.

"No worries, I'm on it," Pop Pop said, kissing her on the forehead before heading down the hall to liberate the beasts.

"Super nice about the tires, hon," Curt said as Phoenix came behind his chair and rested her hands atop his shoulders.

"Yeah...we're both pretty darn lucky to have such great papas," she answered, smiling broadly and making sure Len had heard her.

His smiling eyes told her he had, and the three of them shared a lovely five seconds before they heard Pop Pop's voice yelling from down the hall.

"Hey!! Easy!"

This was immediately followed by a stampede of doggies galloping into the kitchen.

Luke's crazy energy was akin to a bull in a China shop, while (P)Rick trotted in like the country gentleman—while making it known he still had to pee, and Sidney was in Fujita Scale 5 tornado mode, growling and spinning around in tight circles with a blur of energy that threatened to knock down anything in her path.

"Sorry, guys," Pop Pop said as he scurried in behind them, leashes in hand.

"Oh, my..." was all Len could manage.

"Yeah...." Phoenix sighed.

SUN DEVIL CINEMA
PEORIA, ARIZONA
WEDNESDAY, 10:10 AM

The tall chick with the cherry burst hair had the whole theater to herself.

With her hoodie pulled up over her head, Tempest sat in the centermost seat, her feet up on the armrests of the seat in front of her, and her gooey right hand working the bucket of "butter" popcorn she knew must really be doused in something more akin to Pennzoil. She'd dumped three whole boxes of Milk Duds into the bucket to make it her own.

Parking the red van behind the building, she'd opted for the first showing at this second-rate theater complex, as it was showing a second run of a third-rate movie. She hadn't even considered which one; she just needed a place to lay low and think, and she'd already seen *Monsters vs. Aliens*—and with her daughter—which only served to remind her of what a shitty mom she was. *Fuck.*

Her bargain matinee ticket had a gem in store for her today: *He's Just Not That Into You.*

As she chomped into another toxic handful, she shook her head, not appreciating the irony of its title. *Figures...and Ben Affleck...gawd.*

Tempest lasted for all of five minutes before she tuned out the movie completely, her self-medicated mind having little success at making sense of the whirlwind of emotional highs and lows as she set about planning her next move. All rationality was out the window.

Her planning session was briefly interrupted by a gangly, pimply-faced teenaged boy shining a weak flashlight in her face.

"Sir, please take your feet off the seats. Company policy," said the wannabe sheriff.

"Sure thing," Tempest replied as she tucked her feet back onto the floor and the boy walked back up the aisle. *You can go back to changing the motor oil in the popcorn machine.*

Considering her current mood, it was probably lucky for them both she'd left her knife in the glove box of the minivan. *Sir.*

BANNER GOLDFIELD MEDICAL CENTER
APACHE JUNCTION, ARIZONA
WEDNESDAY, 11:15 AM

Phoenix was grateful to be in the capable hands of Nurse Nancy as she replaced the last of the new bandages on her wounds. This one, the deep bite to her left hip, along with the slash across her left thigh, had taken the longest to inspect, and Phoenix could see the concern on her face.

"I mean, they're still all very fresh—we're only starting Day 3—but, all things considered, they look...good. No evidence of further infection, though it'll be a while before they're pretty again."

"So, no jumping jacks for a while, then," Phoenix quipped, a desperate attempt at humor to avoid throwing up at the sight of the stitches.

"Yep, and no twelve-count burpees until further notice," Nancy said with a wink. "You can put your shirt back on. I'll be right back with your Day 3 vaccine," she added, stepping out of the patient room and closing the door behind her.

Phoenix had deliberately worn a loose-fitting button-up Hawaiian shirt she'd brought back from their honeymoon trip. She rarely wore it as she generally preferred tees, plus there was the tacky pineapple pattern, but this might just become her favorite article of clothing for the next few weeks.

She buttoned the front and, her feet dangling over the paper-covered patient bench seat, she perused the many shiny items and the walls' medical posters. The Human Body poster was particularly interesting as it afforded her an artist's three-dimensional rendering of all the muscle and dermis groups the bobcat had torn to smithereens.

A tiny tap on the door announced Nurse Nancy and she had a big needle with Phoenix's name on it.

"Oh, joy," Phoenix said, grimacing for effect.

"Aw, it's not that bad. We'll just have our Day 3 injection today, then we'll see you back here in a few days for your Day 7, and...you get a week off before the Day 14 shot. Easy-peasy."

"Easy-peasy," Phoenix muttered, looking away as she rolled her short sleeve up all the way. She wasn't entirely sure which she hated more: the bobcat, or the frigging needles.

CHAPTER TWENTY-SEVEN

POP'S AUTOMOTIVE
GILBERT, ARIZONA
THURSDAY, 11:35

W ITH THE NEW rubber installed, the wheels balanced, and her front alignment complete, all the Road Runner needed was a little extra cosmetic love to be ready for her closeup.

A simple car wash wouldn't do, Pop Pop decided, so he called in another favor with a customer for whom he'd given a discount on a transmission rebuild a while back. The guy also happened to own a detailing shop a block away, so Pop Pop dropped the car off with him and decided to grab a plate of Pad Thai at the hole in the wall next door. He'd be dining alone today, as Len was doing his own thing.

So as to not be burdensome to his hosts, Len had rented a little Nissan SUV for getting around. He'd already helped Pop Pop deliver a second load of boxes to the apartment that morning, so he'd decided to use the rest of the day to check out the local neighborhoods.

He'd ponied up for the optional dashtop Garmin GPS unit, which helped him navigate the grid and get a feel for area. He'd decided, as a single person and recent retiree, he didn't need a ranch house, and he sure as hell never wanted to mow another lawn. So, he'd decided a two-bedroom condo would work nicely, as long as it had a nice community pool and ideally was within five miles of his new family.

He might be getting ahead of himself, he realized, but he visualized lots of pool play dates with his granddaughter, Rose, and made a mental note to add a pool noodle, some water wings, and a floatie to his shopping list. He'd be picking up the pizza oven utensils on the way home.

POP POP'S RESIDENCE
THURSDAY, 4:55 PM

Phoenix rounded the corner and was three houses away when she heard a very familiar sound.

To her, it was the most beautiful sensory experience in the entire world, and a moment later, its unmistakable source came into view, slowly driving past her and the three pooches on its way to the driveway.

A playful *MEEP-MEEP* honk announced the return of her chariot, and it looked like it must have when it had just rolled off the assembly line in Detroit, some thirty-eight years before. The golden hour sun washed the newly detailed Hemi orange paint in its warmth, and the white lettering on the new tires enhanced the showroom-ready Road Runner's stunning looks.

Phoenix laboriously bent down to pick up Prick and carry him the rest of the way. He was showing more signs of aging every day, she realized, and she had to remember he was like 105 in human years. Luke and Sidney were good and tired, having made a four-mile circuit, and were panting as the pack walked up the drive.

Pop Pop cut the engine, climbed out, and gently closed the driver's door.

"What do you think, kiddo?" he asked, the answer already obvious as Phoenix's gaping jaw provided the reaction he had hoped for.

"Oh. My. Gawd...look at you!" she said as she admired her beautiful baby, now fully restored to a level she'd never before seen. "Pop Pop," she managed, tears welling as she sunk her head into his chest, her arms wrapped around his waist. With the leashed dogs, it made for quite the group hug. "Thank you so much...I love it...and I love you even more!"

"You're more than welcome, sweetie. It's my pleasure," Pop Pop said with a broad smile. "By the way, she got a full detail—inside and out—from the best guy in town, so she's as close to factory fresh as they come, I think. After we put the pooches away, come back out and take a look under the hood."

"Steam cleaned too?" she asked, her eyes wide.

His grin answered her question. "C'mon, let's get these guys inside," he said, grabbing Luke's leash. "Len should be rolling up soon. He called me on the way home and said he was picking up Chinese."

"Woo-hoo!"

Curt had tried his darndest, but after five unsuccessful minutes with his chopsticks, he'd thrown in the towel, resorting to his tried-and-true utensil of choice, the fork. The pineapple veggie-fried rice in particular, he'd found, was impossible to shovel properly with two pieces of wood.

It didn't matter that his seven-year-old daughter had already achieved mastery in this, her first attempt. He was starving and wasn't at all bothered to be the only one not observing tradition.

Rose adroitly delivered a bite of veggie chow mein to her mouth without dropping a single noodle and smiled proudly across the table to Len, her new BFF.

"Good job, sweetheart," he said with a wink of encouragement. "You're doing a better job with those than I am, and I'm a hundred years old," he quipped.

"You're a *hundred...*?"

"Nah, just kidding...but it feels like it sometimes," he replied, looking around the table.

Phoenix finished the last of her curried vegetables and set down her implements. "So, Len, how'd it go out there today? Anything of interest?"

Len set down his half-eaten spring roll, swallowing before speaking, as he'd been taught a hundred years ago to never talk with a mouthful.

"Mmm. Funny you should ask," he replied, pausing for effect while taking a long pull on his bottle of Tsingtao beer. He set the half-full vessel down and smiled. "It went pretty well."

Two sets of chopsticks and one fork shifted into idle as the adults at the table waited for elaboration. Rose continued to shovel.

"Well? You're killing us here," Phoenix said with a chuckle.

"Well, I liked one neighborhood in particular about four miles north of here. Close to a Veterans' hospital, one of those Sprouts markets and, most importantly, close to you all."

"Sounds great, Dad. I hope you find something you like there," Curt said, picking up his fork again and attacking his sweet and sour pork.

"Oh, I did..." Len replied cryptically, crunching in on the second half of his spring roll.

"When you get serious about your search, let me know, Len," Pop Pop said. "I know a great realtor who knows the market. I did some carburetor work on her Mercedes, and—"

"—and I made a contingent offer today!" Len cut in, with a Cheshire Cat grin.

"Wait...what!??" Phoenix blurted. "You...say that again?"

"Made a cash offer, contingent on my selling the Castle Rock condo—which has been paid off for years. That'll sell as soon as it hits the market."

Curt swallowed his bite of heavily breaded pork fat and leaned in. "You're serious."

"As a heart attack, son. Kids—you too, David—we'll soon be almost neighbors. That is, if you'll have me! If you get tired of seeing me, there's that five-mile buffer zone, so...."

"Are you kidding me?! That's the best news I've heard in I don't know how long, Len," Phoenix said, unable to contain her joy. She turned to little Rose. "Did you hear that, sweetie?

Grandpa will be moving into his own house soon—nearby—and we'll get to see him a lot!"

"Yay!!" Rose chirped, hopping out of her chair and making like a koala bear as she jumped into her new grandpa-neighbor's arms. "We can play and color pictures every day, Grandpa!"

"I look forward to spending more time with you, Rose—and all of you," he said, turning to the adults as he continued. "Once I found the right one, the decision became an easy one. It's not a big house or anything—it's a two-bedroom condo unit—but it's on the ground floor, in a good neighborhood, and…" he said, turning back to Rose, "…it has a pool!"

"We can go swimming!?" she chirped.

"You betcha!" he replied. "I'll have to get some water wings for myself!"

"Amazing," Curt said, shaking his head in disbelief. "That's so great, Dad."

Phoenix squeezed Curt's hand under the table, while Pop Pop initiated a congratulatory handshake with Len. The level of joy at this table was palpable, and they each felt confident that things had just made a big turn for the better.

GOOD
FRIDAY

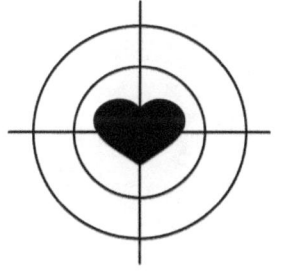

CHAPTER TWENTY-EIGHT

ARIZONA DEPARTMENT OF CHILD SAFETY
PHOENIX, ARIZONA
GOOD FRIDAY, 9:50 AM

Detective Moser had built a rather impressive case file thus far, especially considering all the new forensic evidence that had been added to it this week.

Fingerprint analysis of the drink lid found at the golf course had changed the focus of that investigation from an unfortunate tree-trimming accident to a very probable homicide, placing Tempest Cage at the scene.

Those prints had now been cross-checked and confirmed as a definitive match with prints found on the victim's front door at the trailer park, where said suspect's mother had been brutally slain. Cage's abandoned Tradesman van, a block away from said trailer park, was resplendent with the bondage shackles she'd used to keep Curt Martinsen hostage.

Add to that Cage's prints on the handle of the axe used

as the murder weapon at Lost Dutchman; her prints on her mother's abandoned Maverick; as well as in Paige Peterson's Ford Fiesta. Not to mention Paige's blood found on the passenger seat.

It was damning as hell and all the more reason for Moser to hand deliver a copy of the file the Arizona Department of Child Safety had requested.

This case was too important to sit on a pile atop a desk somewhere.

As much carnage as Tempest Cage had left in her wake—and there was plenty—perhaps the toughest piece for Detective Moser to swallow was the fact that the suspect had essentially disposed of her own child like a piece of refuse, leaving young Abigail on her own as she innocently splashed in the pool at the trailer park, while Cage went about slitting the throat of the child's only other living relative in her double-wide, a scant hundred yards away.

Then left her child behind without so much as a word. Not even a note.

Moser shook her head; she had a difficult time understanding the mindset of such a maniac, and she silently prayed to God this innocent seven-year-old Abigail might eventually find a level of healing and land in the loving home she deserved.

"Detective Moser," the case manager said, snapping Moser out of her thoughts.

"I'm sorry, Miss Andrews. Yes?"

"Call me Ruth, please. I very much appreciate your efforts in this investigation and for driving out here today. This file paints a very troubling picture, to say the least, and serves to prove that Abigail's life going forward will be rife with emotional challenges as she tries to come to terms with her place in the world. She's been put through the wringer at a very young age, and with no suitable blood relatives in the picture, she has a long road ahead."

"I know. I can't get my head around it, really. What about her medical condition?"

"Physically, she's fine, though her nutrition was neglected. Toaster pastries and popcorn aren't the best building blocks for a child's needs, and we're working with a nutritionist to assure her dietary needs are being met. Once she's in foster care—whenever a proper match is found—she would be eligible for medical, dental, vision, and behavioral health services under one health plan. In her case, the behavioral health services are likely to be a lengthy process. Bless her."

"Yes, bless her," Moser agreed quietly. "Uh, please don't hesitate to contact me directly if there's anything else you need, Ruth," Moser said, handing her a card. "And please keep me posted with how Abigail's doing, to the extent allowable, I mean."

"I definitely will, Detective. Thank you again."

"Bethany. Please call me Beth."

POP POP'S RESIDENCE
GOOD FRIDAY, 10:10 AM

Curt was at the kitchen table, coloring hardboiled eggs with Rose, while Phoenix washed the last of the breakfast dishes.

Pop Pop had made two big omelets—one veggie and another with chorizo—for the troops, while Len placed several calls to his realtor in Castle Rock, Colorado.

With those wheels in motion, Pop Pop borrowed the keys to Curt's F-150 so he and Len could fill its bed with the remaining boxes from the granny unit. They'd managed to fit just about everything, with the exception of a couple of dressers and a table they'd deliver tomorrow.

"We're outta here, kiddo," Pop Pop said as he gave Phoenix a peck on the cheek. He turned to the egg decorating committee. "Curt, thanks for the use of your truck. Len will drive it back here later and I'll retrieve mine from the shop after we've loaded these things into the apartment. I'll bet you guys are starting to get a little excited."

"Yeah...it's starting to get real, Pop Pop. Thanks for everything you guys have been doing for us while we're...a little busted up. You're the best."

"Yeah, Pop Pop—you too, Len—love you guys! And I can't believe we'll get to spend our first night there tonight!" Phoenix said, her voice going up an octave with her excitement.

"Indeed. We'll put together your bed while we're there. Rose's new bed hasn't arrived yet, unfortunately," Pop Pop said.

"No worries," Phoenix said, walking him outside to say the next part quietly. The screen door closed behind them.

"Pop Pop, we were actually thinking, if it's okay with

you—and since Rose's bedroom is not all set up yet, it might be nice if she could...maybe...stay here tonight?"

Phoenix had ended the statement with that cutesy little face she made sometimes, the one that usually worked on Pop Pop when she was embarrassed to ask for something.

He didn't leave her hanging for long.

"Totally understand your wanting to spend your first night together in privacy, kiddo. Consider it done. Rose can sleep in my room. The dogs, too. Luke and Prick, anyway. Sidney's still a little on edge with Len in the house, but—"

"We'll take Sidney tonight, Pop Pop."

"Yeah?"

"Absolutely. You're giving us a break tonight; we'll give you a break tonight too," she said, smiling as she came in for a hug. "Thanks, Pop Pop. I love you so much."

"Love you more, sweetheart. Don't make any plans for dinner; I've got that worked out. See ya this afternoon."

Phoenix stood there, dish towel in hand, as she watched her precious adoptive father back Curt's box-laden truck down the driveway. Its full load reminded her of the reruns of *The Beverly Hillbillies* she and Pop Pop used to watch together when she was younger.

"Love *you* more, Pop Pop," she said to herself as he drove away. "*Way* more."

CHAPTER TWENTY-NINE

GILBERT POLICE DEPARTMENT
RAMAGE'S OFFICE
GOOD FRIDAY, 12:35 PM

DETECTIVE RAMAGE SAT at his desk as he slowly and deliberately unwrapped the mystery sandwich his partner had brought him. He took his sweet time with the plain brown wrapper.

"C'mon. I promise it's not booby trapped. It's a veggie sandwich, for crying out loud. On the good Dutch Crunch bread. Not a beet to be found on it, I assure you. It's good for you, and you may even like it," Moser said, shaking her head. It was like she was dealing with a toddler.

"Uh, thanks, partner. Really thoughtful of you," he said as his lunch was fully revealed. "Huh."

Moser parked herself at the side table and had her duplicate sandwich unwrapped in three seconds. She set a napkin on her lap and took a bite. "Mmm."

"Actually, it's not bad—I mean, for a vegetarian deal,"

Ramage said, having assessed his first bite. "What are these little squiggly things?"

"They're called sprouts. Maybe you've heard of 'em," Moser said with a chuckle.

"Okay then," he said, going in for a second bite. He waited until he had a full mouth before he asked his question, which never ceased to amaze his partner.

"Sohowditgowiththechildsafetyfolks?" he mumbled through his cucumbers and sprouts.

"Sorry, I didn't catch the subtitles, but I think you just asked me about my meeting over at Child Safety?" she replied, knowing full well what the Neanderthal had just said. She shook her head as she considered her answer.

"I thought about it the whole drive back here. I mean, we don't have any resolution yet with the case. Meaning, either we finally make an arrest of the child's mom and she's locked away for the rest of her life, or she eludes our capture and dies in an exchange of bullets somewhere. There's no good scenario for that poor child. There's no happily-ever-after ending for that young girl. Breaks my frigging heart if you want to know the truth."

"Roger that," Ramage said softly. "No good outcome there. Still, I hope we catch a break and take Cage into custody before anybody else dies unnecessarily. Let justice sort it out. No matter what, it's always saddest for the kids."

Moser's cheeks ballooned as she let out a sigh of agreement. As they each took another big bite, their cellphones sprang to life in synchrony. He answered his first.

"Whammage."

SUN DEVIL CINEMA
PEORIA, ARIZONA
GOOD FRIDAY, 1:20 PM

There were fewer than a dozen cars in the lot.

"I can't for the life of me figure out how a multiplex like this—with eight screens—can keep the lights on with this kind of turnout," Ramage said as he climbed out of the car. "I mean, it's a holiday week, kids are off from school."

Moser closed her door and came to join him.

"Kind of sad. But I guess you have to factor in a couple of things: one being that the films listed on the marquee are a couple of months removed from being new releases."

"What's the other factor?" Ramage said as they made their way toward the ticket booth.

"It's...Peoria."

"Mmm."

As they reached the window, they saw there was nobody at the register. Ramage leaned forward, cupping his hand against the glass for a better look inside. He turned to his partner.

"And factor three: you can't find an employee, for Chris-sake," he muttered, looking at his watch.

"Here we go," Moser said, as a young, painfully skinny, acne-ravaged flashlight kid entered the booth.

"Which showing?" he asked, none too politely.

"Not interested in seeing a movie today, thanks. I'm Detective Ramage, this is my partner, Detective Moser. We received a call—"

"Oh, yeah. Uh, let me, uh...be right back," he muttered, exiting through the door at the back of the booth.

"Factor four..." Ramage mumbled. "Did you ever work at a theater, Beth?" he asked, turning to her.

"I did, actually. Junior year of high school, I think. Over in Mesa."

"Rewarding work, that? Just curious, because Napoleon Dynamite here seems pretty nonplussed about the gig."

"C'mon, Jeff. You were in high school once. Give him a break. Probably his first minimum wage job."

"Yeah. I worked a few of those a hundred years ago. I used to deliver those giant racks of brontosaurus ribs to the customers' cars over in Bedrock," he said, adding a snicker.

"Once a Neanderthal, always a Neanderthal," she replied with a chuckle.

"Detectives?" came the tinny voice through the speaker.

Moser and Ramage both spun back toward the sound and saw a squat, fortyish woman half smiling at them from behind the glass. She keyed the microphone again.

"Please come around to the front doors and I'll let you in," she said, tucking a long, errant strand of hair back into her unfortunate bun.

Ramage smiled and waved in acknowledgement as they made their way to the entrance. The woman swung the door open so they could step inside and immediately relocked it behind them. It wasn't summer, but the temperature inside the building was cold enough to hang meat.

"I'm Sofie, the manager, the one that called you," she said, blinking rapidly.

"Thank you for calling, Sofie," Ramage said, gesturing to his partner. "Detective Moser, and I'm Detective Ramage."

"Oh, my apologies. I was under the impression your name was Whammage when we talked," she replied.

Ramage glanced at Moser, and he could tell she was trying her best not to snicker. He bit his lip and shook his head almost imperceptibly.

"Yes, well, about your call. Like I said, Sofie, we appreciate your vigilance in reporting your concerns. You believe you saw someone matching the description of our suspect?"

"I do. And my employee—the young man you saw in the ticket office there—he had an interaction with the person as well."

"I see," Ramage said, taking out his notepad. "Is there somewhere we could talk?"

Sofie replied nonverbally, gesturing with her arm as if to say, "This way" as she led them past the concession stand. As they followed the manager, Moser saw the teenager sneak-watching them, utilizing his peripheral as he finished adding what the detective could only guess was a quart or so of 10W-40 to a party bucket of day-old popcorn. Her attention was brought back to the trio when they reached a nondescript door.

Sofie closed the door behind them and gestured to the two folding chairs facing her equally modest desk. "Please," she said, plopping into her own folding throne.

"Sofie, could you please give us a description of who you saw and anything you can remember? No detail is unimportant," Moser said, punctuating her words with a nonthreatening smile.

"Sure, yeah...well. Like I said, my employee and I both saw a customer earlier and—"

"Sorry to interrupt, Sofie," Moser said. "Your employee's name, please?" she asked, taking out her pen.

"That would be Bart. Bartholomew, actually. He's currently working the concessions."

"Bartholomew," Moser repeated softly as she wrote on her pad. It was Ramage's turn to suppress a grin.

"Thank you," Moser said. "And—and I'm sorry to interrupt you, but can you please tell us what time this occurred?"

"Morning...it was the first showing of the day—we open at 10:00—so, probably, I dunno...10:15? 10:30 maybe?"

"Thank you for that," Ramage said. "And what do you remember? What made this person catch your attention?"

"Other than being the only person there—we have eight screens, mind you, but all of 'em were empty, except one—it wasn't like there were a lot of other customers this morning. Tall fella."

Moser's brow furrowed and her ballpoint skidded to a stop. "I'm sorry. Did you say *fella?*"

"Yes. Well, I mean...I think so. Tall, on the thin side, nice features but a bad haircut— from what I could see before they pulled up their hoodie, anyway. Had on one of those lame "I *heart* Arizona" shirts, I think. And a small backpack. Probably smuggling in their own treats, which is against the rules. Left behind three empty Milk Duds boxes, and we don't sell those."

Moser's pen paused at the mention of the candy boxes.

"I hope I'm not wasting your time, Detectives. I mean, I don't read the papers, but the TV news...that's another story. Been following the local crime stories and keeping my eyes out for anything—or anyone—unusual, you know."

"You did the right thing, ma'am," Ramage said. "We—"

"I just hadn't seen this person before, and something just gave me a weird little vibe."

"You never know what lead will be the one that helps, Sofie," Moser interjected. "Now you said there was an interaction."

"Well, I asked Bart to ask the patron to take their feet off the seats. Some folks were born in a barn, I tell ya."

"And Bart asked them to?"

"Yes," Sofie said.

"And the customer complied?"

"Yes, Bart said the customer gave him a little scowl...kind of a threatening one."

"Okay. We may wish to speak to Bart when we're done. Now, Sofie, we'd like to show you a couple of photos if we may, see if there are any similarities to the person you're describing. It would be a big help to us."

"Sure. Why not?"

"Great," Ramage said, nodding to Moser, who had already pulled the three eight-by-ten inch photos from her portfolio. She handed them to her partner as she resumed her notation. He slid the first photo across the desk to the manager.

"This one's a woman, right?" Sofie asked, a bit puzzled.

"This is an enlargement of her driver's license photo, and it's three years old," Ramage admitted.

"Hm...long, blond hair. Pretty gal, but...."

Ramage slid the second photo across to her. "This one was taken more recently. It's a security camera image from a fast-food place, so it's a little grainy, but this is the same person," he said, watching Sofie closely for any reactions.

Sofie studied each image, looking back and forth, shaking her head slightly.

"You mentioned this *fella* had, your words, a bad haircut. I'd like to show you one more photo, this one with a police artist's modification to it. This is what we believe our suspect may currently look like. Please, take your time," Ramage said, revealing the new image.

It was a split screen image of the two previous photos, but each had been modified to reflect the description provided by the young park ranger who'd interacted with her. Sofie's eyes squinted a little as she challenged her memory to compare against the images spread before her. Both Ramage and Moser studied her as she did. A few moments went by before her eyes widened, considerably.

"What is it?" Moser asked.

"Yes," Sofie muttered.

"Yes, what?" Ramage probed.

Sofie brought her thumb and forefinger together and made an *OK* sign, bringing it up to her right eye to peer through as she studied the images further.

"Sorry...I'm trying to envision that face with a hoodie," she said. As she lowered her hoodie-framer, she looked up and met each detective's gaze. "That's him—I mean, her. This is who I saw. I'm positive."

A brief chat with Mr. Loquacious—aka Bart—came to the same conclusion. He had also been asked to put on a pair of latex gloves in order to retrieve the three Milk Duds boxes from the trash.

This second confirmation, in conjunction with a security camera image Sofie had furnished, provided the detectives with proof that the stolen red minivan was indeed their suspect's current mode of transportation—at least as of this morning.

"The way our perp keeps changing vehicles...I swear, she's

a frigging hermit crab," Moser said, climbing into their vehicle. Ramage closed his door and started the ignition.

"Yeah...this hermit crab may've changed her shell again, but she hasn't strayed far from the tidepool."

CHAPTER THIRTY

NORTH 75TH AVENUE
JUST NORTH OF ESTRELLA VILLAGE
TWELVE MILES EAST OF PHOENIX, ARIZONA
GOOD FRIDAY, 3:33 PM

"FUCK. FUCK! FUCK!!"

Tempest had deliberately taken the roads less traveled going south out of Peoria. It was a circuitous route, and would take twice as long, but she wasn't in a hurry, and she wanted to avoid the major highways to the extent possible.

She'd taken the jog south on North 75th Avenue and was a couple of miles from her planned left turn onto West Lower Buckeye Road when the check engine light flashed on.

"Fuck!!!" she screamed again, propping open the hood as she cursed the ridiculous 2.5-liter four-cylinder powerplant. The engine wasn't at all healthy and was spattered with steaming oil spray. A quick look at the dipstick confirmed that its soccer mom owner neglected to check such things.

Tempest scowled, her head emerging from the engine compartment and getting a look at her dismal surroundings. She was out in the boonies but completely exposed. If a cop were to come along, she'd be fucked, all out in the open like this.

Dammit!

She sure as hell wasn't going to call the auto club—she wasn't even a member anyway—and getting a roadside assist from law enforcement wasn't an option. They would undoubtedly be clued in to be on the lookout for a stolen red soccer mom-mobile. There weren't too many of these pieces of shit on the road these days, and probably for good reason.

Tempest reached in her hip pocket and popped a couple of random pills. She didn't even look, as she'd stopped paying attention to which ones. At this point it didn't seem to matter.

None of them were relieving her feelings of mania anyway, and she knew she'd long ago crossed from the borderline region and straight into psycho town.

She was entering into a new realm of her mental illness, fueled by the everchanging crap in her bloodstream and the chemicals sloshing around in her brain matter.

She slumped into the driver's seat, closed the door, and rested her arm on the sill of the open window as she started to sob. The occasional car zipped by, but they were few and far between.

Tempest turned the key in the ignition and was met with a cluster of disco warning lights. *Damn.* She was seconds away from climbing out and starting a very long walk when she heard what sounded like an approaching car, and it was slowing down as it pulled onto the gravel shoulder.

Her hands choked the steering wheel. *Game over.* She

chanced a glance at the rearview, fully expecting to see a cop pulled in behind her.

But it wasn't.

Instead, she saw an older gentleman with a paunch belly and loud slacks, stepping out of his Buick Riviera and walking toward her. He was probably seventy-five, and a quick glimpse at his Canadian license plate confirmed him to be a snowbird.

He came up to the window and Tempest turned to him.

"Everything okay here, miss?" he asked.

"Hi, thanks for stopping. A bit of engine trouble. It's my husband's car; he didn't bother to check the oil, I'm afraid," she answered, trying to muster up a friendly-enough smile to go with the lie.

"Oil, huh? Mmm...that is a problem," he said, removing his tortoise shell glasses and looking around. "Not much around here as far as service stations and such."

"I'm afraid not."

"Mmm. Where're you headed, exactly?"

"Exactly? Well...."

"Perhaps I could give you a lift to a service station and you could arrange for a tow? Should be something on Buckeye, I imagine."

"That's awfully kind of you to offer," Tempest said, hoping she didn't have to kill this guy.

"Offer's a good one and expires in two minutes," he said with a chuckle. "I'm going that way anyway, so if you want a lift, hop in. I promise I'm not a serial killer or anything," he added, holding up his hand in a Scouts Honor gesture.

"Whew, you had me scared there for a minute," Tempest replied. "Sure. Thanks. That would be terrific."

"Reg."

"Excuse me?

"I'm Reg. Short for Reginald," he said, smiling as he initiated a handshake.

"Tem— uh, Tiffany, pleasure," she replied, catching herself. "Let me just grab my daypack."

DWAYNE'S AUTO REPAIR
WEST LOWER BUCKEYE ROAD
TEN MILES WEST OF PHOENIX, ARIZONA
GOOD FRIDAY, 3:55 PM

Reg pulled the Riviera into the lot, parking along the side of the building. The tired, paint-challenged shop looked like it'd been there since the Forties, and there were only two other cars.

Reg unbuckled his seatbelt with a sense of urgency and turned to his passenger.

"Excuse me, young lady, I've got to find a restroom, and pronto, while you talk to the folks about your van," he said, hightailing it into the building.

"No problem," Tempest said with a smile.

She was happy she wouldn't have to hurt this nice man because, little did Reg know, he'd just saved himself by leaving the keys in the ignition.

QUAIL RUN APARTMENTS
APARTMENT 133
GILBERT, ARIZONA
GOOD FRIDAY, 4:15 PM

Phoenix sat on one of the two new barstools that were positioned along the ledge of the kitchen counter. She'd never felt more useless as she watched the beehive of activity swarming around the apartment.

Piles of boxes were stacked in every room now and looked like so many stalagmites. Len walked by with a medium-sized box, which he placed in the hallway, just outside the bathroom.

One of the boxes amongst the living room piles was clearly labeled, *Rose's Bedroom.* As Phoenix got up to take it to its proper destination, Pop Pop shot her a look.

"Nope. Please sit. We've got this. You know what the doc said. What is it?"

"That one...third one down...goes in Rose's room," she said, surrendering.

"Got it," Pop Pop said, liberating it from the stack and relocating it accordingly.

Phoenix turned to Curt, who was feeling even more useless, parked on the other stool.

"I hate not being able to help...it's our stuff, and we can't assist the guys?" she said.

"I feel ya, sweetie. Sucks that we're both out of commission right now. We owe these guys, bigtime," Curt replied with a sigh.

Pop Pop stopped in the middle of the living room, wiped his hands on his jeans, and surveyed the rapidly shrinking space. There was a new loveseat, a TV stand with a forty-two inch plasma thin screen, and a ton of boxes that would need unpacking.

"That's the last of it, sweetheart. That is, until Rose's new bed arrives—but that won't be until next week, with the holiday."

Len walked over, caught his breath, and stood next to Pop Pop. "Well...that was fun! Haven't done that in, like, twenty years," he said, smiling at the youngsters.

"Thank you both, so much. Really..." Curt said. "Sorry we couldn't be more help," he added sheepishly.

"Don't be silly," Len replied. "Besides, if escrow times out like I think it should, I'll be needing both of your help moving my stuff in—when you're healthy enough to, of course."

"Count on it, Len," Phoenix said with a smile.

"Me too, buddy," Pop Pop said, flexing his bicep for comedic relief.

"I'm putting y'all down on my list," Len said, smiling at each.

Pop Pop gave Len a secretive nod, gesturing with his head toward the patio area, which still had its vertical blinds closed.

Len nodded back, almost imperceptibly.

Pop Pop walked into the kitchen and pulled four cold beers from the refrigerator. He'd learned from his many moves over the years, that plugging in the fridge—and stocking it with beer—were the very first steps in ensuring any success-ful move-in.

He placed them on the counter next to Phoenix, popping the caps off the bottles and distributing them to the adults.

"First things first," he said, gesturing with his own bottle. "Here's to your new home, Phoenix and Curt, and to many—"

"Hey!" Rose cut in, having emerged from her bedroom and joining the adults. "It's my new home too!" she chimed, with a half-pout for effect.

"Of course it is, sweetie," Phoenix said, kissing the top of her head.

Pop Pop quickly fished out a juice box, stuck a straw into it, and handed it to Rose.

"We can't forget you, Rose Petal," he said with a smile. "To your new home, Phoenix, Curt, and Rose! May it bless you with many years of joy. Cheers!"

"Cheers!" was the choral adult response.

"Jeers!" Rose said. It was her first time.

Four beers and a juice box came together in celebration, and they each took a pull from their beverages.

"So, kids...listen. Len and I have put together a little housewarming gift—actually a couple of 'em—and, if you'll follow me...watch your step through the maze...over to the patio area...."

Pop Pop led the way with Phoenix right behind him. Curt navigated with care as his crutches competed with the boxes, while Len—carrying Rose—brought up the rear.

Pop Pop grabbed the blinds' plastic rod and paused for effect. "Close your eyes."

Looking around to confirm compliance, Pop Pop rotated the wand to pivot the blinds to the open position. He then dragged the blinds noisily across the track, affording a full view of the patio space.

"Okay...open!"

Phoenix's eyes fluttered open, going full wide at the sight of the caramel brown, fully assembled, three-burner Weber propane grill gracing the back wall of the patio enclosure.

"Wha—wait...what? Nuh-uh!" she said, her face lighting up like a kid with a puppy in their Christmas stocking. "No friggin' way, Pop Pop! Seriously?" she managed, flying into his arms.

"Yes, friggin' way," Pop Pop countered with a chuckle.

"What's frigginway?" Rose asked, looking up at Len.

"Oh, your mama and Pop Pop are just being silly," he said, squeezing her button nose and hoping she wouldn't press further.

"It's beautiful. Holy cow..." Curt said, already imagining his first tri-tip roast on it. "That's beyond generous. Thank you," he said, pulling his right hand from its crutch handle to shake PopPop's.

"But wait, there's more!" Pop Pop said, sounding every bit like the infomercial pitchman. "Len?"

Taking his cue, Len set Rose down next to her mommy and gestured to a blanket-draped table along the shorter wall, adjoining the slider. Under the drape lay a dome-shaped object.

"This is my little contribution to you kids' new start here," he teased, while Phoenix and Curt stared quizzically.

"Maybe I can get Rose to come over and help me with this blanket here. Would you like to help me, Rose?"

"Yeah!" she chirped, climbing out from between her parents and joining him.

"Okay, now when I tell you, Rose, I want you to pull this blanket off the table, honey. Can you do that?"

"Yeah!" she squealed, more excited than anybody.

Phoenix looked over to Curt and shrugged her shoulders. He returned the shrug.

"Okay, Rose, you ready? I'm going to count to three. One...two...three!" Len the Magician said to his lovely assistant. It took her two big pulls to clear the blanket, but as the draping fell to the floor it became immediately evident to the couple that they were staring at their very own new pizza oven.

"What?!" Curt blurted.

"Are you kidding me right now?! Is that what I think it is?" Phoenix said, beaming almost as broadly as the day, several years prior, when Pop Pop had asked her to pull back the sheet that revealed her 1970 Hemi Plymouth Road Runner. It was a close second. Her mouth hung open as she turned to Len, hoping this wasn't a dream she'd wake from.

"Happy New Home, you two!" Len said, hugging them both. "And guess what?"

"What!" Rose cut in, not entirely sure what the excitement was about but going with it.

"We're all having fresh, homemade pizzas tonight. I have all the stuff. Pizza dough balls are already made, and there are a ton of toppings, so...."

"Yay! Pizza!" Rose blurted. "I want prepper pony on mine!"

"Pepperoni?" Curt said, winking at Phoenix. "Me too!"

CHAPTER THIRTY-ONE

GILBERT POLICE DEPARTMENT
RAMAGE'S OFFICE
GOOD FRIDAY, 5:20 PM

ETECTIVES RAMAGE AND Moser were standing
before a wall map of Greater Phoenix and its surroundings, including parts of Pinal County.

There was an assortment of colored highlighter markings
on it, color coded by dates and times, and trajectories. Yellow
lines originated in Surprise, extending to the Coyote Gulch golf
course in Gilbert and the site of Mr. Franco's demise—where
their case originated.

Moser traced her finger along several pink lines, beginning with the Apache Junction bar where Tempest had drugged
and absconded with Phoenix's husband, where their second
case began.

The lines ventured into Pinal County and the Lost Dutchman State Park region before heading back out, going west and
south, to the trailer park in East Mesa where Tempest's mother
had been found. Then back to the Lost Dutchman.

"Jeezus."

"Yeah. And our victim at the campground. Poor guy. Wrong place, wrong time," Ramage said. "And then we have the helicopter fun before she—some friggin' how—manages to find her way back out of the park to..." He paused as he traced a new line—this one green—to the apartment complex. "...to Paige's apartment to kill her...over what? A car? Some pills?"

"Then she steals the van from the campground here," Moser said, pointing to a blue-circled area. "Catches a movie in Peoria," she continued, putting her finger on the red X where they'd just come from.

"And we lose her trail," Ramage muttered, rubbing the angry knot in his neck.

His cell phone both rang and vibrated, jolting him out of his funk. He stabbed the button.

"Ramage..."

Moser turned away from the map, shifting her focus to her partner as she tried to gauge his reaction to the call. She couldn't hear the other end of the conversation, but his eyes were darting back and forth as he listened, like one of those retro Kit-Cat Klocks.

"Where again, exactly?" he said, his brow almost collapsing under its own weight. "Shit...no, no, sorry. No. Good work! Of course...yeah, thanks," he said, ending the call. He spun to Moser and approached the map.

Grabbing a red highlighter, he found the coordinates described in the phone call, circled them, and began drawing a new line heading away from it, going due east.

"Our crab's found herself a new shell, and she's on the move!"

QUAIL RUN APARTMENTS
APARTMENT 133
GILBERT, ARIZONA
GOOD FRIDAY, 7:25 PM

Pop Pop glanced at his watch before bending down to peek back inside the tabletop pizza oven. It was time. The last of the pies was ready to come out, and this one was likely to be his masterpiece.

He grabbed the handle of the twelve by fourteen pizza peel—another part of Len's generous gift to the kids—and slid the thin-yet-surprisingly-sturdy aluminum spatula's surface underneath the crust of the ten-inch spinach-tomato-mushroom-cheese pizza, and gently pulled it out of the fire.

"Oh, would you look at this...it's even more beautiful than the pepperoni and olive one!"

"You've got this thing down, Pop Pop," Phoenix said, beaming at this latest offering. "I'm already full, but I'm going to need a piece of that."

"Coming right up, kiddo," Pop Pop said, sliding the pie onto a cutting board and utilizing the other new gadget: the fourteen-inch rocker-style stainless steel pizza slicer knife. It made quick work of the pizza, as its handler rocked the super-sharp curved edge back and forth four times to create eight uniform slices.

"Can I try that thing, Pop Pop?" Rose pleaded.

"No, honey. This is only for adults to use. Okay? Capiche? It's very, very sharp, honey," he replied, setting it beyond her reach. "But...you can have another piece of pizza if you want."

"No, thank you. There's no prepper pony on that one. And I want ice cream. Please!" she said, catching herself.

"We'll have some of that for you in a few minutes, peanut," he responded with a wink before turning to the others. "Who—besides Phoenix and myself—wants a piece of this? It just may be my best of the night."

Len was seated on a folding chair, his hands resting on his tummy, and his usually jovial expression looking atypically sour. "None for me, thanks...I'm not used to eating like this... oof. I totally overdid it."

"You okay, Dad?" Curt said.

"Hope so, but...excuse me, son, I need to use the restroom," Len said, getting to his feet as Curt shuffled on his crutches and made room for him to pass.

"Your dad doesn't look too good," Phoenix said, biting into her slice.

"Probably just gas," Curt replied.

"Well, just keep an eye on him. I'm gonna get Sidney out of her crate and take her for a quick walk, okay? Poor girl's going stir-crazy."

"Okay, be careful, babe. Love you."

"Probably love you more," Phoenix said, smiling over her shoulder as she went inside.

Pop Pop turned off the knob on the propane canister, removed his apron, and squatted down to eye level with little Rose. "Now, who was it that wanted some ice cream?"

"Me!" she squealed, full Shirley Temple mode.

QUAIL RUN APARTMENTS
STREETSIDE
MOMENTS LATER

Little footlong Sidney was the first to emerge from the parking structure, closely followed by Phoenix, who was at the other end of her four-foot leash.

The little fluffball held her head high, exuding attitude that belied her tiny size. She skipped along down the sidewalk, her little legs moving at the speed dictated by her master.

"Sidney, easy...you can't go any faster than I am," Phoenix said, giving her a slight leash correction. "That's better, good girl."

It was now dark out and both human and pooch senses were heightened a little, Sidney's especially so.

"Grrrrrr."

"What is it?" Phoenix said, looking around to assess any potential dog threats.

"Grrrrrrrr."

"There's nothing there, Sidney. Pick your battles, little girl," she said, distracting the little ragamuffin with a tiny liver treat. "C'mon...you owe mom a poop."

Across the street, and parked away from any streetlights, sat a certain Buick Riviera and—quite possibly—the source of Sidney's discontent.

Tempest had the windows up as she sat there watching the goings on. She'd been sitting there for over an hour, having waited for the cover of night, just her and what was left of her footlong Subway tuna with extra pickles.

She'd already done a bit of recon, noting the Road Runner in the garage. She'd also seen the truck—not Curt's, but the other one she'd seen parked in the driveway at the other house, days before—parked at the curb out front.

Some kind of party. Must've forgotten my invitation.

Tempest watched her side mirror as Phoenix and the hamster she called a dog disappeared down the sidewalk. *Two midgets.* She shook her head and began scarfing down the second half of her sandwich.

She'd wait.

"Good girl, Sidney...good pee and poo!"

Tempest had heard the praise, and it sounded like it was coming from nearby.

She tossed her sandwich wrapper onto the floorboard. Rechecking her side mirror, she saw the source, and they were making their way back along the sidewalk.

Tempest's fingers fumbled around on the side of the leather seat until she found the power recline button. Its motor began to softly whir. *Sweet!* As the seat continued tilting back, she maintained her eyeline on the mirror. The human, and her pooch, were now almost directly across the street and entering the parking structure.

She reclined her seat to its furthest position and glanced at her watch: 8:15

How long's this little party gonna last? Her eyelids surrendered to their weight; it had been another long day in a series of long days, and she'd had a crappy night's sleep—if you could even call it that—in the Fiesta. *Was that...yesterday?*

QUAIL RUN APARTMENTS
APARTMENT 133
GOOD FRIDAY, 8:18 PM

Phoenix carried Sidney inside and returned her to the dog crate stashed in their bedroom. As she came back out to the patio, she found all of the adults sitting there, with the exception of Len.

The move-in, along with his duties as pizza chef, had done it for Pop Pop. He was dozing in his chair, a half glass of Zinfandel still in his hand. Phoenix carefully removed it and placed it on the side table.

Curt had Rose on his lap and her head had sunk into his chest. She'd had a lot of stimuli, too much pizza, and even more ice cream.

"Hey," Phoenix said softly to Curt. "Where's Len?"

"I had him lie down on our bed for a little bit. He's pretty out of sorts and I think we need to get him back to the house—and probably some Pepto."

"Yeah, I'll bet...poor guy. Is Pop Pop going to take him or—?"

"I was thinking I'd probably take him back to the house, get him situated, make him comfortable if I can. Don't want to burden your dad."

"Is Pop Pop okay to drive?"

"Yeah, he's fine. He didn't even finish his glass of wine. He just nodded off a few minutes ago."

"'Kay," Phoenix murmured, processing things.

"If it's anything more than severe heartburn, I think I should be there—just in case."

"No, I understand," she replied, not intending for the tinge of disappointment to be evident in her tone.

"I know these aren't exactly the plans we had for our first night together in the new place," he said, reaching for one of his crutches.

"No worries, babe," she said softly.

"Len still has the guestroom bed there, so maybe you and I can crash on the couch, and Rose can—"

Phoenix shook her head. Too many moving parts. "I have a better idea. How 'bout I stay here tonight, with Rose—she and I can sleep together and—"

"No, honey, I don't want to leave you here and—" he said, cutting her off, before Phoenix returned the favor.

"Nope, it's decided. That way Pop Pop can get a good night sleep too. I'll keep Sidney here 'cause she'll just keep wigging out at Len's presence in the guestroom, and then nobody gets any sleep. It'll be totally fine. It's just one night. Besides, I feel like unpacking our bathroom box anyway. I promise; one box, I won't lift anything heavy. Deal?"

Curt didn't like it, but he too was tired to argue, and Phoenix's debate skills were far superior to his own. She gave him a nod and a tight smile, indicating the discussion was over.

"If you're sure."

"Done deal, sweetie," she whispered, her expression softening now that a decision had been made. "Here, why don't I take the princess while you check on your dad," she said, handing him his crutches, softly kissing his cheek, and collecting Rose. "C'mon, angel," she said softly. "Mommy's got you."

Phoenix had tucked in the princess, given Sidney her bedtime treat, and come back out to the kitchen, only to find Pop Pop finishing up the dishes.

"Pop Pop, you're not supposed to be working. You've already done enough—way more than enough," she chided softly, taking the dishtowel from his hands and giving him a warm hug. "Thank you though. Pizza was the bomb."

"Glad you liked it, kiddo. It was, wasn't it?" he said with a proud smile. "I'm done here anyway. Mostly paper plates... and the Solo cups are in the recycle bag. The pizza spatula deal—the *peel*—and the cutting tool are drying in the strainer there. I think we're all gonna head out here in a minute. Curt's driving Len home in his truck. I'll drive mine."

"You're sure you're good to drive?" she asked, cocking her head.

"Absolutely. I didn't get too far into that good bottle of Zin Len brought, but save me some, okay? Maybe we can barbecue and polish it off tomorrow," he said with a wink.

"Sounds good," she said softly. The smile in her eyes was shining through. "Thank you so much for everything you've done, Pop Pop. Call me in the morning and let me know how Len's doing, okay?"

"Yep. Love you, sweet girl."

"Love you...to the moon and back."

CHAPTER THIRTY-TWO

CURT HAD ASSISTED Len into the cab of his F-150 and quietly pulled out of the spot he'd occupied about fifty yards down the block. They'd already said their goodbyes to Pop Pop, who had promised he'd be about five minutes behind them and would see them back at the house.

8:42 PM

The sound of a truck door slamming, followed by an engine starting, jolted Tempest back into the world.

It took her a few seconds to get her bearings as she blinked herself back into full consciousness. A glance across the street indicated the truck was gone. She checked her rearview, confirming the truck's tail lights as they disappeared down the street.

She glanced at her watch. She'd only been out for about twenty-five minutes, but it had been deep, and it had felt more like a couple of hours.

Tempest slowly whirred the power seat back into the upright position. She had to pee. Taking advantage of the dark, and the fact that nobody else was walking around, she switched off the Riviera's dome lighting, opened the car door and stepped out, gently closing it with a click. *Gotta love a Buick.*

She walked about fifty yards down the street in search of her toilet, deciding upon a darkened driveway with several trash and recycling cans to squat behind. As she finished, and began pulling up her jeans, a large breed dog registered its complaint from inside the house.

"Yeah? Well, screw you too," Tempest muttered as she began walking back. When she reached the Riviera, she stood there, her hand on the door handle, considering her choices.

She pulled the car door open and, instead of planting her butt back in the seat, grabbed something out of her daypack and gently closed the door again.

Fuck it. If I can't have him...nobody can.

Tempest stood there in the dark for a moment and surveyed the neighborhood for any threats. A distant set of headlights approached, and she ducked behind a tree as she watched a black Mercury Cougar pass before disappearing around the corner.

"Black cat crossing my path, really?" she muttered. Things went quiet again.

Crickets. It was time to stir things up a little.

Somewhere, someone. She crossed the street and entered the dimly lit parking structure, initially hiding behind a panel van as she confirmed there wasn't any activity or witnesses to be concerned with. Satisfied, she made her way along the back of the row of cars, toward the rear of the garage, until she reached the orange one.

Tempest regarded the Road Runner's beauty. Even in the sparse lighting provided by the inadequate bulbs, the freshly detailed Hemi orange paint radiated as if glow-in-the-dark paint had been applied at the factory.

She looked at the gorgeous, obviously new tires. They weren't even dirty yet. It seemed like a shame to, but she shrugged the thought away as she retrieved her weapon and pulled open its nearly six-inch blade. It locked into position with a click.

A quick glance in both directions preceded the first jab as she stuck the blade deep into the sidewall of the left rear, inflicting terminal damage. It popped, accompanied by a whoosh of air. It was a little louder than she had hoped for, the parking structure accentuating it some.

Tempest ducked down for a few seconds to assess any reaction, but there was none. Another thrust of the blade took out the left front, and she quickly crawled around the front grill to murder the two tires on the right side.

As she stood, about ready to slink out of the garage, she turned back, her blade still open and locked. Nobody was coming. She touched the razor-sharp tip of the blade against the Road Runner's orange paint, then exuded enough pressure to scar several layers, starting at the taillight and dragging it in a swirling motion along the right rear panel, across the door, and over the front wheel well.

"Ha!" she hissed, shifting to the other side and carving its paint job similarly. "Oops!"

She pushed the blade release button on the rear of the knife and folded it back into its handle. A quick peek over her shoulder brought her huge satisfaction. The bird was sitting low, resting on its rims, and she'd been mortally wounded. *Meep meep.*

Tempest stuffed the knife into her hip pocket and disappeared through the nearby door, the one leading to the rear units.

CHAPTER THIRTY-THREE

QUAIL RUN APARTMENTS
APARTMENT 133
GOOD FRIDAY, 9:02 PM

PHOENIX SAT CROSS-LEGGED on the floor just outside the bathroom, sifting through the toiletries she'd unpacked, when the phone's display lit up.

"Hey, handsome," she whispered. "Thanks for calling. How's your dad feeling?"

"Hey, sweetie. Gave him some of the pink stuff—the one that tastes like chalk. He climbed right into bed, poor guy. Can already hear him snoring down the hall. Hopefully he's feeling better in the morning, otherwise I'll take him to the urgent care place."

"Mmm...okay. Yes, let's hope."

"Did you get the call from Detective Ramage?"

"I don't think so...I think my phone's ringer's been off for a while. When? What's up?"

"He called mine—maybe yours as well—went straight to my voicemail. Just checked it."

"And…?"

"He wanted to let us know that there has been another report of…I hate to even use the name…"

"Your stalker…Tempest?"

"Yeah."

"Jeezus…tell me."

"Well, they said there'd been a sighting—as well as another vehicle theft—and that she may be traveling from Peoria, toward the Phoenix area, maybe even Gilbert. Can't be sure."

"Jeezus…I thought that psycho would've left town—left the *state*—long ago. Did they say anything else?"

"Just to take precautions, just in case. The usual: lock the doors, be vigilant, etcetera. You locked the doors, right? The slider?"

"Yeah. I'm so ready for this whole thing to be done. Excuse my French, but she fucked with the wrong family. She needs to be put away…or put down."

"Agreed, honey. Listen, I didn't mean to freak you out; just passing along the latest. Maybe turn on your ringer, okay?"

"'Kay."

An uncomfortable silence hung in the air. The threat was still there, still real. Curt changed the subject. "Still unpacking that box?"

Phoenix dropped the hairdryer back into the box. "Yeah…I'm about halfway through. Think I'll bail on it for tonight. It can wait till tomorrow," she replied, getting to her feet and padding over to the bedroom door. A quick glance over to the bed confirmed Rose was in la la land, and Sidney was lights-out in her crate. She hoped, five minutes from now, she would be as well.

"Sounds good, honey. I'll call you in the morning. Love you."

"Love you too, baby. Goodnight."

"'Night," Curt replied as the call ended.

At least she'd managed to unpack her toothbrush, paste, and floss. Phoenix tiptoed into the jack-and-jill bathroom and closed the door before turning on the light switch. She'd forgotten that the overhead exhaust fan activated automatically with the light, and she hoped it wasn't loud enough to wake Rose. She shrugged as she fired up her motorized Oral B brush and began her dental regimen—a routine she took seriously.

THE PATH
APARTMENTS 130-140
GOOD FRIDAY, 9:17 PM

The serpentine pathway along this block of apartments was graced by the landscaper's choice of mature, drought-friendly shrubbery that extended the length of it.

This was where Tempest was crouched, behind a cluster of huge agaves and some robust ficus trees. She squatted, taking a knee, as she waited for a young couple to walk by. They were laughing and seemingly a bit liquored. They paid her no mind as they passed, giggling at the door outside Apartment 135 as they fumbled with the key. They disappeared inside and the door closed behind them.

Tempest had already seen the lights go off inside 133. She consulted her watch.

The ginger will be easy. Imagine Curt's surprise at seeing me.
It was "go" time, she'd decided, the fine hair on her fore-arms responding to the surge of adrenaline. Nobody was coming at the moment, so she got out of her crouch and stepped across the cement path. She was now standing outside the designated door.

The porch light had been turned off, which favored her stealth. Tempest regarded the door's hardware, noting what appeared to be a newer deadbolt. She reached out and grabbed the doorknob, giving it a gentle jiggle. *Locked. That would've been too easy.*

Stepping back from the small porch landing, Tempest assessed her next move. Not one to back away from a challenge, she turned her attention to the six-foot-tall patio enclosure to her left. It looked sturdy, constructed of a gray-painted wood, its decorative paneled slats running horizontally along the three outer walls.

Tempest pulled herself up, just high enough to peek over the top, and was delighted to see a sliding glass door leading into the unit. She'd have to navigate the barbecue grill so as to not alert anybody, but there was a clear, scalable section between it and the other thing. *Pizza oven?*

After a quick look in both directions, she jumped, catlike, as she tapped her upper body strength and pulled herself up onto the fence. Propping her elbows atop the flat fence rail, her feet searched for a foothold to assist her over the top.

She stopped kicking. She thought she'd heard something. Hanging there, she listened.

Voices! Shit! They were coming from her left, up the path, getting louder...closer.

Tempest went into high gear, her toe of her right shoe finding the groove between the panels and just enough of a foothold to propel her to the top. As she cleared the top of the fence rail, she dropped quietly, tucking into a crouch on the other side, just as what sounded like two young people walked by.

She closed her eyes, regulating her breath, as she listened for the threat to pass. A moment later, the sound of another door opening and closing told her it had.

Whew.

She got to her feet, mindful not to bump into anything as she stood before the slider. *C'mon.* She grabbed the handle and gave it a gentle nudge to her right. No dice: it wasn't going anywhere. The shaft of light spilling over the wall from the pathway lamp revealed a wooden dowel had been lain along the inside of the slider track as well.

Short of crashing through the sliding door's glass—which would shatter any element of surprise—she seemed to be out of acceptable options. *Dammit.*

That was until she looked down at the base of the wall, just to the left of the slider. *Is...that...?*

It was! *A friggin' doggie door!*

She didn't yet have cause to celebrate, but it might just work. Tempest possessed several gifts, one of them being excellent spatial awareness. She studied the framing around the doggie door. It wasn't huge by any means, but it was obvious it had been designed to accommodate a medium-sized breed. *Way more than adequate for the midget's hamster.*

A quick visual determined its width to be about fifteen inches and its height just short of two feet. With her right foot, Tempest pushed against the plastic flap, pleased to note that it was a dual-flap doggie door and not one of the electronic, collar-activated ones.

This just might work.

Tempest slipped off her tiny daypack and set it off to the side. She also removed her shoes, setting them next to her pack as she laid down on the cool patio cement, maneuvering her statuesque frame onto its side, in a fetal position so as to not kick over the side table.

With her head at eye level with the pet door, she peered into the opening, extending her arm and pushing back the second plastic flap to afford a better look inside.

Aside from the dim illumination coming from the over-the-stove light, the living room was dark. She heard a whirring sound, like some kind of fan, and decided it must be coming from the bedroom.

Tempest inhaled a deep breath and let it out slowly as she began snaking her arms, head, and shoulders through the six-inch deep tunnel.

She had almost cleared her shoulder blades when the source of the fan sound revealed itself. The bathroom door swung open, and the light switched off as Phoenix stepped out.

Tempest froze, her torso almost half exposed and twisting in the proverbial wind as she buried her face in the carpeting. A murderous ostrich in the wide open. *Shit. Shit. Shit!*

Under cover of darkness, and partially obscured by stacks of packing boxes, the intruder slowly rocked her head back, resting on her chin as she opened her eyes just in time to see the midget cross to the kitchen, fill a tiny cup with tap water, and chug it down before disappearing into another room. The door closed with a click.

Jeezus!

Tempest waited a full minute before she resumed slithering the rest of the way into the living room. Her ribcage took the brunt of the abuse as it rubbed along the bottom edge of the pet door frame, but it was manageable.

Her feet had just cleared the pet door when she heard another sound coming from the other room.

Grrrr...

Grrrrr....

"Sidney...shhh," Phoenix whispered, leaning over the bed as she issued a hissed command to the occupant of the crate. "Go to sleep, Sidney."

Rose stirred slightly. The little elf was snuggled next to her mommy, while managing to take up a good two-thirds of the big bed. Phoenix gave Rose's forehead a peck, pulled the bedding up to her chin, and rolled over onto her side. She grimaced as she did, a painful reminder of the Frankenstein stitching holding her still-fresh wounds together.

Phoenix closed her eyes and was seconds away from surrendering to the night when...

Grrrrr....

She reached over the edge of the mattress, gave the crate a thump, and whispered loudly. "Sidney...hush!"

Grrrrrr....

Rose stirred again, her eyes fluttering half-open. "Mommy?"

"It's okay, sweetie. Go back to sleep, baby."

"I'm thirsty."

"Yeah?"

"Can I please have some water?"

"Sure, honey. But just a little bit...otherwise you'll have to go pee, okay?"

"'Kay."

"I'll be right back," Phoenix said, swinging her feet over the edge of the bed and finding her Scooby slippers. "Oy," she sighed, hoping this would be the last speedbump on the highway to slumber town.

As she reached the bedroom door, Sidney again voiced her displeasure. *Grrrr!*

"What's your trip, chocolate chip? You hush now. It's okay; mama will be right back."

Phoenix stepped out into the hallway and closed the door behind her.

Tempest's eyes were wide as saucers at hearing the voices— both human and canine—coming from the next room.

From her vantage point crouched behind the loveseat, Tempest heard the bedroom door close, then the shuffling of slippers heading to the kitchen, followed by a yawn. *The midget.*

Peeking over the top of the furniture and through the box stacks, Tempest watched as Phoenix took a plastic juice glass from the strainer and partially filled it from the tap.

Tempest, sensing this as her best opportunity, got out of her crouch. As she stood, she reached into her right pocket and pulled out her trusty cutting tool. Phoenix had her back to her.

This'll be quick.

Tempest carefully unfolded the deadly blade, liberating it from its handle until it clicked into the fixed and locked position.

Grrrrr....yap!!

Phoenix, tired and annoyed, turned toward the complaints

coming from the bedroom. Sidney had gone to DefCon 2 and was now barking her shrill, high-pitched yaps, which were guaranteed to fully waken Rose. And several of their new neighbors.

Phoenix let out a sigh and was about to correct the pooch in the next room when her peripheral vision sensed an anomaly. She knew she was tired, even loopy, but one of the tall stacks of boxes seemed to be moving. She pivoted the rest of the way to the living room and blinked rapidly because, surely, she was hallucinating.

But she hadn't been imagining things: a tall ghostly figure began to emerge from behind the stacks, and it was slowly and silently approaching. Something else got her attention very quickly: the glint of light reflecting off the long blade this zombie was carrying at her side.

Phoenix's breath caught in her throat. Her heart was pounding a tribal beat as she took a half step backward, then another, until she felt the tile of the sink's counter pressing against her back. She was out of real estate.

The shadowy figure, wearing a ballcap, took another step forward until it emerged into the meager pool of light being offered by the stove's overhead lamp. Even in the dim light, Phoenix could get a good sense of the threat. Towering, athletic, and decidedly evil. Another flash of light bounced off the forged, stainless-steel blade.

"Who—" she started to ask, but the answer was painfully obvious. Her eyes were wide; she was fully awake now. "What—do you want?" Phoenix asked, the urgency now evident in her hushed voice, her heart pounding, threatening to burst through her chest wall.

"I'm sorry...we haven't been properly introduced. You

must be Phoenix," the figure said, taking another step toward her. "I've heard so much about you."

"Tempest," Phoenix murmured, her mama bear instincts rushing to the surface. With her young child in the next room, she couldn't afford to make a mistake here. She'd lost her daughter once, and there was no way she would allow anything to happen to Rose again.

"My husband's in the next room, and he—"

"Oh, you mean Curt? Great...I'll wait."

Phoenix was fixated on the gleaming blade. She let her gaze travel north until it landed on the face of the intruder. The height, the chopped hair, and the facial features she'd studied from the security camera images. Her expression was crazed, and she was clearly jacked up.

It was the maniac who'd kidnapped her husband. The one who'd abandoned her own daughter, killed her own mother, and murdered several other innocent people along the way.

And she wouldn't stop there.

Phoenix looked into the monster's eyes as she felt the bonfire surge, raging in her belly. She did an instantaneous threat assessment, realizing she was outgunned on several fronts. The intruder had a serious height advantage—by a foot—which also meant her limbs had more reach.

Add to that the fucking knife in her hand.

Yap!! Yap!! Yap!! continued from the next room.

Phoenix let the plastic juice glass fall to the floor. It wasn't going to help her. She had to buy some time while she figured things out. There was absolutely no way she was going to let this monster anywhere near that bedroom door.

"What...the...fuck's your trip?" Phoenix ventured. "Tempest? That's your name, right? Or was it Tampax?"

Tempest's expression morphed into a twisted smile at the mention of her name, and the attempted play on it. "Yes... *Tem-pest*. It's so nice to meet you, Phoenix," she said, batting her eyes playfully.

"Yeah, well, I wish I could say the same, but...I've got an idea: how 'bout you get the fuck out of my home."

"Hey, now...that's not very hospitable of you...and after all the trouble I've gone to?" Tempest replied, adjusting her grip on the knife's handle.

"Yeah, well," was all Phoenix could come up with. She has hyper focused on the blade.

"You're even smaller than I'd thought you'd be," Tempest said, enjoying the dig. "I've got to ask: where did you and Curt meet, Phoenix? I mean, did he rescue you from Munchkin Land or something? A midget fetish maybe? Not that I'm one to judge."

Phoenix let the insults slide off her. She knew she was facing a very real threat, yet she was royally pissed at the same time, which she tapped into as she summoned up her primordial energy.

"Is that what you're here for? To fuck with me? Fuck with us some more? Does that give you some sort of twisted...pleasure, Tempest? I mean, you have to resort to stealing someone else's man because you're too...desperate...too pathetic to get one the way everyone else does? Is that it?"

Tempest rolled her shoulders, cocking her neck as she replied. "I can have any man I want, *Fee-Nix*...what kind of fucked up name is that anyway? Was *Peoria* already taken?"

The smile had completely disappeared. A nerve had been touched. Tempest took another step toward Phoenix.

"Is that right? Any man, huh?" Phoenix replied. "So, the

whole date-rape-drug deal...chaining your men up in a fuck-ing van so they can't get away...that's your jam, is it?"

"You'd better watch your little dwarf mouth," Tempest said, reintroducing the knife as a visual aid. She held it up between them, angling the blade back and forth as the reflected light danced across Phoenix's features. "I'm going to rather enjoy this," she added, the twisted smile returning.

"You can do whatever you want to do to me—I'm pretty sliced up already anyway—but you leave my family out of this," Phoenix said, her hands feeling the cold tiled surface of the counter. Her mind was racing, wishing she had a hot pot of coffee within reach to defend herself with. This mama bear was going to defend her little girl at all costs...or die trying.

Tempest took another step forward, accentuating the threat. She was now within striking distance with that knife, Phoenix knew.

Yap-yap-yap-yap-yap!!! Sidney was going ape shit in her crate. Non-stop.

"Mommy?" Rose called out from the bedroom.

"Stay right where you are, honey!"

"Who are you talking to?" the little voice asked.

"Honey, now listen to mommy! Rose, lock the bedroom door and don't come out, do you understand me?" Phoenix cried out.

"Mommy, I'm scared," Rose replied, more of a whimper now. She was starting to cry.

"Rose! Right now! Lock...the...door, and don't you open it! Do it, sweetie!" Phoenix called out louder. Her hands gripped the countertop tightly, her fingers turning white.

"Sweet little girl you have there, Phoenix," Tempest said with a softness that brought extra menace. "I think I'll do her next," she added with a chuckle, momentarily returning her attention toward the bedroom door.

Phoenix seized the moment, acting on a sudden flash of clarity as she remembered the one and only option she had at her disposal. And it wasn't a juice glass.

As Tempest started to turn back toward her, Phoenix pivoted with the grace of a dancer, her right hand finding the wooden handle of the pizza peel. Her fingers choked the handle of the large pizza spatula as she brought it around in a wide sweeping motion like a big leaguer aiming for the fences. The peel's thin aluminum edge raked across her adversary and sunk into her right arm, just above the elbow, hitting bone.

"Aaack!! Fuck!!" Tempest screamed, dropping the knife to the floor. She brought her right foot up and violently pushed Phoenix up against the counter, almost propelling her into the sink basin itself. "I'm so done fucking around with you, you little pissant," Tempest hissed, holding the gashed arm. She bent down and reached for her weapon.

Phoenix fell back onto her feet as she countered with another swing of the peel, this time employing the wide flat surface as it crashed into Tempest's face like a gong, shattering her nose.

"Go fuck yourself!" Phoenix screamed defiantly as she kicked the maniac in the left kneecap, hyperextending it, and noting a cracking sound on impact. Tempest cried out in pain, her long reach enabling her to grab Phoenix's foot on the rebound, pulling the much smaller woman down onto her butt.

Phoenix, on the floor, with her back up against the sink cabinets, looked up at her foe. From her low angle, the menace now looked like an absolute giant as she stared back down at her. Blood was gushing from Tempest's ruined nose and was spattered across her face. She took a step toward Phoenix, hobbling as she favored her right leg, her left hand pressed against the deep gash in her right arm, the knife clutched tightly in her dominant hand.

Phoenix's wannabe weapon was out of her reach now, and her eyes were wide as she considered her fate. Tempest now stood directly in front of her, only a couple of feet away as she slowly lowered herself into an almost crouching position, her left leg not wanting to fully cooperate. She brought the knife's blade up to eye level.

"Mommy?!"

"Did you lock the door, Rose?!" she called out. "Tell mommy you locked the door, baby!"

"Yes, mommy, but I'm scared!! What's happening, mommy?!"

Phoenix closed her eyes tightly, her hands desperately reaching around on the floor for anything she could use to make a last stand before the slaughter.

"You know," Tempest began, launching some blood spittle onto Phoenix's face before continuing, "you're a feisty little thing...I'll give you that. But this is how it ends, Phoenix. You can't save yourself, and you can't save your little girl now. And Curt...if I can't have him, no one can."

Phoenix brought her left hand up and wiped the foul bodily fluids from her face, her eyes searing with intense hatred.

"You know, I almost feel sorry for you—and for your pathetic soul, you miserable, twisted bitch," Phoenix hissed softly. "Somebody must've really fucked you up bad."

Tempest considered this; after all, it was true, but she didn't feel like providing context. She wasn't done, however. Her head rocked back and forth in a mocking motion. She could still rub some salt into the wounds that would follow. "Oh, and I almost forgot," Tempest said, her swollen lips curling into her twisted smile.

"Yeah? What's that?" Phoenix muttered defiantly.

"Um...your car. Sorry about that...it was so pretty, too," Tempest said, throwing her head back as she laughed.

"I figured it was you who slashed my tire. Got it fixed, by the way." *So, there.*

Tempest ramped down her laugh but the maniacal smile and twinkle in her eyes remained as she leaned in to detonate her truth bomb. "Oh, Phoenix...if you could only see her *now*...."

Phoenix's expression flickered as the remainder of her considerable hatred surged to the surface. Tempest delighted in her reaction; her final dig having gotten the desired effect. She let loose another laugh.

Phoenix channeled her fury as she managed to pull open the sink cabinet's door, her fingers grasping at straws as she settled on something familiar. She gripped it tightly and swung it around front, the scouring powder flying from the flap of its open can and blanketing her enemy's face like so much snow.

Tempest screamed like a banshee as the Comet invaded her eyes, her bloodied nostrils, and her open mouth, burning every orifice simultaneously. She fell onto her back, choking, and swiping at her eyes. Her howls of pain were deafening.

Phoenix scooted away on her bottom, her hand finding her assailant's weapon on the floor. As she got to her knees, then to her feet, she reached up to the counter to steady herself, her left hand pulling the dish strainer and its contents crashing down onto the floor instead.

Tempest rolled onto her side, her right leg sweeping Phoenix's feet back out from under her and sending her down onto the deck. She landed awkwardly and the surge of pain coming from her shoulder told her she'd just ripped open her stitches—or worse.

Phoenix lay on her side, the knife having fallen away. It was out of her reach now, and almost within Tempest's as the maniac's arms flailed in a desperate attempt to grab it.

Phoenix gritted her teeth and got to the seated position. Her torso was screaming out in pain, her wounds having reopened. She tried to right herself, her left hand sweeping the floor and brushing against the smattering of kitchen utensils in the process.

Her eyes seemingly on fire, Tempest squinted through the bleachy powder and tears as she focused on the blade, a mere three feet away. She scooted on her stomach toward it.

Two feet...one foot...

Phoenix could only watch as Tempest slithered across the floor, rapidly closing the distance, the knife now only inches from her grasp. Phoenix realized she was powerless to stop her now. *God, help me.*

Phoenix sensed another energy in the room; it was confirmed by the tiny off-white blur that was now charging, growling, and barking bloody murder as it dashed toward the kitchen.

Tempest's fingers walked the final two inches, fumbling for a grip on the weapon's handle. Her fingers wrapped around it, grasping it tightly as she did the equivalent of a boot camp push-up. She sat up, turning toward the sound, her red, chemically scorched eyes something from a horror movie.

First, the mutt!

Before she could fully react, Sidney had already launched into her, making purchase with the handy projection of the back of her right heel. Sidney sunk her razor-sharp teeth into the two foot muscles, her little fangs chomping with the ferocity of a piranha and shaking her entire ankle-biter body for momentum as she tore into it.

Tempest's biggest problem was no longer the scouring powder.

She kicked at the little terrier, trying to break free as she screamed out with a pain she'd never known, but the tenacious pooch now engaged her other heel, inflicting crippling wounds as she growled ferociously. Her mama was hurt, and she was going to protect the leader of the pack at all costs.

Tempest swung the knife around, just missing the dog, which lit a whole new fire within Phoenix. Phoenix's hand found the pizza cutting tool and she switched it to her right hand with the efficiency of Bruce Lee.

Tempest swung her arm out again as she initiated another stabbing motion. As the blade neared Sidney, Phoenix swung the pizza tool down in a chopping motion, making violent contact with Tempest's forearm, cutting through flesh, muscle, and bone like it was so much butter.

The howl of pain was unworldly, seemingly inhuman, as Tempest screamed out, the blade dropping from her nearly severed hand and spurts of blood shot out like geysers.

Phoenix watched the spectacle, confident that Sidney had the upper hand while she set about destroying the lower legs. Sidney took another bite, ripping into Tempest's achilles tendon, as the felled monster flopped about the kitchen floor.

Blood had spilled out onto the living room carpet, and for a fleeting moment, Phoenix considered the fact that they'd probably just lost their deposit on the apartment, but it was the last of her concerns. *Oh, well...enjoy your meal, Sidney.*

Phoenix took a step back and looked up. Standing in the bedroom doorway, her precious daughter was looking at her, her tiny features convulsed in terror and concern, her face smeared with tears. Phoenix picked up the knife and, keeping it from Rose's view, dropped it into a packing box as she made her way over to her daughter, her arms a mile wide.

"Rose...Rose...Rose...my darling, lovey-girl..." she said, smothering her in a hug.

Shoulders heaved and tears flowed as they held each other.

"I'm sorry, Mommy," Rose finally managed, between sobs, as she hung on for dear life.

Phoenix pulled back slightly so she could see her daughter's face. She wiped away her daughter's tears and raked a strand of hair from her face.

"What? What do you mean, honey? You have nothing to be sorry for, lovey."

"You told me not to come out...and I let Sidney out..." little Rose said, her bottom lip quivering like she was expecting a throttling for disobeying a direct order.

"Come here," Phoenix said, smothering her daughter's face with mommy kisses. "You aren't in trouble, my precious girl. You were only trying to help your mommy, honey."

"I know."

A loud groan escaped Tempest as she lay there, sprawled awkwardly on the kitchen floor. She was vanquished and didn't have any fight left in her. Sidney released her crocodile grip on her prey and looked up at her master. Her formerly fluffy-white face was now red and matted with Tempest's blood. The whites of her brown eyes stood out in the dim light.

"Sidney," Phoenix called out to her little savior, smiling before issuing the command. "Come!"

The little pooch shot a quick look at her conquest, then enthusiastically darted toward Phoenix and Rose, leaving a trail of tiny red paw prints in her wake.

"Good girl, Sidney!!" Phoenix declared, praising the proud pup as she jumped up into her arms. "Good girl, baby! Wow..." she said, smothering the diminutive rescue in grateful kisses as she reconsidered the equation of who'd rescued whom.

"Everything's going to be okay, Rose," Phoenix said, turning to her daughter. "Okay?"

Rose slowly nodded unconvincingly.

"Can you bring mommy her phone, please?"

BETTER
SATURDAY

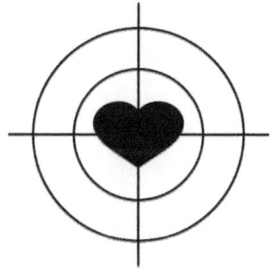

CHAPTER THIRTY-FOUR

GILBERT POLICE DEPARTMENT
CONFERENCE ROOM
SATURDAY, 10:20 AM

D ETECTIVES RAMAGE AND Moser sat at the rectangular conference table. They were joined by Phoenix and Curt Martinsen, along with a ginormous box of assorted donuts. There must have been three dozen of them.

Ramage was tired, having been called to the scene of the Martinsens' apartment twelve hours before, and had foregone any sleep since. He felt atypically celebratory, however, which was reflected in his donut order. He rubbed his eyes and set down his pen atop the legal pad, picking up what was left of his rather impressive maple bar.

Moser sipped her coffee and worked on a plain old fashioned.

Curt's arm was around his wife's shoulder—the good one, where it had been during the past hour of the debrief. Phoenix stared off into space. She was toast. The three donut holes on her napkin remained untouched.

Ramage swallowed his bite, wiped his mouth, and took a swig of his coffee-with-an-add-shot. "We'd like to thank you both, once again, for taking the time this morning and giving your statements. You've been through a lot this past week—sorry, understatement—and it must feel like it's been a year."

"Has it only been a week? Good God," Curt murmured.

"I'm sure this isn't how your family expected to enjoy your Easter week," Moser offered. "That goes for all of us, I guess, but nothing compared to your ordeal. If there's anything we can do...."

Phoenix nodded slightly, mustering up a tight, weak smile of acknowledgement.

"Thank you, Detectives," Curt said.

"Is Rose doing okay?" Moser asked. "The things that little girl has seen..." she added, her voice trailing off.

"We'll know more in coming weeks, I'm sure," Curt said. "We'll resume her therapy sessions next week—and probably double-down on them."

"Sure."

"And you...Curt and Phoenix Martinsen. How are you two doing?" Ramage asked, leaning in. His expression clearly reflected the concern he felt for this family. They had truly been through more than any family should ever expect to experience in a hundred lifetimes.

"We'll be..." Phoenix began, choking up a bit. Curt squeezed her shoulder gently. "We're strong, Detective. Our family has been tested...again. We won't surrender to those who would do us evil. Ever. We'll soldier on, so much, forever," Phoenix managed, a tear rolling down her cheek.

Curt gently tucked her into him, mindful of her

fragile condition. Several moments went by without anybody saying anything.

"Where is Rose today?" Moser ventured.

"With her Pop Pop," Curt said. "He's taking one for the team by catching the early showing of *Hannah Montana: The Movie*. Ramage smiled at the thought.

"Thank you, both," Phoenix said, looking from Moser to Ramage, then back again. "You probably never want to see this family again, which would be all right for us, too...nothing personal, of course," she added with a smile.

"Well, if you're up to it, I hope to see you and the family at the Easter Egg Hunt tomorrow. I'll be there with my daughter, Darla. Think about it, anyway. It might be a nice distraction, for Rose and for you all."

"We'll see...we'll try," Phoenix said, correcting herself and leaving open the possibility.

"Unless you have any more questions for us, I think we're done here," Ramage said, standing and initiating handshakes.

"Just one," Curt said. "What's the status of...you know...?" he asked, refusing to use the maniac's name.

"The suspect should be coming out of surgery any time now," Ramage said, glancing at his watch. "It remains to be seen when she'll be able to walk again, if ever, but she'll be jailed immediately upon discharge from the hospital. Security will remain very tight, I assure you."

Phoenix let out a long sigh. "Can we trust she won't be let out on bail, or...?"

"Not with the charges she facing, which will be many," Moser said as she began rattling off a list. "Let's see...there's harassment, kidnapping, unlawful imprisonment, resisting arrest, child abandonment, assault on police officers, weapons charges...to name a few. Oh, and a few counts of first-degree murder. No, she won't be going anywhere."

"That's a relief, I guess," Phoenix muttered.

"Ready?" Curt asked.

"Guess so."

"Thank you, both," Ramage said. "As before, your show of strength under adversity is admirable...inspiring."

"Happy Easter, Detectives," Phoenix said.

Curt and Phoenix drove in silence as they headed back toward Pop Pop's.

The apartment was still being processed as a crime scene, plus the family wouldn't be returning there until all physical traces of what happened were taken care of. In the meantime, it would be crowded at Pop Pop's, but they'd make it work.

Len was feeling better today, which was encouraging. He'd offered to pay for new carpeting if it was needed, to which Phoenix said she'd consider his kind offer, but only if the carpet cleaners weren't successful.

It remained to be seen if they would ever get past the tainted experience of their first night in the new place. And they'd definitely be wanting some new pizza tools.

Pop Pop had shampooed Sidney three times since the ordeal, and she was pretty much back to her original meringue-like coloring, with a few new pink tones.

A million thoughts were going through each of their heads on the drive home.

"Would you mind stopping at the CVS?" Phoenix asked softly.

"Sure, honey. You okay? You didn't touch your donuts."

"Yeah, just a little nauseous. I'll grab Len some of the cherry flavored Pepto while I'm in there."

"Okay."

"We're all good on Easter candy for Rose, right?"

"So good."

POP POP'S RESIDENCE
THE GRANNY UNIT
SATURDAY, 11:30 AM

Still feeling sick to her stomach, Phoenix had pretty much faceplanted onto the inflatable mattress Pop Pop had set up for them.

He'd picked up a couple of pillows and some emergency bedding from Marshalls, having hastily selected the first package of sheets he'd found. The one with the Hello Kitty pattern all over it.

Their former abode was otherwise empty, save the new toiletries and a couple changes of clothes piled atop the bathroom counter. Phoenix had changed her dressings, which had oozed considerably since the previous night's cage fight. They'd have to last until tomorrow.

Curt had silenced both of their phones, closed the blinds, and plugged in the new nightlight. He had never been a fan of having any kind of light on while he slept, but his recent experience in the cave had changed that for him, possibly forever.

As he emerged from the restroom, Curt retrieved his crutches and picked up the sheet of art paper that lay on the floor; the one Pop Pop had retrieved from the dash of the Road Runner before dropping her off for what would likely be weeks of work at the body shop.

Curt shook his head as he studied Rose's drawing for what had to be the tenth time, taking in every detail of the near-perfect rendering his seven-year-old had created. It raised more questions of how she'd come to draw it, but also served to remind him of his recent stint of solitary confinement, the family's numerous brushes with death, and how close they had all come to losing everything. Again.

Thank you, God.

He set the drawing atop the counter and shuffled over to join Phoenix in what would likely be the deepest of naps. They had a lot to process, and there was nothing quite like the subconscious to do its bidding.

POP POP'S RESIDENCE
THE KITCHEN
SATURDAY, 2:55 PM

Phoenix and Curt were still lights-out, so Pop Pop tried to keep his granddaughter entertained. All three dogs were napping in their crates down the hall, and Sidney had been awarded an extra treat for her bravery.

Pop Pop had survived the movie's hour-and-forty-two-minutes running time, and based on Rose's glowing review of it, he knew they would likely be watching it again, on DVD, once it came out. And they'd watch it a bare minimum of a thousand times.

Anything for his granddaughter. Which was why he was helping her make their third batch of Easter-themed sugar cookies, embedded with every color of M&M candies.

Employing three different cookie cutters, they'd produced one batch of egg-shaped cookies, a batch of bunny-shaped cookies, and another shaped like crosses.

"I think we need some more bunny ones, Pop Pop," Rose said as she surveyed their output.

"Mmm, I think we're probably okay, sweet girl. Besides, Easter's not all about the bunny."

Rose considered this for a moment before signing off on the project. "Okay."

OUT AND ABOUT GILBERT
SATURDAY, 3:15 PM

Len was still out doing errands. Having signed a plethora of loan documents with his realtor, he was working his magic on the blood-spattered areas of the living room carpet at the kids' apartment. He shuddered when he thought about what must have gone down here the night before.

He'd borrowed a bucket and a stiff brush from Pop Pop, rented a heavy-duty carpet cleaning machine, and hoped he had the requisite crime-scene approved chemicals to do the job. He was supplying the elbow grease.

Setting the brush into the bucket, he got off his hands and knees and stepped back into the tiny linoleum kitchen. It was hard to tell, because the carpet would take several hours to properly dry, but he was hopeful he'd brought the Berber back to its pre-crime-scene glory.

If not, his offer of carpet replacement still stood, and he'd coordinate that with the landlord if necessary.

After returning the carpet shampooer, he'd pick up some good Chinese from the place Pop Pop had steered him to, and he'd been asked to bring a little extra for their surprise dinner guest.

RICKY'S RV EMPORIUM
MESA, ARIZONA
SATURDAY, 3:40 PM

Ramage had spent the past three hours scratching an itch he didn't even know he'd had.

Until very recently, anyway.

After getting an impromptu crash course in recreational

vehicles—having explored the pros and cons of every type of rig imaginable, from tent trailers to forty-foot Class A motorhomes—he'd decided it was time to pull the trigger and explore the open road a little.

He didn't need the big bus, so he scratched the Class A off his list. And he didn't have a vehicle suitable for towing anything. Thus, the twenty-four-foot, cabover bed, single-slide out Class C Itasca Impulse was perfect. It had a Triton V-10 gasoline engine, and with its sleeping capacity for three, its size was optimal.

Besides, it was going to be just him—and his fish.

As he pulled off the lot at Ricky's, he wore an insuppressible grin, the likes of which had last been seen when he'd gotten that BB rifle for Christmas several decades before.

The sugar rush from the donuts may have played a part, but this celebratory splurge was bigger than that. They'd just taken a dangerous psychopath off the streets, and the Martinsen family had been made whole once again.

Plus, he and his rock star of a partner would likely receive commendations.

There was much to rejoice.

Ramage honestly couldn't remember the last time he'd taken a proper vacation, and it was time. He figured he'd request a week off around his birthday in June, keep his first shakedown trip close to home, and reserve a spot at a great park...one with a cool ranger, and with a killer name.

Besides, he owed Ranger Danger a beer.

CHAPTER THIRTY-FIVE

POP POP'S RESIDENCE
THE GRANNY UNIT
SATURDAY, 5:20 PM

T HE AROMA OF sweet and sour pork wafting from the main house had awakened Phoenix, and she'd spent the past ten minutes vomiting in the toilet. She emerged from the bathroom and looked over at Curt, who was just now beginning to stir. They'd both slept like the dead for several hours, and they'd been told, pre-nap, that dinner was planned for 6:00.

"You okay, honey? Thought I heard you throwing up."

"Mmm...yeah...I guess," Phoenix replied, carrying the CVS bag with her and placing it in the under sink cabinet. "Queasy though; not sure how hungry I'll be," she said, squeezing a glob of toothpaste onto her brush.

"Sorry, baby," Curt said. "Food smells good...you want the first shower or want me to?"

"Go ahead," she mumbled through a mouthful of foam.

Curt hobbled over to the bathroom with his crutches and got the shower running.

Phoenix spit the foam into the sink. "Need help wrapping your cast?" she called out.

"Nah, I've got it, thanks," he said, grabbing a tall kitchen trash bag and the roll of Saran Wrap off the counter and closing the door behind him. "Pain in the ass," he mumbled.

Phoenix steeled herself as she slid off her shirt and sweatpants and regarded the numerous bruised areas and gauze dressings.

The sutures holding her shoulder wound together were compromised, and one new bruise—the large one on her stomach—served as a fresh reminder of her cage fight the night before. She turned her attention to the weary face staring back at her in the mirror.

"Jeezus." Her red-rimmed eyes, coupled with the dark circles under them, reflected her battle fatigue. Her features were drawn, and the combined effect, in concert with her wounds, frightened her more than a little. She was going to need a long soak in the shower to wash this one away.

POP POP'S RESIDENCE
THE KITCHEN
SATURDAY, 5:55 PM

The semi-restorative shower had been medicinal, and Phoenix had done her best to freshen her look and her dressings. She wore one of her Reyn Spooner Hawaiian shirts, the one with an Arizona Diamondbacks pattern on it.

Pop Pop had used up every square inch of counter space to accommodate the numerous plastic clamshell containers and cardboard to-go boxes of Chinese food Len had come home with.

"Think you brought enough, Dad?" Curt teased as he perused the offerings. "Not that I'm complaining."

There was indeed sufficient sweet & sour pork; veggie chow mein; pineapple veggie fried rice; and beef & broccoli to feed a small army. Add to that the large Styrofoam containers of hot & sour soup; a kid-sized order of sweet & sour tofu for Phoenix; and a gazillion spring rolls.

"A request had been made to get a little extra, so..." Len countered.

"There's an extra place setting on the table, Pop Pop. Want me to put it away?" Phoenix asked.

"Umm, no, but thanks for offering. We may need it," Pop Pop said as he scrounged up every large serving spoon he could find in the drawer. "Hope you're hungry, kiddo."

"Mmm..." came the noncommittal response. "I'll get Rose," Phoenix said, disappearing down the hall.

Pop Pop plated the spring rolls, popped the cap from his bottle of Tsingtao lager, and turned his attention to the sound of a vehicle pulling up the drive. He glanced at his watch. *Right on time.*

"Hey, Curt...do me a favor and grab my phone off the dresser in my bedroom, would you?" Pop Pop asked.

"Sure thing," Curt said, gimping down the hall.

Pop Pop ducked out the door, closing the screen quietly behind him as he made his way out to the driveway. He hadn't needed his phone; it was in his pocket. He was just buying a little time to preserve the element of surprise.

A gleaming silver convertible Mustang had pulled up behind the other trucks and killed the engine. Pop Pop could barely contain his excitement at seeing who was stepping out of it. This would be the icing on the cake after the series of phone calls he'd made, and he was grateful he'd been able to pull it off.

As the muscle car's door closed, Pop Pop met its driver and held out his hand.

"Wingnut!"

"Hey, Dave," the young, pencil-thin man replied as he peeled off his watchman's cap, allowing his impressive ears to flop into their natural position. He tossed the knit cap onto the seat and smiled briefly, revealing a full mouth of braces. Just as quickly, the smile went away, and it was immediately apparent how self-conscious he was about all of the metal in his mouth.

His jaw-droppingly ginormous Dumbo-esque ears, however, were something he was completely comfortable with. Thus, the moniker he'd been stuck with in grade school.

"Please, call me Pop Pop. Or even Pop's fine...anything but Dave," Pop Pop said, initiating a bro hug with Curt's old work chum from Diamond P, the sanitation business where they'd been employed—and subsequently fired from—in California.

"Okay, Pop Pop," Wingnut—whose real name was Jimmy—said, again flashing the nanosecond-long smile.

"Nice wheels."

"Yeah...thanks. Quite the chick magnet," Wingnut said with an embarrassed chuckle.

"Well, c'mon in," Pop Pop said, gesturing. "Nobody has a clue you're coming," he added, grinning in anticipation as they both went inside and the screen door closed behind them with a gentle click.

About ten seconds later, the deafening chorus of greetings spilled outside. Lead by Phoenix and Curt, with variations on the theme, the excited welcomes were unanimous, and probably loud enough for the entire neighborhood to hear.

"WINGNUT!!!"

MOSER RESIDENCE
GILBERT, ARIZONA
SATURDAY, 6:35 PM

Bethany Moser had taken her daughter Darla to the grocery store with her an hour before in order to conduct a little experiment.

Her own mother had done the exact same thing with her when she herself was a young child, and the fact that she remembered it all these years later was testament to the importance of making memories.

The experiment had been exceedingly simple. Her mother had given both her and her older brother a five-dollar bill, which in those days was all the money in the world. She'd told them they could pick out their favorite thing to have for dinner, as long as they kept it within five dollars, and she'd help keep the tally as they shopped.

The only rule was that they couldn't buy any candy.

Darla had taken her ten-dollar bill, adjusted for inflation, and took a whole fifteen minutes to make her selections.

Bethany was delighted to note the things her daughter had chosen, as they were items she wouldn't have otherwise known were her favorites. Similarly, her own mother had, all those years before, been amused by what young Bethany had selected, one of which had been a Chef Boyardee pizza maker kit.

Seated together at the table now, Bethany noted the gleam in young Darla's eye as she ate her fish sticks, canned beets, and portion of boxed macaroni & cheese. It made for a very colorful plate with the red of the beets complimenting the mac's dayglo orange.

It's the little things, Bethany decided, as she poured herself that second glass of chardonnay and enjoyed the last bite of her pan-fried salmon filet.

Tomorrow, they'd join in the annual Easter Egg Hunt at the community park.

She prayed everything would go all right but didn't want to get her hopes up yet.

POP POP'S RESIDENCE
SATURDAY, 7:45 PM

Pop Pop had barely touched his beef with broccoli; he was so enamored by the joy being expressed between Phoenix, Curt, and their old adventure pal they hadn't seen in over eight years.

He'd really hoped his other phone call would have also bore fruit, but his old Navy buddy, Murf, was having a hip replacement this weekend, so he'd sent his regrets. *That would have been something, to get the entirety of both rescue teams together.*

Pop Pop studied Wingnut. He hadn't really had a chance to properly get to know this young man before now, having stayed behind while Phoenix took her fateful road trip out to California.

He flashed back to how, while she was out there, Phoenix had not only established contact with a grandfather she'd never known she had, but also met the love of her life in Curt, and bonded with her husband's partner in crime, Wingnut, as they'd collectively saved her from the clutches of the monster dubbed as the "Pirate"—and all while solving the decades-old murder of her own mother.

But these were happy times, gathered together at this dinner table, and these old friends had picked up right where they had left off like it was all just yesterday.

Curt slapped the table and threw his head back.

"Release the crappin'!" Wingnut blurted to Curt, again

covering his mouth shyly as they shared another private belly laugh.

"What's *crappin*, Mommy?" Rose asked, pulling on the sleeve of her mother's shirt.

"Oh, your daddy and our friend are just being silly, honey," she assured her, punctuating her remark with a little head tilt to the guys, her nonverbal reminder about *language*. "Did you like your pineapple rice?" she asked, redirecting Rose's attention.

"Yes, Mama, but the brockity tastes gross."

"Well, now, you need to eat that because *broccoli* will make you strong...and when you finish it, you'll get some dessert," she said, beaming Rose an excited smile to close the deal.

"'Kay," Rose murmured as she maneuvered the bitesize floret with her chopsticks. She looked across the table and scrutinized their guest's unique features a bit further. She tugged on her mom's sleeve again and Phoenix leaned over to better hear her.

"That man has big elephant ears," Rose whispered softly—an observation, not a judgment.

Phoenix put her lips up to Rose's ear and whispered back, "That's so he can hear everything you say." She winked. "C'mon, let's finish your vegetables."

"Thank you for making the trip out to see us, Wingnut," Pop Pop said. "It was short notice, we know, and a long drive."

"Thanks for inviting me, Pop. My mom recently moved to Scottsdale—after their divorce—so it gives me an excuse to see everybody important to me. And that definitely includes you guys," Wingnut said, looking around the table. He noticed Rose staring at him. "And it's especially nice to meet you, Rosebud!"

"Hey!" she squeaked with a giggle.

"Great to make your acquaintance," Len said warmly as he addressed their visitor. "Thank you for making the effort."

"My pleasure, Len," Wingnut said, scratching his right ear. The appendages were impossible to ignore; they looked more like saucers had been affixed to each side of his head.

Curt pushed his now-empty plate away and took a pull from his Tsingtao. He held up his bottle in a gesture to his old buddy, and they clinked them together. "So, how long you in town, Wing?"

"Uh, not long. Gonna drive out to see my mom tonight. Might stay the night there, depending on how things go. Drive back tomorrow."

"You're serious?" Phoenix cut it. "Can't you stay a few days at least?"

"Wish I could, but I'm overseeing the grand opening of a new store, day after tomorrow. Gotta get back for that."

"So, just a quick In-N-Out trip for you then," Curt quipped, playing on the fact that his friend had become quite the successful burger joint manager since they'd last seen each other.

"Good one. Yeah...quick...especially in the Mustang. I'll be home by tomorrow night."

After dinner, Wingnut had given his solemn pinky-swear promise to not be a stranger, before roaring away in his three hundred-horsepower chariot.

Rose had joined Phoenix as they walked the three dogs around the block, while Curt and Pop Pop cleaned things up and loaded the dishwasher.

"Luke! Leave it!" Phoenix called out, giving the Shepherd's leash a corrective tug as he dropped the nugget of poop he'd picked up from the sidewalk. "Oy!"

"Mama?" Rose asked, coming to a stop.

"Yes, sweetheart? What is it?"

"Will we go back to...that other house?"

Phoenix looked around, surveying the neighborhood as she considered her response. The question was a good one, and she hoped her response was worthy.

"Yes, honey, we will go to the other house, but probably in a few days. It will be our new house, and you'll have your own bedroom, and we'll have pizza and barbecues and—"

"Does the mean lady have to come?" Rose asked, looking up with doe eyes while her bottom lip formed a pout.

Phoenix knelt down to Rose's eye level and mustered a smile of assurance. "No, honey, the mean lady isn't invited, and she will never ever come back."

"Promise?"

"Yes, sweetie. Mommy promises."

BEST
SUNDAY

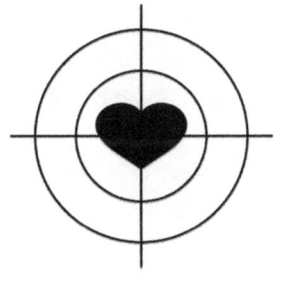

CHAPTER THIRTY-SIX

DISCOVERY PARK
GILBERT, ARIZONA
EASTER SUNDAY, 9:55 AM

POP POP CIRCLED the parking lot for a third time as he searched for a spot nearer the park's main lawn area. It was where the annual Easter Egg Hunt would be taking place, and it was scheduled to start any minute. The place was mobbed with families and little treat-seekers.

"Phoenix, why don't you and Rose get out and you can take her over there while I find a place, okay?"

"Okay, Pop Pop. Let me just grab the baskets and stuff from behind the seat," she replied as she retrieved the items. "C'mon, sweetie. Let's get a move on," she said, unbuckling the safety seat. "Let's go find some eggs!"

"Yay!"

"I'll find you guys," Pop Pop said as Phoenix closed the truck's doors and he pulled away.

Ordinarily, the Road Runner would've fit all five of them,

but with it being out of commission, Len had had to drive his rental car over for Curt and himself.

Several empty Easter baskets hung from their wicker handles, dangling from Phoenix's left forearm like a freakishly huge bracelet. She was also carrying an oversized cardboard box full of cookies, which made it a challenge to hold Rose's hand with her free hand.

"C'mon, honey. It's almost time to start," she reminded her mini-me.

As they approached the crowd gathered there, she saw Curt. He waved with his right crutch when he saw them.

"There you are," he said, giving both his girls a peck. "Where's—?"

"Parking the truck. Len?"

Curt gestured with his crutch, pointing toward his dad. Phoenix looked in the direction he was pointing and saw Len standing off to the side and chatting with an attractive woman who appeared to be in her mid-fifties. "You go, Len," she said with a sly smile, just as the public address system crackled to life with some loud feedback before the emcee managed to squelch it.

"Oops...um...there we go. Good morning, ladies and gentlemen, boys and girls! Happy Easter to one and all, and welcome to this year's Community Easter Egg Hunt!" the portly man in the lime-green sportscoat said from his perch in the park's gazebo.

The man was the town's mayor, and he was joined by a six-foot-tall bunny character who was waving to a legion of young fans. Unbeknownst to the crowd, the lanky nineteen-year-old inside the bunny suit was the mayor's son, and he'd been offered the choice between cleaning the garage or donning the suit for a couple of hours.

"We'll be starting the hunt in just a couple of minutes, but I wanted to tell you all that my friend here has hidden a few special eggs out there, and there will be some fun prizes."

Phoenix noticed a familiar face and smiled as Detective Moser approached them, accompanied by a young girl, a little younger than Rose.

"Detective Moser, Happy Easter!" Phoenix said.

"It's Bethany Moser today, please," she said, offering her hand. "And this is my daughter, Darla. Darla, this is Mrs. Martinsen and her daughter, Rose."

"Hello, very nice to meet you," Darla said, employing the manners she'd been taught.

"Hi, Darla," Rose said. "You want to look for eggs with me?"

"Okay," she answered, checking in with a look to her mama to get her approval.

"That sounds like a great idea, honey," Bethany said, handing her an empty basket. "Thank you, Rose," she added, smiling warmly.

Phoenix handed one of the empty baskets to Rose. "We need to wait for the signal to start, honey, okay?"

"'Kay," Rose acknowledged before turning back to Darla. "I have cookies for after, if you want some."

Bethany Moser patted her daughter on the head and looked up into the crowd. Another woman, about fifty yards away, was looking directly at her, and she looked familiar somehow. As the woman approached and emerged from the crowd, it became immediately evident to Beth why she recognized her.

It was Ruth Andrews, the case manager she'd met with at the Arizona Department of Child Safety, and her arm was guiding a young girl, about Rose's age, by the shoulder.

It was Abigail.

Bethany's heart skipped a beat at seeing the young girl, the one whose mother had abandoned her without a word, and during Easter week. Abby's expression was a blank slate, save the sadness and confusion in her eyes.

"Happy Easter, Beth," Ruth said, smiling as she reached the group.

"Ruth. So nice to see you again. Happy Easter," Beth said, shaking her hand. "And who might this be?" she asked, already knowing the answer.

The case manager looked at the youngster in her charge and smiled. "This...is Abigail. Abigail, I'd like you to meet Miss Moser and..."

"...my daughter, Darla," Beth said, filling in the blank. "And this is Mrs. Martinsen, and her daughter, Rose...and Rose's father, Mr. Martinsen."

"Hi, Abigail," Darla and Rose said in unison.

"Hi," Abigail replied, her gaze turning to the tall man with the crutches. There was a flicker of recognition on her face as she regarded the man who'd been her teacher—for half a day.

Curt met her gaze and winked. "Happy Easter, Abigail." She looked away shyly.

"It's so nice to meet you, Abigail," Phoenix said. "And you, Ruth."

"Pleasure. We thought it might be nice to have Abigail join in the fun here today, and—"

"I have an extra Easter basket, Abigail! You can hunt for eggs with me and Darla!" Rose cut in, her enthusiasm unbridled.

Abigail didn't register any emotion despite the offer, and she took a moment to consider this proposal. She looked up at her case manager, numbly.

"Would you like that, Abigail? Would you like to join Rose and Darla, honey?"

"I guess," she replied softly.

"Here ya go," Rose chimed in, offering her a basket. "We have cookies too," she said, her excitement genuine.

"Thanks."

"Well, that's settled," Ruth said, smiling back at the adults as the PA system crackled back to life.

"We're about to start the Easter Egg Hunt, boys and girls!" the mayor announced. He looked at his watch. "Parents, if you'd please bring your children up here to the base of the gazebo, we'll get things started. Please stay behind the pink ribbon until we officially start...which will be in three minutes. Thank you."

"Did you hear what the man said, girls?" Phoenix asked the threesome.

"Yes, Mommy."

"Yes," Darla agreed.

"Yeah," Abigail answered. She turned to her young peers and her face seemed to lighten just a little, like a cloud was starting to pass. "I like to be called Abby."

"Okay, Abby!" Rose confirmed, beaming a smile.

"That's a cool name, Abby!" Darla agreed.

"Thanks," Abby replied, with the smallest hint of a smile.

Phoenix watched with an eagle eye as they skipped off to join the other children. It was still so hard to let Rose out of her sight—even for an instant—after what had happened in the market's parking lot, and under her very nose, fourteen months before.

"I'll keep an eye on 'em," Curt whispered to Phoenix, sensing her justified unease. It was a feeling he still shared as well.

"Stick close together, girls," Beth called out to them before turning to Ruth. "I think it's great that you brought Abby out here today."

"Yeah, well with everything that poor girl's endured, how could I not. Thank you both for including her in your daughters' fun; she's needing that right now."

"I'm sure," Beth replied. "Any movement on the foster front?"

"Not yet; it's only been about a week, but with the capture and arrest of her mother—and the severity of the charges she's faced with—there's no way any court would grant any parental access to the child. She's a sweet girl, and as you know all too well, she's been through the ringer. We'll be holding out for the best possible scenario and—we hope—the perfect foster family. She deserves nothing less."

"Yes," Beth replied softly.

A loud airhorn got everyone's attention and they turned toward the source. The bunny suit-clad figure had just signaled the start of the event, and several dozen youngsters spread across the large park lawn, giggling and grabbing anything in sight.

"Looks like this party's getting started," Len said, as he joined the group and stuffed a piece of paper into his shirt pocket.

"Hey, there, Casanova," Phoenix teased. "Did you at least get her phone number?"

He patted his breast pocket. "A gentleman never tells," he said, adding a wink.

Some newer objects had been added to the landscape, such as a few faux logs, some potted plants and the like, under which some of the special plastic eggs—the ones that contained clues to special prizes—were hidden. The playground equipment was also littered with them.

The three women, along with Len, and Curt bringing up the rear, made their way over to the festivities, and it was particularly joyful to watch the interaction between the three young girls. Darla found a purple plastic egg sitting on the top step of the slide and as she was about to place it in her basket she reconsidered, instead handing it to Abby.

Rose, who already had several in her basket, discovered another yellow plastic egg in the tall grass and walked over to Abby and placed it in the girl's basket.

Ruth and Beth exchanged looks. Phoenix put her hand to her mouth, looking like she might cry. "So sweet."

Beth Moser turned to Phoenix and nodded, tears welling in her eyes.

Fifteen minutes had elapsed and the sound of the airhorn signaled the end of the hunt, followed by a request for parents to collect their children while the Easter Bunny prepared to announce winners.

"Mommy, look!" Rose squealed, holding out her basket. It was full to the brim.

"Wow, sweetie! Great job!" Phoenix acknowledged enthusiastically.

"Me too!" Darla chirped. Her basket runneth over as well.

"Abby, how about you, honey? Did you have fun?" Ruth asked.

"Look!" Abby said, beaming her first real smile of the day—or the month, for that matter. Her basket was packed to overflowing. "Darla and Rose helped me too," she added.

"Great job, girls. All of you," Beth said with genuine pride and a wink to Ruth.

"May I have your attention, please...the Easter Bunny is here to tell us who the grand prize winner is. Is everybody ready?" the mayor announced, nodding to his son in the suit as the crowd shouted out a collective yes.

The bunny pulled a folded slip of paper from his own basket and handed it to his dad.

"Okay, kids, everybody check your baskets. You're look-ing for a big plastic egg...and it's going to be a purple one!"

The flurry of activity this statement generated was a blur as all of the kids in attendance tore into their hauls in search of any large purple eggs.

"Nope...no purple. I only have two blue ones," Rose said matter-of-factly and without disappointment.

"I have three yellows and a red. No purple," Darla declared, looking up at her mama.

Abby dug down to the bottom of her basket and pulled out a purple egg. It was a large one, too, and she was pretty sure it was the one Darla had given her.

"Like this?" Abby asked softly.

"Wow...yes, sweetheart!" Beth replied with an excited whisper.

"...and inside the egg we are looking for a piece of paper with a special number on it," the mayor added.

Abby's expression was morphing toward a smile as she pulled apart the two halves of the purple egg. There was indeed a folded piece of paper inside. She looked at her peers, then to the adults.

"Has anybody found a large purple egg, with a piece of paper inside, with a number on it?" the mayor asked, his lips touching the mesh of the microphone as he surveyed the crowd.

Abby raised her hand slowly, shyly, but her gesture wasn't seen by the mayor.

"Over here!" one parent cried out. "My son has one!"

"Here too! We have one!" another parent yelled, waving her arms excitedly.

Abby looked up at the adults in her circle, her face registering slight disappointment.

"We have one right here!" Beth Moser yelled, waving and pointing at young Abby.

"Wow...that's great," the mayor said. "Looks like we have... three. Anybody else?"

When there were no other responses, he opened the folded paper in his hand. "Now, to the three children with the large purple eggs, please look at the number on your paper you found inside your purple eggs," he said, giving them time to get ready for the big reveal. "Don't call it out...just look at your number."

Abby removed her scrap of yellow construction paper, but kept it folded.

"Okay?" the mayor asked. "Everybody ready?"

"Yes!!" their parents yelled.

"Great! The winner of this year's Easter Egg Hunt is... number..."

Abby stared at the tiny rectangle of yellow construction paper, listening to the announcer as she unfolded it, prepared for crushing disappointment.

"...thirty three!"

Ruth, Beth, Phoenix, Rose, and Darla were all huddled around Abby as she firmly grasped the piece of paper with the two threes on it.

It was the collective squeal of the two other girls and the three ladies that clued Abby into the fact that she'd indeed won. It might as well have been the Wonka Golden Ticket.

"Yay!!" Rose screamed out.

"Woo-hoo!! Mommy, look!" Darla bellowed.

"We have the winner right here!" Beth declared, beaming at the girl who'd just rediscovered the ability to smile. "Way to go, Abby!"

"That's so awesome, Abby!" Phoenix said, sharing her very real excitement.

"Happy Easter, Abby," Ruth Andrews said, giving the girl's shoulder a squeeze.

"Can we please get our big winner up to the gazebo to join us? Please bring your winning egg, and your adults, with you. The Easter Bunny has a very special prize for you!"

Abby was still absorbing the moment as she looked up at the three women for confirmation.

"Yep, that's you, Abby!" Beth said.

"You go, girl!" Phoenix agreed.

"I'll go up there with you, Abby," Ruth said, taking her by the hand.

"And we'll have cookies after!!" Rose reminded the group.

With great trepidation, Abby took the three steps up to the gazebo and stood alongside her case manager, the big sweaty man, and the creepy-as-hell giant bunny character.

She stared at her shoes mostly, listening to the crowd as they applauded her. The mayor collected her purple egg and verified the winning number on its slip of paper. He held it up high and waved it to the crowd.

"Number thirty-three! We have our winner!" he barked, tucking the microphone under his arm as he handed the egg back to her and shook her hand. He brought the mic back to his lips. "Tell me your name, sweetheart."

"Uh. Abigail."

"Congratulations, Abigail. We—"

"I like to be called Abby," she cut in.

"Of course. Congratulations, Abby!" he said, flashing his best non-threatening smile at her. "Folks, let's all give a big hand to this young lady."

Abby closed her eyes for several moments as she listened to the thunderous applause. It was unlike anything she'd ever heard, and it was equal parts terrifying and something else she'd never really experienced much of in her young life: encouraging.

She opened her eyes and immediately found her people. Phoenix, Rose, Beth, Darla, Miss Ruth, the man with the crutches, and the other man. They were all clapping wildly, smiling broadly, loving unconditionally.

A broad smile spread across Abby's face as she absorbed the enormity of it all.

"Folks, it's time to award Abby her prize," the mayor said, fumbling with the mic's switch. He looked over at the costumed character who was awkwardly making his way up the steps, trying not to trip over his floppy bunny feet.

Adding to the difficulty, the bunny was carrying something with him, one pink and white bunny hand clutching the high-rise handlebar, and the other gripping the long banana seat of a Classic Krate Schwinn Sting-Ray bicycle.

Abby's jaw almost hit the floor, and the crowd's excitement was deafening as the bunny set the gleaming orange bike down and wheeled it over to her.

Tears streamed down her face as she hugged the bunny.

Twenty feet away, tears also streamed down the cheeks of both Bethany Moser and Phoenix. Ruth wiped away one of her own, trying to maintain her professional decorum. She didn't get to see a lot of happy moments in her job, but this was definitely one of them.

After a few photos with her prize and the Easter Bunny, Abby was helped down from the gazebo, and her new bike was delivered to her.

She proudly guided the two-wheeler through the path the crowd had created for her, and she rejoined her tribe, each of whom engaged her in warm hugs while she held tightly to the handlebars of her new prize. After a few awkward moments, Abby started to lay it down on the ground.   "You can use the kickstand, honey," Beth said, pointing to it with a smile.

Abby's expression told her she had no experience with such a contraption.

"Here, sweetie...we just flip it down like...this...and there you go! Tada!" Beth said, demonstrating its ability to make the bike freestanding.

Abby's confused look morphed into an embarrassed smile. "I've never had a bike before."

Beth's smile hiccupped momentarily before she recovered.

"Well, you sure deserve this one, honey." She bit her lip as she made a mental note to buy the sweet girl a proper helmet.

"Time for cookies, Mommy!" Rose declared.

"You are right, honey bunny!" Phoenix agreed.

"Hey!" Rose blurted with a giggle.

Phoenix grabbed the large cardboard container and folded back the top flap as she revealed the colorful assortment of sugar cookies Rose had designed with her Pop Pop.

Darla grabbed a bunny-shaped cookie, while Beth selected an egg-shaped one. Ruth picked out two bunny cookies and handed one to Abby as she took a bite of her own. Rose picked out two, one for her and one for her mom.

"Is one of those for me?" Phoenix asked, setting down the box.

"Yes, Mommy," Rose answered, handing her one of the two cross-shaped cookies she'd selected. Darla and Abby seemed momentarily surprised by her choice of cookies, as theirs seemed more apt for the occasion.

As Rose took a small bite into her cross, she took the opportunity to share a teachable moment with her peers.

"Easter's not all about the bunny," she said, looking up at her proud mama.

Phoenix smiled, gesturing with her own cookie. "That's right, lovey."

Pop Pop made his way through the crowd and joined the group. He was winded, and appeared a bit frustrated, but he stuffed it down, mustering a smile.

"Had to park about three blocks away...did I miss anything?"

CHAPTER THIRTY-SEVEN

POP POP'S RESIDENCE
THE GRANNY UNIT
EASTER SUNDAY, 3:33 PM

P HOENIX'S "DAY 7" rabies vaccination was in the books, as Len had offered to take her and Curt to the clinic after the Easter festivities.

Her wounds were inspected, her dressings refreshed, and she'd been told things were starting to heal. The shoulder would take a little extra time due to the new sutures required. She'd be back to see them in a week for her "Day 14" jab.

Little Rose was curled up like a hamster, and now lights-out in the pink beanbag chair Pop Pop had bought for her. The jellybeans, chocolate eggs, and Easter cookies had done their jobs, supplying her with a sugar rush that had only recently expired, causing her to crash—hard.

The blinds were drawn, and Curt's nightlight was illuminated. Phoenix was tucked up into Curt's armpit as they lay atop the inflatable bed, enjoying the solitude, figuring out the world's problems.

"Rose showed me the drawing she made," Curt said softly.

"Which one? The...new one?" Phoenix asked.

"Yeah...the one of the Superstitions. I still don't know how to process it."

"Did you ask her about it...what inspired her to draw it?"

"She told me. And when I asked her more about her conversations with Willie, her answer was, 'Willie's gone...he's not here anymore.'"

Phoenix propped herself up slightly, enough to make eye contact. "Seriously? She told you that?" she whispered.

Curt nodded, his eyes moistening. "Yeah...something to definitely take up with the therapist next week."

"Wow...yeah...just wow," Phoenix replied incredulously as she lay back down. They both stared at the ceiling for several moments.

"So, I didn't want to read into anything, but did Detective Moser seem a little... I dunno... clingy, maybe—for lack of a better word—around the case manager and Abigail today?" Curt asked softly, staring up at the spider-free ceiling.

"Funny you should ask," Phoenix said, draping her arm across his chest. "She didn't tell me in so many words, but she didn't have much of a poker face either. She might be priming the pump and considering putting in a foster application for Abby. It would depend a lot on how Darla would take it, but they got off to a great start today—as friends, anyway. We'll have to see."

"God, that would be so amazing if that worked out, wouldn't it? Growing the family that way?"

"Hold that thought," Phoenix said, untangling herself and getting up. "I gotta pee."

"'Kay."

The bathroom door closed, and Curt looked over at his

sleeping munchkin. A tiny sliver of light had snuck in through a gap in the blinds and was kissing his little angel's head. God only knew how much the craziness of the past week would set her back with her therapy, but the three of them would go together at the end of the week. They'd get through it together. *Whatever it takes.*

A sigh escaped him. *God, I love my family. Thank You for bringing us back together.*

The sound of the toilet flushing brought Curt back to the present. Phoenix washed her hands and settled back into her saved snuggle spot.

"Whatcha thinking about?" she asked, noting his smile of contentment.

"Just thinking about how much I love you and Rose...our little family," he said, turning to kiss her forehead.

"Mmm..." Phoenix said, kissing him back on the lips. "I'm so glad you feel that way," she added as she handed him the blue and white plastic wand she was holding.

"What's this?" he asked, taking the device, his brow scrunching as he looked at it in the semi-darkened room.

"I don't know...what's it look like?" Phoenix said softly, trying to suppress her grin.

Curt turned the foreign object around in his fingers as he inspected it. "Is it a thermometer?"

"Nope."

"A USB storage device?"

"You're getting colder," she replied with a chuckle. "Read what it says, silly."

Curt held the device out at arm's length to better focus on the tiny display window, like it was one of those Magic 8 Balls with a secret message for him.

"Need me to get you your reading glasses, old man?" she kidded.

"Wait..." he said, turning to his wife. His eyes were wide, his confused look slowly morphing into something resembling a smile.

"Yes?" Phoenix prodded, exuding a new level of radiance.

"Does this say...does it...mean...what I think it does...?"

Phoenix bit her lip.

"I mean, we're sure...?"

Phoenix's big smile provided him with all the answer he needed.

"Happy Easter, Mister Martinsen."

"Oh, honey...this is...incredible," Curt said, his smile fully realized. "How——?"

"About eight weeks, I think... Thank you, *Paul Blart: Mall Cop!*" she said, trying not to laugh. She couldn't possibly know, but it had been the same drive-in theater she herself had been conceived at, and on Easter Sunday, all those years before.

"I love you...so much forever, Missus Martinsen," he managed, the tears in his eyes melding with Phoenix's as they kissed with a passion that had managed to elude them for God knows how long.

Curt let the device slip from his fingers. Landing on the floor face-up, it displayed a single, welcomed, and life-changing word:

Pregnant.

Or was it, *Miracle*? He hadn't used his readers.

THE END...FOR NOW.

AUTHOR'S NOTE

As always, I have a lot of people to thank, so I'll start with you, the reader. Thank you very much for taking a chance on my novel. I hope you know how much I respect your time, and I truly appreciate you coming along for the ride!

To my wonderful frau, Martina, *danke schön* for your patience as I hunkered down in my dark cave for the time it took to write this, sweetheart! I appreciate you. *Mwah!*

To my amazing editorial guru, Lisl, thank you for your brilliance, and for the generous dollops of awesome sauce you always bring to my manuscripts. This is our fourth project together, and I'm grateful to have you in my corner!

My family: you continue to be my rock. I never would have survived the events chronicled in my debut novel, *The Other Cheek*, without you, and I'm grateful you didn't give up on me. Thank you for bringing me back from the void.

And, as we all know, a writer can't march on an empty stomach. Thus, my big thanks to John Gabaldon, Christina Mills, and the staff at Los Dos Molinos Mexican restaurant in Mesa, Arizona. Your game-changer food and your gracious hospitality are the stuff of legend. I can't wait for my next visit—and I already know I'm ordering the "Junior Special."

I'd be remiss if I didn't give a shout out to my brother-in-law, Jack, who, last Christmas, took me out for a spontaneous schlep to the old section of Mesa and the Apache Junction area of Arizona. He was jonesing for some good Pad Thai and wanted to turn me on to his favorite lunch place. While driving about, he deliberately took me down the highway that leads to the Superstition Mountains area. I was unprepared for what I saw. It was right then and there, as the unmistakable shape of that range began to fill our entire windshield's view, I asked him to pull over so I could snap a photo. We were seemingly the only vehicle on that two-lane highway and, in that moment, I knew I'd found the setting for my next book, the one you now hold in your hands. It was meant to be. Thanks, Jack! And yes, that Pad Thai rocked.

As seems to be the case with all of my books, music played an important role once again. There were a few songs I wanted to reference lyrics to, as they were important to the narrative. In the case of the artists' works I chose to use, getting the rights to their usage was particularly challenging because they are no longer living.

This made for some atypically long and circuitous searches for the rightsholders and, once I managed to track them down, I had to go about seeking permission for the licenses to print lyrics. Anyone who knows me well can attest to the fact that I'm doggedly persistent when I choose to be, and this was no different. I'm very grateful to the music publishers referenced on my book's copyright page. And to the brilliant artists, Emitt Rhodes and Dan Fogelberg, thank you for your gifts. Your timeless songs are incredible and your talents immeasurable.

Additional thanks go to my legion of supporters on my social media platforms. I am deeply indebted, in particular, to the incredible admins of my favorite book-related Facebook groups. Your generous support to this indie author is appreciated more than I can properly express. And the same goes for all of my supporters and fans on Facebook, Goodreads, and Instagram. The numbers keep growing, and there are too many to name here, but you know who you are! I couldn't (and wouldn't) do this without you...thank you so, so much!

And to our current lineup of rescue critters, Luke, Barney, Sidney, and Candy, thanks for putting up with Dad's endless stretches at the computer. These stretches must have felt like seven times longer for you than they did for me. I love you all, and I hope you're okay with your characterizations in my books. Sidney, are we good?

As usual, there was a great deal of research involved in the crafting of this story. From plumbing the depths of one character's mental illness, getting up to speed on the incredible backdrop evidenced by the Superstition Mountains, and the indigenous wildlife and topography of Arizona's Maricopa and Pinal counties to travel times as well as certain medical protocols, it all kept me quite busy. I enjoy the process because I want to get it right. That includes the music on my characters' playlists.

Truth be told, I had never envisioned my second novel, *Leaving Phoenix*, becoming the cornerstone of a series. I intended it to be a standalone, and I was beyond pleased to see the positive response from readers. They loved the story and fell in love with the characters. As did I.

When I'd floated the question to my peeps, "What I should write next?" the responses made it abundantly clear that they wanted more Phoenix and her supporting cast. In particular, one reader mentioned she wanted "more Curt!"

Well, file this under "be careful what you ask for" because this one's for you!

If you've enjoyed *So Much Forever*, I hope you'll consider leaving a review on Amazon and/or Goodreads, BookBub, and Barnes & Noble. Please tell a friend and share it as a suggestion on your social media platform(s). Ask your library to carry it if you're so inclined.

Your support means the world to me, and your participation in my books' successes is instrumental in helping them find their place in a very crowded and unlevel playing field.

Thank you again for reading, and this indie author would be beyond grateful if you'd consider spreading the word.

Blessings your way! So much forever.
~ Jafe Danbury

ABOUT THE AUTHOR

Jafe Danbury hails from the trenches of the Hollywood production scene, where he spent decades as a camera operator, director of photography, and director. He has also worked as a teacher and is a decorated U.S. Navy veteran.

He enjoys noodling on the guitar, long road trips, likes his bacon crispy, and loves a good dive bar—especially if it happens to have a twenty-two-foot shuffleboard table. He prefers a leisurely walk to running, unless being chased by a clown with a chainsaw.

Jafe and his lovely bride currently reside in central California and are working on their exit plan. Their children currently consist of several rescue dogs and a wacky umbrella cockatoo, but their house has a revolving door when it comes to rescue critters and may include the occasional owl, abandoned sparrow, or wayward kitten.

So Much Forever is his fourth novel.

ALSO, BY JAFE DANBURY:

Leaving Phoenix
The Other Cheek
X